EBURY PRESS

ANGRIA

Sohail Rekhy was born in Mumbai to actor Waheeda Rehman and businessman Shashi Rekhy and spent several summers and countless weekends on the shores of the Konkan coast. He grew up in Bangalore, fascinated by Indian history, and went on to study literature at the University of Toronto. Sporadic journalism and freelance copywriting always kept him by his pen, as he worked in advertising and television and dabbled in sustainable furniture. This is his first novel, the fruit of years of research and writing. He currently lives with his wife and daughter in Bhutan.

ADVANCE PRAISE FOR THE BOOK

'Sohail Rekhy's *Angria* is an ambitious attempt to evoke the maritime world of the Konkan coast in the late seventeenth century'—Amitav Ghosh

'Gripping and rigorously researched, Sohail Rekhy's *Angria* dredges from the depths of our history the saga of the valorous hero Kanhoji Angre and his resistance to the colonialists. This absorbing saga heralds an excellent debut'—Shashi Tharoor

'A wonderful debut that makes our history come alive through fiction' —Vir Sanghvi

'The saga of Sarkhel Kanhoji Angre! A delightful mix of the real and the imagined'—Uday S. Kulkarni

ANGRIA

A Historical Odyssey

Sohail Rekhy

EBURY
PRESS

An imprint of Penguin Random House

EBURY PRESS

USA | Canada | UK | Ireland | Australia
New Zealand | India | South Africa | China | Singapore

Ebury Press is part of the Penguin Random House group of companies
whose addresses can be found at global.penguinrandomhouse.com

Published by Penguin Random House India Pvt. Ltd
4th Floor, Capital Tower 1, MG Road,
Gurugram 122 002, Haryana, India

First published in Ebury Press by Penguin Random House India 2024

Copyright © Sohail Rekhy 2024
Map by Nitendra Srivastava

All rights reserved

10 9 8 7 6 5 4 3 2 1

ISBN 9780143464105

Typeset in Sabon Lt Std by MAP Systems, Bengaluru, India

www.penguin.co.in

For Ahuratara

Contents

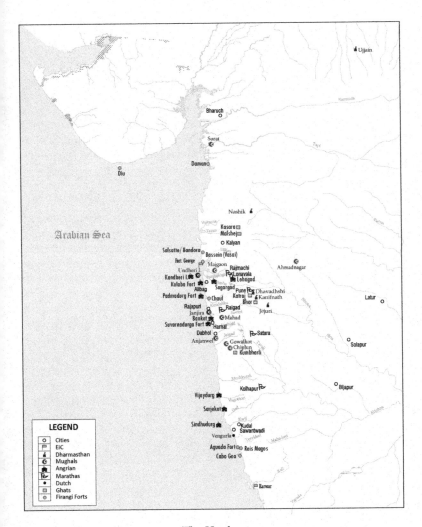

The Konkan

The Last Sankhpal

Shri Ganesh Nameh, Chandravanshi says as he jumps on to his *phatemar,* a small dhow-hulled boat.

Saheb is anxious, he has not left the fort since it was completed last year by the Vaddera masons Maharaj had got from the *Telugu desha.* His skin, off his palms, is encased in basalt stones with thousands of *maunds** of lead that form the foundation of Sindhudurg Fort. Saheb is astride his dun-coloured mare, an Arab of course, but with a mottled white blaze on her face and irregular but decidedly ominous markings along her neck and back. He bought her cheap and if her issue is not so marked with similar misfortune, there will be some gain. Falguni is a gentle and patient beast. She whisks the flies away with her tail as Tukoji speaks to his men at the bastion nearest the Mahadarwaza which he commands with thirteen more on the north-east side.

'Obey Ranga as you obey me and do not slack,' he says to his seventeen captains.

'*Hao,* Saheb,' they respond in unison.

'Ranga will disband you when the rains come and I will see you again at Nariyel Purnima.'

'Hao, Saheb,' they chant. They each lead ten men.

---

* Unit of mass weighing approximately 15 kg.

'Those of you who will stay here over the monsoons: fix your roofs and keep your wood dry. This is not Bijapur, Sholapur or Latur. You will learn what rain is, you will remember the old name of Varuna,' he warns them. A lot of his men are in from the Desha, refugees from the Mughal onslaught, and to survive in the Konkan, they must learn from their Koli compatriots. But what can he tell them? They must feel it and hear it for themselves. The coast is rocky and narrow, cloud-shattering mountains rise in steep gigantic cliffs: the ghats, named for the funerary steps found on riverbanks. The rains gash their green steps and silver blood flows out in a gushing spray. Creeks you can skip over in summer turn to torrents that drown beast and boat, and one wonders how the fish survive such violence.

Those that remain will remain within the fort. Its interior is built with the body of the Konkan itself: pockmarked laterite and hardwood. The stone is red with the blood of twenty-one generations of warriors extinguished one after another. The stone is heavy and heaty, tinged with the metal of Rishi Parshuram's axe. Having given away all the land in the world to the persecuted victims of the corrupt kings he had eradicated, the rishi shot an arrow into this very sea that the Devas and the Asuras had once churned. In deference to the great sage, the Sindhu Sagar retreated to the point of the arrow and revealed the Konkan. The wood these hills are hirsute with—teak, paduk and rosewood—are of the Devi Lakshmi, sprung from the sea, and impervious to decay.

Chandravanshi is at the jetty, and he can see his *yajyaman*[*] ride back on the ramparts towards the main gate. He has been with Tukoji Saheb since he was born, his father with Saheb's father before him. His master has an old name: Sankhpal, but it was given to them here, on the Konkan, by his own Koli people, before the time of the Adil Shahs or the *Firangi*s. The pommel of Saheb's sword is shaped like a conch. The old fisherfolk, marble white hair on smooth dark bodies, say that generations ago they too had

---

[*] Patron of rituals; employer.

kings who refashioned the hilt of the sword that Tukoji's ancestor had ridden down the Desha with. Its grip was wrapped in manta ray hide, its cross-guard fashioned as a tiger, a crocodile was made to serve as a knuckle-guard, a bronze conch pommel was added and the original *ukku** blade from the forges of Vijayanagara resharpened. They rode and fought for the Koli Kings against the Sultans of Bijapur. Then the Firangis came in ships and burnt the coast down, leaving only debris. The Koli Kings vanished. The Sankhpals then offered their horses and swords to the Sultans of Bijapur with their muskets and cannon or the audacious Bhonsales of Sawantwadi and Kudal. The Sankhpals visit every horse fair in the vicinity and have bred them for generations, always unsuccessfully.

Tukoji Sankhpal rides out of the new fort and rides on to their lateen sailed phatemar as Chandravanshi is tying up the last of their cargo.

'Chandu, are we ready to leave?' Tukoji asks his *nakhwa.***

'Hao, Saheb, let me just make Falguni comfortable and then we can push off,' Chandravanshi says, satisfied. He has laid out a comfortable mattress on the covered deck for his mistress.

They will pick up Ambabai *Ai* from the jetty at Sarjekot, at the mouth of the Gad River. Ai has gone to the old Ganpati Mandir to beseech the Remover of Obstacles to clear the path of their mission and make it a success.

But Bapa did not answer the Adil Shah's prayer, or as the current jest goes: as He was preparing to help, the Shah called on another, so the first gave way to the second and on and on and on. The Adil Shah languishes in silver chains, most likely already dead of poison, and his captor, the Mughal Badshah, possesses the mines of Golkonda and further eyes the tri-shored tip and Lanka. For the Badshah thinks what Rama can do, he can do, and what Ravana can do, he can surpass. Gentle Falguni blindfolded and restrained to the mast, Chandravanshi

---

* Wootz steel with high carbon content.

** Boat captain.

orders his eight Koli oarsmen to push off. There are two to an oar and two oars on each side to get in and out of the winds. Each is a good and strong man, pot-bellied and burnt by the sea. Chandravanshi has heard it from his yajyman that the *shastras* say that a man must make his name. Have the Sankhpals lost theirs? It has diminished, but if their mission fails, it will end and be lost forever to time and history.

'*Haiya, haiya, haiya,*' Chandravanshi chants a beat to which the oarsmen draw, united.

Chandravanshi wonders what the Badshah of Dilli wants. They have had a glorious and fearsome name for 600 years—the blood of Genghis and Timur runs in him. His wealth is beyond imagination. Chandu knows what Saheb wants—what he yearns for. Today there are other men and names in the Konkan, and their shadows and reputations loom large like their households.

Chandravanshi sets course, and then leaving a *tindal* at the tiller, he comes up to the helm to join Tukoji.

'The waves don't suit Ai, Saheb,' Chandravanshi worries. Ambabai will at least have one son.

'Nor do the rutted tracks, Chandu. This will be much shorter and safer.'

'It is the right decision. This year, the rains are going to come in early,' Chandu says, reading the clouds.

'Definitely, and it is going to be a big one. See how hot it was this year?'

'Hao, Saheb,' Chandravanshi says and looks out to the ocean. They are sitting on the bow facing the west.

'Saheb, is it true that the Dilli Badshah has made Shivaji Bhonsale a raja?'

'Yes, Chandu,' Tukoji confirms, but seeing Chandravanshi's face blank, continues. 'The Badshah is a samrat. A samrat is a ruler to whom thirty-two or more kings pay tribute and acknowledge as samrat. The ruler of Dilli has been the Samrat of Hindusthan for long, since the time of the Pandavas. He can make and unmake rajas or make rajas into maharajas and maharajas into zamindars. Of course, you need to be from the appropriate *jaati* and have noble antecedents.'

'Don't you want to be a raja?'

'To be the first and last Sankhpal Raja? Tukoji Sankhpal! Raja of the North-east Walls of Sindhudurg?'

'No, Saheb, I did not mean it like that. Just see, Baba Kanifnath is all powerful, I will have a brother soon.'

'From your lips to the ears of Khandoba,' Tukoji says, raising his joined palms to the sky.

'Tell me of the Dilli Badshah?' Chandravanshi says, trying to change the subject and the mood.

'He imprisoned his father and killed all his brothers. But they tend to do that. He chopped off Dara, his eldest brother's head, their father's favourite, and sent it to his imprisoned and dying father.'

A shiver runs down Chandravanshi's spine. But it is not the wind which their sail has picked up. Chandravanshi has the oars pulled and after resetting course, returns to the bow.

'How did he beat the Yuvraj Dara?'

'Because he is a warrior. He cares not for comfort or wealth. His brother, on the other hand, was a scholar: a student of the Upanishads and the Vedas, a *rasik**. None of the brothers were any match to the current Badshah, militarily.'

'Is he unstoppable then?'

'He was. But now we have Raje, and the Badshah knows Raje's worth. He wishes he had one mansabdar equal to Raje and not having any, he wishes Raje would join him.'

'Will we have to pay the tax?'

'Never. Though it will be the Badshah's undoing, just wait and see,' predicts Tukoji.

'Will Raje join him? Has he?'

---

*Connoisseur.

'In the realm Raje moves in, nothing is fixed and permanent. His grandfather Maloji fought with the great *Habshi** Malik Ambar and then too broke the spine of the Mughal. His father Shahji was the Senapati of the Adil Shahs of Bijapur when Raje killed Afzal Khan of Bijapur. All Shivaji Raje wants is the Sardeshmukhi of the Dhakkan. He will send to Dilli what is owed to Dilli,' Tukoji explains.

They pass the small fort of Rajkot, built on a promontory and little more than a watchtower, as they head to the Gad's mouth.

Hiroji Indulkar, Shivaji's ingenious architect, had built Rajkot as an extension to Sindhudurg. The best come to work for Shivaji Bhonsale. Firangi and Angrez marine engineers come for better salaries and Daulat Khan and the Darya Sarang come because he is the ascending sun who shines on all faiths, the Kolis, Bhandaris and Agaris come because he sees no caste. Saheb joined him because he said he was a decent and good man.

'Soon, we will control the Konkan. All the way from Kutch to the Malabar,' Tukoji notes.

'What about the Firangi ships?'

'Well . . .' Tukoji mulls the impossible size and weaponry of the Firangi leviathans that slide up and down the coast with the self-assurance of the largest whale.

'Raje will deal with the Firangis too, once we can make our own ships and cannon and shot,' Tukoji says.

'At least someone is finally bothered about the Konkan, Chandu. I hear Raje plans to rule from Raigad Killa; that means his heart is still in the Malvan and Konkan. We are amidst a new age, Chandu, a golden and prosperous one. If only I can bring a child into it,' Saheb says.

'Hao, Saheb, just see, it will come to pass,' Chandravanshi says as he slips the sail and orders his oars dipped.

---

* Abyssinian.

Sea Lions

The phatemar lurches up after hitting a wave and its prow momentarily blocks the setting sun. Ambabai is clutching on to the bulwark on the covered deck, expelling her hungry and empty stomach into the sea. A pod of dolphins is escorting the boat, hunting in its bow wave. Seagulls fly in raucous gangs close overhead. Her head is spinning. How do these Habshis do this? From the corner of her eye, she spots something floating on the sea. Coconuts? A head? A limb? She shouts for her husband.

They pull out a boy, a pair of immense coconut shells tied to his armpits. He is green-eyed and blue-lipped.

'Can we keep him?' says Ambabai.

'What do you mean keep him? He's not a stray cat.'

'Not a cat, but Karna. This is a sign from above. A gift. Maybe I was supposed to find him. As our child, of course.'

'No, you know we can't. I mean, look at him. It's obvious what he is,' Tukoji says anxiously to his wife.

'How can we leave him alone? He has no one,' she says, looking at the boy with affection.

'He's just fallen off a boat. It must have been his first time at sea, and he must have gotten really seasick. You know, they cling to the side of the boat, retching their guts out and sometimes they just

7

fall in. It happens all the time. He's fallen off one of the boats ahead of us and he is lucky we saw him. We will ask him when he comes to.'

'Look how young he is,' Ambabai says to her husband.

'It would have been a gift if he was a Maratha.'

'What will we do with him?' she wonders as she dries his hair with the corner of her *pallu.**

'He's most probably from Chiplun. Rehman Ali will put him on the next ferry back to Dabhol and then upriver to Chiplun.'

'How much longer till we make landfall?' she asks her husband.

'We just crossed Janjira,' he assures her and takes the boy from her. The mention of the dreaded fort sends a shiver down her spine. When they were children and would not sleep, their mother would threaten her and her sister: 'The Siddi eats up all the children who are not asleep, he can see the white of their eyes shining in the night.'

Her younger sister lost one child and then the second one was born still. But now, she has a girl and two boys, having lost a few in between. Ambabai feels that she had cursed herself, for when she got married to the strapping Tukoji, she had let her imagination run riot. Her son would be a courageous and daring warrior like Senapati Shahji's son. It is too late now, and she has jinxed herself and for the past twelve years she has been childless. Aunts and cousins titter: a barren field ploughed by a strong ox. Her husband has been continually harassed to take on a more fertile partner. He is after all a Sankhpal, hereditary warriors serving the kings of this ancient and rich coast.

They dock at the mouth of the Kundalika River at the jetty at Revdanda. They will spend the night at Rehman Ali's guest house; he's an associate and colleague of her husband who lives nearby. Chandu is off to the local Firangi *mandovi*** to have his papers and their vessel checked, and then he follows the same procedure at the Janjira Mahal's custom house. She watches as her husband hands

---

* Loose end of a sari worn over the head or shoulder.

** Customs office.

the still sleeping boy, wrapped in a white cotton dhoti, to Rehman Ali when they reach his house. It is an immense compound with lumber yards, warehouses, a jackfruit orchard and a plantation of supari trees.

'I am taking her on pilgrimage to the Nath Guru,' he explains to Rehman Ali, 'we found him in the water. When he came to, he said his name was Vishnu and he was kidnapped on his way to Kashi. He jumped.'

'Smart boy. Don't worry, I will send him back to Chiplun.'

'Hao. Looks Chiplunkar, no?'

'Without a doubt,' says Rehman Ali. The Konkani may sport a variety of skin tones, eye colour, hair texture and features and each is a clue as much as a family name.

Ambabai is ushered into the zenana as she overhears Rehman Ali whisper the latest rumour doing the rounds in Rajapuri: the Habshi commander, the Siddi of the Mahal of Janjira—the impregnable island fort to the south—is looking for a new master. Rehman Ali's wife breaks purdah and brings her children and Ambabai back where the men are sitting under tiger skins and *barasingha*[*] antlers. She is not a Habshi, but a Konkani Mussalman and Ambabai feels safer. A silver *thaal* with a bevy of colourful juices and fruit enters. Ambabai counts their children, they are fine healthy specimens with good teeth and dark smooth skin. She notices how muscled and athletic they all are, even the girls.

'Bhau saheb, what news of Shivaji?' Rehman Ali's pregnant wife asks and the eldest girl, who is of marriageable age, giggles. She herself is in her mid-twenties and feels like an old maid well past the age of childbearing.

'It is rumoured that he will make Raigad his capital, that will be good for the Konkan,' Tukoji says.

'In exchange for 35 per cent of the revenue, a fourth in Chauth for security measures and 10 per cent in the hereditary *Sardeshmukhi*

---

[*] Swamp deer.

for revenue collection, the Badshah can return to Dilli and leave
the Dhakkan in the capable hands of Senapati Shahaji's son,' adds
Rehman Ali.

'He must be rich beyond measure. I mean, after Surat, maybe he
is looking for another wife?' says the Begum.

'Ammi, Shivaji is not like other men. He moves like the wind and
spends like a river. On forts, shipbuilders and shipyards. The price of
teak has doubled. He could have taken several women, but instead
maintained their dignity,' explains Rehman Ali's eldest and irritated
son, a boy of ten, to his foolish mother.

'Listen to your son, he is right. This man is brilliant, he doesn't
waste his time on nonsense. He is building a navy of warships that
can patrol the rich ports of the Konkan and wrest back all the *jung-
jazeeras* that are now scattered amongst several masters: the Firangis,
the Siddis, the crafty Topikars and the constantly drunk and red-
faced Angrezi *vanias**,' states the patriarch, as Ambabai lovingly
looks on at Tukoji, who has taught her of the Habshis. The Habshis
had come from across the sea. They had been sailing to the ancient
and rich bazaars in Dabhol, Champawati—the very same Chaul**
that is ruled by the Firangis—Thana and Sopara for millennia. Their
ancient queen, known to Mussalmans and Firangis as Sheba, married
Suleman, famed for his agate mines and anecdotal wisdom. It was
this line that the God of the Christians and the Prophet of the
Mussalmans, Isa, was from. The Arabs and the Habshis controlled
both sides of the Red Sea and the route on to *Misar**** and *Yavan*****.
There are large communities of Habshis from Gujarat down to Keral.
Most married local Koli, Agari or Bhandari women, like Rehman Ali's
begum, and their offspring never want for sustenance, for they have
their boats, and the stars, the moon and the sea speak to them as clearly

---

* Trader/Mercantile caste.

** Modern name of Champawati.

*** Egypt.

**** Greek.

as any *purohit*. They know the unmarked roads on the sea as well as her people know the smallest paths on the Ghats.

'So, both of you have thrown in your lot with Shivaji Bhonsale?' says the Begum. She isn't much smaller than her towering husband.

'I am a mere sailor and boat builder, it is Tukoji here who has made the right choice at last. There is no reason for any man regardless of his race, religion, caste or financial background to not find cause with Raja Shivaji and be charged with his uplifting energy. He finances the building of the boats and creation of the necessary infrastructure to service them, and I profit. One day his sardars from the Dhakkan will provide the necessary land forces and they will overwhelm the coast. It will be the end of the Firangi, we Siddis will all join him.'

'Saheb has definitely been more energetic,' Ambabai says coyly, 'buying and breeding his mares.'

'Tukoji, damn your horses. Just trade like your father did. They are more delicate than women, the wretched beasts. This is no place to breed them. Let the Arab do it in their dry waterless desert. Hindustan is no place to breed horses,' Rehman Ali emphatically tells his friend, to Ambabai's joy.

'They do breed horses on the Desha,' Tukoji defends his investments.

'In the desert or where they have pasture, forget the Konkan, buy *Tai* some nice emeralds,' Rehman Ali chuckles.

'Buy me some emeralds *Mian*, your daughter is to be married within the year,' the Begum admonishes.

'Kaka, the Siddi of Janjira is joining the Dilli Badshah,' says Rehman Ali's boy, putting rest to the rumour.

Fire in the Belly

They are sitting in the back of a covered bullock cart, well-appointed with mattresses that fail to soften the unending shocks. Tukoji has pulled the flap down and lies back as they bump up to Lonavala on the rutted mountain path, seeking the cave of Kanifnath. He knows she is praying to Khandoba for a son imbued with all the qualities of their Raja. Ahead lies the path to the Samadhi of Kanifnath, a small cave on top of a mountain.

They arrive the next afternoon. Tukoji leads Ambabai up the hill to where the cave is. She isn't allowed to come into the cave itself as no woman has ever crawled in there. Tukoji unties his long-sleeved kurta and takes it off as all devotees must enter bare-chested. Looking at the small slit that leads into the temple, Tukoji wonders if he is too fat. But the *bhagat* who is outside the cave's entrance instructs the well-built Tukoji on how to corkscrew himself through the arm long and foot wide opening into the cave that holds the *samadhi*. He can feel the presence of Kanifnathji who has taken samadhi there. That great yogi, a soul liberated to a point where he made no distinction between life and death, had been buried alive here, and his heart, like the immortal Parshuram's, still beats in the cave. It is a small cave with no other opening. There is Kanifnathji's samadhi mound and a fire burning in a recessed hole in front of it. There is only one pujari in the cave, which cannot hold any more than eight or ten people at a time. Today it is only him and the pujari and Kanifnathji. He prays fervently, asking for a son for him and Ambabai. The walls close in and Tukoji is drenched in sweat. The pujari who has been in the cave since the *darshan* began in the morning, is dry and unbothered by the heat. The priest puts his hand into the fire and picks up a glowing orange ember and offers it to Tukoji. Tukoji is expecting *vibhuti*—the ashes of the sacred fire—but he puts his hand out stoically to receive the *prasad*, the blessed sacrament of the great *Navnath* yogi. As the glowing ember touches Tukoji's palm, instead of burning him, a warmth spreads through his entire body, into his head, up his spine and then down to his loins. The orange ember is transformed into a lump of ash, grey and cool.

'Give this to the child's mother,' says the pujari.

Cupping the vibhuti in his palm, Tukoji crawls out of the cave feet first. Tukoji straightens himself and turns to his wife who is sitting cross-legged in prayer. She opens her eyes as he approaches her. He offers her the prasad and she takes it in her cupped right hand and swallows it. It disintegrates into a fine dust and mixing with her saliva enters her body. She too can feel the growing warmth that washes over her entire body. It is the warmth of a hot bath on a cold morning. She smiles, knowing she is blessed at last. She can feel it in her heart and in her womb.

Bal Kanhoji

It is the month of Shravan.* A squadron of hawks keeps watch, circling amidst low clouds. After a pampered pregnancy and fat with fried mackerel roe, Ambabai gives birth to a son on *Ravivar.*** It is the auspicious day of Nariyel Purnima. Ambabai has returned to her father's house in Shitole to give birth. Tukoji is in Suvarnadurg preparing for the homecoming of his son. His son's nursery is painted yellow with turmeric and limestone, and he makes sure the newly painted room is scrubbed with generous amounts of cow dung and urine slurry. But Tukoji cannot wait. His son is already two weeks old, so he goes up to Shitole on his finest steed with the most thoughtfully appointed carts to bring his beloved wife and his young son back home.

For the birth of his son, he had made sure a *jyothshi**** was at hand in Shitole to record the time of his birth and draw his astrological chart. The moon did not set that day. The jyothshi checks twice and then once again with the assistance of his clearer-eyed assistant. The *Navagrahas* have aligned for his birth. His *rashi* is Kumbha.

---

* Fifth month of the Hindu calendar.

** Sunday.

*** Astrologer who calculates birth charts.

'This boy is protected by the Sun, Moon and Sea. His chart looks like that of a king, a king with many sons,' the jyothshi informs Tukoji.

Overjoyed, Tukoji bathes the harbinger of prosperous calculations in borrowed silver coins.

Tukoji in his thirties is more patient but has eyes only for his eldest, looking at his son with great amusement and letting him do what he wills. The boy is deliciously fat: every ponytailed girl and toothless hag takes turns to count the rings he has on his arms and thighs, comparing him to the butter thief god. They name him Kanho. His dark eyes are alive and sparkling with curiosity and his neck is always straining to look farther and farther. Ambabai holds him to her chest for the first two years and then he must share a breast with the younger sister. As he begins to toddle, a maid and his *sais*'s* son replace Ambabai's constant surveillance. They attempt to follow the growing boy as he licks, tears and pokes at everything around him. He likes being carried outside and directs with an outstretched finger the way up to the bastions and chuckles with the sea breeze on his face where his mother has dabbed two—for good measure—big black circles of kajal to ward off envious eyes.

When the monsoon comes and he has had a taste of its fat cooling drops, he constantly wails till he is taken outside. There are arguments between husband and wife.

'He will die of the cold and fever. Who takes the child out in rain like that?' she says.

Tukoji does, astride his favourite mare, his son sitting in front of him, his palm shielding the boy's ecstatic face, laughing in the rain.

With the grace of Khandoba of Jejuri, Kanho is healthy and strong-limbed. Curious and energetic, his cheeks have melted away and he resists sleeping. His days are spent clambering the rocks and catching crabs and starfish with the toddlers from the adjacent fishing village.

---

* Horse groom.

On the evening of a harrying day, Tukoji overhears Kanho's maid: 'If you don't go to sleep, the big *naag* that lives in the wall will bite your eyes.'

He is livid and scolds her for scaring his son. The next day, the woman is absent: unwell with fear.

Ambabai tells Tukoji she can't replace such a dedicated guardian, her second child is just a four-month-old infant, and has come out early, 'so don't scare everyone away'.

Tukoji is the senior of the two Sarnaubats at Suvarnadurg. With Killedar Mohite always away at his estate at Talsure, he runs the fort. They have three rooms not far from the water reservoir and a few servants to look after their needs. Their life is simple and Ambabai has some silver, but very little gold. His stable, always teetering and tottering, is doing better. He found a new sais, hanging by a short noose, on a pipal tree, the Pashtoon incarnation of Ashvavira. Tukoji cut him down, and now for shelter and anonymity, he works for him.

Tukoji and his family all sleep in the same room. The infant sleeps in a cradle beside Ambabai, and Kanho is between her and Tukoji's side by the door. Having eaten before dusk, his wife and children are in bed early: too early for little Kanho. The infant is fast asleep snuggling against her mother. Kanho's legs are in the air as he tries to somersault to where his father sleeps.

'Go to sleep,' Ambabai admonishes Kanho.

'After Baba comes. Where is Baba?' Kanho asks his mother.

'He is busy with the Majumdar, go to sleep, close your eyes,' she commands.

Kanho is bored.

'Tell me a story,' he asks.

'There once was a king called Dasratha.'

'No, not the same one, another story.'

Ambabai tells him of the Siddi, a line of Abyssinian warlords who hold twelve forts along the coast, including the impregnable one off Rajpura called Janjira.

'Hundreds and hundreds of years ago, a giant Habshi hid himself and his men in barrels and lay adrift near Janjira,' she tells him. The story describes how the first Siddi, a corsair for the Sultan of Ahmednagar, smuggled his troops into the fort in crates and barrels, for that was the only way to enter this ancient fort, with guile.

'They are still there, his successors—elected from amongst the Habshi captains of the Konkan. It is blessed by four freshwater springs though the fort sits surrounded by the sea,' she says.

'So let him sit in his fort,' is Kanho's response.

'Oh, that he does during the day, but at night he comes out from a secret tunnel that connects to Rajapuri. Black against the black night, he is invisible,' Ambabai says.

'Then what does he do?'

'First he looks for little children who are playing outside after the sun has set. He can smell them because they have not taken a bath. After he catches all of them, he starts looking for children who are awake.'

'What does he do with them?' Kanho asks anxiously.

'Some he eats and others he packs into dhows and sends them across the seas for his giant family to eat,' she says in a scary voice.

Tukoji comes in, having bathed, and lies down on his bed and listens to the rest of Ambabai's story.

'They are not giants or *rakshasas**,' Tukoji assures his son. He will need to find a *gurukul* for the boy.

Kanho is up with his father. In his little hands, the slingshot is a formidable and accurate weapon the fauna of the Konkan dread. Tukoji pays Kanho a *dam* for every rodent he can slay. He has just traded a colt for a rare and new kind of musket. Made in some Firangistan, it has a wheellock. It is self-igniting and does not have a flare. It can be used in a little rain too. To the horror of the local parrots and his wife, Tukoji gives the weapon to Kanhoji. The next day, Tukoji takes Kanho down to the market to meet a Firangi called

---

* Demons.

Campos. This old man can fix powder-powered weapons and if a wound must be sealed with fire and powder, this is the man to do it. Campos opens the musket up and shows him its different parts. Then he teaches Kanho how to clean it. Next, he tells him where to put the powder and where to drop the shot.

'First, pull the cock back to the full cock position,' he demonstrates.

He loads the pan with *barud* before closing the pan's cover. Then he winds the striking wheel and engages the safety.

'This is the *kutri*,' Campos transliterates the word dog, and shows him how to set the spring-loaded arm. Kanho is tickled with the word.

'Now when you pull the trigger, this pan will open and . . .' aiming the trigger at a broken pot in his courtyard, Campos fires. The cock falls back and brings the pyrites in contact with the jagged edge, which ignites sparks that light the charge in the pan. The pot explodes. There is noxious smoke everywhere and Kanho runs away in a fit of coughing.

He soon starts calling his new weapon Kutri, and when his mother admonishes him for it, he explains why with great enthusiasm. Tukoji drills into him the habit of cleaning his musket. His ward now is the pockmarked Pashtun sais who is keeping his father's meagre stable from the brink of collapse. Ambabai insists he is a murderer and Tukoji agrees. Obviously must have been somebody from his own *kabila*—for he shuns his own race. He can cure colic and keep them sweating through the year. He knows how to keep their hooves dry. He whispers in their ears, and they grunt back to him, and he nods his head knowingly. In the Konkan, men are replaceable, horses less so and Ambabai knows she must put up with Basheer Khan. She does not mind Chandu Koli, her husband's shadow, her husband's nakhwa and if her husband were to lose a hand, its ready surrogate.

Basheer Khan, perpetually squinting, carries Kanho on his shoulders as he works the horses. Chandu's son, Suryavanshi, runs between his feet, catching grasshoppers and butterflies. Basheer puts a saddle on the breeding mare. Tukoji calls her Sunheri, her coat has a metallic golden sheen. Basheer chose her at the Kalyan fair, bought from a Turkmeni horse trader from Kandahar. She is a noble and intelligent lady of the Akhal Teke: a breed known for stamina and the ability to endure extreme weather and terrain. Basheer shortens the stirrup belts and puts Kanho on Sunheri's back. It's not the boy's first time, but today Basheer is going to teach him how to trot.

In the heat of the afternoon, Kanho swims with Surya. They wear white *langots*, which are stripped off and held over their heads whilst they cross the fray of creeks or swim up to barges and dhows to extract a toll. They spear fish at the coral reefs to the south. Kanho's arms are burnt, and legs scarred by barnacle encrusted rocks and thorny bushes. At dusk, his name reverberates across the fort, above the rocks below and the fields around. Ambabai complains and Tukoji smiles proudly.

The rains come and Tukoji has taken them to his ancestral village, where his mother and blind father live. It is not far from the basalt fortress of Kulaba, which Tukoji heard was once their family seat. Sekhoji Sankhpal has had an old arquebus found and gifts it to his precious grandson: the first born of his firstborn. Its broken tripod has been repaired and it is a welcome addition to Kanho's wheel-lock which is now tied and retied with copper wire along the length of its barrel. The next morning, Kanho sets up at the edge of his grandfather's paddy field and threatens the sharecroppers in jest. Tukoji sees him and gives him a slap across the back of his head. Little Kanho is stunned; it's the first time.

'Never point a gun at anybody or unsheathe your sword unless you mean to kill. These are not toys, they are weapons. Don't be frivolous with the instruments of death, it is a perverse power one derives from them that can very soon turn you into an animal.'

Kanho is embarrassed and he apologizes to his father. He stops pointing his weapons at the two-legged animal: Khandoba preserve the rest. He walks in one morning holding an immense squirrel by the tail, there is blood on the floor and Ambabai is livid. Kanho deftly blocks the copper *kadchchi* his mother has thrown and sprints away. Ambabai tells Tukoji of his son's bloodlust. Tukoji wonders how else the boy's aim will improve. She suspects Kanho and Surya have eaten the squirrel and is disgusted when Tukoji laughs it off.

Kanhoji has formed a *paltan* of boys who ride out on three horses, the loyal sais being forced to commandeer his own master's horse in an unsuccessful chase. The gang consists of Kanhoji astride a stallion called Uchhaisravas, Suryavanshi holding on behind him, a nephew of the Raja of Kudal on his own steed, accompanied by Manu Mohite, the killedar of Suvarnadurg's son. The sixteen-*bigha** fort is older than time itself. Seven years ago, the outermost walls of the fort were expanded by Shivaji Maharaj to include fields, stables and housing; while an inner string of fortifications had been built by the Bahmani Shahs to defend an ancient fortress hewn out of the solid rock cliff. The ancient citadel that sat in the heart of the fort was an impenetrable basalt tower much like Gheria to the south. The children were free to play anywhere except the powder store which was always under guard and off-limits to the children, Kanho included.

Increasingly the days and nights are spent in the fields and jungles around the fort. Straying livestock is collateral damage while they search for tigers, leopards and bears at night. Leopards and wild boars are aplenty but most of the glowing eyes or a rustling back they fire on turn out to be nightjars, goats and the occasional pig that has strayed too far from its sty. When Basheer can afford it, he recompenses the aggrieved owner of the maimed or dead animal from his meagre allowance, but when he is out of pocket Ambabai must make the compensatory payments. She henceforth disallows Basheer from cowing down the aggrieved peasants and instead commands him that he should bring the aggrieved party to her for any reparations.

Whether it is a stick between their legs or riding a donkey, the children of the Konkan emulate their brave new king and his ever

---

* Measurement of land equal to 0.6 of an acre.

willing and wily sardars. They re-enact famous battles and the attacks on Afzal and Shaista Khan—all of them rearing to grow up and join the ranks of their king's army. Early one morning, a little before dawn, the boys are besieging a tiny village behind Harnai; they shoot a *lota* off under a farmer relieving himself in the fields. Basheer plays tough, but when the villagers assemble and threaten to tell Tukoji, he falls at their feet. This is not the first time, they remind him. They know of the boy; he is a menace. Why don't they stick to stealing fruits like regular children?

Basheer promises a silver lota to replace the copper one and an oath that the children will never return.

Later in the season, Basheer's loyalty is tested. He overhears Kanho planning to attack a Siddi patrol. He chooses his employer over his ward and his relationship with Kanho is forever damaged. Tukoji is not overly worried: boys will be boys. But he realizes his son needs discipline, the authority of a guru. Ambabai feels her son needs a wife.

Brahmachari

Ambabai prevails.

Tukoji has a word with Kanhoji that evening.

'Shivaji Maharaj has many wives, and he took his first one when he was younger than you. This is the way it is. Mathura will stay with her parents even after you are married and come to you when she is a woman.'

Kanho listens intently. It isn't often his father is present or is in the habit of interfering with his son's life, so Kanhoji listens intently and agrees to do whatever his father decides. Though Tukoji himself was keener on finding his son a suitable tutor, he throws himself behind his wife's desire to pick and choose her daughter-in-law. As the mother of two children, the third died; Ambabai's place in the universe has drastically improved after the fourteen barren and painful years.

On his wedding day, Tukoji presents Kanhoji with his first full-sized steel sword. It has a simple but beautifully finished scabbard in silver, filigreed with golden tigers, cranes and bears. It too was made in the smitheries of Vijayanagara and the blade is made of intricately patterned ukku steel. It is almost as big as Kanhoji, and he holds it so it doesn't drag on the floor.

Eight-year-old Mathurabai Bhonsale turns out to be a head taller than her husband. The top of his burgundy turban equals her height; they make an impressive pair even at this young age. She is thin and lanky with a head full of thick hair. Kanhoji is dark and a formidable chest is just beginning to take shape under the baby fat. A ubiquitous comment is that their inherent differences in height and colour will render their progeny very beautiful. Mathura has already heard all her cousins gush about her husband-to-be and she is as happy as her anxiety permits. Tied together in a fine shawl, Mathura and Kanhoji proceed by touching the feet of the elders, beginning with the grandparents all the way down to aunts and uncles, some of whom are still younger than they are and take their blessings in turn.

'Please meet Pandit Joshi,' says Kanhoji's father-in-law to Tukoji, 'it was he who read their *kundli*.'*

'Their kundlis are suitable,' says Pandit Joshi to Tukoji dismissively. The Pandit is a slightly built man with an aquiline nose and grey eyes. Tukoji marvels at the freshness and cleanliness this Brahmin exudes: every hair, every crease of the dhoti is in place. He smells of petrichor.

'My son has just finished his schooling with Guruji, and I am forever indebted to him for his efforts. Let me tell you, he can straighten a pig's tail,' says Kanho's father-in-law.

'Hard work and diligence can straighten the most crooked branch, I have nothing to do with it,' says Pandit Joshi with uncharacteristic humility.

'But he is quite old, you should have sent him to a gurukul already. The stable and jungle are not much of an education,' Pandit Joshi quickly adds.

'Oh, you know how mothers are, Guruji,' says Bhonsaleji, trying to save his in-law's face.

'I too am to blame as much. We had him after a long wait and want him with us, but Guruji, meeting you here is providence indeed,' says Tukoji, a little embarrassed.

---

* Astrological birth chart.

'It's not that he hasn't been trying to find his son a tutor, he was unable to find someone suitable. I must tell you, the boy is in dire need of schooling,' says Bhonsaleji in the spirit of the new family.

'Oh, Guruji is the best teacher in the Konkan, you would be most fortunate if he accepts Kanho,' he gushes further as Pandit Joshi silently accepts the compliment.

'Please Guruji, teach my son-in-law as you have taught my son,' Bhonsaleji finally insists. 'The boy truly needs you, or we will have a bandit on our hands,' he says laughing.

They all laugh and Tukoji is only slightly relieved that Kanho's reputation, though having preceded him, has not prevented the betrothal at least.

'Send him to me before the month of *Shravan*, I am not far from Suvarnadurg. On the ghat up from Harnai; Bhonsaleji knows the way.'

'Kanhoji,' calls Bhonsaleji loudly, and Kanho comes running along, his sword clutched to his side. He performs a *namaskar mudra* to all the elders present.

'So, I heard you are a good shot?' asks Kanhoji's father-in-law.

'If the barrel is straight, why should I miss?' he says cockily.

Everybody laughs but Tukoji is perturbed by what he finds to be insolence and he glares at his son.

'Let's see then. I have many straight barrels and a tiger or two out in the jungles behind the old fort. Tomorrow we go out for a hunt.'

Kanho almost jumps in joy, and bowing low, takes his leave of a laughing audience.

'*Bhau*,' Bhonsaleji later whispers to Tukoji, hugging him warmly in a private moment: 'We are proud of Kanhoji. There is nothing to worry about. I am glad my daughter is married to a tiger with fire in him. Boys will be boys. Pandit Joshi will make a man of him yet. I have spoken to him, and I will pay whatever shortfall there is in the *gurudakshina*.'

'Not at all, Bhonsaleji, I have a stable full of colts, but it is very kind of you,' says Tukoji.

Gurukul

On the morning Kanho is due to leave, Ambabai arranges a puja for an auspicious start to his studies. She thumbs a *tilak* of the finest sandalwood paste on to her son's broad forehead and prays it will be full of knowledge. Kanho is excited. This is the first time he will be staying away from home. Tukoji and his son get on separate horses and are accompanied by a small retinue of retainers that includes Chandravanshi and Basheer, who are also mounted. They ride to the border of the Waghave forest to the east. Suryavanshi comes running to say goodbye and winks, asking him to 'learn for the both of us'. He will miss Kanho the most as they are constant companions and the truest of friends. Kanhoji wonders aloud why Suryavanshi can't come along too to study?

Tukoji does not bother to answer. Kanho is slowly beginning to realize that there are some imposed differences between people that everybody sticks to, no matter what they feel. But he asks his father anyway.

'Well, Kanhoji, gurukuls are not for everyone. But he will grow up to be a great mariner and a swimmer like his father.'

'I am as good a swimmer as Surya and can hold my breath for longer. But he's good with a sword and can really throw a spear,' Kanho says.

'It's because you are a few years younger than him,' says his father.

The path starts winding uphill and soon father and son get off their horses and trudge up the narrow and risky mule path along the escarpment. Creepers hang down from the branches of the tall trees impeding their every move, and Chandravanshi takes the lead and slashes away at the bramble. They make a turn along the ridge and enter a series of fields nesting on the hillside. A stone-paved road opens on to a little plateau, and on its left side is a short wall with blooming creepers that block the view of the sea. The gurukul is impressive from the moment one walks through its bamboo gate, and both father and son are pleased enough just to walk around unannounced and admire the place. Tukoji has never seen anything like it. Laterite pathways lead them to gardens full of *champa* trees in full bloom. There are *tulsi* plants everywhere, and coconut and banana trees are plentiful. The most awesome aspect is the sea to the west behind the main house. There are two other structures there and everything is immaculately clean and manicured. It is all very tastefully and carefully done and delightful to any eye. They are only about 200–300 *dand** above sea level, but it is enough to transform the horizon into a magically vast silver expanse, cooled by a gently blowing breeze. The fronds of the coconut trees rustle crisply and flowers lilt eastward in the wind, spreading their pleasant aromas.

It is not long before Pandit Joshi emerges, assisted by a couple of young boys in their mid-teens—moustaches sprouting hesitatingly from their pursed lips. Panditji does not ask Tukoji to even freshen up, and their parting is over before either Tukoji or Kanhoji realize. The boys tell Kanho where to put his bedroll and the teak trunk that contains his clothes, lota and sandals. As he disappears inside, Tukoji is bidden farewell by Pandit Joshi, and he leaves a little surprised.

When Kanho has been allocated a place in the annex that boards the students, he comes out with the two boys—Bala and Pandurao—to find his father gone. They have shown him where he can take a bath and have him take one and change into a short white dhoti.

---

* Unit of measurement equalling 6 feet.

He has been told by one of the boys, called Pandurao, to remove all and any rings, necklaces and armbands, and return them to his father. Finding his father gone, Kanho dumps them in his wooden box. The boys take him into the row of rooms that stands behind the two other residential structures: Guruji's on the left and the hostel on the right. The students' accommodation is recessed and under the shade of a massive *kokum* tree and there is a row of jackfruit trees along a protective wall in the rear. A mass of ivy and creepers grow on the wall and roof of this third structure. It is essentially a large porch that accesses four adjoining rooms. The rooms are cool and have large windows that bring in a lot of light.

The room on the eastern side is Guruji's library and office, where he sits throughout the day reading the various scrolls, *patris* and books he has. Half a *kos* away lives a family of Mehtars. The father, a young man with two boys, comes in the night to take away the excreta of Panditji's family and the students through a little gate at the back. His payment is a corner at the edge of the field and the leftover food the Pandit's wife makes for her family and the students, and it is left near the students' latrine.

That afternoon, Panditji calls Kanho to his library to assess how much the boy knows.

'Let's see what you know first,' Pandit Joshi tells Kanhoji as he sits down across from him for his first interview. Kanho spends the rest of the day with Pandit Joshi, writing his name out for him in his indecipherable handwriting, fumbling through the most basic Marathi texts and answering all sorts of questions on his family life, beliefs and friendships. What history did he know? What stories had he heard? Kanho, always loved and supported, is always forthright with his answers. He knows what he knows and what he does not know, is because he has never heard of it before. He is unashamed.

'And what are you?' Guruji finally asks the young boy.

Kanhoji gives his genealogy the best he can, finishing with 'we are *kshatriyas**, sworn to protect the Koli Raja, and therefore called

---

* Martial and aristocratic caste.

the Sankhpals, the protectors of the Sankha Kings and my father
Tukoji has joined Shivaji Maharaj'.

'Kshatriya?' Pandit Joshi brings his pointy nose towards Kanho.

'Tell me one thing, Kanhoji Sankhpal, how is it that when Lord
Parshuram annihilated twenty-one generations of kshatriyas, one
after another, so not a single individual of that race would be left—
how did he let your family go? He washed their blood off his axe
into this very ocean you see here,' he says pointing outside to the
glimmering sea.

'Well, Guruji, maybe my great-great-great-grandfather pretended
he was dead and lay down with all the dead kshatriyas and then later
when Lord Parshuram was gone, he escaped into the jungle.'

'Well, now that I have met you, that is obviously very much a
possibility. Well, Kanho, that's all I need to know about you and your
character inherited from your lucky ancestors, who painted their own
bodies with the blood of fallen kinsmen and hid behind the corpses
of their relatives only so that they could slink away like snakes in
the night.'

Kanho is crestfallen. What happened? What has he said and what
was he meant to say? He is thoroughly confused as he walks back with
a black ball of anguish jammed in his throat. He has brought shame
upon his entire family on his first meeting with his guru. He smacks
his forehead in anger and at his own stupidity and impertinence.
He does not want to be here another minute and is equally scared
of going home. Distraught, homesick and ashamed, Kanhoji walks
around the gurukul by himself as he hears a gong being struck. All
the boys eat separately, the Brahmins with Pandit Joshi's family in
the kitchen, Pandurao and the vania boys in the adjoining room and
Kanho is served on the veranda with the weaver's sons.

By the end of his first day at Pandit Joshi's gurukul, Kanhoji knows
his fate is sealed. Panditji's son comes to wake Kanhoji in the morning,
though it is closer to the middle of the night. Kanho is allowed but
just a little time to relieve himself. He is then led to one menial task
after another, and then a little after dawn he is given a stick and asked

to graze the cows. The other students at the gurukul begin their day with a session of hatha yoga, after which they all take their first bath of the day. A boy, a few years older than Kanho, accompanies him out the first few times and then Kanho is left to his own devices. The first two days, Kanho's paralysing regret tides him over but on the third day he is visibly miserable and starts to sob in his bed at night.

'Are you okay? What happened?' asks a boy a few years older than him who shares his room with two others.

Kanho turns around to see a pair of big grey eyes peering at him in concern.

'I'm Bala Bhat. Can I get you something?'

'I'm Kanho. Water. I'm thirsty.'

Balaji gives him a copper lota of water and Kanho raises it from his lips and lets the water stream in. He returns the lota to Balaji and sits up fully.

'I know Panditji is rightfully punishing me, but if I just herd cows the whole year—what will I learn? And then Baba and Ai will find out what I said.'

They talk until Panditji's eldest son, Vithal, comes in to rouse Kanho for his duties. They immediately pretend to be asleep as soon as they hear him. On this morning, the bug-eyed boy called Pandurao, who has made it his special mission to taunt and torture Kanho at every given opportunity, accompanies Vithal. Pandurao kicks Kanho.

'Get up, you lazy cowherd,' Pandu says.

It takes Kanho another two days and Bala's presence to muster the courage and dive for Pandit Joshi's swiftly shuffling feet.

'Well, it is my duty to teach you, but since you come from such a crafty family, you need only half the time to learn. After midday, you can relieve Bhikya from the fields and he can help around the gurukul,' Panditji says with a stony voice.

Kanho starts the morning sessions with the other students at the gurukul. He makes friends with another student, Venkoji Kamath, whose grandfather is one of the biggest traders in the Konkan and a pillar of the Konkanasth Chitpavan community. Kanho instinctively realizes that when Venko is around, Guruji is kinder. Kanho, an energetic and already well-built boy, starts doing push-ups and squats every morning once their session of hatha yoga is concluded.

Later in the week, Pandurao informs Panditji that he has witnessed Kanhoji and the cow-herder roasting up little birds and eating them. When Panditji asks Kanho about it, Kanhoji says that he did not know it was disallowed. Pandit Joshi whips him with a cane and sends him to be bathed and purified. Now he is served his meals outside the house, in the yard.

One afternoon, just as Bhikya leaves and Kanho is searching for round pebbles for his afternoon hunt, a group of eight men and boys come upon him. Some are younger than him and most are as old as his father, though one is so old, he is almost dust. They carry on their business paying no heed to Kanhoji or the cows. A thin scrawny boy, a little older than him, greets him and they get talking. All of them are uniformly bony with large elbow bones and knees. They are tall and wear large colourful turbans and small langots and carry big sacks on their shoulders and wield long bamboo sticks. They are looking for *ghoos*, the large field rodents that burrow unseen everywhere and are the bane of every farmer.

'We are *musahar*s, come in from the south. Have you seen any snakes?'

'Oh yeah, several. Hit a couple with my slingshot—dead on the head. But they just run away,' he lies.

He doesn't want to admit that if he were to see a snake, he would be atop the nearest rock or up the closest tree. He can't even stand to think of them, and their mention gives him the shivers.

'We can catch any snake, even *naagrajas*,' says the musahar boy.

The musahar elders have located a snake and are patiently poking it out of a labyrinth of bandicoot burrows under the ground. They light little fires at the entrances of the burrows and blow smoke into them. The disturbed snake, a sand-coloured cobra with two eye-like designs on the back of its head emerges to confront the musahars. They deftly distract it and in a second it is in one of their shoulder sacks. By evening the women in their tribe have materialized and have erected tents of greasy sheets of calico hung on hastily chopped down branches.

Kanhoji relates all that has happened that evening to Bala with his usual embellishments, for Kanhoji worries for his sallow friend as much as Bala worries for him.

'I wish you can join me in the afternoons. It's much better than reading and mathematics.'

'I'll come tomorrow. I have a plan. We were just reading it today: about Lord Krishna and the *shesh nag*,' Bala turns to Kanho and says excitedly.

Mid-morning, Bala complains of severe and constant diarrhoea. He secretly disposes the concoction of neem leaves and haldi the Panditji's wife has instantly prepared and slips over the wall where Kanho is waiting. They head for Bhikya who is just finishing his lunch of *jowar rotis** with a heap of moringa masala, which he eats every day. Once they reach the grazing grounds where the musahars are camped out, Bala immediately heads towards the oldest looking member of the snake hunting tribe.

'Can you stuff your snakes?' he asks him without preamble.

'What do you mean stuff them?'

'I don't know, maybe with hay. We want to play a joke on our friend, and we want you to make a dummy snake from a real one. But one with five heads.'

'Five heads one body. Like this,' Bala says, picking up a twig and scratching the body of a five-headed snake on the ground.

'And it has to stand up on its own and look realistic.'

'Of course, I can. We will put sand in the tail to balance it out. It will cost you more than you have though.'

'Don't assume what we have and don't have,' Bala shoots back at the old man.

---

* Unleavened sorghum bread.

'He will show you your payment tomorrow and once we have seen what you have made, then we will pay you.'

'Well let's see what you bring tomorrow,' says the emaciated musahar elder and returns to his bandicoot tracking.

The next day, Kanhoji takes a gold ring with a small ruby set in it. He still has some rings and jewellery he hadn't been able to return to his father, but some of it seems to be missing.

The old musahar bites into the gold band and squints at the red stone.

'Give me two days,' he says, eyeing Kanho suspiciously.

When Bhikya is gone, a musahar boy called Kondu invites Kanhoji to join them for a snake hunt.

'I hate snakes. Can't really stand them. I don't know why Bala wants them,' he tells Kondu.

'Oh, don't worry. I feared snakes too. Hated them and found them repulsive. But after I killed a few, the fear went away.'

A few days later, as it was approaching dusk, Bala starts whispering worriedly to Venkoji and the other boys, about the whereabouts of Kanhoji. He still isn't back, and it is much past the time of his return with the three cows and the calf. Panditji soon hears the whispers, the white hairs on his ears tingling, and shouts for Bhikya to look for Kanho. Bhikya returns soon enough with the cows, which he says he found quietly grazing nearby. Pandit Joshi is anxious now. What if a tiger or a leopard got to the boy? It is after all the fate of most shepherds. What if Tukoji or Bhonsaleji were to ask him what he was doing grazing cattle? He calls for Vithal and the elder students and they set out with Bhikya leading the way. Soon a couple of the other students and Bala trail along behind them, helping them look for Kanho. They all search for him, calling his name out intermittently only to be squawked back at by monkeys and peacocks. They make their way past the fields towards the jungle. Bala has quietly taken the lead.

They come to a rocky hummock and Pandit Joshi climbs the mound of conglomerated mud and stone to get a better view.

The boys are excitedly chattering behind him and suddenly he puts his right hand up to silence them. He calls Vithal who clambers up the hump to his father's side. They look ahead dumbfounded and soon all the boys creep up alongside them. Kanho is sleeping in a patch of grass in front of some bushes and shading him is a five-headed naagaraj. A stone noisily rolls out of the hummock as the boys clamber on to it for a better view and the miracle they are all witnessing vanishes before their eyes. All of them are speechless, finding it hard to believe their senses, and they look at each other in confirmation. Pandurao is aghast and just as he begins to run towards Kanho, Bala motions to Kondu, who is hidden in the grass with the effigy he has just pulled back into the bushes with a string tied to its tail. Seeing the signal, he slinks away with the hydra.

'Kanho,' Bala screams at the top of his lungs and Kanhoji who has been lying on a tuft of grass across the gully from where Panditji and the group of boys are, slowly lifts his body and peers at them. He quickly gets up when he sees Guruji and runs towards them, meeting Pandurao halfway, who returns with him. Kanho runs back, first down the banks of the dry gully and then up the mound where Panditji is standing with the rest of the students. Pandurao follows him back flat-footed.

'Where's the sun?' Pandurao mumbles to himself.

Kanho immediately lunges for his Guruji's feet. Pandit Joshi is still insensate and trying to come to terms with what he has just witnessed.

'Please forgive me, Guruji, I dozed off; please forgive me. Oh no, where are the cows? Have I lost the cows? Oh, please forgive me,' Kanho pleads profusely.

'It's okay, it's okay, the cows have come home,' is all that Pandit Joshi can say.

Returning to the gurukul in twilight, Pandit Joshi periodically turns to look at Kanhoji. Pandit Joshi is in a hurry. He needs to head back to his library and consult Kanhoji's kundli again. Bhonsaleji had given him Kanho's astrological birth-chart when he wanted to check its suitability with his daughter's, at the time of the proposal. He needs to rush back and see what he missed the first time. Long after the boys are asleep, the lamp in Panditji's library remains lit as he pores over Kanhoji's birth chart recalculating it through the night. This student of his is going to grow up to be someone extraordinary, a king at least, for the planets in his chart all point towards a samrat.

First Blood

Hanuman Jayanti is just a few days away and Pandit Joshi sends Vithal along with Kanho, Bala and Venko to Harnai. Bhikya carries the torch for them but is not to touch the provisions that are needed for the puja. At the bazaar, Kanhoji contacts Basheer and cajoles the boys into visiting his father at the fort. He is missing his wheel-lock pistol and has got Basheer to get it for him along with some powder and a pouch full of shot. Basheer feels that it is best that he tells Tukoji and seeks his permission before giving the weapon to Kanhoji.

'Good, at least he hasn't lost his instincts. What's the harm?' says Tukoji and goes in and gets a heavily wrapped parcel.

'Might as well give it to him now,' he says to Basheer and asks him to call his son in without the other boys.

Kanho comes in with Bala and prostrates in namaskar to his father, touching his feet. Bala follows suit.

'Learning anything or just daydreaming?' Tukoji asks his son.

'Learning. Baba; this is Balaji Vishwanath Bhat. His elder brother works for the Siddi.'

Tukoji smiles at the boy trying to size him up.

'I know Basheer wanted me to come alone but Balaji is like my elder brother.'

'So, I have another son it seems. Well, here it is, never seen one like this. Got it off a Topikar in Vengurla. But I didn't know when I will see you next, so take it with you.'

Kanhoji accepts the wrapped parcel and starts to peel it open eagerly. When he gets past the final velvet cover, he shrieks in delight.

'Baba, what is this?' he says incredulously.

'It's called a *badakpai*. It's for close combat on ships.'

It is a pistol much like his wheellock, but with four barrels splayed out like a duck's webbed foot.

'Thank you, Baba,' Kanhoji gushes, hugging his father and loving him for always being greater and more giving than his own imagination.

'I bet no one else in the whole Konkan has a gun like this,' gasps Balaji.

'I doubt it too,' says Tukoji dryly and puts his index finger to his lips, and both the boys nod. Then Tukoji makes sure all of them are fed by the Killedar's Brahmin cook. When he is told of their consumption, he laughs as tears trickle down his cheek.

The boys are then taken by Tukoji's bullock cart along with the ghee and curd he has sent for Pandit Joshi to the house where they are to collect all the provisions they have purchased. Here they rest while the sun is at its zenith. The bullock cart takes them as far as it can, and then the boys get off carrying their loads the best they can. The cart turns around and returns towards the fort. As the cart driver returns, he hears the heartbreaking and life-altering news that has come in from Raigad. As soon as Tukoji hears the news, he sends two riders to catch up with his son and the other boys, as he knows the Siddi is bound to mark his territory anew.

Fifteen kos up the coast, sitting in the best-protected and most impregnable sea fort on the entire Konkan coast, Siddi Kasim, the ennobled Yakut Khan, Admiral of the Mughal Navy, sighs in relief as he hears that Chhatrapati Shivaji is dead. He immediately orders the famous 600 maund Kalal Bangdi canon to be fired as a mark of respect to his most constant enemy. As soon as the canon goes off, an order is given for fireworks to be lit and a celebratory feast enjoined. Then he orders for an immediate increase in patrolling around all his dominions and gives an order to engage the enemy at sight.

The boys on the rock-strewn mud path back to Pandit Joshi's purposefully inaccessible homestead, hear the cannon reverberate in the distance.

'Are you following *Karnabharam*? Where have you reached?' Vithal asks Kanho gently.

'So, what animals have you shot?' interrupts Venko as they are trudging up the forested hill.

'Lots of things. Leopards, wild boars, deer, sambar, barasinghas, porcupines, birds, squirrels, goats and once, almost a man taking a dump.'

'You mean all those animals are here? In this jungle?' asks Venkoji, suddenly alert and uncomfortable at the teeming fanged possibilities.

'What do you mean? Of course, there are even tigers here. Several tigers.'

'Never shot a tiger, *hunh*?' asks Vithal.

'Not yet, but one of these days, luck is going to run out for one of them.'

'And don't forget snakes—pythons, boas, cobras and spitting vipers,' adds Bala behind glinting grey eyes. Everybody glances at Kanho.

'What if a tiger attacks us?' butts in Venko nervously.

'I will just have to run faster than you, Venko,' replies Bala.

'Never climb up a tree or even try to, they'll get you for sure. Their paws are this big,' he says cupping his palms chest apart to show them the size of a tiger's paw.

'When have you ever seen one?' wonders Vithal.

'At my father-in-law's house. He has shot several and has the skins on his walls. I could fit my head into the stuffed tiger's open mouth.'

'Well, I just hope we don't come across one on our way back,' Vithal prays as he realizes it will soon be dark.

'Relax, I'm here,' says Kanhoji in his usual self-assured way, 'I'll handle it.' Kanhoji is in his element and feeling very much still at home.

Soon it is dark and Vithal has Bhikya light the *mashaal* and lead the way. Scores of unseen crickets are rubbing their legs and the chirr-chirring pervades the forest. Monkeys cackle and owls hoot intermittently. Soon they can see an array of yellow, orange, green and red eyes peering at them through the undergrowth and from the canopy above. The boys are on edge and Venko is trying as hard as possible to not show the overpowering terror he feels. Kanho is not scared but prefers to be prepared. He pretends to relieve himself while he pulls out his two pistols and loads all the five barrels, and tucks both into his dhoti.

The exhausted boys, carrying pots of ghee and oil and sacks of rice, flour and pulses reach the fork on the hill path. Vithal suggests that they take the steep shortcut, as it would be much quicker. Kanhoji wants to take the longer but easier road, saying it wouldn't matter if they get there an hour earlier or later. They start up the long path that sensibly zigzags up the hill's gradient. It is wider and free of branches and underbrush, and all along, they keep their distracting banter up. They see some light up ahead on the path and assume it to be farmers rushing to Harnai or farther home. As they turn the corner, the boys come face to face with four Siddi patrolmen and their mashaal carrier.

'And where are you boys going to at this time of night and what is all this you have with you?' asks one of the patrolmen.

'Just taking some provisions home for the puja,' says Bhikya, his voice quavering at the sight of their glistening swords.

'Puja for your dead king?' the patrolman shoots back.

'Well, let's see what provisions you have in there,' pants an immensely fat patrolman.

'Forget it, let's not waste our time, they are just young boys,' says the third Siddi patrolman.

'Young boys are not much different than ripe girls,' the fat one says as he walks into view. He is rubbing his crotch and leering at

Bala and Venko. The four patrolmen start giggling as they advance towards the boys.

'Later, we can get a good price for them,' their fat commander assures his men as he unsheathes his sword.

Bhikya and Kanho have been keeping an eye on each other, and as the commander followed by two of his men walks towards Balaji and Venkoji, Kanhoji whips out his duck-foot pistol, removes the safety and fires. Four explosions rip through the air and echo against the hillside. Kanho disappears in a cloud of smoke. The commander and the fat patrolman slump to the ground while the third's elbow is macerated and his forearm hanging on a strip of skin. Bhikya smashes his mashaal into the patrolman standing next to him. The patrolman is burnt and screams in pain as he clutches his face. He stumbles and gets up again and launches himself at Bhikya. Kanhoji already has his trusty wheel-lock drawn and pulls the trigger at the patrolman. The shot hits him on his cheek and he collapses in front of Bhikya. Bhikya quickly grabs the sword and rushes the patrolman with the swinging forearm who is advancing towards Kanhoji with a spear in his good hand. Bhikya slashes him across his back and opens the base of his skull. The patrolman falls with the sword still stuck in his spine at Kanhoji's feet. Their *mashaalwala*, a boy of eight or nine and unarmed, darts back the way they had come.

Their own mashaal is lying on the ground and its scattered embers light up the four log-like lumps on the path, which are bleeding out. Kanhoji grabs a spear and stabs each of the bodies in the throat. Bhikya kicks them to make sure they are dead. Then both boys bend over, breathing heavily at first and then retching their guts out. Their knees are trembling, and they collapse on the ground.

Bala runs over to Kanho to check for injuries. Finding none, he helps him up and gives him water.

'Bala, you and your *chikna* ass. Always getting us into trouble,' says Kanho laughing between heavy breaths, his adrenaline forcing out a dark humour. Bala is wide-eyed and does not reply.

'Let's get the bodies off the road,' says Kanho, and Bhikya replies that they shouldn't have let the mashaalwala go.

Venko has wet himself, but nobody is bothered as Vithal has too. They wait for Venko to come to his senses and clean him up after he has a bout of vomiting. Then they roll the heavy corpses over the cliff.

'What the hell was that?' Vithal finally asks Kanho.

'Luck, my friend, luck. Can you believe it, my father gave this to me today?'

'You just killed four people, both of you,' Vithal says looking at Kanhoji.

'So?' Kanho says and starts laughing. Bhikya starts laughing too.

A shiver runs down Vithal's spine and his hair stands on end, his body suddenly covered with goosebumps. He picks up the mashaal and after restuffing and lighting it, leads them back home. Balaji and Kanhoji are both discussing what the patrolman had meant when he said their king was dead. It cannot be, Shivaji Maharaj is their king, and he is still young and fighting fit.

Hanuman Jayanti proceeds sombrely. Everybody is on their knees weeping, old and young, man and woman. Each has torn their chest apart revealing the idol of their king that they hold in their hearts. The righteous umbrella under whom they had taken shade and sought protection is gone, and they burn in the sordid sun and are drenched in the apocalyptic rain. Kanhoji, sitting outside as it drizzles, is shattered. How is this possible? He had seen it play out so many times in his mind: Shivaji, standing in *tandav*, his left heel on the Padishah's chest; making him the subedar of the Konkan. He could see his father beaming at his side and Suryavanshi cheering him, the Arabian Sea in the backdrop. In his dreams this scene is always set at the bastion at Suvarnadurg Fort, which has the flagpole planted by Maharaj.

'Too soon, too soon,' mutters Panditji under his breath. All the children but Bala mistake it for a mantra.

The mudras and mantras of the puja having been performed exactly, perhaps with an unusual urgency, Panditji leaves everyone to their own devices and retreats to his study to consult the *kundli* of the new Chhatrapati. Balaji finds Kanhoji sitting with Bhikya on the paved road outside their compound in a teary drizzle. They are trying to recreate the chain of events and remember what transpired the night before as blinding flashes, sulphuric smoke and adrenaline obfuscate their memories.

'What happened yesterday?' Bhikya asks Bala as he sits down with them.

'Kanhoji had removed his gun before I saw them. I saw him remove the gun when he put the sacks down to take a piss. I know he had it on him. He was just in front of me. Then, suddenly—bang and there was so much smoke.'

'I heard Guruji is going to meet your father,' Bhikya says to Kanho.

'Let him, I don't care. What did I do wrong? If he wants to send me back to grazing, I don't care about that. I am not going to become a *munshi** anyway.' Looking at Bala he adds, 'Not that there's anything wrong with that, but I am a Sankhpal, and as you can see, I can well perform my own dharma.'

'*Arre*, I will tell them what happened. If you hadn't reacted and didn't have your badakpai, you and I would have been fine, but Shriman Balaji, Shriman Venkoji and Shriman Vithalji would have been the fair damsel slaves of the Siddi.'

All three of them laugh, well knowing it would have probably been true.

'Kanho, you are a kshatriya who has proven himself in battle,' assures Bala directly.

'Guruji wants to tell your father about the other thing,' says Bala.

'Well then, saving your pink bottom was the least I could do for you after what you have done for me.'

'These things I don't keep an account of Kanho,' Bala winks at Kanho.

'Of course not, we are friends,' says Kanho, putting out his raised hands and the other two boys reach out and clasp their hands together—Bhikya hesitating till Kanho pulls him in.

---

* Accountant.

'So, Bala, what do you think is going to happen now, with Maharaj gone?' Kanho asks his much wiser friend.

'Aurangzeb will be thanking his stars. If he wins, then we've all had it,' Bala says, making a slicing motion over his penis.

'We are not finished, Sambhaji Raje will lead the fight,' says Kanho.

Bala makes a tippling motion with his hands.

'*Bakwas*,' shouts Kanhoji angrily.

'You are a *Bahman*, you can't understand. Everybody drinks. My father drinks sometimes and my uncle drinks all day. It's no big deal, we Marathas drink. Sambhaji Raje escaped from Agra with Maharaj as a child,' Kanho reminds them.

'Yes, actually that is true,' says Bala, shaken and surprised at his young friend's loyalty.

'Eating meat, onions and garlic heat the blood up which is good for fighting, but the side effect is drinking and insatiable carnal desires. Just like the Siddi who will be rearing for a fight,' Bala further adds in everybody's defence.

'Then what—look at Bhikya. He's always eating meat and always sporting a lance ready for battle,' Kanhoji jokes.

'Actually, Kanhoji, you saved the patrolmen by killing them, otherwise Bhikya would have given it to them in the rear,' Bala says, trying to be crude.

They laugh forcibly, drowning out their terror.

Through the gate, Pandurao Phangaskar, the resident moral policeman, appears.

'What are you guys laughing about? Maharaj is dead and you boys are laughing?' Pandurao accuses them.

'Nothing,' Kanhoji says and continues to chuckle.

'It's how we deal with grief,' Bala offers.

Bhikya looks down in guilt and fear for being found with his friends.

'Always laughing like monkeys and wasting time. And what is this filthy *achyut*[*] doing here?' Pandurao says seething with vitriol.

---

[*] Untouchable.

'How dare you keep sitting when I am here?' he says directly to Bhikya and kicks a stone towards him that cuts his cheek. Kanhoji jumps up and takes a step towards Pandurao and punches the air in front of the much taller boy's face, and Pandurao, shielding himself with raised arms, shouts for Vithal as he retreats scared.

'Guruji is calling the both of you,' he lies, to Bala adding: 'You better take a bath before you dirty us all.'

'Go milk the cows,' he barks at Bhikya, not knowing it is not milking time.

Pandurao turns around and leaves as if distracted with a multitude of worries and chores, muttering abuses under his breath: 'Lazy, filthy, untouchables, good for nothings.'

'What did you say?' Kanho shouts at Pandurao, who just quickens his pace without responding and then breaks into a run towards the safety of Panditji's wife's kitchen.

'Don't mind him. Bhikyu, he is only here because his father promised eightfold gurudakshina.'

'He's an arse,' says Bala as Bhikya looks down in shame.

'I think I should go and see my father—they will need recruits for the coming battles,' says Kanho once Pandurao is gone.

'Don't even think about it; after what happened yesterday, the area will be full of the Siddi's troops. The mashaalwala is not going to report that they were bested by a bunch of boys,' shoots back Bala.

'I'll join up with you, if your father will have me,' says Bhikya as he gets up waving, letting them know he will meet up later, and heads to the well. Both the boys go in to see what Guruji wants only to realize that he is unaware of having called for them.

Gurudakshina

It is late in the evening and the sun has set. As the deputy commander of Suvarnadurg, Tukoji's duty never ends. He is physically tied to the fort, as his superior isn't. Achloji Mohite, who is the killedar, lives on a breezy hillock amidst a leafy estate of jackfruit, mango, areca nut and coconut trees. The estate is farther inland in the village of Talsure. There, in a preposterous palace with an arid courtyard, he visits his junior wife, son Mankoji and his three daughters whenever he comes in from Kolhapur or Raigad. Achloji is currently at Raigad attending the funerary ceremonies of the departed Chhatrapati.

'Sarnaubat *Saheb*,' one of his guards says, running up to him.

'I am sorry to disturb you—but you have a visitor,' he says and from behind him out pops Kanhoji.

Tukoji stands up in alarm and rushes to his child, 'What happened? How are you here? Did you not go back?'

'We did go back. The two men you sent after us are still at the gurukul.'

Relieved but curious, Tukoji dismisses the guard, telling him to send up his manservant and calls his son to the room that functions as his command post.

'Is everything all right, Kanhoji?' Tukoji asks anxiously.

'I did something, or rather let someone do it for me. I mean, it was his idea, but I really liked it and let it happen,' says Kanhoji.

'Tell me, Kanhoji, it doesn't matter. I need to know because then I can try to stop something worse coming of it, now, before it gets too complicated. What did you do?'

Kanhoji tells him about meeting the musahars and the ring he traded with them, and Panditji and the boys finding him in the jungle.

'But why were you grazing the cows in the first place?'

Kanhoji tells him about his exchange with Panditji.

Tukoji chuckles. Kanhoji's dread melts off his shoulders.

'You must be very respectful of your teachers, Kanhoji. What does your ai always tell you? *Guru Mata Paramathma*—in that order.'

'Hao, Baba,' says Kanhoji, relieved.

'Kanhoji, if you can take one thing from me, take this: always be aligned with the truth and keep away from fraud and lies. Anyway, now that it's done, just don't say anything about it any more. That same Balaji, who had come with you?'

'Yes Baba, he's extremely intelligent: the sharpest person I have ever met.'

'More like cunning,' qualifies Tukoji.

Tukoji's manservant comes in to take Kanhoji to wash up and meet his mother.

'Oh, yeah, yesterday on the way up, I shot four patrolmen who wanted to take us for slaves.'

'Wait, what, what?' Tukoji shouts.

A little later, Tukoji is shaking Ambabai awake. He is beaming with pride, and she wakes up to him exulting: 'Your son is a tiger. You gave birth to a fiery tiger.'

When Kanhoji retraces what happened that night—the gaps filled in by Tukoji as if he too had been there, Ambabai is horrified and starts to cry uncontrollably. Tukoji returns to his post while his family goes to sleep. Chandravanshi, who had rushed up to Tukoji the second he heard his boss's eldest son was at the fort unexpectedly, is the next to hear of the encounter. The two men talk into the morning as they sip from clay tumblers. It was well worth the long wait he and Ambabai suffered, Tukoji says. Chandu believes a part of Maharaj's *atman* has entered young Kanho.

As soon as he is up and bathed the next morning, Kanhoji goes to find his father. Kanhoji is famous. Everybody is hailing his name and waving out to him. They are calling him a tiger and a warrior. Obviously, word of the escapade has spread. He finds his father at the flagpole bastion with Chandu.

'Angria,' Chandravanshi says to Kanhoji, clasping him to his chest and patting his back.

Kanhoji touches his father's feet.

'Baba, is the Siddi going to attack?'

'Well son, at a time like this when we are mourning our dead king and busy with the change of guard—it makes sense to attack.'

'Can I join you? I mean the navy, the defence of the *Swaraj*.'

'Does Pandit Joshiji know you are here or did you run away?' Tukoji counters.

'Whatever Panditji is teaching us, Balaji is learning. We will work together as a team. With Suryavanshi and Bhikya who are going to join us too.'

'Well, that's just not how life works, son. You need to be independently competent, educated and intelligent.'

'Please? Don't you think it would be better if I learnt practical things?'

'We'll teach you everything there is to learn,' says Chandravanshi.

'What nonsense, Chandravanshi. First, he must educate himself, know how to read and write well, know the *shastras*, know about other people and their customs, know how to speak with confidence, quote scriptures to make a point when need be. Education is standing on the shoulders of our ancestors. These things are very important in life. Soldiering is a dog's world.'

'Saheb is right,' Chandravanshi says apologetically.

'Let Panditji call you what he wants, swallow your pride and learn and absorb everything he has to offer. That is intelligence and humility.'

'I have to go back?' asks Kanhoji sullenly.

'Immediately; your teacher has sent a message with the riders. He wishes to speak to me and now I know of several reasons why he would. So, you will be taken up and Panditji brought down.'

Tukoji has himself seen and experienced the calm fortitude of Maharaja Chhatrapati and seen his dreadnought eyes. The Chhatrapati's humility towards the learned Brahmins and his unvarying decency towards women, slave or prisoner, has been the hallmark of his righteousness. It had given him the mandate to increase his dominion and lengthen the spokes of his umbrella and shade the farmers and the craftsmen in peace and security. Tukoji wants his son to be a similar person: fearless and humble. Humility, though, has never been his son's strong point. The young boy has an insatiable desire to be a better rider than his Pathan sais and a better swordsman than himself. The winds have fanned the ember.

Back at the gurukul, one rain-drenched afternoon, Balaji's *mama*[*] unexpectedly arrives from Chiplun. He seeks out Pandit Joshi and has a private word with him. Balaji is called in and Panditji has a long talk with him. When Balaji comes out with his mama, he is crying uncontrollably. All Kanhoji can catch while he helps Balaji pack his meagre possessions is that his elder brother has died. Kanhoji does not press him for any information, as he is sobbing uncontrollably— the always-astute Balaji is debilitated. Balaji's mama leaves with him as soon as he has come. Kanhoji is shattered; 'We had a few more years together,' he thinks, 'nothing ever goes according to plan.'

Kanhoji runs to Pandit Joshi demanding to be told what has happened to his best friend. Pandit Joshi explains the convoluted situation Balaji has been knotted in. Balaji's elder brother, who had taken on the mantle of the provider of the family, had been employed at the Siddi's extensive salt pans and depot in Chiplun. This was one of the largest salt pans in the area, only superseded by the pans near Thana and Bhiwandi, which have been supplying the Desha for centuries. Salt from

---

[*] Maternal uncle.

these coastal areas crosses over the Himalayas and reaches Tibet while Chinese and Javanese junks trade the salt as far away as Nihong. The charge was still unclear, but the Siddi's troops had sewn Balaji's brother into a sack while he was still alive and thrown him into the Vashishti flowing nearby. Punished but still indebted, Balaji's dead brother was now held to recompense for the losses incurred or imagined. The dead young man not having any material wealth, the Siddi decided to confiscate his mother and younger brother as slaves, and they were auctioned off. Balaji's mama had bought them on a loan taken by indenturing his sister and nephew to the very same Siddi. This way, they did have a chance of regaining their freedom once the loan was repaid. Kanhoji understands and is disgusted.

Kanhoji's time at the gurukul ends and his father comes up to get his son and pay Pandit Joshi the gurudakshina—the fees for all the knowledge he has bestowed upon his son. The investiture ceremony is a *havan** with invocations to Saraswati Devi. In turn, the students receive a sandalwood tilak on their foreheads and a white cotton shawl from their guruji, they touch his feet and present him with their gurudakshina. It is Kanhoji's turn, he respectfully touches his guruji's feet and bows his head in namaskar. Tukoji steps up and two of his men bring a chest laden with silks and fine cotton on which lies a purse of silver and some gold coins. There are baskets of fruits and sacks of rice, grain and pulses besides, which have been left in the kitchen.

Pandit Joshi brings his hands together in a namaskar and addresses Kanhoji: 'Son, there is only one thing I ask as gurudakshina, and I ask it from you. I want nothing from your father, without in the least wishing to disrespect him.'

'Of course, Guruji, whatever it is, please tell me?' asks Kanhoji, very curious about where this new turn will take him.

'All I want is that you make sure I always have this house and my surrounding fields, what I already have now. Let me always have this and leave this to me.'

---

* Ritual burning of offerings, especially ghee.

'Yes, of course, Guruji,' replies Kanhoji without comprehension.

Tukoji understands what Guruji is getting at and has his son repeat the promise to Pandit Joshi with an addendum on providing security.

'Who is that boy?' Kamath Seth, who is behind Tukoji, asks his son Venko.

The School of Life

Kanhoji climbs on to a beautiful piebald colt, which the almost blind and white-bearded Basheer hands to him and they ride down to Harnai. Ambabai cries tears of joy to see Kanho and cannot believe how much he has changed from the last time they met. She teases him about a moustache he is trying to rear and says at least it has more follicles than foals his father has managed. The father and son are inseparable as they talk throughout the day. Kanhoji has another well dug, leading his father's labourers in its construction. Then he expands the stables for the breeding mares his father has got from Kathiawar and Mewar. The plan is to breed them with the best imported Arab stallions crossing through the Konkan gateway.

'What do you want to do now?' Tukoji asks his son. He is proud of his boy's strong frame and the fine features he has inherited from his mother.

'I want to join Maharaj,' says Kanho with surety.

'You know, if I could go back to when I was younger and had just known a little bit more about what was around me, it would have helped me immensely. No harm in knowing the lay of the land. Why don't you travel around the coast? Go to Surat, go to Keral, Lanka even.'

'Sightseeing or on pilgrimage?' asks Kanhoji sarcastically.

'Whichever you wish,' says Tukoji.

'I already know how to handle a sword, fire a gun and a cannon. I want to fight against Aurangzeb.'

'We are Konkani, we will stay in the Konkan and protect it from him or anybody else. But my boy, in the Konkan, you must know the sea and you must know boats, and to truly know the secrets of the waves, you need to learn it from a Habshi.'

'So, you want me to join the Siddi?'

'Not the Siddi but a Siddi. As a true Konkani Maratha, you must master the boat and the waves as well as the horse and its reins,' Tukoji reminds his son.

'I already know how to sail,' Kanho says sullenly.

'Tomorrow you will take a letter to Habshi Rehman Ali,' Tukoji instructs his son.

Kanhoji detours to Chiplun. He must find Balaji, know if he still lives. Once he gets to the salt pans, he asks the Agaris working the pans where he can find Balaji Vishwanath Bhat. No one has heard of him there, so Kanhoji asks for the storehouses, where, if his friend were still around, he would most probably be working. Kanhoji removes his turban as he approaches and tries to blend in with the heavy traffic of workers going in and out of the storehouse blocks. There are several rows of high-roofed stone structures with small entrances that lie behind the large depot where the loose salt comes in on bullock carts. From the depot, it is weighed and stitched into coir or hemp gunny bags. They are then manually carried to the storehouses, where they are measured again before being accounted for and stored in massive stacks. Kanhoji sees a line of workers moving a stack of sacks into the storehouse and he gets into line. Two workers on a slightly raised platform put a bag on his shoulders and he follows the man in front of him to the storehouse. Once he has entered the first row of storehouses, he puts the bag down and goes looking for Balaji. He sees a distinctively Chitpavan Brahmin man working at some ledgers and asks him about Balaji. Without looking up, the accountant raises his hand and points to the room behind him, continuing with the double-checking of his entries.

Kanhoji walks into the room to find Balaji in the position he most often saw him in, sitting on the floor in front of a low desk intently reading or writing something.

'Balaji,' Kanhoji says softly to the only boy in the room still engrossed in his work. Balaji looks up and his grey eyes almost pop out of their sockets.

'Kanhoji, is that you?' says Balaji ecstatic.

'Then who? Manoharibai Chhanchanwali? I was hoping you were still alive,' says Kanhoji as if they had just met yesterday.

They agree to meet at the gate once Balaji's day at the warehouse is done.

In the evening they walk along the banks of the Vashishti River and Balaji shows him the spot where he is told they threw his brother in, bound in a sack.

'How is your mother?'

'She works for the Mazumdar's wife. Household work. But at least they didn't send her to the pans. Only the Agaris can survive that,' Bala says morosely.

Kanhoji takes off all the jewellery he has, including a silver armband his grandmother gave him and shoves it towards Balaji.

'I don't know if this will be enough but put it towards her release.'

'No, no, Kanhoji, I can't,' Balaji protests, pushing the gift back.

Kanhoji forces his ornaments into Balaji's hands and loudly says: 'You well can, and you well will. She is my mother too. Think of her.'

Balaji looks down as tears run down his cheeks.

Kanhoji shakes him gently by the shoulders saying: 'You know this is going to change—your luck and your life.'

Balaji joins his palms in prayer and looks up at the sky, wishing Kanhoji's words would fly straight to the ears of Parshuram as he chokes up in grief.

'Anyway, tell me, who was that girl at the salt works?' says Kanhoji, trying to lighten the mood. He has to report to the Habshi soon.

'Which girl? There are so many girls working there,' says Balaji composing himself.

'The one who was stitching the bags at the scales?'

'I don't know.'

'Are you crazy? Did you see her? How could you not have noticed her yet?'

'Which one? High cheekbones, full lips, dark with long hair?'

'You dog, you know exactly which one I'm talking about. I need to see her tomorrow and then I'm off to Mahad to work for Siddi Rehman Ali.'

'Oh yeah, his people transport a lot of salt from here,' Balaji says, recognizing the name. 'He's got a whole fleet of barges.'

He bids Balaji goodbye and makes his way to Rehman Ali's depot in Mahad, fifteen kos upriver on the Savitri.

It is a prosperous inland depot, its banks thick with warehouses. Rehman Ali's river barges travel down the Savitri to an ancient entrepôt on the sea. The mouth of each river has one, usually guarded by a pair of forts on either bank. Bankot protects the Savitri and is held by the Siddis. Their chief, a nawab, the Yakut Khan, sits at Janjira, the Imperial Coast Guard. Him, Kanhoji pays at the will and whimsy of his extortionary commanders who rove the entire coast. But the Firangis are the accepted masters of this coast with their massive and heavily armed galleons escorted by even deadlier Men of War with their triple gun decks. Kanhoji purchases their cartaz from the mandovi at Chaul if he must take his goods north. At some ports like Dabhol and Harihareshwar, one must pay them both. These payments are ostensibly for use of ports and essentially guarantee them protection from the stray pirate but primarily from themselves. If the vessel lacks the Firangi permit—the cartaz—and a Firangi vessel comes across it—it can be sunk, confiscated or fined depending on the mood of the Firangi captain.

Rehman Ali poses his final test. A shipment of saltpetre from Karwar to the jetty near the Mumba Devi *dharmasthan** in a dhow called Akbari. The princess of the Firangis had married an Angrez king and her *dahej*** included a cluster of rocks south of the island of Shaisti. Kanhoji delivers the cargo at Pallva Bandar and visits Shaisti. He has heard it has a large population of black leopards. Here on the

---

* Temple or place of religious significance.

** Dowry.

island of Shaisti, Kanhoji first loses his wits to a girl. He refuses to
leave the village where she lives till she speaks to him. Her father is a
Topashi, a community that has formed through the marriages of the
Firangi soldiers with Konkani women and sometimes, though rarely,
the other way. Kanhoji is seduced himself with her singular features:
she has large brown saucers for eyes and frizzy light-coloured hair,
the likes of which he has never seen. Her name is Shandra and she
lived in a fishing village half a kos down from the Firangi fort. He
had gone there for a walk and saw her combing her hair in a window.

When a solid gold bangle his grandmother has recently gifted
him is rejected by her, he brings a melanic leopard's carcass to
her house. After a few days, a worried Rehman Ali's son is sent to
retrieve him. They return to Chaul where he is the cause of much
mirth and teasing. Rehman Ali's daughter, much tickled by what
her brothers have told her about this new *majnu*[*], conspires
to bump into him in their courtyard. It is the start of a long and
intimate relationship fraught with mortal risk for both—making it
for both again, the most exciting times they can spend with another
person. Rehman Ali acquiesces to Kanhoji's conspiracy of taking as
many trips to Bandora as possible, not knowing what is happening in
his own house. Kanho is not at all like his father Tukoji in this one
matter: Tukoji, who stuck it out with his barren wife for fourteen
years, never taking up with another woman. But Rehman Ali will
keep that to himself.

Once home, Kanho sheepishly inquires as to where Mathura is
and when she will come and stay with them.

'No time for that, boy. Sambhaji Maharaj is going to attack Yakut
Khan at Janjira. Maharaj is coming down himself to lead the attack.
You are to leave tomorrow morning for Padmadurg.'

'Who do I meet there?'

'Don't worry, son, I am going to accompany you tomorrow.'

'With your back?'

'I'm fine,' Tukoji snorts happily.

---

[*] Romeo.

Padmadurg

Lord Indra on his solar chariot reins his horses in behind the last of the staggering clouds returning at the end of the monsoon: the weather is cool and amiable. Another season of war has finally commenced after the paralysing rains that had inundated both the Konkan and the Desha. The trees are taller, the thicker undergrowth bursting with the sounds of insects, the fish have laid their roe and the pools in the jungles are full of water.

Chhatrapati Shivaji's heir has come to the Konkan at last to lay rest to the constant dilemma of the Siddi of Janjira. He is now at Padmadurg, a fort built expressly for this purpose a few kos from Janjira. Sitting under a royal saffron-hued umbrella held by its bearer, Chhatrapati Sambhaji Maharaj is very much his father's son as far as his handsome face, his athletic build and even his swordsmanship and bravery go. His legendary father had been equally famous for his generosity and compassion as he was for his martial acumen and courage. His son, born a high prince and therefore untouched and unexposed to hardships or personal suffering or even witness to it, develops an impulsive streak worsened by constant drinking of wines and liquors gifted by foreign dignitaries. He sits on a makeshift throne under an umbrella on the highest bastion watching the preparations for the coming war. His mother, the Rajmata, always tells him that he needs to be with his people or at least seen to be there. So, he sits there, sweating in the sun for his mother while hoping the miserly breeze will open her arms and fan him with more vigour than his incompetent *pankhawalas*.

Across the sea to the south sits the impregnable Fortress of Janjira—and not for the lack of trying. Shivaji Maharaj had built Padmadurg on an island one kos to the north. Maharaj had laid siege to the fortress, and when the monsoon came, Varuna's wet minions forced his eager troops to retreat. Any boat left in the sea is battered to pulp between the surging waves and the anvil of the basalt coastline. It was Sambhaji's great father who had seen the need for a naval arm and pioneered one that could guard the coast and attack coastal forts and harbours. The old generals of Shivaji Maharaj are glad that the son is following suit in his attention to the navy. He has commissioned several *galbats*, boats powered by a team of sixteen to twenty-four oarsmen that also feature one or two masts with attendant triangular main sails. Sambhaji Maharaj gets up to stretch his legs, and his coterie, which includes the wily Santaji Ghorpade and Siddi Daulat Khan, follow him to the edge of the parapet. There are masons, carpenters and a bevy of labourers carrying wicker pans of sand and stone, further fortifying the walls. Behind them on the jetty, men are loading the galbats and *ghurabs** with shot and bags of powder.

'Who is that boy?' Sambhaji points to a shirtless youth carrying twice the number of gunpowder bags men around him are.

The coterie around him peer at the jetty with shaded eyes trying to make out whom the Maharaj has meant.

'That tough little thing carrying all that load,' Sambhaji qualifies.

'Maharaj, that is the retired Sarnaubat of Suvarnadurg Tukoji Sankhpal's son Kanhoji Sankhpal,' says a sardar.

'Why then is he slaving like that?'

'Maharaj, Sarnaubat Saheb dropped him off yesterday and personally requested me that I show no partiality in treatment to him. As for the labour, it's of the boy's own wish,' says Daulat Khan.

---

* Larger vessels with twin or triple sails.

'Maharaj, I was charged to lead him into battle and pray for his safety,' the Daria Sarang continues.

'Well, just don't put him in the front line. Call him up. I want to meet him.'

'Angria,' shouts Daulat Khan towards the jetty and everybody stops their work and looks up.

'Come up, Angria,' Daulat Khan shouts as loud as he can as he motions to him.

As Kanho makes his way up to the bastion followed by every eye on the fort, Daulat Khan tells Maharaj about how as a boy he killed four Siddi patrolmen.

'He's still a boy,' Maharaj responds.

The boy has a name and now everyone there knows it and the face that goes with the name.

The First Battle

Suryavanshi is livid with himself for not being present.

'So, what did Maharaj say to you?' asks Suryavanshi curiously, thoroughly regretting not having met his monarch too.

'Nothing much, just pleasantries,' Kanhoji replies blushing.

'Come on, that is not fair. I wasn't there; describe the whole thing to me in detail. What exactly did Maharaj say?' Suryavanshi persists.

'Maharaj was only interested in knowing about you. He wants to find you a bride.'

'Shut up. Don't do this—tell me what Maharaj said.' Surya pleads with Kanho.

'Maharaj said that I was the handsomest Maratha he has ever seen and then Maharaj told me to give you this,' he says, fishing out a dagger and giving it to Suryavanshi, son of Chandravanshi. It's the first instalment of your dahej—your Baba even said yes.'

'Bakwas,' shoots back Surya but his retort is softened by the awe he is in. He dares not remove the blade from its beautifully engraved scabbard.

'Sultan Akbar gave it to Maharaj when Maharaj helped him escape to Persia,' says Kanho, repeating what the Maharaj had told him when he gifted him the dagger.

'Sultan? You mean Aurangzeb's son?' asks Surya.

'The one and the same.'

'What did he give you?' asks Suryavanshi as he holds the manta ray hide hilt and draws the gleaming steel blade out of its exquisite scabbard to test its sharpness.

'Blessings. Plenty of them.'

Surya puts the dagger back into its scabbard and returns it to Kanho.

'I know you are lying. Maharaj gave this to you. I can't keep it,' Surya says, trying to hand the dagger back to Kanho.

'Look, I can't disobey a command from my king. If you don't believe me, then ask Maharaj yourself when he comes back.'

'Where is he going?'

'Raigad.'

'Why?'

'Because the entire Mughal army is moving towards us.'

'You handle the situation here while I quickly deal with the Mughals and return,' is what his king, Chhatrapati Sambhaji Maharaj, had told him yesterday evening after blessing him with a long and prosperous life.

'You better take me with you the next time Maharaj sends for you.'

'I would have this time too; I was just confused as to what was happening.'

'Well then, Angria, it looks like I better make a name for myself too in the coming battle.'

'I can't wait,' says Kanhoji, bristling with energy as his mind plays out the heroic scenarios that are bound to unfold.

The next few days pass in exciting anticipation as the commanders wait for a day favourable to both the God of War and those that manifest weather. Kanho and Surya are in a state of feverish anticipation themselves as they walk around their camp at Padmadurg: Surya, with the dagger proudly on his waist and Kanho blushing every time someone hails him with his new moniker.

That favourable day dawns on the assembled Maratha Navy as well as the Badshah's *Wazir* and Chief Admiral, Kasim: the Yakut Khan of Janjira. Sambhaji Maharaj directs his artillery to the mainland opposite Janjira Fort. The Marathas set up a series of batteries on the beaches of Rajapuri whilst their infantry divisions wait anxiously at the jetty of Ekdara beside shoals of small canoes, fishing boats and galbats to ford the impending breach. Kanhoji and Suryavanshi distinctly hear the first cannon fire a kos down coast and before they can gulp the lumps in their throats, the next shot is fired. The down on their arms has risen and the back of their necks feel cold. After that, the firing continues unabated for two nerve-fraying weeks. Kanhoji and Suryavanshi, eagerly anticipating their call, are going out of their minds with excitement. Rumours buzz around irritatingly like sandflies sitting on steaming heaps of lies: Maharaj has been hit; the Wazir has been hit; a breach was made in the fort wall; our powder stores have blown up; the Siddi has surrendered; Maharaj has left for Raigad; the Siddi's mermaids are picking up soldiers on the beaches.

Finally on the fifteenth day the navy is signalled to man positions and be on the ready. Kanhoji is a sight on the deck of the galbat he and his boys have been assigned to, and everybody turns to look at the small boy with a musket bigger than himself standing dwarfed beside the stocky and broad-shouldered musketeers. His firing speed—acquired through a childhood spent repeating the different steps involved in loading and firing a musket—has earned him a spot beside the veterans on board. Suryavanshi is in the galley with the other rowers. As the nakhwa of his galbat waits for his commander's orders, Kanhoji sees more than thirty boats head south towards the black stone walls of Janjira Fort.

'Why aren't we moving?' he asks a Topaz gunner dressed in the Firangi style of *patloons*, sweat-soaked undershirt and a threadbare coat standing to his right.

'Why would you want us to move? Luckily we are in the rearguard and there is a good chance we might survive the day.'

Kanhoji looks at the man in disgust and counts twelve other galbats and two ghurabs that remain behind with them. The remaining vessels bob up and down with their troops and gunners on board and their oars in the water. Strands of time, stretched by the juices of fear, drag each moment out on the repeating waves. A signal must have come for the oarsmen to start rowing, which is accompanied by a synchronizing chant: *haiya haiya*. All the infantrymen, gunners and musketeers on board cheer as the galbat moves out of the jetty. When they are out of the harbour, the oarsmen in the galley retrieve their oars and the sails fill up and push them slowly south towards Padmadurg.

The fortnight-long Maratha barrage against the eastern wall of the fort has caused a lot of damage but it is unsuccessful in creating a passable breach. The navy has been called in to soften the northern and western sides of the fort walls. As a tri-masted *Pau* with forty thirty-pound cannons leads a fleet of a dozen ghurabs and twice as many galbats south-east towards Janjira Fort, the Mughal Wazir's fleet encounters them midway. The equestrian-minded, Dhakkani-trained commanders charge their vessels into the Siddi's fleet to bring them within arm's reach. In their natural element and following tested battle procedures, the Siddi's captains break the Maratha line in two places. Dissected into three sections and outmanoeuvred by the Habshi captains, the Maratha commanders charge their ships towards every Siddi vessel they see, yelling at the captains to turn this way and that like their horses could. Then the reserve vessels are called up.

The sound of the shelling from the mainland and from Janjira Fort grows louder. An explosion, overpowering the other blasts is heard, with a distinctive high-pitched whistle trailing its air-crushing boom.

'That's the Kalal Bangdi cannon, the largest in the Konkan,' points out the unruffled Topaz to Kanhoji. This Topashi, whose father was Firangi, had joined up with his cousins instead of his deceased father's people. The young infantryman behind him is frothing at the mouth with excitement and babbling to himself. There are so many different explosions he can hear and tremors he can feel, some louder than others and some emanating from closer by, but he finds them to be coming from all directions and being in the exact centre of the devastation. It sounds like the clouds themselves are exploding and the sky cracking and then splintering down like an abandoned roof. Whistling, imperceptible, an iron ball smashes through the hull of their galbat.

The vessel turns towards the coast in a jerking abrupt arc as it chops through the wind. Kanhoji cannot see anything but the back of his own shipmates and he tries to push through to the other side. The explosions are closer now. The musketeers and cannons on his galbat start firing back. The deck is covered in low-hanging clouds of thick and grey sulphuric smoke from the musket and cannon as Kanho feels the galbat shudder as a couple more cannonballs smash through the prow of the boat. An explosion of cherry shot—a multitude of irons balls as wide as your thumb—clears the deck of the soldiers in front of Kanhoji, and as they fall over, Kanhoji wipes some brain and gristle out of his eye and sees the broadside of a Siddi vessel shelling them from less than 100 *gaj* away. Kanhoji vomits and then takes the opportunity and steps forward through the thinning troop and sets up his old flintlock arquebus. Kanho can see the gunners on the Siddi vessel reloading their cannons, and choosing a group huddled behind their gun, starts patiently firing at them with the utmost precision he can muster on the swaying and rocking boat. It is not possible to dodge or escape the wanton and chaotic destruction that is going on around him. His safety is in the hands of Khandoba. Shot and splinter come from all directions and there is no way to anticipate invariable death. Soon he will die: a splinter or shot through his head. He concentrates on his slow and careful shooting as the world falls around him, and is blown out of his vision.

'You got one, you got one,' shouts the infantryman standing behind him. The excited man is beside him now and is sobbing between fits of laughter. He is holding a musket picked up from one of the dead troops, but he fumbles, his hands are trembling. As Kanho is ramming his next shot in, the first of the battered retreating Maratha ships crosses him. The few survivors left on the deck are indicating 'retreat' by sweeping their raised hands back towards

Padmadurg. Kanho is trying to aim through the passing Maratha vessels that are now taking the pounding directed at his galbat when he is reprimanded by an injured musketeer beside him. Their galbat reverses its direction of rowing and retreats too. Kanhoji is ordered down to the galley with the rest of the surviving troops to replace the dead oarsmen below.

'Kanho, come here, come here,' he hears Surya scream in the blood- and gut-splattered galley. There are chunks of intestines he can see, elongated scarlet queen ants in clumps. He clambers over the slippery bodies and takes his place beside Surya, who despite being covered with blood, is looking grey. Surya has splinters on his face and arms and an inch-thick wedge of wood is embedded in his shoulder.

'Are you hurt badly?'

'No, I was really lucky.'

'Look at that,' Surya says, pointing to a face, perfectly sliced, like halwa with a wire.

Kanho looks and then averts his eyes. The air is heavy with the smell of faeces and bilious last meals.

The deflated Maratha armada returns to Padmadurg to tend to their wounds. Kanho hears that Chhatrapati Sambhaji has left Padmadurg after the battle at Janjira and headed towards Burhanpur. He hadn't liked the galbats; you couldn't turn them like horses or bring your personal arms to bear upon the enemy. He wanted solid ground beneath his feet. He had 20,000 cavalry still behind him with the daring of veteran sardars like Hambirao Mohite. He would attack the Mughals in Burhanpur while Tana Shah of Golkonda and Sultan Sikandar of Bijapur kept them busy in the east and south-east.

War

On the roads of the Dhakkan, dust is in the air as the blistered feet of refugees from the recently conquered kingdom of Bijapur make their way west and south. Chhatrapati Sambhaji is at his durbar at Raigad Fort with only his most trusted sardars in attendance.

'Sikandar Adil Shah is in chains, though they be of silver; locked up in Daulatabad Fort,' Sambhaji Maharaj tells the assembled sardars.

There is silence in the court.

'Betrayed by his most trusted commanders who sold their salt for a few coins of gold,' he thunders in anger.

'Jhavle and Kalu Shaikh fought to the end for Bijapur,' says Dadaji Suryanath Desphpande.

'What good can two men do? Bijapur is no more,' Sambhaji Maharaj shouts, throwing his silver goblet at the floor and glaring at Dadaji.

'Why are you here? Have you completed your works at Janjira?'

'Maharaj,' Dadaji replies cautiously, 'we are filling up the channel between the mainland and Janjira Fort. The work is progressing well, and I have left both my sons in charge. I thought, with the capture of Sultan Sikandar of Bijapur and the siege of Golkonda, I best return to the Desha.'

'Yours is not to think, Dadaji, yours is to do. Why hasn't the channel been filled yet? Water is no place to fight, I need Mother Earth beneath my feet,' Sambhaji Maharaj says unsatisfied.

It is a gargantuan task with 800 gaj of the coastal channel, more than ten gaj deep in parts that is being filled with earthworks.

'Dadaji, you doddering fool,' Kavi Kalash says impetuously, 'hasn't Maharaj said that he would personally lead the charge against the Siddi once your channel is filled?'

'Yes, but we cannot find enough labour,' Dadaji replies with all honesty.

'No labour? Why half of Bijapur has come down to our lands,' Kavi Kalash counters.

'Dancers, musicians and poets,' says Dadaji to Kavi Kalash, 'have taken the refuge you have offered, but the masons and stone-cutters we need, Aurangzeb has pressed for himself.'

'I will send you the poets then and the Brahmin clerks that have come from Bijapur,' Kavi Kalash sneers.

Dadaji and the other sardars shake their heads in dismay at their king's favourite adviser.

'The Angrez, despite having treaties in place with Sambhaji Maharaj, have betrayed him and given the Siddi's ships access to his docks at Mazgaon,' Kavi Kalash says, bringing up his master's concern.

'What does that have to do with me?' the wizened Dadaji wonders.

'Did you not visit their fort just before coming to Raigad?'

'Yes, I did,' Dadaji says, raising his voice at the insinuation.

'To purchase cannon to protect the labour working on the *bundh*, with my own funds, while you . . .'

'Funds that I hear have increased a lot lately,' Kavi Kalash says smiling.

'Maharaj,' Dadaji splutters at Chhatrapati Sambhaji in appeal.

'Enough of this,' shouts Sambhaji Maharaj. 'Dadaji, return to the Konkan and finish the channel, I will send someone to deal with the traitorous little vanias at Mumba Devi.'

Dadaji bows and takes his leave as Kavi Kalash smirks for all to see.

Sambhaji Maharaj now removes a small and much-folded letter from his cummerbund. Written in Persian, it had arrived after many tribulations from the impregnable fortress of Golkonda, accompanied by a purse of cherry-sized diamonds.

'It is from my friend Tana Shah,' Sambhaji Maharaj says and gives it to Kavi Kalash.

'I will translate it into Marathi as few of you know Persian,' Kavi says condescendingly to men who have fought alongside Shivaji Maharaj:

> Brother Sambhaji, I write to you one last time as the Qutb Shahi Sultan. His Imperial Majesty is already moving to Gulbarga on the pretext of a pilgrimage, and he inches towards the annihilation of my Sultaniyat's ancient birthright every passing day. He is livid with Sultan Mu'azzam for the peace we concluded with Your Royal and amenable Self, and is contriving to accuse me of supporting your insurrection with the lakh of pagodas I had sent you for the shrines and temples of Chaul and for the feeding of poor and learned Brahmins. Hazrat Gesu Daraaz taught us that we are atheists when we pray for fame and hypocritical cheats when we pray out of fear. I pray for the preservation of all the people in this ancient land that took our ancestors in and enriched them; I pray every colour remain; every note of music be heard; every mudra manipulated; every saint emulated, and every god deified. Does he not see that when he proclaims the one God it divides that very god from its manifest existence? I have only one prayer for you, my strong and independent brother: protect the tomb of Bande Nawaz and keep his *murids* safe from his murderous sword. *Khuda hafiz*, Tana.

Sambhaji Maharaj takes the letter back from Kavi and folds the little note, knowing it is the last one he would receive from this most amiable and generous of his friends.

'*Har ki murid gesu daraaz, shud vallah khilaaf-e-nast, ki uu ishq baaz shud*,'[*] Sambhaji Maharaj silently quotes Bande Nawaz in reply, as his friend is too far away to hear him even if he screamed.

'Now, there is only one sultan left between Delhi and us. Kaka,' he says to Mohite, 'show the Mughal what we are made of; burn all the crops and destroy his grain stores and annihilate his supply lines. If he makes my friend starve, then starve him too.'

Hambirao Mohite steps forward and bows, honoured with the responsibility.

'Ghorpade will go with you and besiege the besiegers,' Sambhaji Maharaj adds.

---

[*] Syed Gesu Daraaz has pledged his obeisance; there is nothing wrong in it because he has deeply fallen in love.

Balaji Bhat

Kanhoji has ridden to Chiplun with Suryavanshi. They are accompanied by two attendants and an extra horse for his friend. He is carrying his childhood wheellock along with a couple of old flintlock muskets. All their barrels have been repeatedly tied with brass wires to keep them from shattering. His latest acquisition is strapped to the side of Betaal, a dappled Arab stallion with inauspicious markings his father was unable to sell. He has brought Pushpa, Mathura's own genteel Marwari mare, for Balaji. They have cleared the red and brown fields sprouting mustard green and now head into a thick jungle on a path overgrown with purple and orange blossomed creepers and fat leafed vines.

'How can you be my friend and not be able to ride a horse? How is that even possible?'

'Horses are beautiful at a distance, obscene when you are on them,' says Balaji, clinging on to his wide-shouldered friend's taut midriff.

'Where are you taking me?' Kanhoji asks Balaji for the fifth time that hour. Balaji had sent a message to Kanhoji for him to come immediately to Chiplun.

Balaji would not tell him where he was taking him. After falling off Pushpa twice, Kanhoji had thought it safest that his slight-framed friend ride with him on his own horse, and like two children, they ride tandem.

'To Viratnagari, to meet the Pandavas,' Balaji replies laughing.

'Come on, I'm no longer a layabout, I'm the Sarnaubat of Suvarnadurg Fort, I can't just gallivant around like this. Come on, Bala, tell me where you are taking me.'

'We are going to Ajinkyatara Fort,' Balaji finally says.

'Are we going to meet Maharaj?'

'I will tell you everything when we get there. We are not going to the fort, just towards it. We need to make for Vygragad Fort and then on to the river.'

'Well, at least we will get some game. Need to try my new flintlock out. But who are we going to see in the middle of the jungle?'

'I am working now for Dhanaji Yadav, as an informant,' says Balaji, trying to change the subject.

'That is wonderful, but can't you leave the Siddi now? Isn't the bond paid back?'

'Oh, it is. I can leave; I am no longer his slave. But they have come to trust me, and we need someone close to the Siddi.'

'How did you meet Dhanaji Yadav?' Kanhoji inquires, always wondering about the intricate and sublime machinations his friend's mind is capable of.

'Pure dumb luck. His mashaalwala had the shits running down his legs and I volunteered to carry his mashaal.'

'What did you feed the poor man?' Kanhoji laughs.

'Did you meet him in Satara?' he asks his tricky friend.

'No, he had come to Chiplun.'

'*Wah*, Bala, the sardars of the world come to you and ask you to light their way.'

'Kanho, you are the sardar whose path I want to light with my learning and experiences. You need to pay attention to your job and stay at home more. Remember your dream?'

'Chhatrapati Sambhaji called me up to the bastion at Padmadurg!'

'Don't gloat, I heard all about it. You were a boy and you almost got yourself killed in that ridiculous charge—like you were riding horses.'

'Well, boats sure don't turn like horses. The galbats pitch a lot, it's so much harder trying to shoot a musket. I had no idea what was going on.'

'Keep your muskets for hunting, on boats, the only way to go is cannon, and Kanhoji, keep your life and your mind for thinking of strategy. You are destined to be a commander.'

'No way in hell!' says Kanhoji excitedly,

'I'm not going to be another Achloji Mohite fawning over silks and his mango orchards. He's not a fighter; he's a bloody businessman. Ever felt his hands? Mathura's are rougher. You need to feel his hands, like a baby's.'

'Kanho, the men already respect you. You are lucky to have a reputation precede you.'

'A fake made-up one,' Kanhoji says softly.

'What about the four men you killed? You are the toughest Maratha I know. You are a brilliant shot, and an excellent swordsman and a born rider. Your father let your destiny shape you well—he let you be a man when you were still a child.'

'Khandoba, make me your warden for this beautiful stretch of land—I don't want to be an emperor, just a caretaker: the *bhagyadar* of the Konkan,' Kanhoji says, looking up to the vast blue sky. Balaji smiles and relaxes and hopes that the coming meeting will go well.

'*Woahhh*,' says Suryavanshi in a loud whisper and raises his hand. All the riders stop in their tracks. Angria looks at Surya who is five gaj in front of him. Surya has made their sign for a sambar—three crooked raised fingers and has pointed to the right. Angria sees the soft brown antlers of a sambar and some of its rump poking out from the tall monsoon-fed undergrowth.

Angria pulls out his musket from the saddle as Surya is already loading his. Surya waits for Angria to load his black powder, pad and shot and carefully take the shot. The head and the chest of the sambar are hidden, and he makes a calculated guess. There is an enormous explosion with a lot of grey smoke and a sulphurous stink. As the smoke of the musket shot clears, a sambar steps into the open. Its bottom jaw is hanging at a right angle, as it stands stunned with a pitiful look in its wet eye. Another shot rings out, hitting it above its foreleg. The sambar leaps once and then staggers to a drop, putting its head down to the ground as the last of its life thromboses out of it.

The muzzle of Angria's musket has shattered, and he looks at Bala to check whether any shrapnel has hurt him. They are both fine, but Bala is bent over vomiting at the grisly sight.

They all unhorse and Kanho helps Bala down. They give him some water to wash and drink with. Surya and Kanho are laughing all along as the two attendants run to the dead sambar with their butchering knives.

'Are you okay, Bala?' asks Kanho, knowing the queasiness of his friend well.

'Just no more hunting on the way there. Do it on our way back.'

'Whatever you say, we already have dinner. Fresh from the jungle, the best meat any man can eat.'

'We can't take the meat there. We are going to meet a *sant.*'

'What sant? Are you serious? You can't be? All this way? Important? Come immediately?' says Kanhoji dismayed. He is not given to meeting tantriks and seers and finds almost all of them to be charlatans preying on the superstitions of the poorest. It is anyway Mathura's domain.

'You should have taken your sister-in-law, not me,' Kanho says testily.

Balaji was hoping it would not come to this, but it eventually has despite assiduously trying to avoid the topic, well knowing what his friend's reaction will be.

'Please Kanho, you need to meet him. It's just a few more hours away. Please, for me, please.'

'Alright,' huffs Kanhoji, 'but if he has a beautiful daughter or a young wife even, then don't blame me.'

'*Chee*,' says Balaji, 'don't talk like that, he's a holy man.'

'Well, then let's ride a little more, make camp for the night, have some roasted sambar and we will head to your saint's house tomorrow—unless of course he can magically transport us to his place overnight?' mocks Kanhoji.

Bala eats poha at the rudimentary camp Surya had trussed up while Kanhoji roasts a leg of the sambar. He has burnt the butt of his musket in the bonfire, disgusted with his weapon. Surya has wisely held on to the rest of the mechanism, not knowing when it could be required for parts.

The next day they set off as soon as the sun rises, but are lost for several hours after they cross the Vygraghad Fort, until they find a shepherd who directs them to the hut of the Chitpavan sage. The sage was born on a small farmstead not far from here. He has been to Benares and studied with the greatest teachers. He has now come to live and meditate on the banks of the Koyna River on a spot both far from and close to the chief city in the area. The shepherd has pointed them south on a well-worn path wide enough for a bullock cart.

The path they are on descends to the river, narrowing down to a row of rocks. A hundred yards below they spot a compound marked by a low wall of laterite blocks that encloses a temple with a simple conical roof. A large hut made of stone and several smaller ones made of mud-lathered twig-walls and thatched roofs can be seen. The larger hut and the temple are both made of stone blocks plastered in white limestone and they shine, reflecting the sun.

'How did you meet him?' asks Kanhoji.

'I had run away from the salt works once. I came here, to the river and found him by chance. When the Siddi's guards came looking for me, he told them I was his uncle, and I was not running away and had come to see him. They did not believe him, so he even bribed them. He made a prophecy about me: that I would rise to the highest office in the land!'

'What's his name?' asks Kanhoji.

He was born Vishnu Pant Dixit, but now he is known as Brahmendra Swami. He is a great man. Wise. Just wait and see, you will be surprised,' assures Balaji.

The Mahapurush

'The temple is of my own design. The *bhakts** completed it before the rains began. It has not leaked or anything. I hope to improve the design the next time around,' Brahmendra Swami says, taking them towards the Parshuram Temple with wide verandas on all four sides sloping down in the Konkan style. The small square roof in the centre rises to a conical mound shaped like a diya flame. Kanhoji is surprised. He was expecting to meet an old, bearded sadhu or tantrik not a young spritely man, clean-shaven and dressed in the finest white muslin dhoti he has ever seen. Unlike most Brahmins who either have excessively lean or fat bodies, the Swami's physique is as toned as his own and his well-formed arm and chest muscles impress Kanhoji immensely.

'I love to swim, used to swim across the *Ganga Maiya* herself,' the athletic Swami says to Kanhoji when he sees him looking at his arms.

'I must say, you have an extremely broad chest and strong arms yourself,' the Swami counters, flattered by Kanhoji's attention.

'Push-ups and squats every morning Swamiji,' Kanhoji explains humbly.

---

* Devotees.

'You can call me Vishnu, Brahmendra Swami is for the people. Bala tells me you are his oldest and closest friend. That you have been a brother to him.'

'He has been a brother to me, Swamiji,' replies Kanhoji.

'Thank you. Yes, it's best you just call me Swami. But we are friends here. Do you understand? Friends!'

They remove their footwear and go into the temple to pay obeisance and Brahmendra Swami offers them prasad after the *aarti* and blesses both with tilaks. He shows them around his little ashram, and Kanhoji finds it as charming as his host. Swamiji knows everything about everything and everyone.

In the evening, the three of them sit on mattresses and bolsters laid out under a tree. Vishnu insists that Kanhoji have the tipple of his choice but Kanhoji declines. A black enamelled hookah is brought out for the Swami and his attendant keeps it filled and purring with fragrant herbs and *som booti* the entire evening.

'So, Angria, what does the future bode for you?' Brahmendra Swami asks through a cloud of smoke rising through the dying dusk light.

'I don't know, I hope I stay lucky,' Kanhoji replies, unsure of both the question and any possible answer.

'Your future,' Vishnu says, his grey eyes looking flatly at Kanhoji, 'your prosperous future is assured. You will always have more than enough to feed your horses and ride like a king. This I assure you of.'

'Through trade? I have no interest. I want to do something.'

'What thing?'

'I don't know, something to make my mark, something to add value to this place and our lives.'

'Your friend, my devotee,' Vishnu says, looking at Balaji, 'is a man after my own heart, cut from the same cloth we are.'

Balaji nods silently.

'Tell me, Balaji, what is in the *Uttara Desha* besides gods, mountains and rivers?'

Balaji nods again, well versed in the ways of Swamiji.

'The wealth of this land is in the south. The diamonds are in the south as is all the wood, the silk and the cotton and all the craftsmen. And the *mirih masala* the Firangis take back—as if they have never seen it before. Your little Konkan gives salt to the entire continent. There are traders here from lands so distant and they all are here for what we have, and we have everything.'

'Except good guns and horses,' says Kanhoji automatically.

'Well, they can take what they want of ours in exchange for what we want of theirs, and, my dear Angria, it all comes in and goes out from the ports of your beloved Konkan, except for Surat of course.'

'Even though a lot of the goods arrive at Surat, they then are shipped back south to go to Java, Chin and beyond,' Kanhoji adds.

'Exactly!' exclaims Vishnu. 'The Firangis and the Angrez and their pink-nosed cousins have cut the Arabs out and are taking it south and west over the ocean and around Habshistan and it gets to Istanbul and Rum from the west.'

Kanhoji and Balaji nod.

'Do you know, Angria, that the oldest and richest ports dotted your coast like a string of fireflies beckoning every trader and adventurer for thousands of years?'

'Well, Swamiji, to tell you the truth, the Firangis at Gomantak and the Habshis at Janjira rule the coast. I am a chowkidar at the fort, neither guarding anything beyond my walls nor controlling anything beyond cannon range. I am unable to protect barges and cargo of our own kith and kin.'

'Hmm,' Vishnu responds dramatically. 'What do you think of your Yajyman?'

'Mohite doesn't even maintain half of what he is supposed to. I pay and maintain my twenty men and he maintains ten instead of 200.'

Vishnu let him finish and then corrected him: 'I meant your real Yajyman, Chhatrapati Sambhaji?'

Kanhoji looks at Vishnu.

'He is strong and a great fighter,' Kanhoji finally replies.

'No doubt, yet he kills his father's advisers and turns to charlatans and *kalushas* from Kanauj. His behaviour is very unlike Shivaji Maharaj's. His most esteemed father commanded honour and respect across communities, especially amongst his enemies. That is the mark of a true king.'

Kanhoji does not respond and instead looks at Balaji first and then searches the riverbank and the mountain behind. Bala knows his friend is questioning the loyalty of their host as he shuffles his crossed legs and looks around agitatedly.

'Your future, Angria, and yours, Balaji, are entwined as one body. It is your strong body, Angria, and your sharp mind, Balaji, that must be the new force that takes the cause forward: Maratha brawn and Chitpavan brain,' he concludes, chuckling over the hookah pipe.

Brahmendra Swami motions to his attendant and points to Kanhoji gesticulating 'give, give', with rapid and generous movements of his hands.

The attendant whisks away silently and returns with a pair of men carrying several large flat boxes and a pair of mashaalwalas carrying extra torches to illuminate their contents. The boxes are placed in front of Kanhoji, and Vishnu says: 'For you. May you always have your heart's desire.'

Kanhoji, not expecting any gifts, is surprised and thanks Swamiji with a simple namaste and he gets up on his haunches to open the gifts. There are two large boxes and one smaller one, and Kanhoji immediately recognizes them to be gun cases. He almost opens the first one before he sits back, wondering if his childhood friend has sold them out to this overly smart and well-dressed sage.

Vishnu sends all the attendants away and laughs to himself and says to Balaji: 'Your friend has been offended by me,' and then looking at Kanhoji, his cat eyes become serene, and in a calm voice the young Swami asks of Kanhoji: 'Tell me, Kanhoji Angre, who would you be more loyal to—if you had to choose between your mother and Chhatrapati Sambhaji?'

Kanhoji clenches his fists, controlling his natural reaction to strike the insolent interrogator, as Balaji quickly cuts in, 'It's just a mental exercise, Kanho, Swamiji means no offence.'

Kanhoji's eyes rise towards Bala, though his face is turned to the bonfire.

'My esteemed mother is the wife of a man who was a loyal soldier of Shivaji Maharaj and the mother of a loyal soldier of Chhatrapati Sambhaji. There is no choice to be made, the question does not arise—even hypothetically.'

'Muqarab Khan has been deputed to deal with us. Have you heard of him?' asks Vishnu.

'Who hasn't?' responds Kanho petulantly.

'The fate of Golkonda was sealed the day he switched to the Mughals. Now his troops from Telugu Desha join Aurangzeb's entire force including the Imperial Guard—the finest warriors from Rajputana.'

'I pray to Khandoba he comes to the Konkan,' says Kanho.

'Oh, his convoys travel through here, but he has bought land in Agra,' Vishnu intones, pursing his lips and closing his eyes as if in profound thought.

'The commander of your fort, Achloji Mohite, is your superior and instated by Chhatrapati himself. What if he were to surrender the fort?' he asks, breaking out of his reverie.

Kanhoji is silent.

'Well, know this: that Mohite's loyalties lie first with himself as do those of any king and many a man. But yours, as Shivaji Maharaj's were, and should be, only lie with the good of this land and its people. You eat of this land and drink its water; you are Her and your loyalties must lie with this primal mother of yours—the mother of your mothers.' People come and go whether they be kings or commanders. I was just wondering as to your prime loyalty,' Vishnu explains.

'Look, I don't know all these things. What I do know is that I am loyal to Chhatrapati Sambhaji, who I will have you know, is a brave and valorous man who will not give up the Swarajya.'

'The wonderful thing about you, Angria, is that you don't mind saying you don't know. I love that. Everybody these days always seems to know everything.'

'Kanhoji says he doesn't know even when he knows, Swamiji, it is a childhood habit of his,' Balaji adds laughing.

Vishnu takes the break in mood to call back the mashaalwalas to illuminate the cases and says to Kanhoji: 'I'm not trying to buy your loyalty, my friend, we already share it, but it is one of my *sankalps* that you have the best collection of guns in the Konkan.' Kanhoji pulls the topmost walnut box towards him and opens the twin brass latches on either side and lifts the lid of the case. The inside of the case is lined with blue felt. The case holds a pair of what he first thinks are axes. They are partially, but on closer inspection he finds on the handle a trigger mechanism with a protruding wheel above it and his favourite doghead cock on top. Alongside lies the entire accoutrements for the pair of pistols and a set of tools. Kanhoji closes the box and raises it towards his head in thanks and sets it aside. He moves closer to the second wooden case, as it is at least three gaj long and a *hath* wide. He opens it to find three muskets that have seen a lot of use and are of a simple and unadorned construction.

'For your men,' explains Vishnu as Kanhoji closes the case after having examined the guns. They have a circular mechanism over the trigger and their entire bodies from wooden butt to brass barrel are glistening with oil.

'All *payawaals*, no *rassi*,' says Vishnu happily. 'You hunters too prefer them I hear.'

'In our wet weather, we need them, but I don't need them only for hunting any more,' replies Kanhoji, well knowing that the matchlocks are not meant for the humid Konkan as the rain or dew dripping from the canopy could extinguish the slow burning ammonia-dipped ropes that light the powder of most muskets. Flintlocks are not very reliable and often did not spark the powder, unlike a spinning wheellock musket. These weapons are of the latest technology and extremely rare.

Kanhoji pushes back the second case and pulls the last one towards him. This case is heavier and made of a beautifully grained red wood he has never seen before. It has a black double-headed eagle enamelled on to its centre. He unhinges the brass latches, two on the sides and four in the front, he gasps as he lifts the wooden lid. Kanhoji wipes his hands on his dhoti before picking out the musket and staring at it flabbergasted. He turns it every which way and finds the ramming rod missing before he carefully checks the mechanism.

'Do you know what this is, Swamiji?' he asks Vishnu, unsure if the Brahmin would know anything about guns.

'Yes, I do, and the rod isn't missing, but I will show you in the morning and let us see if good Balaji here can hit at least one target tomorrow.'

Kanhoji cannot sleep and much before dawn, he tracks Surya down. They figure out the weapon's breech-loading capacity and are targeting a mashaal as light breaks. After the morning ablutions and oblations, the Swami shows them how they can make cartridges of black powder and shot wrapped in *tendu* leaves, padded down with a little dry cow dung. Balaji gives up with a bruised cheek after he has fired his first and only shot.

Grahaspati

Kanho returns from the old fort, north of Gheria after studying the natural defences it offers, hoping they could be recreated at Suvarnadurg. But it is not in his hands and above his commission. Achloji is an indolent commander and has only the fame and indulgence of his powerful and aristocratic uncle Hambirao to thank. Mohite has never taken any initiative and considers an inert maintenance of the status quo as his only duty. After the unsuccessful assault against Janjira, Chhatrapati Sambhaji had ordered an assault against the greatest power in the Konkan: the Firangis based out of Goa at the southern tip of the Konkan. At first the Marathas had succeeded in taking over Anjandiva, only to be run out of it a few months later. After that there was no Maratha action in the Konkan and hulls rotted, and drilled and adrenaline-shaped muscles fell slack. The challenge Shivaji Maharaj had instigated in claiming his suzerainty over the Konkan has dissipated in the past six–seven years, and the Firangis and the Habshis continue to control the coast and all its valuable trade. He was at both actions and the scars on his arms and back are constant reminders of failure.

'How can anybody come in as it is? I feel so safe here,' says Mathura while she is feeding her infant son.

'We are safe from thieves, if that is what you mean, but assume if tomorrow Maharaj has to take refuge here and Aurangzeb and

Muqarab Khan are at the walls with lakhs of troops, their entire artillery aimed at our walls—we don't stand a chance.'

'That will never happen. You always imagine the most improbable negative scenario,' she says, soothing herself and her child.

'Well, if that last scenario is sorted, then there is nothing to worry about, is there?' he says irritated.

'What's bothering you?' asks Mathura, sensing something amiss. 'It's Father, he has gotten much worse.'

'Let's go to Kulaba for a few weeks. Why don't you ask Mohite Saheb, he would never say no. The baby will bring the home much-needed joy.'

'I think I will, it's not like anything is happening. Might as well go home for a bit before the rains set in,' Kanho agrees and goes back to cleaning the musket Brahmendra Swami had given him earlier in the year. He has put it to good use, making sure his family and his men have plenty of antelope or boar meat and jungle fowl soup to keep them strong.

'So, when do you plan to ask him, next week?' Mathura asks testily. Kanho rolls his eyes and then smiles at his wife.

'Right now, my life, commander and my queen,' says Kanho to Mathura as he puts away the musket and comes over to kiss his wife and son. He kisses them both as Mathura coyly resists and then he makes his way to his commander's estate on the mainland where Achloji is currently residing. Kanhoji is not as confident as Mathura on the permission to leave being granted, as Achloji himself is invariably away at Raigad or his estate and expects Kanhoji to hold it in his stead. Kanho is pleasantly surprised with his commander's ready willingness to allow him a sojourn.

'Let your men off for a fortnight too, they need the break, especially your man Suryavanshi. He's always on duty it seems: Don't these fisherfolk ever sleep? Or do they sleep with their eyes open like the fish?' wonders Achloji affably as he readily gives his permission for Kanho to disband.

Kanho rushes back to Mathura with the news, telling Surya they could disband for the fortnight. Surya's wife is nearing the end of her expectancy with their second child, and he is glad he would be back for his child's birth. Surya insists that he will accompany them to Alibag, to Tukoji's estate. He has arranged for a private barge to leave the day after in the morning with the seaward winds, and Kanho and Surya immediately get busy preparing for their departure.

Kanho does not like the idea of not leaving one of his men behind. At the least it would look irresponsible, not that he cares how things look to others. But Achloji is an incapable soul, and he needs to leave at least a pair of eyes and ears behind. Surya volunteers to stay back but Kanho is not having any of that. They could leave Golu as he has nowhere to go, but then they would need another person to be his mouth. Surya, too, will have none of it as he finds it hard to accept Golu as a bona fide human being. But Golu must remain.

A palanquin carries Mathura and her infant son down to the beachhead on the north-eastern side of the island where Surya is waiting for them. Suvarnadurg Fort does not have a jetty. It has been built on a boot-shaped rock, the soles of which are parallel to the mainland and the ankle points north-west. The only exit and entry the fort's rocky shoreline permits is a narrow stretch of beach right on the heel of the island that is approachable only by small rowboats. Kanhoji comes down to the rowboat once he has issued his final instructions to Bhikya and Manu and given them a few *dam*. They will remain with Golu. The rest of his *paltan* will leave later in the day. The little boat starts for Harnai Bander, which lies 600 gaj to the south where they can visit the bazaar before embarking on the barge that has been chartered for them.

At Harnai, Mathura goes to the Radha temple as one of their servants hurries to Achloji's estate to pick up the box of his deservedly famous *hafus* mangoes he wants to send to Tukoji. Kanho decides to survey the little 700-bigha island to the south of Harnai Bandar. The little island is 150 gaj to the south and connected by a strip of rocks to the mainland, and this feature acts as a natural tide-breaker for the port. Kanhoji has long wondered if it would be an appropriate site for an expansion to a complex of defensive forts. As Kanho makes his way over to the strip of rocks disappearing into the small isle, one of his servants comes running up to him followed by a young bald Brahmin boy in a dhoti.

'Saheb, saheb,' his servant calls after him and Kanho turns to look.

'Sardar Saheb, this boy was wanting to go to the fort to meet you. He says he has come from Chiplun. He says he has been sent by Balaji Vishwanath Pant.'

'How do I know you are the bloodthirsty Kanhoji Angria?' asks the little boy.

'How dare you?' screams Kanhoji's servant as he moves to sock the impudent boy on his bald little head.

Kanho raises his hand to stop his guard and replies to the boy: 'But aren't I the handsomest Maratha you have ever seen?', confirming the code Bala and he had decided on, for recognizing couriers.

'Beauty thirsts for blood,' he completes the code.

'Duty before beauty,' the courier confirms and Kanhoji calls him closer.

'Saheb, Pantji has a message for you.'

'Repeat the message,' Kanho replies.

The boy closes his eyes in concentration and repeats the message he has memorized by rote: 'Siddi Kasim has requisitioned Rs 2 lakh from the treasury at the salt works. They are being sent under guard to Dabhol. Pandurao Phangaskar was recently at Janjira and is accompanying Kasim to Dabhol with a fleet of thirty ships and over 400 men. From there he is planning to proceed to Suvarnadurg. I have apprised Dhanaji Yadav of the situation.'

Kanho bends his ears to the boy's lips so his voice could break through any obfuscating wave crashes.

'Repeat it again,' says Kanho, and the boy repeats the message exactly as he just did.

Kanhoji tips the boy a full silver rupee and heads to Harnai to find himself a horse. He borrows an old horse loitering unsaddled at one of Habshi Rehman Ali's warehouses, which are adjacent to the jetty. The Seth's staff do not mind in the least as they have seen him come and go over the years at all times of the day and night. Kanho reins the horse east and on to the road heading south to Palande. He knows Achloji is not at Suvarnadurg, and he must find Surya too. He abandons a brief gallop for a steady trot when he sees Surya seated beside Mathurabai's servant and a bullock cart driver coming down the road.

'Is he up there?' asks Kanhoji as he approaches them.

'Mohite? Yes. Got these baskets of mangoes and some other *tarkari*[*] he has sent, this fellow could not find the place, so he requested me,' replies Surya, pointing to Mathurabai's manservant.

'What is Achloji doing? What was he asking you?' Kanhoji asks.

'He was getting ready to go to the fort, said he'd enjoy the sea breeze for the next couple of weeks. He's got his whole retinue coming with him. Why?'

'Retinue, soldiers or women?'

'The whole household it seems,' Surya replies. 'He's finally commissioned some men. Piloji was there with twenty men. We needn't worry, the fort will be safe while we are away.'

'Take the mangoes to the Radha Temple in Harnai, near the jetty,' Kanhoji instructs the bullock cart driver and has Surya join him on the old horse. They turn around and head back to the port town.

'How can you be sure?' Surya says once Kanho has related the message he has just received from Balaji.

'What else can it mean? It's not a force big enough to take us and it's coming with money that sounds too much like the right amount to hand over the keys to the fort.'

'But Pandurao Phangaskar works for the Firangis, why is he coming as the Siddi's representative?'

'Know this and know it well, Pandurao Dhanapat Phangaskar works for nobody but himself—he uses the Firangis and the Siddi to his own end.'

'You know him well.'

---

[*] Vegetables.

'Well? Like the back of my hand, if my hand was a scorpion's tail hidden in a jar. He was at the gurukul with Bala and me.'

'What do you want to do? What can we do?'

Kanhoji has no idea what he is going to do.

'When do you think they will come?' Surya asks.

'Tonight, or the next night. Tonight. When I have just left. But Mohite only found out I would be gone day before.'

'That's enough time for a message to go to Janjira and be back with a reply. They want it before the rains set in. If they miss their chance now, they will have to wait another year,' Surya calculates.

'We have to get back into the fort without anyone finding out.'

'A lot of the men left right after us, and Jaideo and Balav left in the morning.'

'Forget the other men—even if we had all of them,' Kanhoji trails off pensively.

'Ho Khandoba, the Swamiji had predicted this,' Kanho says as each hair on his body rises.

After Kanhoji fetches the pregnant Mathurabai, Surya along with the remaining members of his paltan in Harnai secretly return to Suvarnadurg Fort on a tiny rowboat. There is a secret entrance at the southern side of the fort, and Kanho has always carried a key to the small door that descends below the foundation of the wall. They return to their quarters unnoticed and have the doors block-latched from the outside. Surya finds an opportune time to corner Golu, Bhikya and Manu. They keep away from Narsoji and his ten men that remain at the fort. Narsoji is as young as Kanho but nowhere as experienced or keen. He is a distant nephew of Achloji's and hails from Karad. He spends most of his time flying kites and has always looked at Kanho with a childish gleam of admiration.

Kanho calls all his men into his personal armoury, situated to the rear of his quarters. Kanho has five men, excluding himself and Surya. He will carry his infamous Badakpai. It has only been used a few times, but its legend has grown. He gives Surya his new wheellock and his old one to Bhikya. The new flintlocks are distributed between Manu, Shambhu and Kori dada who have already trained on similar muskets. Golu is given the pair of axe-pistols to look even more ferocious. Kanhoji forbade Golu to cut any of his hair and encourages him to try new and more menacing styles. Golu's attempt at a wild-haired Polygar chieftain is quite fetching and fearsome.

Kanhoji is still unsure about what he is supposed to do.

'Kori dada, you are the eldest here,' he says to the oldest member of his platoon, one who has served with his father, 'you need to stand beside me and back me up with whatever I say. They need to see age on our side.'

'Why don't you talk to Narsoji now, intimidate him a little and turn him before his uncle comes,' offers Kori dada.

Kanho and Surya exchange glances.

'If he isn't in on the plot, he will never believe it.'

'Kanhoji Saheb,' Kori dada butts in, 'please send a letter to the court, addressed to the Ashtha Pradhan, saying what you are about to do is based on the information you have received from a spy of Dhanaji Jadhav, and all actions will be temporary pending approval from His Majesty.'

'Good idea,' says Surya, seconding the seasoned soldier.

'We have nobody to send now, I think we should talk to Narsoji, tell him it is temporary and subject to proof,' Kanhoji says.

'No, Saheb, I am sorry, but I insist. We will be thought of as traitors. I have a boy with me who is capable enough to take the letter to Raigad.'

'Do it, Sardar, you don't know how people like Mohite can turn it around and frame you.'

'Alright, I will, but don't worry, I am solely responsible for what we do,' he assures Kori dada and his other men.

Narsoji has posted two men at the beachhead to inform him when his uncle is coming while he makes efficient use of the brisk afternoon wind to fly his newest kite. His mama's *saala** is due for the

---

* Brother-in-law.

weekend. He has been promised a holiday and can leave the day after with a bonus of twenty silver rupees. The kites he could buy with the money. Narsoji has his eyes set on a red Chinese lantern kite that can hold a candle in it. He is by himself when Kanhoji and all his five men appear at the bastion where he is flying his kite.

Golu grunts menacingly as Manu and Bhikya hold his arms and his kite escapes into the sun-scorched sky.

'Are you also in on it?' screams Kanhoji.

Narsoji is terrified and breaks into tears.

'In on what?'

'How much has he promised you?' shouts Kanhoji brandishing his Badakpai at the shaken youth.

'Promised what? The bonus?' says the trembling boy.

'Ah, so that's what you call a treasonous bribe?' Kanhoji screams at Narsoji.

'Saheb, saheb, there has been some misunderstanding. I am not part of any treason. I don't understand what you are saying.'

'Your mama is selling the fort to the Siddi. Which part of that do you not understand?'

'Saheb, he is my mama's saala's *kaka**. All he told me was that I could go back to Karad for the monsoon, and I would get ten silver rupees for myself and one each for my ten men. I am to leave day after. There was nothing of the Siddi or abandoning the fort. I thought it was the norm.'

'Free money? A norm?' Kori dada asks, clucking his tongue in suspicion.

'Dhanaji Jadhav is personally on his way here, and till he gets here, you can decide whether you are loyal to Chhatrapati Sambhaji or are loyal to your treasonous uncle,' Kanhoji shouts at the boy as his men leer and rattle their blades.

Narsoji folds his hands and falls to Kanhoji's feet crying and shaking.

---

* Paternal uncle.

'I have nothing to do with that man, I would never betray Maharaj, nor you. Please do not count me as one of them,' he pleads.

Kanhoji picks Narsoji up and brushes his tears off.

'We will know your involvement only once we have interrogated Achloji,' adds Kori dada.

'Sardar, do you have any proof of it though? Why would he after so many years? He is close to retirement,' Narsoji asks as a little doubt seeps back in.

'It's his last chance to retire with a fortune, more than he ever made in all his life. The traitor!' screams Surya as Golu grimaces and shoves him.

'I am not a traitor,' says Narsoji.

'Just let it play out. We don't know whether it is going to happen tonight or tomorrow night. If nothing happens, well and good, but if we let anything happen, it would mean we have given up the fort. An agent is due with a bribe. If he comes, we arrest Achloji,' says Kanhoji.

'And what if he doesn't come?' asks Narsoji.

'Then I will resign my commission and you may arrest me for treason against my killedar,' says Kanhoji.

'Look, we don't know who is involved and who isn't. We found out in the nick of time or all of us would be away by now. Just tell your men to let you know when Achloji arrives. Receive him and take him up to the *Juna Daftar*.'

'I will do it, but Sardar Angria, I am not a traitor. I do not know anything of this,' Narsoji says as the kites of his childhood drift away forever.

As dusk approaches, Narsoji comes running to Kanhoji who has stationed himself in the Juna Daftar. It is the ancient hall of the pre-Adil Shahi commanders who had built this part of the fort.

'It's not Achloji, but somebody else is coming, with a paltan of troops and ten or fifteen other people, in four rowboats.'

'It must be Piloji. Let them come, but don't let any of them come in here. You don't go down till Achloji comes and then direct him here.'

'Got it,' says Narsoji, who has in the past hour risen from his shaken state to one of ecstasy. This is so much better than flying kites.

He runs back not ten minutes later and informs Kanhoji that he has spotted Achloji approaching on a barge with five rowboats.

'Don't let anyone but Achloji and Piloji enter in here. My guys are outside watching. I need all your men at the fort gate. Narsoji?'

'Yes, Sardar Angria?' asks Narsoji as he turns.

'You need to trust me, if you get confused now, each one of us within the fort, both you and I included, will die. Let's do this like intelligent men and loyal Maratha soldiers.'

'Got it, Sardar Angria,' says Narsoji as he runs to the beachhead already panting with excitement.

Kanhoji has Kori dada and Manu with him; Surya will be the last one to enter the door of the Juna Daftar with Golu and Bhikya.

The Juna Daftar had been the headquarters when only a small but high-walled defensive structure had existed on the island. It predated the extension work the Bijapurkars had done to it over a couple of hundred years—adding walls, ramparts and other structures as the need arose. The Juna Daftar had at its entrance a similar turtle carving as was found at the entry of the fort. Shivaji Maharaj had done extensive work at the fort and built a series of bastions encircling it. Maharaj had an image of Lord Hanuman engraved near the turtle at the gate. The rooms here were not that large and were separated by narrow passages. The thick walls were constructed with massive basalt megaliths. The Juna Daftar could only be entered through a steep and narrow staircase that led right up to the door of a bright and airy room full of square niches in the wall.

'Do you think this will work?' asks Manu nervously as they impatiently wait for Achloji to arrive.

'If we arrest Mohite now, we won't be able to catch the Siddi's man or have any solid proof. Mohite can just deny it,' says Kori dada.

'I don't know. Maybe we should have waited for Pandurao to arrive and . . .' suddenly Kanho swears at himself.

'Let's get out of here, I have screwed up,' he says as they both run down the staircase to the lower level. They jump out of a window and head to the corner where Surya and Golu are hiding.

'What the hell are you doing here?' whispers Surya loudly.

'This is wrong. It won't work. We need to hide again. I was thinking while I was up there. Let's go now.'

'What about Narsoji?'

'Manu, has Mohite ever seen you?'

'I don't think so, Sardar: when is he ever here?'

'Good. You find Narsoji and tell him it's off. Tell him to come to his quarters when everybody has settled in. It would be better if we catch Pandurao at the jetty. Maybe I can talk to Piloji before that,' Kanhoji says.

'Bhau, are you sure? Have you thought about it this time?' checks Surya.

'I wish Balaji was here,' says Kanhoji, sorely missing his friend's quick-thinking resolve.

'I hope Balaji is right,' adds Surya.

'Yes, I'm sure now. Surya, you take Bhikya and Golu and hide near the beachhead. I'll keep Dada with me,' Kanhoji says quickly.

'Manu, you join me at the beach once you speak to Narsoji,' says Surya as they slink away in the growing darkness.

Narsoji is baffled. Angria's man has just whispered in his ear, and he is not sure what he has heard. Is Angria trying to set him up or playing some game? Has something happened to Angria? Has Mohite found out? Narsoji wonders to himself as he makes his way to his quarters. He kicks the door open and makes for his store of cashew nuts.

'Narsoji, close the door,' someone says to him.

'Who is that?' says the alarmed Narsoji reaching for his Firangi crab sword.

'It's me, Kanho.'

Narsoji shuts the door and finds Kanhoji sticking to a wall in the corner.

'What are you doing here? How could you call it off? He was wondering where I was taking him all the time.'

'Relax, nothing happened, did it?'

'So, what are you going to do now? Achloji is here with Piloji and his twenty men.'

'Where are your men?'

'They have the gate. But what are you planning to do?'

'We need Pandurao to get to the fort with the money. If we arrest Mohite now, he can call it off. There must be a signal that says: "all well, proceed". We need to wait till Achloji sends that signal, then we can arrest him and Pandurao.'

'What's the signal going to be? And who is Pandurao?'

'I don't know: a flare or a cannon shot. Something they can see or hear out at sea. I think we should talk to Piloji.'

'He's getting paid 200 *rupaiya* for a weekend of work. He told me Achloji said he was due for an inspection and needed Piloji and his men for a couple of days to make things look good.'

'Then why would he send me away? Do you see that he is lying?'

'I don't know what to think. He seems so jolly. As if nothing is about to happen.'

'But if he was due an inspection from the Parasnis's office, why would he send me or you away? He could have asked us to wait a week.'

'True,' ponders Narsoji, realizing more and more that though Angria does not actually have a plan, his suspicions seem correct.

'Let's go meet Piloji, in fact, why don't you call him here. Show him some of your kites.'

'I don't have any fancy kites, yet.'

'Well, just say you do, or whatever. Please get him here.'

Narsoji goes to find Piloji whose father had accompanied Shivaji Maharaj on his Surat raid. The gossip associated with the family was that Piloji's father had helped himself at a jeweller's establishment during the raid. He had supposedly secreted large stones within the nether regions of his body and thus they were never accounted for.

The family had never worked as soldiers since but retained all the trappings and maintained a small troop that convoyed their own cargo and that of other traders for a fee.

Narsoji is gone for more than an hour when he returns with Piloji who has an attendant with him carrying his tumblers and *tadi*. They are a couple of drinks down when they enter quite merrily. Narsoji closes the door behind them and asks Piloji's attendant to wait outside.

'Eh, why are you keeping the most important person out? What's going on?'

'*Shrimant* Piloji Raje, *Pranaam*,' Kanhoji says.

Piloji is wearing a pair of large rubies on his earlobes that match his turban. Around his neck is a delicate emerald necklace, glinting on his silk kurta.

'Kanhoji, what a pleasant surprise. Forget your kites Narsu; let Kanho take us out hunting. What say? We'll have peacock for breakfast,' Piloji says cheerily.

'I need to talk to you,' says Kanhoji.

'Achloji said you were gone to Alibag,' says Piloji, anticipating the hunt.

'Piloji Raje, I had to stay back. Come sit. I need your full attention.'

'I am in my senses,' says Piloji offended. 'I've just had one drink—just about wet the tongue,' says Piloji winking.

'Then listen,' Kanhoji says, 'Achloji plans to hand over this fort.'

'To whom?' asks Piloji, suddenly very serious.

'To Siddi Kasim, for Rs 2 lakh that is on its way from Dabhol. Mohite is going to receive it either tonight or tomorrow night and let the Siddi's men in.'

'I don't know anything about this,' says Piloji recoiling. 'He offered me Rs 200 and a further rupee a day for as many men as I could muster up and make look like soldiers. For the inspection.'

'He has let me and my troops leave yesterday and is letting Narsoji go tomorrow too. Why would he do that if he had an inspection?'

Piloji wipes his brow in growing anxiety. He knows of the machinations of men.

'Help us arrest Mohite and I'll triple it,' says Kanhoji.

'There's Rs 2 lakh coming in. Take your cut, Narsoji, his bonus and the rest we will see, and you remain outside any conspiracy to surrender the fort,' he adds.

'What if it's not true and no one comes but the Parasnis?'

'Well, in that case, as Khandoba is my witness: you can have all my guns. I wouldn't need them where I would be anyway.'

'You are on,' says Piloji immediately.

'Including the Badakpai?' Piloji confirms.

'Of course, the Badakpai and a pair of axe guns I just got,' assures Kanhoji. Though he has always envied Kanhoji's collection of well-used firearms and swords, he still hopes that this is not how he would come to possess them.

'So, what is your plan? I hope it doesn't involve fighting because my cooks and *dhobis* look like right fighters but can't fight a mouse. Only my musket works, the other two which my men have are just for show,' says Piloji.

'We need to let Mohite give the signal. Once he does that, they will initiate contact and send somebody here to the fort. Once that happens, we arrest Mohite and seal the doors. No one gets in or out. In a couple of days, Dhanaji Yadav will be here, who knows maybe Maharaj himself.'

At last, like a ghost arisen from his words, Kanhoji has a plan.

Kanhoji's and Narsoji's men keep watch for any flares or orders to fire the cannon. There are only eight gunners in the fort and Kanhoji knows them well. He has not risked talking to them though and will instead just wait and watch. There is nothing but shooting stars that night and the first of the sagging and low-hanging clouds come in the next day. It rains in the afternoon as Kanhoji and his men bide their time. Narsoji comes in with some news just as the rain ceases.

'Mohite has told Piloji to be ready to welcome the auditor, who is coming tonight. He will confirm it at the start of the last watch. Piloji is to bring the auditor up to him. He has told me to get to bed early, as I am to escort him down to the beach and on to a barge before dawn. He says he is going to Valukeshwar for a darshan.'

'Good, that means it is most definitely tonight. You also need to be on the beach with your men. I have no idea how many people are coming but I want to stay out of sight as Pandurao can recognize me.'

At the start of the last watch Kanhoji sees a sulphurous flare burst from the ramparts and wriggle across the sky before falling in a diminishing fireball. He realizes he can hear his heart thumping against his ribcage and his throat is suddenly parched.

Kanhoji and Surya head straight for Achloji Mohite's rarely used quarters as decided. Narsoji is there waiting with his men, and Piloji is already inside trying to open a bottle of Firangi wine.

Bidhe, Mohite's right-hand man and bodyguard, is drinking water beside a clay pot when Surya shoots him down well before entering the room. Mohite is stunned as he watches his man crumple over and then he sees Kanhoji, with his Badakpai in his left hand and a *dandpatta** in his right rush up to him. A young man, who turns out to be Bidhe's son, draws his sword and is felled by a single chest shot from Golu's axe pistol. Everybody else there is too stunned and scared to even flinch.

'Achloji says that Bidhe was merely trying out a new flare they had got,' says Piloji, no longer blind to his commander's treasonous intentions.

'You are under arrest for treason,' shouts Kanhoji, staring at his pot-bellied commander.

'Piloji, Narsoji,' Achloji screams in horror as both come to stand behind him and grab his pale arms.

'Tie him up, and all his men and keep all of them locked in the granary,' commands Kanhoji

'There is enough for all of us,' Achloji screams as Golu grabs him from Narsoji.

---

* Gauntlet sword.

Bhikya had been instructed by Kanhoji to do just one thing: keep Piloji in his sights and shoot him dead the second he wavered. He now stares at Piloji through all the din and smoke from the two blasts, his finger on the trigger.

'Earn to earn tomorrow,' Piloji says to Mohite as Golu lifts him out with a pistol to his head, adding: 'You are finished, old man.'

Bhikya stays on alert though Kanhoji feels a knot of doubting cobras ease out from the burrows in his head.

'Let's round up all his men and secure them and then we can head to the landing beach.'

By the time they get to the fort's gate, they can see that two rowboats have grounded themselves at the landing beach. Kanhoji waits in front of the main gate, which is left slightly ajar. Piloji and Narsoji go to meet whoever has landed on the island.

Soon Kanho and Narsoji can make out a party of nine men on the beach.

'Rat-like teeth and a rat-like face. Is that Pandurao?' Narsoji inquires of Kanho as he comes back to report to him.

'Undoubtedly,' affirms Kanho.

'He has four small chests, he says they are for the Killedar's eyes only and as they are too small to carry a person, he does not want them opened.'

'Auditors bringing chests. See?' Angria gloats, 'Let him come in—but by himself.'

'He says that four people carrying the boxes and four guards will accompany him to the Killedar's door.'

'Who are the guards?'

'Can't say,' Narsoji says.

'Okay, let him in, but only two guards,' Kanho says as Narsoji goes to relay the plan to Piloji.

Pandurao Dhanapant of Phangas enters the fort in front of his men and impatiently asks the way to the Killedar's daftar. As soon as Pandurao is in, Piloji and Narsoji re-enter the fort along with

Kanho's and their own men and they latch the main gate. Kanhoji and Surya step out of the shadows from opposite sides of the gate and poke their barrels at Pandurao's guards and shoot them at point-blank range. Piloji's dhobi has his sword at Pandurao's throat, who is startled and surprised.

'Narayan, Narayan,' Pandu says, choking against the blade.

'Pandu, we meet again,' Kanhoji says to his former schoolmate who is looking quite unduly aged with his thin moustache and rounded gut.

'You have no right to manhandle me. I was sent with some packages for your killedar. Let me go,' Pandurao protests to no avail.

'You bring shame to our guru and our gurukul,' Kanho says, slapping Pandurao hard across the face. He then spits on the ground and turns away in disgust.

Pandurao is taken to the *Kalbatkhaana* after the boxes he has brought in are checked. While three of them contain silver Bijapuri larin coins, the third is filled with gold hons.

Surya comes into the treasury where Kanhoji is conferring with Piloji and Narsoji.

'There are about twenty ships with cannon on the western side of the fort, and twelve boats are landing troops on the beach,' he tells them.

'Let's show them the meaning of stepping on Suvarnadurg,' says Kanhoji headily.

'I'll guard the prisoners in the granary, if you don't mind,' adds Piloji quickly.

'I'll come with you,' says Narsoji, 'let's show them what we are made of.'

As they head towards the main gate, Surya tries to dissuade Kanho.

'Let's just call it a night, they can't get in.'

'No, we need to scare them off,' Kanhoji snaps. 'You stay back, I will go with a couple of guys. I want to shoot some of them down, the treacherous bastards, they have to pay for trying.'

'I am coming with you,' Surya says.

'No,' Kanho insists, 'you need to hold at the gate, just in case something happens to me.'

Surya shakes his head at his friend's stubbornness and follows him to the gates of the fortress. Kanhoji, forsaking the security of the high walls and unbreachable Mahadarwaza, heads out of the fort followed by Narsoji and his man who have a musket each and Bhikya and Manu who are primed and loaded too.

Khairiyat Khan

Kanho and Narsoji run out of the gate and turn towards the beach. The moonless night is sparkling with every star in the firmament. The sea and the sky behind them are dark. Silhouettes of dhows bob on the surf in the distance. They spot several Habshi infantrymen walking up the surf towards them. Kanho halts and raises his musket as his compatriots line up beside him.

'Ready,' Kanho says as they steady themselves.

Narsoji and his men are loading their powder and ball.

Kanhoji shouts: 'Fire.'

Bhikya, Manu and Kanhoji make their shots as Narsoji and his men raise their muskets. Before Narsoji and his two men can fire, a volley of shots flash brightly from the dark rocks to the left of them. Narsoji falls as a ball of lead enters his earhole. Manu and Narsoji's man have been hit on the legs by the crouching Habshis. Kanhoji turns and fires his Badakpai at the smoke on the left of him, when a muzzleloader's thick heavy butt swings out from the smoke. It catches him behind the ear and sends him crashing to the ground. Surya, accompanied by two men, rushes out of the gate firing with his musket and screaming death.

The Habshis retreat, dragging Kanho with them to a rowboat rocking in the surf. They make straight for their commander's dhow.

Khairiyat Khan has been waiting for the gates of the fort to be thrown open to his men, so he may follow them in and take his prize.

'What is the delay?' he screams as the landing party returns. His hair is braided like a *jathadaari** and his suit is crimson and gold.

'Who is he? Where is Pandurao?' Khairiyat screams, his wide nostrils flaring, as he scans Kanhoji.

A bucket of water is thrown on Kanho. One of his men slaps Kanho awake and then hurls more bilge water at his face. Kanho is disoriented from the severe concussion and unable to see clearly. Sounds come and go. But his eyes are open, and his captors assume he can hear them. He is being uncooperative. They try to make him cooperate.

'Who are you?' shouts Siddi Khairiyat loudly over the cacophony of other voices and all others pipe down.

'Kanhoji Angria,' he mumbles through his bleeding and swollen lips.

All the voices within earshot of Kanho fall silent.

'Oh, I've heard of you, haven't I?' demands Siddi Khairiyat.

'From your mother,' spits back Kanhoji.

Siddi Khairiyat smashes his fist into Kanhoji's face, who slumps to his knees. Khairiyat laughs, throwing his chiselled head back.

'Why were you running from the fort, where were you going?' he asks Kanhoji, still laughing.

'Running away? I came out to kill you.'

Khairiyat smashes his foot into Kanho's knee.

'Where is Munshi Pandurao?' Khairiyat asks, now gently, in a low voice.

'Pandu is dead. Achloji is under arrest. His plan was discovered days ago. Santaji Ghorpade and Dhanaji Yadav are on their way down to Harnai. Now go home Habshi, the fort is closed.'

Siddi Khairiyat stomps down on Kanhoji's shoulder and when he falls back, he stomps his boots on his chest.

---

* Unshorn dreadlocked hair.

'Take him down to the hold and tie him up, I'll deal with him later,' commands Khairiyat as four troops surround Kanhoji and drag him aft.

The war dhow lurches in the dark water. Kanho cannot see. His eyes are swollen and caked with glutinous blood. Two men carry Kanho: their arms around his shoulders, they drag his limp body across the deck. The other two guards walk in front, clearing the crowded deck swarming with curious soldiers. Kanho wrenches one eye open to get his bearings. They are at the aft of the vessel on the way down to the hold. After the first guard has disappeared down the ladder and the second guard is on the second step, Kanho springs alive. With every ounce of energy he can muster, he grabs his guards' heads and knocks them together. He then flops over the collapsing guard and the curved bulwark into the sea. The remaining guard raises an alarm and every musket on board empties its charges off into the dark sea around the dhow. Kanho dives down, and with his one sensate hand working furiously, swims in the stinging and tarry brine. Kanho's lungs are aching, and his pounding chest heaves in pain and exhaustion. He does not know in what direction he is going. He goes on and on. It seems endless and impossible. Each stroke, each kick from a broken leg. A rock scrapes his leg, and it jolts him awake. There is something solid beneath him. He passes out. He lies on the cold and sandy beach and tries to regain his breath. Before he has, he lifts himself up to his macerated knees and crawls on them. In a few moments he is up on his feet, and he limps towards Harnai, keeping to the shadows.

The port town is crawling with the Siddi's troops. At least he knows it better than them. He limps through shoulder-wide alleys and backyards, and stumbling over low walls, Kanho heads through a maze of throbbing pain to Rehman Ali's warehouses where he knows he can die in safety. He patiently waits to cross undetected, hoping his breaths' heavy rasping won't betray him to the pairs of lancers that patrol the bazaar and the dockyard streets. Kanho ducks behind a wall as two soldiers suddenly turn into and illuminate the alley he needs to cross. He crouches behind the *kathaa*** and phlegm-stained wall, a troika of fuzzy beige puppies surround him and lick the blood that is oozing from his legs. A pup's sharp tooth finds the gash in his thigh and Kanho bites his hand to keep from screaming. The patrol turns off the street and Kanho dashes across, the pups chasing him and nipping his bare toes and bloody ankles.

Kanho wakes up throbbing and disoriented. He may be in the chowkidars' house, an old and trusted retainer of Rehman Ali's family. Or he may be revisiting his sins. He has been here many times. Kanho's eyes come to focus, and he sees the old man—long retired—squatting at the door looking at him in great worry. Kanho drinks several miniature clay cups of water from a rotund clay pot as he puts on a pyjama that is hanging on a peg on the mud wall. His body has been cleaned and his wounds wrapped in clean muslin. He can see the ochre stain of the turmeric and honey that has been applied to his wounds. Fresh blood, pink against the muslin, is beginning to stain again.

'I have to get back to the fort,' he says to the man, who many years ago, found Kanho in bed with his daughter.

'They are looking for you,' the old chowkidar says.

The girl who had been found in bed enters the room from an adjacent one. She is a pregnant woman now and her husband peers at Kanho from over her shoulder.

'Come,' she says, trying to hide her smile.

'You must hide under our charpai, they are already at the gate,' she says.

Kanho follows her into the room and gets under the charpai. As she gets on to the charpai, her husband puts a rolled *chattai*** under the charpai to hide Kanho and lays down on an open one just at the foot of his wife's bed. When the soldiers come to check, the husband is mortified at their attempt to sully her dignity and modesty and raises a cry to the Almighty.

---

* Catechu.

** Reed mat.

The Sons of Saraswati

Seth Narayan Kamath is in the comfort of his own twin-masted *dubash*—though his dubash is not on board this cargo vessel named for that profession: the translators they invariably carry. Pesiji has been sent with Ramaji to Surat. His younger son Venko is playing the role of translator on their trip to Karwar. He is now fanning his father as he lies on a charpai whose feet are nailed to the deck. Venko had handled the matter impressively when a Portuguese caravel had boarded them. Behind it a massive galleon, decks lined with cannon, had loomed a few hundred yards farther out to sea and yet cast its long shadow on their little dubash. The captain of the caravel had demanded a cartaz, which they had earlier paid for at the Reis Margo Custom House on the mouth of the Mandovi River. Narayan Kamath had not disclosed the truth about all the contents of his cargo. Goa did not give any exemption on religious works if they did not involve Catholic churches, so Narayan Kamath omitted mentioning the silver idol of the Goddess Saraswati along with her ornaments that he is taking back to Palva Bandar. The idol will be consecrated and installed at the temple that members of the community have constructed within the Angrezi Fort that lay between Palva Bandar and Dongri. The silver-maned Narayan Kamath had been a pioneer and then a pillar of the Konkanasth community in this vile and lucrative little port. The Firangis had overrun these islands over 200 years ago, and when the Firangi Rani married the Angrez Raja, these outcrops were given away as dahej to the Angrezi Raja. But it stood on this little strip of land that was the export route of all the kingdoms that lay above the steep slopes of the ghat. The port that was offering the most profitable opportunities would always change, up and down the Konkan, but it would always be some safe little land head by an estuary on this coast. Narayan had put his lot in with the Angrez. Like him, they were traders and not warriors, and like him, they seemed practical when it came to profit. Of course, he had to manage the inevitable pollution that came with the territory.

The captain of the caravel had sent two guards with a Topaz inspector on board to tally the cargo on board with what had been listed and levied. The inspector found a four-foot-tall solid silver statue of a four-armed goddess sitting on a life-sized silver swan. There was an intricate model veena made in silver and filigreed with gold and a chest containing a solid gold crown and bangles, bejewelled necklaces, earrings and *payals*[*], all made in gold and encrusted with rubies and emeralds. None of these items was found mentioned on the cartaz. Venkoji spoke to the Firangis in Portuguese and showed him the English permit that allowed free transport of the idol and ornaments for the temple. Of course, Venkoji admitted that the English permit was worthless and only good for carting goods on the streets of Bom Bahia. These waters were the State of Portugal and now the goods must be confiscated for deliberate avoidance of custom duties. Venkoji persisted, first in their native tongue and then in the universal tongue, for they did not care that these were for a temple and belonged to the whole community who had entrusted its senior-most member to acquire and transport them from the Karnatak. The matter was settled in the hold where the inspector had descended. Venkoji paid just the three of them all in gold *reais*[**], saying in his fluent Portuguese

[*] Ankle ornaments.

[**] Portuguese gold currency.

that he could not afford to pay the captain but could give half the captain's share to the three of them. Venkoji, unlike Ramaji, had been very quick to learn the ropes and was also more ambitious than his elder brother had been at his age. Narayan attributed this to the costly education he had been able to afford for his son with a famed *acharya** of the Konkan. Venkoji's time there had changed him for the better, Narayan felt. Education could never go to waste he thought as he carried the Goddess of Learning and Wisdom to the temple the Konkanasths had built. It was not a grand temple but beautifully constructed. Granite blocks and pillars had been carved in Mysore and then shipped up the coast from Cochin. Every inch of this temple to learning had been intricately and carefully carved or cast by masters of their craft.

'Enough, Venkoji, stop fanning me. Where is the pankhawala?'

'*Apu***, he has just gone for lunch, he has been fanning you the entire day.'

'In that case, I can take a few minutes' break from being fanned myself. Come in and sit here,' Narayan says, motioning to his cot as he gets up to sit.

'Don't worry, Apu, I am not tired, this is nothing and you are not well. I don't want you getting all red and sick again,' he says to his beloved father. He is the favourite; everybody knows it and accepts it. Rama is not jealous, as he is as much a father to his much younger brother as Narayan Kamath is, only sterner. Narayan Kamath was still making his fortune when Rama was young. Venko was born a prince.

'You should have paid them in *siccas****,' admonishes Narayan when Venkoji finally sits down, wiping sweat off his forehead.

'Apu, I carry a separate bag for siccas, for the Habshis and Marathas. Firangis, with what we have on board, I did not want the

---

* Spiritual master.

** Father.

*** Coin.

captain to come down. Then he would have confiscated the *murti*[*] without a doubt.'

'Couldn't the captain have also been paid in siccas?'

'Apu, the common soldier or inspector or custom guard does not care, the more liquid the better. But their higher-ups would not have passed this murti up. It is a conquest for them, maybe. But I know they actively hunt for such things and the items of the greatest quality are sent to their kings in Rum and Portugal.'

'How much you know, *hah*?' Narayan says proudly, combing back his silver mane with his slender fingers.

'Aren't you glad I sent you to Harnai?'

'Apu, that was almost ten years ago. Everything of value that I have learnt is from you and from Rama *dada*,' replies Venkoji. 'Guruji could learn a thing or two from Rama dada,' he adds proudly.

'Don't insult your guru, he is the emanation of Saraswati on earth,' chides Narayan though thoroughly amused.

'Guruji had some ideas about them, though, the Firangis and especially the Angrez.'

'Are you in touch with some of your friends from the gurukul?'

'Of course, Pandurao is often in town, you know him.'

'I mean other than him. Venko, quite frankly, he is one friend of yours who . . .' Narayan trails off, either not wanting to influence his son or not knowing quite how to describe the uncomfortable feeling the overbearing and unbearably sweet boy inspires in him. Venko has conveniently forgotten to mention his closest friend, the hot-blooded, meat-devouring Maratha: Kanhoji Sankhpal.

'*Matlabi*[**], I know, Apu. All he's ever interested is in knowing what deal Dada is up to.'

'What do you say?' wonders Narayan.

'He doesn't ever ask directly, but I know what he's getting at, so I tell him just the opposite of whatever Dada is doing or where he is

---

[*] Idol.

[**] Opportunist.

going. If Dada is going to Surat, I say Vengurla. If he's buying rice, I say selling.'

Narayan Seth laughs and stretches in contentment.

The sun beats down and the wooden boat is blown north on its two lateen sails. The oarsmen in the hold sleep. Narayan has the captain of his boat head starboard into the sea to avoid the Siddi's patrols nearer to the coast. This dubash could, if he wanted, easily venture up to fifty kos into the deep sea. This vessel was initially a *balav*, built in Mazgaon by Pesi's brother-in-law, Keki Udwadia, and is made entirely out of prime teak logs from Dindelli and the masts are constructed with Malabari rosewood. The attendants have the deck in the fore, and the members of his syndicate, and he, take the aft deck. Keki and Pesi are both from Bharuch, and Narayan had met Pesi in Surat.

'You are not a dubash but a *navbhash**,' Narayan had said, amazed when he had witnessed Pesi's linguistic ability. Foreign tongues were incomprehensible to Narayan who spoke only in his own Konkanasth dialect and Marathi. Ramaji had an ear for languages, but Venkoji had surpassed all in the community. Narayan knew it was as much to do with Pesi Dubash as it was with his son's rarefied Sanskrit education. His boy spoke Marathi like a Maratha, Persian like a Mughal courtier, Firangi like a padre and could jabber with the Angrez at Fort George or the Dutch who were his father's main clients in their saltpetre trade.

'Sethji, Sethji,' his nakhwa shouts, running towards him. But Narayan Kamath has already heard the alarm and gotten up. Venkoji is already up and looking at the pair of triple-masted ships that have raised their captain's alarm.

'Ships, Sethji, signalling us to drop our sails.'

'Who are they?'

'The ships look Angrezi to me,' says the veteran Nakhwa.

---

* Speaker of nine languages.

'They are English,' concurs Venkoji, 'it's all right. Pull the sails, we have permits from them too.'

The nakhwa orders their large and smaller lateen sails to be dropped as Narayan's dubash slowly drifts towards the smaller of the two frigates. Venkoji can clearly see that both the vessels are East Indiamen of the English design. He peers at the men who are standing on the deck.

'Strike sails, strike sails,' Venkoji suddenly screams to the nakhwa as he runs to his father.

'Apu, stay here, don't come out, they aren't wearing any uniforms,' he says, unable to relay his confusion to his father.

It is too late though as iron grappling hooks are cast out from the ship entangling their little boat. As their dubash comes to rest upon the hull of the smaller East Indiaman, several men jump on to their craft from the ship.

'I have all required permits from the Company and bear a personal letter from the Honourable President of Bombay and simultaneously carry cartaz issued by the Government of Goa,' Venkoji clearly enunciates in English, confronting the group of men who have jumped in.

'Do ya?' says a red-haired bare-bodied man carrying a cudgel.

'Pity we can't read, aye?,' says the other who has a sabre in each arm.

'May I please speak to your captain?'

'What nice white sails ya have,' leers another barefoot sunburnt man.

'"It" can speak, by Jove,' says the red-haired man.

'Gonna keep this 'un,' says a massive, bearded man in a sweat-drenched leather waistcoat, 'got me a speakin' monkey,' he continues as he grabs Venkoji by the head. Narayan Kamath's nakhwa and tindals charge as they see their Seth's greatest prize touched and are knocked down. The two lone guards Kamath has with him tremble as they try to load their muskets. They are immediately shot down. Narayan Seth emerges on to a smoke-covered deck as soon as he can no longer hear his son's voice.

He approaches one of the pirates with his arms raised and his palms joined in a namaskar over his head, trying to plead reason: Narayan Kamath is struck by the butt of a matchlock pistol, and he crumples to the freshly swabbed teak deck of his dubash.

Salt

When Parshuram washed his axe in the sea, Varuna recoiled in disgust and retreated. Parshuram then shot arrows into the seabed reclaiming the land for himself. The blood of twenty-one generations of Kshatriyas had mixed with the ocean and made it saline. Varuna would deposit that blood's salt on Parshuram's doorstep to remind him of his genocide. This salt would then travel back into the mainland to replenish the blood of its children. Ganpatbhau Lokhande would add to that salinity the sweat that dripped off his people's burnt bodies and the blood from their cracked feet as they worked the corrosive *agars*[*]. But not the sweat of his children, he had sworn to that. Other people believed—and he knew this as they had told him themselves—that Agaris had a special quality to their skin that allowed them to work in the salt pans. It was true, they said, because they knew that the hands and feet of dead Agaris were almost impossible to burn as they were naturally imbued with some protection. Ganpat had witnessed his younger brother's cremation. The boy was fifteen years old when he had died, and his feet and hands burnt without a problem. Shards of crystal salt would constantly wound the Agaris and if they were not taken out entirely, they would grow into rocks in the hands or feet of the afflicted person.

---

[*] Salt pans.

Ganpat did not know whether salt had been a gift from Varuna or a curse from Parshuram, whom his ancestors along with a Koli woman, had pleaded with to limit the reclamation. For him and his ancestors, it had been a life of constant toil through the ages without either gain or change. He was determined to change the life of his people who had no rights to the pans they worked or the profit they helped generate for the traders. Salt was worth its weight in copper, but it had always belonged to whichever king was then ruling as he claimed rights to the land and then taxed the salt. There was a time when his people were a community of ingenious technicians. His ancestors had devised a way to turn the salty and all-encompassing sea into a free raw material and use the sun and wind and scorching labour to grow salt. Without their effort, it was only available in the hills of Punjab, Mandi and Tibet, where it was mined. His people had not just stood idly by and waited for the sun to evaporate the water as most people perceived the process to be. Perfectly flat pans had to be dug in places with clayey soil. The pans were as deep as the midpoint between a man's heel and his knee. There were two kinds of ponds, and the first set was layered with hay. Seawater was channelled into a series of shallow tanks where the infinite crushed shells of billions of minute sea creatures calcified and separated from the salt crystals. The crystals were then moved to the second set of carefully flattened pans where they would be farmed into large crystals on a diet of briny water. No animal could help these people in their work, and the dry winds and the blazing sun burnt their skin and blinded their eyes. Eons ago, communities of Agaris had built and owned those pans and worked them together. The salt was shared amongst the different families depending on the work they had put in. Now kings owned the salt and when we ate it, we came to belong to them. Now he shakes these ancient memories from his head.

The sun has just risen and Ganpat is at his salt pans in Kharegaon. His pans are on a bend where the River Ulhas meets the copper-coloured sea. He has taken a round of the pans while it was still dark and cool and now it is time to find shade. Ganpat sees an oddly shaped high cart drawn by a single massive bullock approaching on the bundh. He heads towards it, not recognizing its passenger from that distance.

'Namaskar, Lokhandeji,' Rama says, resplendent in his shining white dhoti and kurta. He has a month's worth of hair on his recently shorn head.

'Any news of Venkoji?' asks Ganpatbhau sincerely.

'Nothing at all, Sethji, not a word, not a clue.'

'Don't worry, we will find him,' says Ganpat reassuringly.

'I hope and I just pray he is safe and unhurt till then.'

'Why would they kill an able-bodied man? These sea bandits are slavers, and let me tell you, he was so well educated and presentable, he must have been sold as a munshi,' Ganpatbhau hopes as much as he reasons.

'I pray you are right, Lokhandeji.'

Ganpat takes Rama to a simple shelter made of wooden poles that are covered with a patchwork of thick jute and hemp sacks. The structure has a high roof and the shade within it is deliciously cool. Rama waits while Lokhande and a few foremen meet and discuss work for the coming day. Ganpat lets Rama know he is ready to leave, and they make their way to the funny little bullock cart.

'What is this?' asks Ganpat as he climbs a short ladder to a high bench not much wider than the giant bullock.

'You came from Kalyan in this?'

'No, Sethji, from the jetty. I take this bull and the cart with me on board the *machua**.'

'Wonderful, Ramaji, what can I say? You have inherited your father's élan and surpassed it even.'

Rama and Ganpat head to the jetty where Rama's machua is docked. The cart driver sits just behind the bull, and the two wooden benches in the back are raised on a platform that starts at his head. The large wheels of the cart are under the seating platform and that

---

* Fishing boat.

makes the entire cart much slimmer. This uncommon configuration also afforded Ganpat a view of his pans he had never seen before.

'*Wah*, what a view, they look so clean and pure, so grand,' Ganpat says, admiring the neat gridwork of the pans.

'Sethji, I was wondering that if on our way to Mumba Devi, we can meet Abdul Seth in Bhandup, and you can impress upon him to join us for the meeting?'

Ganpat now understands why Rama has come all the way to him even if he is on his way back from Kalyan. Seth Narayan Kamath's death and his younger son's abduction at the hand of sea thugs had shaken the genteel sections of trading society and affected him personally. They had been comfortable and happy partners. Though Rama was still looking for his passionate and fragile brother, he had channelled the anger and grief of his father's death into a desire to improve the decaying safety of the Konkan coast. The seas were a dangerous place for unarmed and civil people these days. There were stray Malayan pirates who had been plaguing the coast as did Siddi captains gone rogue, and Arabs came and went as Allah and opportunity provided them, but they were just thieves in little boats. But now they came in ships first stolen from their own countrymen to terrorize this distant coast.

'And Sethji, I would also request you and Abdul Seth to decide who amongst the both of you will spearhead the activities now that Appa is gone. I am not in a position to do so.'

'We will see, son. We will see,' Lokhande muses.

The cart driver drives the bullock straight up the boarding plank into Rama's machua. It has four oarsmen on each side in the hold and is twin-masted with lateen sails.

'Wah, this is the way to travel, not a speck of dust or splash of mud,' Ganpat says, impressed as he gingerly gets down from the high carriage. Pesi Dubash welcomes both the Seths on board as they settle on to the matted floor of the rear deck. The nakhwa instructs the oarsmen to push off as he navigates the machua through the creek south towards the open sea. Flocks of flamingos paint the dull marshy banks orange and pink on both sides. After passing Airoli and Ghansoli villages on the mainland, the nakhwa has the oarsmen row the machua into the Bhandup inlet when he spots a distant minaret behind the mangroves. They make for the jetty and then to Abdul Seth's salt pans nestled inside a huge forest of mangroves on Rama's high carriage.

Abdul Seth is helped up the steps of the special high carriage and the three seths return to Rama's machua. Once the nakhwa has navigated the machua out of the crowded creek, he has the sails struck and they sail south again, down the Thana River to the archipelago at its tip. On one of those tree-topped and rocky islands lies the warehouses of the Angrez. They sail past hundreds of barges and boats plying their cargo from Thana and Kalyan to the several depots that dot the coast down to Kanyakumari.

Saltpetre

Pesi, with his trimmed beard and manicured fingers, has known Ganpat Seth and Abdul Seth for decades. Most people knew them as amongst the countless salt pan owners manufacturing salt for up-country trade or export to Persia and Arabia, but Pesi knows them for what they truly are: the Kharatpanna Gang. A syndicate of saltpetre exporters that had been led by his late employer. Narayan Seth had made them all Seths and amongst the most prosperous of the lot, by sourcing saltpetre from Malwa and Mysore which they then sold to the Persians and the Dutch. The demand for saltpetre was outstripping their ability to procure it but that did not really matter as the Swedes and the French would pay exorbitantly for it. Dorab Patel, who worked at the President's office in Bombay, had told him that the Seths in London had been commanded by their king to either carry a fifth of their cargo back as saltpetre or pay duty on the silver they were sending out to buy goods here. It was good that Rama had got his father's partners with him because many of the people at the meeting also knew who they were, and despite their humble origins and demeanour, how rich they were.

Lokhande Seth decides that he prefers getting off at Wadi Bandar instead of Palva Bandar. Rama directs his captain to dock there instead, and the three Seths and Pesi Dubash get off in Rama's high carriage. Abdul Seth is glad to see the bustling streets after so many months. Everybody knows everybody and it is a long procession of namaskars and small talk.

'We might as well have walked,' Abdul Seth says, exasperated at the constant chatter and gossip.

'Rama, too many people looking at us,' Lokhande says, embarrassed as people turn to look at the odd carriage. Here the shopkeepers and merchants have seen an assortment of eccentric little cabs and grand ungainly carriages that the Angrez use, but this they know belongs to young Kamath.

'Trust me, Sethji, this half daand more of height changes the entire perspective.'

'Undoubtedly,' agrees Ganpat, 'but what about getting a horse?'

'He never sits on anything with a mind of its own Sethji,' Pesi butts in.

'Well, I just hope you don't take that attitude to bed,' teases Abdul Seth as Rama blushes and smiles awkwardly.

'Rama, what do you mean to achieve today?' Abdul asks, turning to the work at hand.

'Sethji, Father is already gone, and I don't think we will ever see Venko again, but for our business to continue the way it has and even grow, we need security in the region. Between the Siddi, the Firangis and the Angrez, none can keep the shores safe.'

Though it was an exaggeration when people claimed that every grain of rice eaten in the Mughal Empire passed through Seth Mangatram's hands, it wouldn't have been incorrect to say a tenth of it did. His power came from the consortium of moneylenders and rich investors from his community whom he had organized into an efficient and lucrative bank that could tilt the axis of power. He had bet on the unpleasant and miserly Prince Moiuddin against the generous and compassionate Crown Prince Dara exactly for those reasons of character. Always bet on the parsimonious, his father had told him. It had paid off and though the rest of his Kayasth community was daily being replaced by clerks and munshis from Persia and generals from the Pashtun wilderness, his enterprise had grown against all odds and safeguarded the wealth and power of his community. Under the emperors Akbar and Jehangir, the Kayasths had come to dominate the administration of the Mughal treasuries and armies. The Rajput secretly considered them their rivals as much as they could admit, being sun-born kshatriyas that ostensibly shunned trade themselves.

The Kharatpanna Gang made its way past bighas of stacked timber and endless warehouses stocking bales of calico, muslin and an infinite variety of cotton weaves, towards Seth Atmaram's haveli farther inland. The mud streets passed through jackfruit and mango orchards interspersed with paddy fields as they went farther west. Contrary to popular belief, Seth Mangatram had not shut shop in Thana; they were not in that business. They had instead acquired warehousing premises between Mazgaon and the English fort farther south. When Atmaram had suggested the idea to his father, the old man had dismissed it. It was just not worth their while dealing with the new batch of pinker Firangis. Their red upturned noses bothered him. Mangatram had known their breed as quack doctors and purveyors of trinkets and wondered what trade they could possibly offer. Atmaram though, started diverting goods to the Portuguese in Daman and to the Dutch, English and Swedish traders he met in Surat. They paid in sparkling silver and gold coins of standard and reliable weight and purity. Atmaram consigned these payments back to his father in Agra with the projected estimates for the coming year based on the understandings he had entered. Atmaram moved to Thana from Surat where another brother replaced him from Daulatabad. Soon he had warehouses in Palva Bandar and Bassein and was planning a trip to Vengurla to post an agent there or maybe even open another warehouse. The Kamaths had warehouses and a comfortable *bungala* in Vengurla and were on very good terms with the traders from the Nederlands. At first their requirements were limited to nuts and masala, then they grew to include muslin, pigments and exceedingly saltpetre. Despite all the muskets and cannons they had, the poor sods did not have the most important ingredient required for making *barud*—the black gunpowder that lit every shot of musket and cannon fire. Narayan Kamath had, sometime ago, realized the importance of the long white crystals that were grown out of liquids extracted from the soil. The Padishah had a monopoly in Agra and Bihar, and Adil Shah in Bijapur, and they were the primary consumers too. But now people who had nothing to do with the Padishah or Sultans wanted it and were willing to pay for it in hard silver and softer gold. So Narayan's son had offered Atmaram help in Vengurla if he could supply him with saltpetre from Agra. Lokhande had saltpetre sources in war-ravaged Malwa and Abdul in Mysuru but they still were unable to meet the demand even at highly profitable prices, because everybody wanted gunpowder—as much, if not more, than they needed salt.

Their carriage turns on to a cobbled lane that runs through a formal Mughal garden that is still under construction. Gangs of lanky muscled men in dirty langots and colourful pagdis work on laying a gridwork of pipes as tile layers work in fountain wells and *malis* plant saplings and even attempt rose bushes. The haveli has scaffolding on one end where masons are finishing corniches and balcony-sized *jharokas*. It is a double-storeyed structure made with mortar in the *Lakhnawi* style with large windows and high walls indented with a row of small open *mehrabs* just under the roof. There are horses and their retainers milling around at the entrance of the haveli to the left side of the entry stairs and bullock and horse carriages parked on the other. *Palkhiwalas** shyly hide behind the palanquins they have shouldered here. Rama recognizes Ratan Chand Sahu milling around outside under an umbrella held by a servant. As the carriage comes to a stop in front of the stairs leading into the haveli, the three Seths climb down from their perches and greet Ratan Chand, inquiring about his father, Som Chand Sahu.

'Why are you outside in the sun?' asks Rama.

---

* Palanquin bearers.

'Pandurao Phangaskar is here, trying to meet Seth Mangatram. Why did you call him?' Ratan Chand says testily.

'I definitely did not call him,' says Rama, wondering how that little snake smelt it and slithered his way in.

'Well, then maybe Atmaram did? They are the best of friends,' suggests Ratan Chand.

'No, not at all, highly unlikely, I told Atmaram to keep it to himself.'

'Don't be so naive, Pandurao gets him girls and anything else he wants.'

'Are you scared of him, Ratan, that you are hiding from him outside?'

'Scared my ass, I just don't want him picking my pocket,' Ratan Chand replies, making everybody laugh.

'Don't fear people like that, you boys. See, some people want to play the game forever and take it to a new level, as you do because of the families you come from. And then, there are people who think the game is *chuna lagao*. But you can do it only once to a person before you must move on to somebody new,' the elderly Seth Abdul advises Rama and Ratan Chand.

'Unless you find an idiot, then you can con him repeatedly,' Lokhande corrects, 'and the world is teeming with impressionable fools.'

'So, who all have you called?' Ratan asks Rama.

'Your father, us and I also asked Seth Dhanjibhoy, Teli Seth Kihimkar, Kapus Seth, Trimbukji Meghji, Seth Nimisbhai, Dadi Seth, Thakker Seth and Dorabji Nanabhai, a trusted Patel working for the English Company to also join us.'

'I don't know, Rama, what am I doing with all these big Seths?'

'*Chup*, Ganpat Seth, if only they knew what you hide under your simple dhoti,' replies Abdul immediately, though Lokhande has voiced an uneasiness he shares.

'Sethji, everybody knows who the three of you are,' Rama says to Ganpat, forgetting he has replaced his father.

'*Arrey*, don't worry, Lokhande, I'm just here to see if it's actually true that Mangatram's teeth are made of pearls and his bottom gold,' says the ever-irreverent Abdul.

'Quietly, somebody will hear you,' says Lokhande nervously.

Lokhande and Abdul gasp when they enter a huge hall with high ceilings. An immense crystal chandelier hangs from one of the massive teak beams supporting the roof. The walls are covered with astonishingly lifelike paintings in ornate gold frames. The massive room is populated by a naked citizenry of petrified and marbled children with bows and arrows amongst naked athletes, warriors and brooding women. Lokhande checks to make sure a life-sized boy is not in fact a real human sealed within the glossy stone. Abdul Seth, for all his ribaldry, is embarrassed at some of the images on display but his eyes keep dragging him to a naked and corpulent woman standing in a large open clam shell amidst the ocean waves. Rama heads to a painting of an orange amongst three pale green pears he had seen the last time he was here. It is unbelievably lifelike and the bright fruit bowl sitting on a dark table seems to emerge out of the frame.

'Ramaji, Ratan Chand,' greets Atmaram as he walks into the room to receive his guests. He is a short, almost delicate man and smells of roses. Atmaram greets Ganpatbhau and Abdul Seth formally and tells them how much he has heard about them from Rama as he leads them to an adjoining room.

'I hope there aren't any Firangis or Angrez here or I'll have to take a bath before going to the *dargah*,' Abdul whispers to Ganpat as they enter a large room covered with mattresses and bolsters along both walls. There are also eight heavily carved rosewood chairs on each side of the room where the mattressed sitting area ends. Brass spittoons, gold *pandaans* and silver hookahs are in attendance beside the several business magnates that are sitting or reclining on the mattresses. Bucolic tapestries cover the walls of the room, as realistic and fascinating as the ones in the hall.

'Ah, the notorious Kharatpanna Gang,' Pandurao Phangas immediately voices loudly in welcome.

They ignore him as they take the empty spots along the row of mattresses on either side. Lokhande and Abdul go to the far side of the room, settling beside the amiable Nimis Seth.

'*Kem cho, Sethji?*' Abdul politely inquires as Lokhande mumbles the same.

Rama greets each of the Seths individually as they condole his father's passing and his brother's abduction. Trimbukji makes place for him closer towards the raised daybed at the head of the room.

Rama has sold the meeting as an opportunity to meet the famous Seth Mangatram who rarely if ever leaves Agra and even if he does, it is never to visit the Konkan.

'So, the mountain comes to Mohamad?' Trimbukji asks Rama, wondering what brings the great Seth to their humble coast.

'Seth Mangatram is on his way to Kanchipuram, he arrived from Surat yesterday. Tomorrow he will leave for Calicut.'

'Kanchipuram? Is he going to build a temple or take *sanyaas?*' Trimbukji whispers into Rama's ears.

'Just a pilgrimage,' Rama whispers back.

'I hear he has made a substantial loan to Mukarab Khan,' Trimbukji quietly tells Rama as Atmaram re-enters the room with his father. Seth Mangatram is a surprisingly diminutive man with an ample belly and full jowls. His massive white turban raises him another hand as every eye in the room is transfixed by an egg-sized ruby glowing like blood at its centre. He is wearing a miniature silk kurta in its natural golden shade buttoned with pearls. Everybody stands up, the Parsi Seths and Pandurao from their chairs and the rest from their mattresses. Mangatram climbs up on to the raised mattress and greets his guests with his palm facing himself in the *dehelvi* style. Atmaram stands at his side as his father surveys the Seths bedecked in their grandest attire.

'*Pitaji,*' Atmaram says, directing his father's attention to Ratan Chand: 'This is Hiranand Sahu Mushirabadi's grandson, Ratan Chand,' he says in his deferential Urdu.

'You people have reached here too?' Mangatram asks Ratan Chand. 'Then there must be something of value here,' he says to Atmaram.

'Namaskar, Sethji,' Ratan Chand replies, bowing and raising his cupped palms to his forehead.

'Tell your grandfather to leave the rest of us some little corner in this large land,' Mangatram compliments his rapidly gaining competitor.

'Pitaji, may I present Ramaji Kamath, and he can introduce his friends whom he has invited here, their coffers are the beacons that light these shores,' Atmaram says looking at Rama who looks back at him and then at Pandurao.

'Pitaji, I have also requested Pandurao Dhanapant Phangaskar, a representative of the Firangi Nawab and a trader with great insight and acumen to join us—if you don't mind Rama?'

Rama purses his eyes and lips articulating it is no matter.

'*Pranaam*, Sethji,' Rama folds his hands in greeting.

'When Seth Atmaramji told me you were gracing our little jetty, we could hardly believe it. Your acumen and your deals are legend in all four directions, and we are honoured with your darshan, so please forgive this imposition on your valuable time,' Rama says in clear though slightly accented Urdu.

Seth Atmaram asks Rama to continue with a slight nod.

'May I please present to you Dadi Seth, who has been a bastion of trading in Kalyan even before the Angrez took over from the Firangis.'

Rama chooses to introduce the equals in order of age seniority. Dadi Seth bows his head in a salaam and sits down in a chair.

'Abdulbhai Pilatar, salt; Bharanji Thakkar, horses; Khoja Phanoos Kalandar of Hayastan, everything under the sun to lands that have none; Ibrahim Chaulkar, oil; Lokhande Seth, salt and also my business partner; Nimis bhai is here representing his father Chandubhai.'

'*Kem cho Motaseth*?' Nimis wishes Mangatram casually, and the banker from Agra touches his belly consciously.

'And finally, this is Trimbukji Meghji of Alibag, who trades in everything from horses and cannon to silk and ropes.'

'The pleasure is entirely mine. This has been most fortuitous as I was asking Atmaram to introduce me to some of the good men of Konkan Desh.'

'Seth Mangatram Galgotia *daulat e riyasat, Hujoor*, you have blessed this land by stepping on to it,' gushes Pandurao immediately.

'His Excellency Don Castro is most eager you stop for an afternoon on your way south. He would be most honoured to entreat you.'

'Young man, let me be clear with you, the Padishah Alamgir is much annoyed with the arrogance of the Firangis and quite frankly I don't think they could manage what I am used to.'

'Sethji, it is merely a misunderstanding, the distance between the august Badshah and their king in Portugal is so distant, miscommunications are bound to arise.'

'Well then, shall I arrange for someone closer home to buy his *jagir* and his ships if it is too distant for the Portuguese King to manage?'

'Sethji, they pay in the best gold and silver,' Pandurao parries an indisputable fact.

'And their ships,' he adds, whistling and spreading his arms to denote their immense size.

'Kamath, I am sorry about your father. Atmaram says you wish to unite the business community and increase our strength?'

'Merely some security, Sethji. As you now travel down the coast, it is a matter of concern that you are not assaulted in any way by *pariah dakus* and thugs as my father was. We pay the Firangis their cartaz, and the Siddi at their ports too for passage of goods. Each has a fort, often right next to each other where they waylay our cargo and penalize us but cannot provide any semblance of safety.'

'Son, the Wazir himself will escort me down the coast. Is that not safe enough?'

'Of course, Sethji, for yourself of course. But, say tomorrow Atmaramji must go to Lanka or to Vengurla, I don't think the Wazir would afford him personal protection or even send out a convoy to escort him.'

'Good point, Kamath, I must tell him to send some troops with Atmaram when he travels. I'm told he is a Habshi. But I see your point,' Seth Mangatram says in chaste Urdu.

'The seas are no longer safe,' says the Yehudi oil manufacturer and exporter in Marathi. Rama translates it for Mangatram into Urdu for his friend from Chaul.

'There is no way to recoup any of these losses and these bandits destroy even what they choose to leave behind. Always drunk and terrorizing the poor people on the boats,' adds the Armenian Kapus Seth.

'We were under the assumption that the Habshi Wazir was in control—total control of the situation here,' Mangatram says.

'Sethji, here in the Konkan, even power follows the ebb and flow of the waves. The control of forts and the jurisdiction of areas under them change hands every week. The farmers often are forced to pay the same taxes to the Siddi and to the Marathas. Now the Angrez are imposing their taxes.'

'I pay all taxes and duties four times over: to the Siddi, to the Marathas; to the Firangis or Angrez and finally to righteous Ahura Mazda and I see no problem. There is still enough profit to be made,' intones the hawk-nosed Dadi Seth.

'What about the constant danger?' asks Ramaji in his accented Urdu.

'Why do we Seths have to venture out? It is not our calling to brave infested waters. We have *dalals** and munshis for such work. It is better we choose the shadow of some fort and stay safe behind its walls,' Dadi Seth rejoins, throwing his hands up.

---

* Agents.

'Sethji, my late father had made the trip personally as I was away in Vengurla and the cargo was the murti and materials for our Saraswati Mandir. It was his personal responsibility, and he lost his life trying to accomplish it.'

'No need to make excuses, Rama, why should Kamath Seth have not gone? Why are we being terrorized into sitting at home rolling out *bhakri* like women?' Lokhande Seth says in Marathi.

'Thakkerji, what thoughts do you have on the matter?' Mangatram asks the senior Gujrati trader.

'When there are too many daughters-in-law in the kitchen, the taste and quality of the meal invariably suffers. That is why we keep a *maharaj**, so even if the *sethani* dies the food neither changes nor decreases in any way,' Thakkerji says sagaciously.

'Well, Sethji, then it is a matter of too many maharajein,' says Ratan Chand.

'That is about to change. *Shrimaan*, let me tell you a thing or two about the Padishah. He is an able administrator, and more importantly, he is not wasteful. He means business. He is not here to build gardens and pleasure houses. I cannot tell you the amount of wealth that was dissipated by his ancestors. Forget the countless *arabs*** on a single mausoleum, but the lakhs spent every day on just food and clothing. He has brought about a sea of change. All the nonsensical pageantry is gone. His gold and silver go to maintaining troops. He has fought his whole life and always come up on top. The entire land will be connected and governed by one authority. This is his plan. Shivaji was an aberration that has delayed his plan. But now there is no stopping him. Mukarab Khan Zaman is the finest general of our times. He was a stalwart of the Qutb Shahi's before their venerable house was turned into a veritable *kotha**** by a *qalandar*. He now leads the Padishah's armies in the south, and he will

---

* Head cook in Gujrati households.

** Billion.

*** Brothel.

not stop before he reaches Keral. This I can assure you of. Bide this time till better days come and come they certainly will,' Mangatram says with finality.

'The best days are already here, Sethji,' Pandurao fawns.

'The Honourable English Company eagerly wait upon this era, Sethji, and daily pray for such a day to come to pass. As your most loyal subjects, we take it upon ourselves to provide security for vessels trading out of Bombay . . .' says the Patel of the Angrezi traders.

'I must point out, Dorabji Saheb, that father had and always did take permits and, on this occasion, had a letter from the Honourable Child Saheb himself.'

'Ramaji, it was most unfortunate, an accident and a tragedy but our own ships are taken without mercy . . .'

Rama rolls his eyes, exasperated: 'Often by men who till recently were in the employ of your company. The line between these brigands and your company is very fine indeed, Sahebji.'

Lokhande signals to Rama from down the room, gesturing patience and restraint with his eyes and his palm. Dorabji invites Ramaji to come and meet Sir John Child. Each Seth probes the other amiably for some news or information as they compare their recent successes. Trimbukji and Chaulkar Seth excuse themselves and make to the jetty from where they will sail directly to Kulaba.

The Habshis

At the mouth of the Rajapuri creek stands the island fortress of Janjira across a wooded bay near the ancient 'City of Kings'. Near its unbreachable entrance is an ancient carving of a mythical lioness trampling an elephant. The fortress has two freshwater springs and ample housing for its officers and some private citizens too, who live there with the reigning Siddi's family. The Yakut Khan of Janjira is ensconced in this citadel that overlooks the Arabian Sea out to his ancestral homeland beyond the horizon. His troop of fighting sailors are ever ready at his feet and his navy anchored in the inlet nearby. Centuries ago, his ancestors had captured the island from the Koli king Rama Itbarao through deception. It has never left their hands since and serves as their base in the northern Konkan. Kasim is now Wazir and if he ever ventures inland to court, he would be standing amongst the first line of ministers and grandees. Kasim knows that though he is protected against any external enemies, the people most dangerous to his career are those that are always at arm's length. For arms often end in sleeves that conceal daggers. Pandurao Phangaskar is haranguing him on a guest he has been requested to meet by the padishah's imperious though minuscule banker. Kasim feels Pandurao owes him the money he had lost at the failed takeover of Suvarnadurg despite there being a mole in his operation. The word had got out either from Janjira or Chiplun, and now Pandurao is trying to implicate a minor accountant at the salt works along with Rama Kamath and Kanhoji Angria.

'Your Excellency, I had the misfortune of knowing these boys from childhood. That munshi in Chiplun is the smartest of the lot and he was working for you till he disappeared right after the incident. He is working for Dhanaji Yadav now. He was as thick as thieves with Angria and Rama. That Bala—it is in his blood. You had his elder brother drowned for causing you great losses and he is taking revenge.'

'That was not I. That was before I was Yakut Khan,' Kasim corrects him.

'You said Rama's brother just now, the one who is missing?' the Wazir asks.

'They were both there,' Pandurao lies.

'Now, Rama is trying to raise a private militia—a naval militia,' he continues.

'What nonsense. You know that is impossible?' says the Wazir.

'Why? He was saying that if the Angrez and the Firangis can protect their cargo, then he has the same rights.'

'There is a big difference, they take their ships out to the deep sea, on the coast, there is no need. The waters are safe—as safe as they have ever been.'

'Rama was very clear on that issue in front of all the Seths and especially Mangatram bhau. When I pointed out that you were the only legal authority here, Rama said you were incapable or unwilling to exercise it and that you wouldn't even help Mangatram's son if required.'

'I am not every baniya's private *sipahi*[*],' thunders the roused Kasim, 'I am Yakut Khan, Wazir to the House of Timur: the Emperor's sword on the seas,' the Wazir thunders.

'But with your money which Bala and Angria took from Mohite, Rama thinks he can start his own navy,' Pandurao digs in.

---

[*] Infantryman.

'Angria is just a hot-blooded boy, he is nothing. The Marathas are finished. Sambhaji's days are numbered and then they will be finished,' the Wazir says smugly.

'But somebody like Angria, you will still have to force out of that fort when the time comes,' Pandurao reminds him.

'Anyway, what does this merchant want from me?'

'Seth Mangatram wanted him to address any complaints or raise any concerns directly with you.'

'He did mention him,' the Wazir admits.

'There is one more thing you need to know about Rama Kamath. He is the biggest barud smuggler in the Konkan. He and his syndicate sell *kharatpanna** to all the Topikars including the Angrez.'

'Find that munshi from Chiplun first before you accuse my house of treachery. Now call him up,' Kasim commands Phangaskar who slips away to get Rama whom he has kept waiting on his boat. Rama comes up into the citadel followed by two pairs of retainers who are carrying *nazrana*** for the Wazir.

'Just speak your mind, the Wazir is a fair and honourable man,' Phangaskar advises Rama on their way up to the dark citadel.

Rama bows respectfully and presents the nazrana to the Wazir.

Rama recounts the events of that fateful day when his brother went missing.

'They should not have been so far from the coast. Had they sailed past us here, they would never have been assaulted. We often see boats trying to bypass us by going deeper into the ocean. Pay your duties and travel safely under the shadow of our cannons.'

'It is a policy with our dalals and nakhwas to always pay for the necessary cartaz and duties,' rejoins Ramaji.

'It is a pity,' says Kasim, not feeling anything. It is getting late, and he wishes to meet his astrologer who has been waiting for him.

---

* Saltpetre.

** A gift given by a supplicant.

'What specifically do you want from me?' Kasim asks curtly. Rama can feel the man's impatience nor find any sympathy in his voice. A cheetah on a chain barks as a baboon in a cage starts howling.

'Your indulgence. A consortium of traders can make available a fund that supports a naval coastguard that patrols the coast and keeps it safe, of course, under your expert guidance and authority.'

'If you want me to become a chowkidar for baniyas, then you must pay for it. Let me know how much you can pay every year and I will let you know what I can do about it. Or you can always make the same offer to your friend Kanhoji Angria.'

Rama is confused, he has heard of the name Angria from his brother Venkoji but is himself unacquainted with the man. Assuming Kasim has mistaken him for his brother, he lets it pass without qualification.

'Ho Huzoor, I heartfully thank you for making the time,' Rama says as he bows out. He is not about to waste any more time and the Wazir dismisses him adding: 'I am sure you are well aware that kharatpanna manufacture and sale is the sole preserve of the Padishah.'

'Of course, Huzoor, it is a fact accepted and adhered to by all,' says Rama, bowing in deference as he leaves the citadel. There is no hope here. The Siddi is as likely to go raiding on a long day as an Angrezi *daku**, and he seems to suspect his involvement in saltpetre production.

---

* Dacoit.

Gunpowder

Rama finds his machua at the village of Owale on the Savitri River where he has left his capable nakhwa Mangu. The yellow-eyed Mangu had expertly navigated the bends of the river as they passed by the villages of Warathi, Mhapral, Kondgaon and Shigvan that grow paddy on the riverbanks. They cross Shipole's cashew nut orchards before they sail out to the Arabian Sea and then head south for Suvarnadurg. The coast is an array of verdure over black cliffs, and human habitation is marked by groves of the thin-stemmed flowers that the coconut trees look like from a distance. Curious dolphins and clamouring seagulls escort them south while the turtles choose to ignore their boat as it sails on the seaward wind. As the boat approaches Suvarnadurg, it runs into a raucous armada that is anchored to the north and west of the island. There are black painted dhows and galbats flying the Wazir's red pennant. On the pinnacle of the highest mast of a large dhow flutters a golden fish glimmering on a green silk pennant.

His dark skin gleaming like obsidian, the unflappable Mangu is being heartily abused, shouted at and threatened to return the way they have come but he takes his craft right up to the outermost dhow. Rama palms a copper sicca to one of the soldiers who is screaming at them to leave. Their eyes meet and with a gleam of future profit understood, the soldier pulls Rama up on to his own dhow.

'Just take me to your commander—I'll make it worth your while,'
Rama winks at the well-fed musketeer. They cross a bridge of dhow
decks and then get into a little rowboat. They make their way over to
a vessel with a line of dead black eyes running along its sides. Rama
has impressed upon his escort that he is a poor Brahmin astrologer
who has come to see Kanhoji Angre with a proposal of marriage.
When Siddi Khairiyat hears the tale, he is amused and permits Rama
to leave without any payment.

'What wonderful news: Angria getting married again. Tell him
not to waste his time and join us. Tell him I will dance at his wedding
if he does. His king is dead if he doesn't know, tell him that too,'
Khairiyat good-heartedly advises Rama who is glad he has gotten
away virtually free: he is made to read Khairiyat's hand and tells him
that he will be the father of many brave and prosperous sons.

'Pandit, you will live with her curses,' shouts a soldier as the
assembled troops all laugh. They will search his boat before it
can head to the fort. Rama pays his escort a few more rupees and
with happiness and cheer all around, leads him back to have his
machua searched.

Mangu pilots his rowers towards the small beach that
affords landing. Rama is gingerly helped into a small dugout canoe
that has been lowered into the water and is rowed by a single
oarsman to the beach as the garrison on Suvarnadurg's walls
wonder who their dainty visitor is. He makes his way to the fort
gate and speaks to the soldiers peering down at him with their
muskets aimed at his head.

'I am here to see Kanhoji Angre. Tell him I am Venkoji Kamath's
elder brother Rama Kamath,' he enunciates loudly over the waves.

A good amount of time passes before the tall brass strapped
gate creaks open and a soldier pulls Rama in. As the gate is opening,
a salvo of cannon fire smashes into the surf behind Rama and the
Siddi's troops cheer and sing randy songs portraying Angria. Rama
is taken up the several flights of stone stairs that periodically appear
between the rising courtyards. Coming lithely down a flight of stairs
he sees a young man with curled whiskers approaching him.

'Seth Ramaji Kamath, welcome, welcome. I am Kanho. Please come,' he says bowing and inviting him in. Though his host's tone is genuinely warm and inviting, his eyes and his face are serious and even aggrieved.

'I am blessed indeed to have you as my guest. It was my intention to come and meet you but as you can see, I am a little distracted at the moment.'

He suggests Rama freshen up and later meets him in a simply set meeting room.

'Two Angrezi ships had waylaid my father's dubash. Kanhoji, my father died of a head wound and my brother has been abducted. Our nakhwa himself made an offer to the dacoits for Venko's release right then and there but they took him away, nonetheless. My father can talk himself out of most situations and he would have tried his best too. People in our community are actually accusing Venko of running away with a silver murti of Saraswati Devi and the accoutrements and jewellery!'

'I know,' says Kanho.

'How?' asks Ramaji.

'Venko was my friend. I am very sorry for your loss,' Kanho condoles. 'Your brother did not run away. He was taken and then,' he slows down and controls his tempo and his tone, 'he is no more.'

'How do you know this?' Rama screams back at Kanhoji as his hopes for his brother make one last attempt.

'I could not prevent it, but do you think I did not find out. Had he told me, I would have provided an escort for him. He did not tell me about this trip. But I found out. I mean everybody knows we are friends, and we did spend a lot of time together. Angrezi dakus. One of them could not believe that Venko could speak Angrezi, and he took him.'

'Then?' Rama asks as Kanhoji quietens down again.

'By the time my man found Venko, he had already given up hope,' Kanho's voice trails into a choked whisper. Rama can see Kanho's affection for his brother and the sorrow of a lost friend in his eyes.

'We may have been able to get him back.'

'Then why didn't they take the ransom then?'

'Because they are animals. My man asked. They said they would enjoy him for a bit and sell him for a good price as a translator.'

Rama falls silent with visions of his brother's pain encompassing him.

'If it is of any solace, his oppressors are dead,' Kanho says.

Kanho offers Rama a pandaan that is readily accepted. Rama expertly folds the chopped betel nuts into a lime-smeared betel leaf along with some cardamom seeds, sticks of clove and a splat of katha.

Kanhoji shouts out for an attendant who is then privately instructed to get something.

'It's no consolation, but when my man found the dakus who had taken your brother, he did get back the Devi.'

Rama cannot believe his ears. At least his brother's and his family's reputation wouldn't be tarnished, and the rumours would be put to rest.

Pairs of attendants dressed in spotless white kurtas and dhotis return bearing the chests that had been looted from Rama's father. On a wooden pallet sits the silver Saraswati idol covered by a white cotton cloth. Kanhoji has it removed so Rama can inspect the statue. Rama gets up and bows in namaskar to the much younger man.

'The reputation of my family has been saved and I am indebted to you Kanhoji,' he says, still in disbelief over this most unexpected restitution.

'I couldn't send this across Khairiyat to you to Palva Bandar,' Kanhoji says as Rama looks on still dumbfounded. 'Well, at least not cheaply.'

'There is no hurry. I will pay back whatever you paid to get this back,' Rama assures Kanhoji, suddenly realizing the fortune that would have gone into buying back the idol, her pedestal and the golden veena.

'Please don't bother. This is courtesy Pandurao. I ransomed him back to his family and it more or less covered the costs.'

As Rama feels unburdened by his family's escape from ignominy, a hollowing pain gushes into his heart with an aching desire to make his brother alive again.

'No, no. Kanhoji, what you have done for me, I will never be able to repay. It is so much more than silver and gold.'

'Ramaji, with all respect please do not talk like this. Venko was my brother too.'

'I did not realize you were so close,' Ramaji says.

'Venko and me, we had big plans, you know. It was he who remembered that Swamiji had old texts in his library on how to distil saltpetre from the soil and on how to mix it with charcoal and sulphur to make excellent quality barud. Given your father's involvement in the trade already, we were planning to manufacture our own barud here. Do you know that all the kharatpanna in the world goes out either through the Konkan or *Bangal*?'

'Yes, on the caravan routes over land to Persia and China,' adds Ramaji.

'But let me tell you, sailing anything up is much easier, especially if it is heavy or bulky.'

'So, you were planning to manufacture gunpowder?'

'Lots of people already do that. We were planning to manufacture the best gunpowder in the market for the Maratha kingdom: the purest and in the right proportions of *gandhak**, kharatpanna and *koyla.***'

'And you knew the right proportions?'

'We still do. It's all there and Venko made copies and I have them with me. From medicinal use to explosives—it's all there.'

'We could still do it?' Rama lilts, raising his silver cup.

'Of course, and we shall,' Kanho thunders, smiling.

'For my muskets, a powder made of one-part *vanjula* koyla, two parts gandhak and seven parts kharatpanna is the best mix,

---

* Sulphur.
** Coal.

and now that I have command over the guns and gunners of both Suvarnadurg and Gheria, we can figure it out for the cannon too.'

'Talking of the Maratha kingdom, what are you going to do now?'

'What do you mean Sethji?'

'I mean, do you seriously believe there is a future with the Bhonsales? Honestly, do you think they can last?' asks Ramaji, his inhibitions drowned.

'Well, that bloody *Khadoos* doesn't ever seem to die. As a boy I was so sure that Shivaji Maharaj would outlive Old Alamgir, I would have bet my life on it.'

'Well, he has outlived both Shivaji Maharaj and his son,' Ramaji points out.

'But other sons remain. Sethji, I don't want to make gunpowder to sell it, I want it for our guns. I want to control the quality, not make a hon. What we can't afford is for our guns to not fire each and every time or blow their own breeches up.'

'The Maratha kingdom will survive, and it will flourish. As far as the Konkan goes, unlike my supervisors I am glad they ignore it because I can and will do it on my own. I mean with a little help from my friends, but we can do it here.'

'Do what?'

'Control the coast, from Surat to Lanka: A fort every 30 kilometres down the coast and an armada to patrol it. Let everyone come pay their duties and trade and flourish in safety.'

'Excuse me, Kanhoji, but are you speaking of fantasies you had as children or are you speaking of the present?' Ramaji presses.

'Ramaji, as detested as the old man is by the gods, one day they will forgive him and let him rest. What then? Are you aware of the rebellions in Punjab? Mewar? Having killed his own brothers, what are the *shahzadas** expected to do when their father dies?'

'You keep on top of things, don't you?'

---

* Crown princes.

'Isn't everything connected? That's what Swamiji has demonstrated to us, and to deny this all-pervasive connectedness is sheer stupidity. Ignorance, he says, is a crime we alone are responsible for.'

'You are talking of Brahmendra Swami?'

Rama wants confirmation.

'Yes,' Kanho says and laughs out aloud when he sees Rama's expression of disgust—his nose wrinkled like it just realized it was inhaling a dog's fart.

'I have seen better magicians at *melas**, Kanhoji, he is a charlatan of the highest order. I can't believe both you and Balaji follow him.'

'Look, he does tricks to astonish the simplest-minded folk and they imbue him with a reputation of power and respect; for the more worldly-wise, like my friend Kudal and the Siddi, he makes flattering predictions and prescribes suitably expensive pujas in exchange for wealth and prestige, and for people like us, he has great insight and wisdom.'

'In exchange for?'

'The ability to effect change, that's what he uses people like us for.'

'He also is a *sahukar,*** I hear?'

'Why not? Do you not loan out money, or borrow when you need to and be glad of paying or charging for the privilege?'

'Of course, but it is my profession and my dharma—I never claimed to be a *sant*.'

'Ramaji, are you not a Brahmin too and was not your esteemed heavenly father also?'

Rama must acquiesce to that fact.

'But I just find the mixing of religion and business abhorrent. Those that have given up the world must then stay away from its matters—this is a dictate of the shastras,' he clarifies, not wanting Kanhoji to think he has something personal against his guru.

'I actually do not need anybody else. Once I took over here, I realized that it's nothing but insatiable greed that keeps us from

---

* Fairs.

** Moneylender.

doing what we should have. My father or I have not paid for this posting, it was given to me by Chhatrapati Sambhaji in recognition of my unswerving loyalty. I was also given several villages, the revenue of these being sufficient for the upkeep and improvement of this fort. As soon as this lout Khairiyat leaves, as he will when the rains begin or when he gets bored, I am going to construct two more forts on the mainland. First, I am going to control the coast between Suvarnadurg and Gheria, it's forty kos. This is where everything comes from to go to Goa, Surat and Thana.'

'The Firangis and the Wazir?'

'First I have to deal with the Firangis.'

'You are dreaming of attacking the Firangis while the Wazir's navy besieges you?' Rama gently mocks his host. The tongues and hearts of both men are loosened by wine and their love of Venkoji and as they talk, an attendant comes in to light the various diyas and the wall torches.

'Let me tell you something: Gheria above all, then Janjira and this fort Suvarnadurg cannot be taken from the outside. Anyone who has commanded them knows this, as does Siddi Kasim. But now that he is Yakut, he will never again leave Janjira, for remaining within is the only way to hold it. That is why they neglect the sea. Before the Firangis came, Rajapuri and Dabhol were the biggest ports and if you had a fort at the entrance, you controlled all the trade that passed through it. Rajapuri had Janjira and Dabhol had Gopalgad.'

'Is Gopalgad under you?'

'That was then. Anyway, now it is a Maratha possession currently under Bhawanji Mohite. Today, the game has changed with the Firangis and all the Angrezi and Topikar traders coming in and making their fortified *godams** along the entire coast where their cargo is stored. Today, you need to control the waters; the forts are just your bases and dry docks. We need to be out there on the sea making our presence felt and reminding them that these are our waters.'

---

* Godowns.

'How could you ever take on the Firangi ships? Some of them seem bigger than forts themselves and carry more cannon.'

'Swamiji told me to keep something in mind, he said that "a person or a thing's greatest asset is also invariably its greatest weakness". As far as the Firangi or Angrezi ships go, their problem is that they are too big for the coast.'

'What is stopping you then?' wonders Ramaji.

'Funds, of course. See, currently the only ships on patrol are the Firangis and these too only around their mandovis. Most coastal traders head out to sea to avoid the custom houses they pass along the coast and then they get picked up as happened to Venko. However, if you get your *dastaks** from me, I will guarantee that you are not assaulted by anyone because it will enable me to build ships and get them out on the seas filled with armed soldiers. Currently, you have protection only within the range of a fort's cannonball, whether it be Siddi, Firangi or Maratha.'

'Kanhoji, for it to work it would require the majority of the trading community to back you. I will as I am indebted to you, but to most other people . . . and you are an unknown quantity,' Rama says as plainly as he can.

'I don't mean now, but in the near future, once both my quantities and qualities become known,' Kanho says as he gets up.

'Ramaji, I have made arrangements for your stay here tonight, please excuse me while I let my gunners get some night practice. Khairiyat has been so kind in obliging to be our target.'

Rama decides to follow Kanho up to the ramparts of the fort but soon decides to return to his assigned quarters as the sound of the cannon is painful to his ears. By the time Rama reaches his room, the firing has stopped, as has the ringing in his ears. His dreams are tinged with excitement and eagerness to return to Palva Bandar with the Devi's idol, and he sees his father smiling and his brother swinging by the neck in them.

---

* Permits.

Sarnaubat

Rama wakes up the next day to a barrage of cannon fire Siddi Khairiyat has commanded as an *azan*[*] to wake all the faithful. It almost puts all thoughts of returning to Palva Bandar out of Rama's head. But he is equally eager to return with the Goddess and her accoutrements and clear his brother's name. Rama completes his morning ablutions and rituals and seeks out Kanhoji. The fort is abuzz with a martial fervour that seems to emanate from its commander's own unceasing energy and interest. Rama finds it in everything, from the jogging water carriers to the flying sparks of the metalsmith's grinder. It flashes in the morning sun as Surya is leading a close combat training session for an oiled troop assembled in the northern courtyard. Kanhoji is at the southern end of the fort, mounted on a large grey Arabian stallion. His musketeers are also on the backs of chestnut and piebald mounts. Kanho trots along the sideline while he watches his riders charge and fire their muskets. In pairs the *silhadars* gallop out with shouldered muskets, which they then set, aim and fire. They are required to holster the fired musket and reach out for the second one that is strapped to the saddle right behind their seats. Often the rider drops the first musket or the second, and some try to come to a halt or slowdown in the manoeuvre while cocking the gun.

---

[*] Islamic call to prayer.

The small field is blanketed with dark sulphurous smoke and dust every so often and the riders wait for it to clear as they are egged on by Kanhoji to experience actual battle conditions of blinding smoke. Overcome by the spreading smoke and dust, Rama dares himself on to the western bastions of the fort, from where he can see an armada of twenty-odd war dhows and galbats of various sizes, all bristling with cannon. As he walks around the ramparts, he can see sweepers and cleaners in every direction sweeping the courtyards and mopping the stairs. Each cannon on the fort has a pair of gunners sitting beside it and Piloji is training sharpshooters from the ramparts of a massive octangular bastion. Piloji introduces himself to Rama and condoles him on Venko's passing.

'Are forts always this busy? Or is it because of the siege?'

'It is because of Sardar Angria,' Piloji proudly replies.

The slim and well-mannered Piloji wears pearls and emeralds in abundance. Today they match his lime-green kurta. He is clean-shaven and the aroma of *oud* lingers around his body.

'Sethji, every shot fired costs money. Most people would never waste powder and shot and risk damaging the guns in practice. Not our Kanhoji. He trains us constantly, all out of his own pocket,' he explains.

'How come no one has a bow and arrow?' Rama asks.

'Sethji, mastering a bow is a tedious and difficult art and not for everyone, whereas I have seen a street performer's trained monkey load and fire a musket. Shooting a gun is just repetition, it requires no skill.'

'Really?' wonders Rama, and adds: 'I had no idea he was so disciplined.'

'All the powder is checked before it is distributed. There are two people assigned to this duty. He has ensured the best *payawali* guns for all of us but if you slack in cleaning or maintaining them, then he will have your head. Discipline? Riding, sword fighting and firing a gun is his dharma. As is running this fort. I have never seen anything like this anywhere before.'

'What about the Siddi?'

'Oh, nothing to worry about. He's just here posturing because of Chhatrapati Sambhaji's death, hoping Angria will sell him the fort's possession and move out.'

'So how long is he going to stay around?'

'Who knows? Till the rains come and he must go back or next week. Can't tell really.'

Rama is quite dismayed hearing this as he hopes to return at the soonest.

'If you want to go back, it can easily be arranged, but if you want to go back with your things, then that will cost you. Khairiyat is a very amenable man.'

'So it seems, but I think I would rather wait.'

'You must, you must—stay here awhile: Sardar Angria likes you. He misses Venkoji. They would go out riding in the mornings,' Piloji says.

'My father was with Shivaji Maharaj at Surat and my mother is the grandniece of Hambirao. Let us meet in the evening,' Piloji adds, confirming his pedigree.

'Definitely,' Rama says as he makes his way back down to his assigned quarters to take another bath. He is tired from all the walking and watching exhausting training, and Rama has a snooze while the sun is at its zenith.

Golu, wearing a halo of peacock feathers on his head, comes to fetch Rama in the afternoon, indicating that Kanhoji is calling for him. He is taken up to a row of rooms below the south-western ramparts. A cool breeze is blowing through the small square windows that let in oblique posts of light. Rama finds Kanhoji being congratulated by his troops as Piloji and Surya look on cheering: 'Jai Sarnaubat Kanhoji Angria!'

Golu takes Rama straight to Kanhoji who smiles warmly at him.

'Ramaji, you have brought me great luck. Chhatrapati Rajaram is on his way to Jinji and has appointed Sidhoji Gujar the *Sarkhel** and Bhawanji Mohite and me as his *Sarnaubats*.**

---

* Admiral.

**Vice admiral.

'Congratulations, Kanhoji!' Rama shouts out amongst the cheering soldiers.

'I have independent charge of the Northern Fleet, now Rama, you must help me build the fleet,' he says laughing. Kanhoji raises his hand and Surya shouts everyone to silence.

'Before we celebrate,' Kanhoji says to the assembled crowd, 'we must remember our murdered king and swear loyalty to his younger brother.'

'Jai Chhatrapati Rajaram Maharaj!' Kanhoji booms as everybody assembled echoes twentyfold back.

'Sambhaji Maharaj, as you know, was betrayed by Kavi Kalash to Aurangzeb's general Taqrib Khan.'

People in the room hiss and curse when they hear the Padishah's name.

'But do you know that when he was taken to the Old Man, he was offered riches beyond belief, a mansabdari and the Old Man's own daughter in marriage? Did he accept?' Kanhoji shouts out at the crowd.

'No,' they all echo back: 'never.'

'They tore out his tongue. They told him he would live if he converted and submitted to their god. Blood dripping from his mouth, he wrote: "Not even if I was given the throne," so they cut off his hand.'

The assembled garrison cheers again.

'Aurangzeb divided his troops up in two lines and made Maharaj run in between while every soldier—low and high—beat our brave and unyielding king. They then cut off both his arms and his legs and finally cut his beating heart out of his chest.'

The room fills with the vilest invectives against Aurangzeb and the Siddi. Kanhoji raises his hand which holds a piece of stiff paper, and he waves it around shouting: 'I received this a few hours ago from our friend Siddi Khairiyat offering me 5 lakh siccas to give up the fort,' and he tears the paper up as everybody cheers him, shouting, 'Jai Chhatrapati Rajaram! Jai Kanhoji Angre!'

'This is our land and will forever remain our land, we will not sell our mothers—ever.'

Now they cheer Kanhoji as he walks out of the hall and into the adjoining yard where more of his troops and workers in the fort have assembled. Chanting 'Jai Chhatrapati Rajaram Maharaj', he walks to the edge of the rampart and throws the crumpled paper towards the Siddi's fleet below. Surya orders the gun captains to fire all the cannons in the fort as everybody erupts into celebration. The *dhols** are out and soon follows the tadi.

That evening as Ramaji sits with Kanhoji, they are joined by Piloji and Surya. Surya remains standing and every so often disappears for some moments. Everybody is excited and talk is now all business. Kanhoji shows them the proof of a seal he is having made. It reads in the *devnagari* Marathi script: '*Shree // Rajaram charni sadar Tukoji sut Kanhoji Angre nirantar.*'

'Kanhoji, son of Tukoji Angre, is forever at the service of Chhatrapati Rajaram,' says Piloji looking at the text.

'Ramaji, now at least I have the authority, if not the cognizance.'

'Indeed, you do, Kanhoji, now we pray that His Royal Highness Chhatrapati Rajaram live a long and prosperous life,' Ramaji says. Rama knows it ultimately depends on the ability of the Bhonsale clan to keep other Maratha clans united with them and themselves away from the jaws of the ravenous Mughal.

'With this, I too have a better offer to take back to the traders in Thana, Kalyan and Chaul,' Ramaji says.

'Don't forget Vengurla,' Kanhoji reminds him. 'You don't have to set up any fund or pay me in any other way than the Dastak we issue which is at 2.5 per cent of the goods' value. If anything is proven to be looted, then I will underwrite the value of those goods—but of course I will be the judge of that once all the evidence has been produced. But it's a better deal than the cartaz or your Angrezi permit, which is nothing but a Maratha permit sold illegally.'

That evening Siddi Khairiyat sends an emissary to Kanhoji who presents him with a fine dagger in congratulations on his promotion. The Siddi's munshi reads out his master's letter:

---

*Drums.

'Siddi Khairiyat says that Allah is on the side of Kanhoji Angria. He not only escaped my clutches but also has been awarded for his loyalty and bravery. I further congratulate him on his impending wedding, where I hope to be invited to celebrate. As a token of my respect, please accept this small knife forged in the celebrated forges of Vijinagiri.'

Kanhoji accepts the gift and in return has his cooks give two roasted sambars to Siddi Khairiyat.

When the emissary leaves, Rama inquires about this odd overture of friendship made by Siddi Khairiyat.

'Last year, he kicked my face in, and if he hadn't killed me, he would have sold me back to my father for all we were worth. But he is just a soldier, like me. He has nothing personal against me. A few months ago, I met him at Swamiji's ashram. I have been trying to get him to join me and now he was hoping I would join them. But unlike me, he is a free agent, out to carve his own kingdom.'

'He is not with the Siddi of Janjira?'

'Nothing is permanent. Kasim deposed Siddi Fateh by switching sides to Aurangzeb from the Bijapurkars. All alliances are temporary as far as they are concerned, and loyalty is to the highest bidder. Of course, there is always the matter of trust, so you generally go with your own kind and people you have known.'

'Isn't that true of everyone?' Rama wonders.

'Yes, almost invariably if you are looking at the short term. But we who are of this land and have no other place to go best consolidate our own power.'

The very next day Siddi Khairiyat slips his anchors and returns north to the docks at Janjira. His men return to their fields and workshops. Rama waits another day as he must head up in the same direction. His machua has been moored at Harnai and it is sent for once he is ready to depart for home. Rama gets on to his vessel along with the Devi and her golden veena, and they are escorted by two galbats all the way to Palva Bandar.

Refuge

Khandoba himself had overheard Seth Rama's lie to Khairiyat, as Kanhoji is soon married to a young Maratha girl who is the daughter of his father's compatriot, Tulaji Jadhav. The astrologer compared their star charts and changed her name to Lakshmi.

True to his word, Rama returns once the monsoon has come and gone. As a small token of irredeemable appreciation and a wedding gift, he has brought several brass telescoping spyglasses that he has acquired from his Dutch partners. The finest of the lot, inlaid with contrasting silver and wrapped in sealskin, is separately presented to Kanho in a walnut case. Kanho is touched by the thought that has gone into such a welcome gift. A clear and powerful spyglass is hard to come by, and it is a vital logistical tool in Kanhoji's arsenal. Rama has also brought with him a Firangi called Hansuji and his Dubash Pesiji. Hansuji is as odd-looking as Firangis came. Instead of the usual red or brown hair, Hansuji's is a pale yellow that renders his eyelashes and his eyebrows invisible against his exceedingly pale skin. He has discoloured spots on his large nose and cheeks, and his eyes are tiny swirls of indigo in milk. Pesi translates as the browless man speaks: 'My name is Hans Stohr, and I am from the town of Suhl in Thuringia. I am a very good gun maker. I can make the most amazing guns in the world. But there was an accident. A client of mine, a crown prince, very rich and very powerful, like the son of the

Padishah, the gun blew up in his hand. He had put bad powder—too strong. He lost his hand, and they came after me. I hear you could use the services of a man like me.'

'Now you have crossed the seven seas to blow up my hand? Then there will be no place for you to go,' Kanhoji says, laughing at the lash-less man as Pesi translates.

Hansu speaks again and Pesi translates: 'Hansuji says that the guns he makes are very special. He says they can fire repeated shots. You fill the gunpowder for several shots along with eight or ten lead balls and you can then fire them repeatedly.'

'Impossible; tell him I have no place for magicians in the foundry,' Kanhoji says testily.

Hans gesticulates that he could make the gun and that he would test it himself and before Pesi can translate, Kanhoji tells him that he can try.

'Also tell him that you will be gone soon, and he should learn Marathi,' Kanhoji advises Pesi.

Hansuji nods and salutes Kanhoji in the Firangi way with his hand to his chest. Kanhoji brings his hands together in a namaste and says: 'Food and lodging and then we will see,' which is relayed to the satisfied gunsmith.

Once an attendant leads Hansuji away, Kanhoji points out the gunsmith's blaming the gunpowder for the explosion of his gun to Ramaji.

'It is very important to have a standard quality of barud, mixed wet and then well sieved when dry. The grains must be of equal size.'

'I can get you all the saltpetre you could process,' Ramaji assures.

'What about the people and place to process it?'

'It can be arranged; I know somebody who would be very interested. I will bring him the next time around.'

'Who is it? Can you send for him now?' Kanhoji says impatiently.

'Now?' Ramaji laughs. 'Yes, that can be arranged,' Rama says, appreciating the haste. It is a rare quality and one he possesses himself and often finds wanting in the Firangi and Maratha administration.

Maybe the Konkan climate is exhausting, though young Kanhoji seems impervious to it.

Rama instructs Pesi to request Lokhande Seth personally and to tell him to bring his son along with him as the Maratha Sarnaubat has requested a meeting.

'Dubashji, also any shipbuilders you know and trust, I can give them a very comfortable life here,' Kanhoji says to the departing Pesi who makes straight for his employer's dubash.

Kanhoji takes Rama to the mainland across from the fort where hundreds of near naked men are working on the construction of a new fortified complex.

'What are you making here?' Rama wonders at the immense throng of stonecutters, their chisels chipping away at laterite blocks.

'Three more forts,' Kanho points south over the dusty red percussion of the stonecutters: 'Kanakdurg and Fattegad, and here we are standing in Gova. I swam to that beach when I escaped from Khairiyat.'

'Isn't the fact that the fort is on an island enough to protect it? You seemed very unbothered with the Siddi at your doorsteps.'

'This will make it even safer, truly impregnable. Then their land forces do not have a chance to harass you with artillery from the east and you have absolute control of the moat in between. If you have one foot on the mainland, it also enables you to engage their land forces and have easier access to provisions.'

'They say there is a *bhuyaar* from the Janjira Fort to Rajapuri?'

'Yes, there is and once this fort is complete, I am going to dig a tunnel too and connect this fort to Suvarnadurg.'

'Is it possible?'

'Anything is possible if one has the funds and commitment.'

'Kanhoji, it all looks very expensive,' Ramaji says, as he wonders how much interest Brahmendra Swami is charging his devotee.

'It is. But it needs to be done. This is an investment for the future and a necessary foundation that I need before we step into the water. Look, Ramaji, today all I have authority over is Gheria and

Suvarnadurg and five or six galbats. First, I need to make all my three bases impregnable and then I need to make my presence felt at sea. Today, you and any other trader will always prefer a Firangi cartaz, will you not?'

'Of course, it is the law. They are masters of the entire coast and everyone including the Angrezi or other *Topikar*** ships also must drop their sails to them. Only the Siddi does not bother to pay heed as he feels he is the rightful master.'

'Well, Ramaji, soon a Maratha dastak will become equally necessary. I am not building these walls to sit behind them.'

Rama is witness. The sons of the fishermen, coconut harvesters and salt pan workers form the teams of willing youth that he is drilling in his handful of galbats. He had initially dismissed Kanhoji's talk as the dreamy phantasm of fiery youth. But this young man seems relentless in his pursuit, and the fire in his eyes reminds Rama of the story his brother had told him about the young Kanho. Hadn't Angria been favoured by the gods with a blessing of royalty and greatness as a child? Venko's tale from when he was at the gurukul, excitedly related to the whole family and immediately dismissed as fanciful, comes back to him in a flash as Rama looks up at Kanhoji and wonders if he is destined to be another Shivaji—a Konkan Shivaji?

'What are you thinking about? Don't get so worried, Sethji, I will give you the best terms—friends and family discount,' Kanhoji says to Rama who has suddenly gone silent.

'Actually, Kanhoji, I would like to pay my dastak in advance. I will give you 2 lakh siccas now and you can adjust it in the months to come,' Rama offers Kanho.

Though Rama has lost all faith in the Bhonsales to provide security and stability in the region, he must hedge his bets against this rising rough diamond, which in his own estimation will supersede

---

* Hat-wearers, a reference to Europeans.

his masters in lustre. It would also be a way for Rama to repay the monetary part of the reacquisition of his father's lost cargo.

'It is the grace of Lord Khandoba,' Kanhoji says to Rama as he thanks him and lets Rama unburden some of the debt that seems to be wearing him down. Kanhoji calls for his *sachiv* who is hovering around under an umbrella. Kanhoji's secretary puts down the umbrella and rushes to his master's side, all the while removing his paper and charcoal pencil to make his notes.

'Let it be known that Seth Ramaji Kamath is a loyal subject of Chhatrapati Rajaram and has offered his support by financing the Sarnaubat of Suvarnadurg 1 lakh rupees for the building of vessels and 1 lakh rupees towards the purchase of weapons. As recognition of his loyalty, all his cargo will only be charged at 1.5 per cent of the value of goods instead of the usual 2.5. Send one copy to the mazumdar and get the other signed by him and send it with the Jinji *dak*.'*

Kanho turns to Rama and does a deep and thankful namaskar again.

'I am most thankful for your support Ramaji, and your help means even more now, when I need it. You have hastened up my plan and we will reap our harvests sooner.'

'Why do tomorrow what we can do today?' Ramaji says.

'And why do today what we can do now?' Kanhoji completes the aphorism.

'Are you sure this gunpowder plan will work? We have tremendous demand for saltpetre, more than we can provide. The Persians, the Sultana of Aceh and especially Chin, their demand is constant and insatiable, and it can reach anywhere safely unlike gunpowder which they make themselves. Who do you plan to sell it to?'

'Sell it? I want to make it for myself, and Bala feels that a standard is vital to warfare. When Bala can, he will bring it up with Dhanaji

---

* Mail.

and the other *senapatis**. Look, Ramaji, you are the businessman, and these things are out of my depth, but I need for you to make it pay for itself.'

'We will need some other customers then.'

'The Punjabis need it, as do all other rebels against the Empire. Earlier the Royal Bijapuri and Golkondan factories were selling it to their enemy's enemies, now we shall, and once the old man dies, then every raja and nawab who doesn't have his own facilities will need it. Trust me, Ramaji, as far as businesses go, it is better than anything else in the world.'

'Ganpatji makes the best salt in the area. He also processes all our saltpetre that comes in to further purify it and has started making his own saltpetre in Mysuru. He will be the best man for the job. His son is a bright boy, and he can run the operation. You need to provide a safe place where we don't have the Siddi's people or the Firangi's poking around.'

'I will give him the place and I will provide the security too, don't fret about that,' Kanhoji says as they head to the second outpost Kanho is building on an isthmus of basalt rocks that protect Harnai port from the open sea.

As the burnt orange sun descends to the horizon, Sarnaubat Kanhoji Angre and Seth Ramaji Kamath head back to the fort. Kanhoji suggests a night out hunting but Rama excuses himself. Unlike his younger brother, he is not particularly keen on the outdoors and the multitude of insects and serpents it promises. As Kanhoji heads back to the mainland with his new Firangi gun maker, Rama spends most of the night in Kanhoji's personal library. Rama has requested to study the copies of the texts on gunpowder processing, so Kanhoji arranges for his sachiv Gangadhar to escort him to a large untidy room that is attached to Angria's official meeting hall. Gangadhar is a Konkanasth Brahmin like Ramaji and had been a pupil of Pandit Joshi's like his master. He unlocks the heavily carved teak door and

---

* Military commanders.

lets Rama in after lighting the several diyas and small wall torches. Once Rama has read the sheaf of papers Gangadhar had handed to him and taken notes on them, he moves on to the plethora of patris and palm-leaf manuscripts that clutter Kanhoji's library. There are bound illustrated books in Persian, patris in Sanskrit and scrolls in Marathi and Braj amongst maps of the world and the celestial sky. Besides the texts, there are models of Arab dhows, galbats and even European ships. An entire shelf recessed into the basalt wall has a collection of spyglasses, and another holds every possible shape and size of nautical and martial tool. Kanhoji also possesses something Rama has never seen outside of any nautical vessel: logs of the captains and quartermasters. He finds copies of ledgers from Goan mandovis along with other records of trade and shipping which Kanhoji has no business having. Ramaji wonders to himself how his host could have acquired these items. Still wondering, he moves on to the various curiosities that function as paperweights on the large European-style rosewood table that takes up a fourth of the room and is covered with maps in Chinese and Malayalam and celestial charts in Arabic besides the usual Persian maps. There are several upturned steel helmets filled with coins in various metals and shapes.

Kanhoji finds Ramaji studying a three-foot high globe that stands on its bronze feet when he returns from his hunt well after the sun has risen.

'It is a copy of a *naksha* of the world on a model of the planet itself,' Kanho explains.

'Where did you get it from?'

'It was a gift from Swamiji. It is a copy of one that belongs to the Sultan of Istanbul, or so he says.'

Kanho shows Rama where they are on the globe as Rama inquires about the hunt.

'Well, I hope Ganpatji likes wild boar, and if he doesn't, Surya has got us as much *titar** and *chakor* as his heart desires,' says Kanhoji.

---

* Partridge.

'He's a carnivore of the highest order, he'd be delighted for sure,' confirms Balaji.

'What is this?' Rama asks picking up a narwhal's horn.

'It's a white dolphin's horn, and those dolphins are found here,' Kanhoji says pointing to the topmost land mass on the brightly coloured globe.

'They live in a sea surrounded by deserts of snow. Have you ever seen snow, Ramaji? I really want to see some snow.'

'I haven't yet but I must say you have quite a collection here,' Rama compliments Kanhoji on his eclectic curiosity.

'Just trinkets you come across, most of them are taken away by my son Sekhoji as toys.'

'A lot of books too.'

'Surprised? Do I look that illiterate? Is my neck too thick?' Kanhoji says laughing.

'Venkoji read a lot, did he not?'

'It is a habit that was beaten into us by Pandit Joshi while our hides were still supple,' Kanhoji chuckles appreciatively.

Tigers

Sukhdeo, hair rustled by the sea winds, looks back at his father in pride. Unlike his own feet, his father's occasionally crack open and bleed. He is in the prow of Seth Ramaji's vessel with Pesi Dubash who summoned them in great haste. In the covered deck, Pesi's brother-in-law, Keki, a burly man with big forearms and a larger nose, is telling his father and his father's partner Abdul the faults of the vessel they are sailing in.

'He told me my head was too big,' Sukhdeo tells Pesi over the flapping sails. He no longer wants to meet Angria with his big head.

'He corrects my pronunciation in languages he does not speak, but he knows how to build boats,' Pesi says laughing out loud.

Pesi continues his song as Sukhdeo looks east at the craggy coast they are passing.

'Gheria,' says Pesi, and almost at his command, the sail is dropped and the oars dipped.

'Are we to meet Angria today?' Sukhdeo asks apprehensively.

'Most likely you will meet him immediately, he has to meet Keki too,' says Pesi.

'But I must wash before I meet him,' the boy tells the Dubash.

The vessel docks and Pesi takes the four men up to the gate where Kanhoji is already waiting for them. Kanhoji takes them up to the main bastion and shows them the flagpole where Chhatrapati

Shivaji Maharaj had personally raised the *bhagwa**** pennant. They all touch the pole reverentially, reaching across time to touch Shivaji Maharaj. Kanhoji has arranged for mattresses and bolsters to be set out on the wide *naal*****, where it meets the bastion. Kanhoji plies them with refreshments of kokam juice, solkadi and a variety of fritters before offering his guests separate hookahs.

Ganpatbhau and Abdul begin to unconsciously share a hookah out of habit, as Sukhdeo teaches his distinguished and elderly audience the process of making pure saltpetre crystals. They have identified a village called Rangantithu, which is near Mysuru in the Karnatak. The forests in the area have abundant birds and countless bats that leave their caves at night to fly over the adjoining fields that are trod by cattle and men during the day.

'In what season do they do this? Or can you mine it all year long?' Kanhoji asks the young man.

'One needs to mine the soil during *Phalgun******, and one has to mine it from a different location every season. The extracted soil is dissolved with water and then using a system of fine bamboo filters, saltpetre liquor is extracted and then cooked till it is concentrated. Then this concentrate is left to cool and crust overnight. Once it has solidified, the remaining water is thrown away and the most impure form of saltpetre emerges: the *jharia*. In the imperial territories the jharia is to be solely collected by the Padishah's agents.'

'Is this what you buy?'

This is what Lokhande and Abdul bought from small extractors along the trunk roads and brought it back, hidden in their returning caravans. The jharia was then further refined through continuous boiling and removal of the precipitated salty sediments that would form in the wide and shallow iron pans. The remaining liquid was scooped up from the tank and left to settle. Again, it would be drained from the top and the process repeated. The third time around, the

---

* Saffron coloured.

** Ramparts.

*** Twelfth month of the Hindu lunar calendar.

sticky white liquid was poured into a shallow pit in the ground that had a fine bamboo *jaali** suspended across it. Here, the solution was left to crystallize for a week. The crystals were then washed in cold water and left to dry on a split bamboo sieve.

'The more you clean it, the purer it gets,' Abdul burbles through his gurgling hookah.

'Well, that is everything about kharatpanna I presume, but what about barud?'

'We have not made barud yet,' says Seth Abdul, 'it's a very dangerous business, saltpetre cannot blow up.'

'I have been to a small factory in Mysuru where they make barud,' Sukhdeo says, looking at his father from the corner of his eyes.

'How often do they blow themselves up?'

'They told me it happened once. Six people were killed. But quite some time ago as there has never been an instance in the past four–five years.'

'What proportions are these people using for the barud?'

'Equal parts of charcoal, saltpetre and sulphur,' says Sukhdeo promptly.

'Barud is dangerous, especially what I will be asking of you: seven and a half parts saltpetre, one and a half of sulphur and one part of koyla,'

'Now, that is a dangerous recipe,' says Sukhdeo in awe. Not only has he met Angria, but he has been lecturing him. The same Angria that boarded a Siddi vessel and single-handedly fought its commander and crew before escaping through the sea. Now Sukhdeo is entering into a venture with his hero, the legendary hunter.

'Saheb, I too have shot a tiger,' slips out of Sukhdeo's mouth.

'It's not easy, is it? There is a male I have been after since I was a boy. I once clipped its ear, and you can still identify it. It's at least a *kathi* long now, the biggest I have ever seen.'

'Saheb, Mysuru too is just teeming with tigers.'

'I'm sure of it, Sukhdeo, but never forget that barud is a more dangerous beast and you must treat it with greater respect.'

---

* Mesh.

Babel

After gently depositing a dry Ramaji at Vijaydurg, Pesi Dubash turns his vessel upriver to his brother-in-law's boatyard. Keki has expanded the dry docks built on the Vagothan by Shivaji Maharaj and created a large shipyard adjoining it. He is glad of the dry plums his brother-in-law has brought.

'Two years ago, a week after you first arrived here, you sent for clothes, last year you sent for my sister and my nephews and niece. What happened, Keki? Such a long meeting?' Pesi asks, unable to not laugh at his running jest.

'As you can see,' Keki says sweeping his hands across the industrious vista, 'I have been busy since our meeting: a dozen galbats and a ghurab already complete.'

'What about those Firangi ships?' inquires Pesi.

'You will enjoy it here too, the languages that are spoken here! Saheb welcomes all, and all come. Sarnaubat Saheb is often here, studying their designs, their weaknesses,' he says knowingly.

Javan and Chinese junks are berthed next to Dutch fluyts and Omani dhows. Pesi then meets Hansuji at his foundry at Gheria where he produces everything from nails, grappling hooks, anchors to lead shot and fixes muskets. He repeats the joke about Keki to Hansuji in Marathi. Hansuji can now make a sturdy and unadorned wheellock musket but refuses to try his hand at cannon.

157

That evening, they travel upriver with Kanhoji to visit Sukhdeo's barud factory. Sukhdeo has been able to manage his responsibilities in Mysuru with those at Kharepattan primarily because his father has appointed a son-in-law to be deputed to the Karnatak permanently. Pesi follows Sethji and the Sarnaubat around the jharia purification works that makes a perfectly clear saltpetre. Sukhdeo shows them samples of the prescribed willows for making the most appropriate charcoal and samples of the purified gandhak. Kanhoji is impressed with the two pairs of massive granite stones that look like the wheels of a temple chariot. Each pair is placed in stone cisterns that hold the damp mixture of the three inert materials that are transformed into an explosive when combined. These are housed at two mills, roofless structures made of thick laterite walls on four sides, and each constructed at a distance from the other. Over Sukhdeo's Konkani, Pesi can hear shouts of effort and warning in Telugu and Tamil, and what he presumes could only be Kannada.

They return to the sea and head to the mouth of the Vashishti River. Kanhoji halts at the Swayambhu Navnath Mandir to seek the blessings of the very deity whose fire feeds his soul. Pesi, waiting outside the sanctum, can hear the ancient Sanskrit intonations that remind him of his own temple. At Dabhol, a full boatload of fruits, vegetables and bales of fine muslin and cotton are waiting to join them onwards. The nakhwa leads his oarsmen in a hectic chant as they zip over the calm waters of the Vashishti followed by a second galbat. The river is full of stubborn chonok—badamundis—hunting ample blooms of shrimp and strategy-minded dolphins chasing delicious *bekti** and *rawas*** as they escape upriver. They are all sitting at the prow, an impatient Suryavanshi cursing the crowds of barges, dhows and smaller dugouts and rowboats that fill the river to make way for the Sarnaubat. Kanhoji is joyous at the bustling trade and doesn't mind as he explains to Ramaji: 'Sarnaubat Bhawanji Mohite

---

* Sea bass.

** Indian salmon.

has charge of both Gopalgad and Anjanvel, which we took from the Firangis of Gomantak. But all he cares for are his mangoes,' says Kanhoji as they pass under Gopalgad.

Ramaji sends Pesi to fetch a gift that Ibrahim Chaulkar has sent for him. Pesi brings it to the covered deck they are sitting in. Pesi opens the thin pallet and gives a package wrapped in brown waxed paper to Rama who then gently proceeds to untie the twine and unwrap the waxed paper. Kanhoji is so astonished at the image he sees that he gets up to take a closer look. It is a domestic picture of a man washing his hands, the water pouring out of a white porcelain jug.

'What amazing craftsmanship, you can see the light, or is it . . .' Kanhoji plays with the angle of the sunlight hitting the painting to see if it moves—No, it's the painting. If the artist had made him full-sized, one could easily be fooled into thinking it's a real man. Where did he get this from?

'From the Topikars of Vengurla, the painting was pawned to a silk merchant who gifted it to Ibrahim Seth. The silk merchant says Ibrahim's oil has gone into making this painting.'

'Where did the Topikar get it from? Persia or Chin?'

'No, no, it's done by a *Dus Topikar**.'

'By an artist called Vermeer,' Pesi adds.

'I find that hard to believe,' Kanhoji says.

'I tell you it is. Seth Atmaram has a collection of them at his haveli, some are life-size images.'

'I would have never imagined they are capable of such art.'

'To tell you the truth, the Dus Topikars have been gifting these to powers that be and their local partners, simply to impress upon them that they are not as uncivilized as we feel.'

'Come now, Sethji, in this matter you are exactly like Venko. You like their toys. I have them too and loved them as a child but other than their trinkets and curiosities, they are, to say the least, a filthy lot.

---

* The Dutch.

I mean how can you call them civilized when they do not follow the basic principles of hygiene.'

'Kanhoji, they are quick to learn and disciplined in their nature.'

'You are wasting your time with them. Anyway, please do thank Ibrahim. In fact, you must tell him to come and see me whenever he wishes. His oil will be safe under my watch.'

Kanhoji has every person on the two vessels line up to see the picture of what he had assumed was of a Circassian slave washing his hands. The painting is then rewrapped and taken down to the hold. Kanhoji, though impressed by the gift, is happier about the fact that a merchant of Ibrahim Chaulkar's standing is sending him a gift: if not yet a force to reckon with, at least now they were hedging him into the equation. The traffic on the river is a joyful inconvenience to all on board except the nakhwas. They carefully slide upstream as they manage to keep from colliding into each other or having their rowers' oars clash.

They deboard at Gowalkat Fort, the ancient seat of the Chougle Rajwada on the southern banks of the river. This too is in the possession of the ever-absent Bhawanji, and the Sarnaubat is disgusted at the indiscipline and sloth that besets an otherwise important fort. Shivaji Maharaj had wrested it from the Siddi of Janjira and renamed it Govindgad though the old name continues to stick. Pesi misses Rama Seth's bullock cart as he sits cross-legged on the low platform of a mule cart as they make their way west to Brahmendra Swami's ashram. The Koyna River valley is teeming with game, and according to the Sarnaubat, it would be remiss to pass through its verdant valleys without a little hunting. They spend the night at Vasota Fort before heading to the ashram next day, reaching it only in the late afternoon. The Sarnaubat has ridden ahead while Surya has stayed back with Ramaji who wobbles along on his toy cart with Pesi and Gangadhar.

Ramaji and Surya arrive much after Kanhoji has settled into his little *kuttiya** at Brahmendra Swami's ashram. Brahmendra Swami

---

* Hut.

is warm in his welcome as young acolytes porter Ramaji into the manicured ashram.

'It's good you have come when you did—any later and you wouldn't have seen this place,' starts Vishnu immediately.

'Why? Is it being reclaimed by its actual owner?' asks Ramaji.

'No, no, Khairiyat has made a grant of lands in Dhavaddshi, we are moving there,' says the Swami.

'Swamiji, Ramaji has brought something most wonderous for you,' Kanho cuts in as he sends Gangadhar to fetch the painting.

'Why must you insist on presenting me with nazrana every time you come, Kanhoji Raje? It is I who should be presenting the nazrana to you, chosen by Nav Nath and blessed by Lord Vishnu himself,' Swamiji says as Kanhoji blushes over his brown cheeks.

'Do you know that he was marked as a child?' Brahmendra Swami asks Ramaji.

'So I have heard, Swamiji,' Rama replies.

'Well, what do you think? Now that you have met him?'

'The devas cannot be wrong, they have made the right choice.'

'Well, just don't forget to repeat that in front of our guest this evening,' the Swami tells Rama with a naughty sparkle in his eye.

'Who is to be your guest, Swamiji?'

'Our guest,' the Swami corrects Ramaji, 'is a true and ardent *chela** of mine.'

Gangadhar has fetched the painting and opens it up for Brahmendra Swami to see.

'This is from the Topikars, I presume. Made in that style. No, Raje, you must send this on to Jinji, to Chhatrapati Rajaram Maharaj, with your next dispatch.'

'You are too generous and wise, Swamiji,' Kanhoji replies. As a bevy of eager young initiates directs Ramaji's *khidmatdar* to a cottage assigned to his master, others take Pesi to his quarters. Ramaji is surprised at Kanhoji giving away the painting to Brahmendra Swami, but more surprised at the Swami's selfless advice. Ramaji takes a

---

* Acolyte.

bath and then puts on a cream-coloured dhoti and kurta with a black *angavastram* over his shoulders. He puts on a pair of charcoal grey pearl earrings to match his angavastram and combs his thick mane repeatedly till it shines and then covers it with a black turban. Lastly, he puts on a necklace of pearls that are a pair of strings, one black and the other cream-coloured like his dhoti.

A disciple comes to get Ramaji and leads him to a courtyard at the centre of which is a large jackfruit tree—as dangerous a place as any to sit under. Half a dozen charpais have been laid out with soft cotton mattresses that are covered in fine white cotton sheets and bolsters. Brahmendra Swami is sitting cross-legged on one, while Kanhoji and another man sit on the edge of their individual charpais. As Ramaji comes to occupy a charpai assigned to him, Swamiji introduces him to the tall dark man with curly hair: 'Siddi Khairiyat, please meet Ramaji Kamath, a great trader and a banker and an intimate friend of Seth Mangatram's son.'

'Yes, of course, you were at Janjira a few years ago to see Kasim with the *bhadwa** Pandurao, and then you pretended to be a marriage broker when I was besieging Angria saheb.'

'That is right, Siddi Saheb. I am sorry I did not recognize you,' Ramaji replies.

'Well, that's because today I have taken a bath. Anyway, I am very sorry to hear about your father and brother,' a domestic Khairiyat replies. He is looking resplendent in a red velvet kurta over a tight fitted black churidar. A rich maroon sleeveless coat embroidered in gold matches the maroon fez on his head.

'If the coast is better guarded against brigands, it wouldn't have happened,' Ramaji laments.

'Ramaji that is why I like to sit here under this heavy fruit that could at any moment crash down on our heads and kill us. It makes us realize how important each moment is and that it could be our last,' says Brahmendra Swami.

---

* Pimp.

Ramaji and Khairiyat both look up to check if there are any fruit right above their heads. Khairiyat shifts on his charpai to a safer place. Surya, who is standing behind Angre's charpai, unsheathes his sword looking up at any fruit that would dare assault his sarnaubat.

'We can and do go away suddenly, do we not? We have no control as to how or when. Therefore, when you are alive—live.'

Khairiyat, who is listening to Swamiji, reverentially nods in agreement.

'And know this: there has been no better time to be alive. We are at a cusp—a time of great change, renewal—we are entering a new phase of this Yuga. The velocity of the planets and the universe are changing, and we must use this time well. We cannot allow incidents such as what happened to Narayan Seth and Venko ever again.'

'I want you both,' Brahmendra Swami says, looking first at Kanhoji and then at Khairiyat, 'to ensure the security of the merchants and their cargo. How could it have happened so close to our coast? It is just not done.'

'Siddi Kasim . . .' Khairiyat begins in defence.

'Forget Kasim, forget Bhawanji and forget everybody else. That was in the past. There are the two of you now and that should be enough.'

Brahmendra Swami makes a motion with his hand and pulls a piece of eight out of thin air. Khairiyat is flabbergasted and Rama's eyes roll up.

'The both of you have to unite against this,' Vishnu says, showing them the golden Portuguese coin.

'Do you know how they found this?'

'No, Swamiji,' Khairiyat says with his mouth still open.

'From the same place they got mirih, *kaju* and *batata*. The Firangi Raja was looking for a route that would put them directly in contact with the Konkan, so he sent his captains west to bypass the Sultans of Istanbul and the Shah of Persia. Instead of reaching the Konkan, they found a continent full of emeralds and gold, and those inhabitants not having horses or muskets, soon became their slaves and gave up the secrets of their limitless mines. Let me tell you, the Firangis and Angrez and the rest of the Topikars have nothing but wool to offer from their own lands. However, they can bring us gold from distant mines and for that we must welcome them. But you cannot let them sink their bronze claws into our sacred land: the land of Rishi Parshuram.'

'The Firangi are already the greatest power here, Swamiji, and were even before Angria or I were born,' says Siddi Khairiyat.

'But now both of you are here. Are you not? So, forget the past and begin anew is what I keep telling you.'

'What do you suggest, Swamiji?' Kanhoji asks.

'Khairiyat needs a secure base for himself, otherwise he is totally dependent on Kasim, so let him have Anjanvel,' Swamiji says to Kanhoji.

'But Swamiji, that is not even under me. Gopalgad is Bhawanji Mohite's,' Kanhoji says, throwing his hands up, amazed at Swamiji's treasonous suggestion.

Brahmendra Swami gets up from his seat and calls Kanhoji to follow him. They stroll away into seeping dusk and out of earshot.

'It will be treason,' Kanhoji says as soon as he feels they can't be heard.

'No, it's not. We need him on our side. You must look at the long game, bhau. Kasim is a politician and though he may have the Old Man's backing, he needs to be prodded out of his harem with threats into any kind of action. Khairiyat is the man to watch out for. Be at peace with him and you can move against the Firangis like you should. You need to make an impact on the seas, and you will not be able to if he is at your back. Nothing must be done immediately either. Say yes now, and then we will see later,' Brahmendra Swami says, winking at Kanhoji.

They walk back to their respective charpais and Kanhoji agrees to help Khairiyat with Anjanvel.

'But Khairiyat, you need to be patient. First, you must entreat with Kanhoji Angre and promise that you will not attack him under any circumstances for the next few years, at the end of which, if

Gopalgad is still not under him, he will turn a blind eye or be otherwise preoccupied in another skirmish when you take it from Mohite.'

'As you say, Swamiji,' Khairiyat says as he brings his raised hands together in front of his forehead in thanks.

Brahmendra Swami raises his hand and spins his wrist in a thoroughly practised manner and materializes a *taveez* in the palm of his hand. Khairiyat jumps out of his charpai and approaches Swamiji on his knees whence he is blessed, and the amulet tied around his bicep.

'This will protect you for the next seven years when Shani enters Uranus, and your star will be on the ascendant. Have patience till then,' Vishnu says as Khairiyat takes his leave, salaaming everyone and hugging Kanhoji three times.

'What news from Palva Bandar?' Brahmendra Swami asks Ramaji. This is a valuable man, Vishnu thinks to himself: neither easily impressed nor a flattering scrounger, a man such as this is a valuable source of information and the best sort of ally. Venko had been taken in with Vishnu's familiarity and sense of humour, but Vishnu is finding his elder brother to be a much harder mark.

'I thank Laxmi Devi for the markets of Chin. Fortunately, the demand is constant, and customers keep increasing every year. But that brings in more entrants and competition. I am sure you know the vagaries of business well, Swamiji—it's constantly going up and down. Persian trade is a little down though Aceh and Java are booming. There are a lot more Hayastanis around. Demand from Mombasa and Malindi has gone up. I know the Angrezi ships have been commanded by their authorities to carry saltpetre as ballast.'

'Forget them, they are meaningless. What of your friends, the Topikars?'

'They fought a war with the Angrez and were bested. I don't know how, for they are invariably more capable, and their guns and ships seem to be better built. They must now drop their sails for passing Angrez ships and they are taking freight on in Kannur as the factory in Vengurla has been shut.'

'That means their sailors and gunners will be looking for work.'

'Yes, Palva Bandar is full of them.'

'Well then—can you find some reliable gunners for Sarnaubat Saheb here?'

'I will definitely ask around.'

'Do it discreetly. But good ones, not any old *gora**, otherwise we *chitpavans*** could have become gunners. There are so many goras pretending to be doctors and gunners when they don't know anything. Get some people with experience and rank,' Brahmendra Swami says.

'Anyway, I just got news that the monsoon has failed in Malwa,' Swamiji adds, and as Rama calculates the increase in his fortune, the evening turns more congenial.

---

* Fair-skinned.

** Fire-purified.

Ladubai

It is flamingos and egrets that fly; time flashes ahead unseen, only a brief reflection caught in the height of children and trees. Ladubai is three, sitting on his lap. Her father has got an elephant for her mothers and herself to ride in. Her brothers lead on stallions bred by her father. He has shown her the teak trees he planted on her birthday and the forts at Bankot he has constructed for her brothers to guard. Baba and his men have been busy. Ai says he picks each man personally. Now every vessel that crosses a galbat made by Keki kaka must pay for a dastak issued by Baba. He takes their big guns away, so they don't harm each other.

The rains are just about ending, and the weather is pleasant for travelling up-country. It will be a few months before the roads turn to dust and the sky to its acrid heat. They are going to Gulshanabad.

'When will we get there?' asks Ladubai not long after they have deboarded at Kalyan and gotten on to the hired elephants. She does not want the journey to end. Baba has been away for too long. Always working.

'Do you even know the way, Baba?'

'Yes, we are going to Panchavati, up in the mountains. You know what happened in Panchavati, thousands and thousands of years ago?'

'No, what happened, Baba?'

Kanhoji begins to narrate the story right from the beginning, as they have many days of travelling ahead of them: 'There was a king called Dashratha who had four wives . . .'

By the time Lord Rama has been exiled, both Sekho and Shambhu are in Kanhoji's howdah, and he speeds up to the part where Laxman lops off Surpanakha's nose in these very jungles.

'Are there still Rakshasas around, Baba?' asks her eldest brother.

'Only a couple of them. So be on your guard and make sure they don't attack our caravan.'

'Yes, Baba,' Sekhoji says as he turns to scan the canopy of the forested hills they are passing through.

They will first go to the Shiv mandir at Triambakeshvar, where the sacred Godavari originates and then to the Sita Gufaa and the Kapleshwar Mandir.

'Will you go away again, after the rains? To the new Ai and Tula dada?' asks Ladu.

'Shut up, Baba is there to fight the Firangis, he doesn't care about Tula or the new Ai,' snaps Shambhu, who has been named in honour of Chhatrapati Sambhaji.

The Ganj-i-Sawai

A special durbar has been called at Janjira and the quorum has congregated at the Siddi's dank and humid court. The hall is full of Siddi and Koli nakhwas and the entire European population of Rajpura. Trembling slaves in all hues fan the room with ostrich-feather fans. Kasim is uncomfortable. The taste of bile and the veal curry he has eaten at lunch swirls inside his mouth. His throat and his chest burn and gases leak from his hard bloated stomach and creep up behind his eyes, which are throbbing with pain. Kasim summoned the Angrez from Mumbadevi on pain of destruction of the entire settlement. The Governor Mr Grey has feigned sickness and has sent Rustomji Dorabji in his stead. The young Patel is now shuffling in his spot while counting the threads on his shoes. Kasim, dark as he is, is now glowing a violent shade of purple. The Padishah's personal war dhow—the Ganj-i-Sawai—has been boarded and captured by Angrezi bandits. The armed dhow was taken on the high seas. The large *ghanjah* dhow, constructed in the marshes of Kutch, had, like every season, taken its cargo of pilgrims—each clothed in a single piece of white cotton or wool—and the Padishah's personal cargo for export to the markets of Mocha and Makkah. On its way back, it was not only carrying Rs 52 lakh worth of gold but innocent pilgrims that included a granddaughter of Aurangzeb's. It was a calamity and, as the Chief of Aurangzeb's navy and the provider of its escort ship the *Fatheh Mohammadi*, Kasim's neck is on the block. An elderly cousin of the Padishah had been repeatedly raped till her hips broke. His granddaughter is missing, and the rumour mill is claiming she is happily married to her *kaffir* abductor. An image of his own head on a platter being presented to the Padishah flashes in Kasim's mind as his gut creaks.

'How dare you claim excuse from responsibility? I will burn your little shithole of a port down and lynch each one of you,' Kasim screams.

'But truly . . .'

'Truly, I will crush your head,' Kasim says as he smashes his fist upon the ground beside him.

'They raped old women. I need not know anything more about the race of your masters. The Padishah demands vengeance, and he will have it, Munshi, tell your masters that,' his baritone thunders in the pillared hall.

'Your Exalted Highness, Avery has nothing to do with my employers at Bombay. He just happens to be English and . . .'

'Don't split hairs, all of them are the same. It does not matter. You must take responsibility for the low and shameful deeds committed by the men of your master's land. What are the revenues from your little shit-pot of *supari** and *nariyel*? 20,000? 30,000? And what is the entire revenue from trade of your banias at the fort? 20 lakh? You are a bunch of bandits waving specious documents from ridiculous and meaningless little dogs you call their kings.'

'Your Highness, the Governor trades with the permission of the Padishah,' Rustomji squeaks back, the sweat weighing down his fine muslin turban.

'If they were mere bandits as you claim, how is it that they knew only to attack ships on their way back, not the ones heading west with goods? This is the second time in two years. The Royal Grandmother Maryam Makani's ship was taken some decades ago

---

* Betel nut.

and that was the end of our truck with the Firangis of Goa, and this will be the end of you, you miserable pieces of pig's shit,' the Siddi shouts at Rustomji.

'Let those who ask why it is called the Strait of Tears know that its water has been seasoned by my tears,' quotes Kasim to the assembled sailors.

'Read Khafi Khan's report,' Siddi Kasim says to his munshi.

'The whole of the ship came under their control, and they carried away all the gold and silver along with many prisoners to their ship. When their ship, the *Charles II*, named for their king, became overloaded, they brought the imperial ship to the sea coast near one of their settlements. They stripped the men of their clothes and dishonoured women both young and old, some women getting an opportunity, threw themselves into the sea or committed suicide using what blades they could find,' the munshi reads out the report Siddi Kasim has received.

'Your Exalted Highness, Nawab Saheb, what can we expect of these people who do not even wash after they take a shit—just scrape it off with whatever's at hand,' says Pandurao as he pushes through the first line of attendees to stand in front of Siddi Kasim's throne.

'I don't need your nonsense now, Pandurao,' Kasim shouts. 'If you don't have anything of value to add—begone.'

'Your Exalted Highness, Nawab Saheb, maybe one needs to first ascertain this settlement that is mentioned. It was not Bambai.'

'If it was Bombay, you would have known about it,' jumps in Rustomji.

'What are you getting at, Panduraoji? Out with it before I have you thrown out.'

'Angria's ports offer services, sales and repair to all, regardless of who they are—roving sea bandits or Javanese cut-throats.'

'What nonsense! The settlement was in Arbistan,' Siddi Khairiyat says to all.

'The name of the settlement is not mentioned in the report,' Pandurao says.

'Because if Angria was involved, I would know of it,' Khairiyat says.

'Indeed, you would Siddi Saheb, you are such good friends with Angria.'

'What nonsense, I would know because my dhows are there and I would know if the raiders of the Ganj had sought refuge with Angria as my eyes are ever on him,' Khairiyat says at the top of his voice, all the while glaring at Pandurao.

'But it is a possibility, is it not? The enemies of his enemies are his friends. Khairiyat, I want you to find out if Angria helped or associated with any of these Angrezi bandits,' Siddi Kasim says.

'Nawab Saheb, I have already . . .'

'Then do it again,' Kasim snaps back at Khairiyat.

'Yes, Your Excellency,' Khairiyat says, bowing and stepping into a far corner of the Durbar.

'The matter remains of the Shahzadi,' Kasim's munshi says. 'Avery has kidnapped her and has headed towards Goa.'

'I have heard that they have gone west to Malagasy Desha after they took on provisions in Gheria,' Pandurao Phangaskar pipes in.

'I don't care if he has gone to Chin, I want his head and I want the Shahzadi back safely,' Kasim demands.

'Patel, you better tell your masters to find their man and bring him to me by the time they celebrate Hazrat Isa's birthday, or I will be paying them a visit that day and I will send them all to attend it in heaven itself.'

Rustomji has been beaten. He hadn't been able to complete a sentence, let alone present his case. The perpetrator had doubtless been an Englishman, Henry Avery, formerly of the Royal Navy. He had led a mutiny on the ship he was first mate on and was then elected captain by the mutinous crew. Avery had spent the last five years terrorizing the East African coast and the Gulf of Aden. Now there were talks of vengeance against the Company's warehouses in Surat, and his boss, Mr John Gayer, the Governor of Bombay Fort, was petrified. Rustomji seeks Siddi Khairiyat out, to make the case to him, as he hasn't had the courage to remind Siddi Kasim of the similarities between the English and the Siddis. Weren't there Siddis who were independent of him? Who had allied themselves with the Marathas? Siddis who had coursed the coast, pillaging and enslaving? Was the exalted Nawab responsible for the action of every Habshi in the Konkan? But he hadn't been able to open his mouth while that gigantic man was frothing in anger.

The Durbar dismissed, Kasim is now alone with his captains and commanders, and he lays out his plan. He sends his commanders in all directions from Mogadishu to Malindi and up to the Bab al Mandeb where the *Ganj-i-Sawai* had been taken. But before he can conclude the meeting, Kasim's colon can't hold itself scrunched any longer and he springs up from his throne and commands his men to 'board every Angrezi *jahaz* you come across and exact righteous vengeance upon them', and he races to the *gusal khana.*

Alliances

Kanhoji smiles inwardly at the ritualized dance he and Siddi Khairiyat have so naturally settled into. The large concave umbrella Golu holds in his left hand, as his right hand caresses the axe-headed musket that has become his signature weapon, shades Kanhoji's face and its mirthful features. As the small teak landing boat sways and gently rocks to its rendezvous outside Gheria, Kanhoji feels calm and content: Mathurabai is in Kulaba with the children and the Badshah is pulling his whitened hairs out by their roots. A half-dozen spyglasses each on the walls of Gheria and Khairiyat's war dhow bear witness as Kanhoji and Khairiyat are rowed out to an honourable middle distance that will not tarnish the prestige of either man. They have two oarsmen each and a person each to shade and fan them as Khairiyat's tall female attendant is now doing with her second arm. Surya, ever cautious, has taken on the duty of Kanhoji's oarsman, and now comes up against the small dugout canoe Khairiyat is sitting in. An oarsman from each boat facing the other pulls their oars out and clamps on to the side of the other boat, joining them as one.

As the two warlords face each other, Khairiyat breaks into a smile and salaams Angre who reciprocates with folded hands.

'What a beautiful little boat, Angria saheb,' Khairiyat says, marvelling at the glistening landing boat. On both, the bow and stern is a flat deck that rises to the gunwale, each made of grooved planks of teak. In the centre are three rows of thwarts for the oarsmen and passengers to sit. The polished brass row crutches are shining like gold.

'And what a beautiful big *chatriwali*, Khairiyat saheb,' Kanhoji says winking. 'This is merely something for our lady folk, Siddi Saheb: easier for them to step on and off with their saris and jewels,' Kanhoji explains.

'Indeed, goatskins would do well enough for you and me,' Khairiyat replies.

'What is this about, Khairiyat?'

'The *Ganj*, saheb. Everything now is about the *Ganj*.'

'A pity. My condolences to the Badshah,' Kanhoji says, and then putting his hand to his chest: 'and I am truly aggrieved at the treatment that was suffered by the women of his family.'

'As are we all, Sarnaubat Saheb,' Khairiyat replies gravely.

'But,' he continues, 'I have been commanded by Siddi Kasim to ascertain the truth behind the rumours that you have been in touch with the *Haramis* that attacked the Padishah's august house or have any knowledge of it,' Khairiyat says as he throws up his hands in a gesture of frustration.

Kanhoji throws his head back in genuine laughter, tickled at the thought.

'Fifty-two lakhs? You think I would have settled for *dus takka* for victualling them?'

'Saheb, I must know from your own mouth. Though it was Phangaskar who put it in Siddi Kasim's ear. You shouldn't have let him go, when you had him at Suvarnadurg.'

'*Chhah*,' Kanhoji spits in the water, 'he's just a pimp. But you can tell Kasim that the success of my little shipbuilding and victualling enterprise at Gheria is due to better workmanship than what Janjira can offer and better rates than Kalyan. The *Javani* come to us for provisions and repairs, as do Habshis, the Hayastanis come and so do the Cheen. As for the Angrez who come to us instead of going across to their own brothers at Palva Bandar—they tell us the Angrezi vanias there are snakes in the grass who would eat their own young.'

'I will definitely relay your answer to Nawab Kasim but do know that your friend Phangaskar is a trader in rumours and fabrications. The world would have been a better place without him darting about.'

'You are correct there, Siddi Saheb, but forget about him. However, do impress upon the exalted Nawab that if I was such a person and Aabri had been ten kos of me, wouldn't I have been offering Nawab Kasim 52 lakhs for Janjira? And to you I say, that I am a soldier of the house of Chhatrapati Shivaji Maharaj, if Aabri would have come to me, I would have boiled them all alive. Tell Kasim to talk to the Angrez, for Aabri is Angrezi.'

'Kasim knows that they were Angrezi. The Angrez are shitting their tight little patloons. They sent their Parsi Dubash with no one to translate for to Janjira when Kasim summoned them.'

'What do you expect from vanias? Anyway, where did you get this woman?' Kanhoji says looking at the gigantic Masai slave woman who is fanning Khairiyat.

'A gift from Kasim's son. Should I send her over later?'

'Only if you have a ladder that goes with her,' Kanhoji replies as they both burst out laughing.

The slave woman, who cannot understand their Konkani but can sense that they are talking about her, covers herself unconsciously as her eyes grow wide.

'May I step on to your boat?' Khairiyat asks, 'I am intrigued.'

'Yes, of course,' Kanhoji says, ignoring the wide-eyed warning from Surya.

Khairiyat gingerly steps over his oarsman on to the polished deck aft and opens his arms to embrace Kanhoji. As Surya raises his musket, Kanhoji steps in front of it and hugs the dark giant.

'Kasim and the Firangis are planning to attack you jointly, within this moon. Your dastak has not gone down well with them. I will hold to our agreement,' Khairiyat whispers in Kanhoji's ear and disengages. Then, over the lapping of the waves he says to Kanhoji and all in earshot as he stamps the deck to check its stability: 'Your landing boat for the slave.'

'Siddi Saheb, how your fist tightens in covetousness? You were just going to gift her to me,' Kanhoji chuckles.

'Agreed, but I'll take the boat for the ladder,' Khairiyat laughs and returns to his boat. The two oarsmen unclamp and push off.

Kanhoji tells Golu that he has found him a wife worthy of him at last.

The Firangi Raja

His Excellency Dom Pedro Antonio de Menesses Noronha de Albuquerque, Viceroy of the Estado de India, is, after devouring a pair of fried mackerels, cutting into his first sausage, when a clerk disturbs the morning meal of the most powerful man on the coast, who is enjoying it on an expansive and well-manicured lawn overlooking it. It's an urgent request from Senhor Pandro. The clerk waits as the Viceroy masticates on the first link and wonders how much the purveyor has bribed his clerk to disturb his breakfast. Having swallowed the first link, he demands an answer from his clerk as he taps his greasy fingers on the tablecloth. The clerk unpockets the bribe of two small silver coins and leaves it on the Viceroy's table as he is dismissed with the wave of a hand that has come to resemble a quintet of pink sausages sprouting from the spine of a white capon palm. The mention of Pandurao's name has birthed vivid images of the nastiest harlots to the Viceroy's mind. His Excellency turns to a plump chicken that has been braised in garlic and vinegar. He moves on to a stew of red beans and pork that he vanquishes with an armada of little bread buns. Sated and slightly aroused, the Viceroy sends for Senhor Pandro as a large platter of fruits is ushered on to his table.

Pandurao stumbles as he is escorted into the garden, and as he crosses a marble birdbath, he speedily wets his fingers and dabs his brow with the water. He sets his face to one of extreme sorrow and vexation.

'Hah, Pandro, what have you brought us today?'

'Information, Your Excellency: Angria has taken a barge that was heading to Daman. He has imprisoned and tortured the *capitao* along with the crew and distributed the cargo amongst the traders of Harnai.'

'On what charge and authority?' Pandro says breathlessly in Portuguese.

'He says it did not have a dastak issued by the King Rajaram of the Marathas.'

'What was the cargo?'

'Pepper, cashews, silk . . .'

'Were you able to get your hands on anything, Senhor Pandro?' Dom Pedro chuckles as he spits the glossy black *sitaphal* seeds on to the lawn.

'Yes, no, of course I came straight here,' Pandurao flubbers back. Pandurao silently curses the ruddy man with a bowel disease.

'Is this why you have disturbed me, the Viceroy, you fool? Have you lost your senses? Do you bring nothing of interest?'

'Your Excellency, Angria has sworn to reduce the Portuguese on the Konkan. As we speak, his mazumdars are recruiting the local fishermen and boatsmen and commandeering their vessels . . .'

The Viceroy laughs at the little man's joke but immediately comes to be irritated when he realizes there is no woman to be had.

'You idiot, you scare me with the ambition of some second-rate fort commander with dugouts and fishing boats?'

'Your Excellency, I would not have come if I did not think it serious. I personally have witnessed preparation for war. He is stocking Gheria and Suvarnadurg's granaries with rice and millet, goat and fowl, dried fish, fruits and vegetables.'

'That indeed is a cause for concern,' the Viceroy says sarcastically, adding: 'and what of his wife? What new clothes and jewellery has she purchased?'

'Your Excellency, this past year he has trained his rowers and gunners. He has built four new ghurabs and has a dozen galbats, all armed with cannon.'

'His king is in exile on the other side of the continent and the Mogul is at their heel,' the Viceroy reminds Pandurao.

'Precisely, Your Excellency. Angria is taking the opportunity to carve out his own little kingdom. He is brewing rebellion amongst the Siddis, and Nawab Kasim is of the view that it is wise to nip his ambition before it flowers into a poisonous fruit.'

The Viceroy bites into a piece of papaya as he mulls Kasim's offer.

His Excellency knew the Marathas were only in their element on their ponies on rutted hill tracks. There were no Africans with Angria and the one his king had in his service was long dead. Anyway, both Angria and his nephew were the same age, and the Good Lady was on the side of Dom Alfonso who after all had been named for the Great Afonso, creator of the Estado. They would crush Angria.

'I will send the three largest ships I have: the *Nossa Senhora da Saude*, she is an old Nau that looms over the two largest galleons I have at Margo Reis, the *Bom Jesus* and the *Santo Antonio de Tana*. Their sheer size will strike terror into the hearts of the Marathas on their dwarfed and insignificant canoes,' the Viceroy says haughtily.

Pandurao knows that both the three-masted galleons have forty 30-pound canons on their three decks and their main sails seem to hold entire clouds in their billowing canvas.

'Manuel de Castro, an experienced sailor, will be my nephew Dom Alfonso's first mate, and Dom Carvalho will be given the *Santo Antonio* and Dom Moraes the *Bom Jesus*. *Nossa Senhora* will sail as the flagship under the command of Mor Capitao Dom Alfonso de Alburquerque. It will be such an awesome show of might that no Maratha would dare to even contemplate the exercise,' the Viceroy says, sounding out the plan for himself and concluding the matter.

'Tell the Admiral of the Mogul that he is wise. After all, we do both believe in the One God of Abraham. Let us unite against a common enemy while his king is still away. Suvarnadurg to him and Gheria to us,' Dom Pedro says.

The Viceroy knows exactly what he must do: he will put the fear of God into this insolent upstart before eradicating him from the face of this bountiful and Christian Earth, half of which has been granted to his own king.

As Pandurao turns to leave, His Excellency commands: 'Bring me someone this evening, someone young, cultured and sophisticated—a European and don't ever come empty-handed again, you imbecile.'

Goliaths

A curved sliver of the pale moon, like an errant aureole, shows itself in the dark night sky. On the banks of the Terekhol, a lady of the night, after a visit by a drunk Firangi capitao, sends a homing pigeon into the dark night, a note tied to its ankle.

The moon has waxed to a silhouette of a breast against a dark sky. Spyglasses rise in the hands of fishermen strung along coastal villages as three Firangi ships lumber on north. Each of the sails has an enormous square cross, the colour of Christ's fresh blood on it. Atop the main mast, the violet pennant of the Noronha Alburquerque flutters impatiently. Capitao Manuel wishes he were on one of the galleons instead of this lumbering oak behemoth that must sail away from the shallow coast. The galleons are several leagues further north and much closer to shore than his own vessel, which Manuel assiduously keeps off the perilous rocks that wait patiently for erring copper-bottoms to be ground on.

As the immense *Nossa Senhora* sails north, passing the mouth of the Terekhol River, that lady's pulse quickens, and a lump of anxiety sticks in her betel-juiced throat. Manuji was correct, there are just three of them and one of the ships is enormous. It is sailing starboard of the two smaller though immense galleons and lagging behind them considerably. She extricates her spyglass from the mirrored chest, and she can swear that she has spotted Manuji on the topmost deck of the largest vessel.

Manuel, hiccupping, heads to the Capitao Mor's cabin astern, as he has to apprise young Dom Alfonso of their direction and then have it confirmed and commanded back to himself by the sunny lad. Manuel suggests Dom Alfonso walk the poop deck and see the passing country. Dom Alfonso steps out for a few minutes before returning to his cabin bored. It all looks the same to him, whether it is Sao Salvador, Luanda or Goa: the sea is muddy, and the mostly rocky shores are topped with a wig of wild green, whose composite species he cannot make out at this distance.

'Call for me when you have sighted Bassein,' he commands Manuel, as he picks up his flute and puts the embouchure to his flattened lower lip.

When the ship disappears from her eyeglass, the lady feels nothing for Manuji, neither loss nor joy: just another customer come and gone and forgotten.

Bassein is days away.

The Revolver

The Karli River travels west till she reaches the two egg-shaped Shivlings ensconced at the Mahapurush Temple, and then she turns south like a bent finger of an elderly grandmother giving her grandchild sweets. She remains separated from the sea by the veil of a narrow peninsula till she reaches Devbagh, where she finally meets her sisters. Here, silent and still, Kanhoji and his forces crouch behind the tip of the peninsula—as large dun-coloured crocodiles lurk unseen by the sandbanks. With them are hidden sixteen galbats and thirty-odd rowboats teeming with turmeric-smeared Kolis armed with grappling hooks, sickles, axes and choppers.

It is a little past midday, and the sun has begun its arced descent towards the distant horizon. It flashes briefly, reflecting off a highly polished brass plate, held by one of Kanhoji's sentries sitting on the top of Trimukhi Rock. Kanhoji stands on the prow of his largest ghurab, raises his right hand in the air and rotates his cuff twice, and then bending his arm at the elbow, points it west. Twenty pairs of oars from each of the galbats gently break the lapping waves in unison, pushing off towards their gigantic prey. In a few moments, the ghurabs start moving, towed by the galbats ahead. Behind them, a plethora of little dugouts and rowboats, crammed with innumerable Koli boys and young men, kick off from the sandy shore.

The galbats drag the ghurabs out to sea and on Kanhoji's signal, disengage the cables from them and proceed farther west making straight for the stern of the copper-bottomed *Nau*, which is inching her way north. Once they hit the Firangi leviathan's wake, the galbats turn north assuming a U-shaped formation and row towards their quarry in a pair of parallel lines led by a lead galbat under the command of Surya.

As the point galbat enters the shadow cast by the sails of the *Nossa Senhora*, it fires both its upper and lower cannons stationed at its prow and then veers to the right making place for the next galbat. The cannons on all the upper decks of the galbats have been issued with chained shots and the cannons in the hold with 12-lb shot. The chained shot from the upper cannon falls short of the mizzenmast and smashes into the stern as the 9-lb shot of the lower cannon harmlessly digs out a chunk of brine from the sea.

'Higher, higher,' Surya shouts and gesticulates to the galbat that has just taken their place at the point. The gunners of the next galbat hammer a wooden wedge under their cannon's barrels to give the shots higher arcs and fire. This time both the shots reach the *Nossa Senhora* and smash into the oak stern of the fat-bottomed Nau.

'Higher still, higher still,' shouts the gun captain of the second galbat as he moves away to the right, making space for the third. The chain shot of the third galbat punctures the bonaventure sail, and the correct angle the cannons need to be at to make contact is relayed down the line. The galbats now fire in rotation from the *Nossa Senhora*'s wake, like encircling sharks waiting their turn to take a bite.

A few leagues up the coast, Dom Carvalho on hearing the distant echo of cannons, rushes out of his cabin. The sound is carried upwind from the south, so he runs to his stern and puts his spyglass to his eye. He can see four small ghurabs lined up with their broadsides facing the *Nossa Senhora*. But the ghurabs are not firing their guns at all and are instead sailing north towards him. Yet he can hear the booming of cannons and every now and then, a hole appears in the *Nossa Senhora*'s foresails, or her rigging is sliced and swings away towards her deck. He commands his first mate to signal the *Bom Jesus*—still farther north—to turn around. Then he orders his own to turn tack.

The first impact of a 9-lb shot on the hull of the *Nossa Senhora* causes Dom Alfonso to drop his flute and scurry for cover under his nailed cot. Surprised and confused, Capitao Manuel Castro, ever on deck, runs to the stern to see an unfamiliar tactic being employed on his rear by a flotilla of minuscule galbats. He commands the *Bombardeiros* of the stern chasers to fire at will and then proceeds towards the wheelhouse to turn his broadside to the pesky galbats. Manuel reaches the wheel to find a hapless helmsman unable to steer the venerable *Senhora*. Guessing it is the capstan, he runs below decks to have it fixed as chain shot tears into the shrouds, ratlines and cables above, dislodging several yardarms and splintering the masts. Manuel discovers that the rudder cable has been severed by a lucky shot. As he is having it tied, he hears a massive crash amidst the cacophonous thumps his Nau is suffering. His first mate comes down to inform him that the mizzenmast has been brought down. Manuel knows there is only one thing left to do.

Kanhoji signals for the dugouts and small rowboats, teeming with the Koli boarding party to head towards the beleaguered *Senhora*, and jumps into one of the passing boats with Golu just behind him. As he steadies himself in the wildly rocking boat, crammed with his Kolis, the ghurab he has been on takes a direct hit from one of *Santo Antonio's* 22-pounders. Kanhoji does not look back and instead urges the rowers to head straight for the *Nossa Senhora*. Her gunwale is crowded with helmeted musketeers gathered to defend her, and they shoot at the approaching swarm of boats as they brave splinters and crumbling masts and lines. The flotilla of small boats with the boarding parties congregates at the two edges of the stern, safe from the Nau's cannon but not from the musketeers on deck. The Portuguese Marines in armour and the chemise-wearing Topashis on deck fire at the pates of the swarms below them and many in the boats fall dead.

'Rama, this ship must be 80 daand high,' remarks a young Koli man echoing the sentiments of many.

'Saheb, what are you doing? We will all die,' screams a glistening pot-bellied man on Kanhoji's boat as they approach the impossibly high oak hull of the Nau. Around him, men who are essentially fishermen stare at him in abject terror. Kanhoji, who at that very moment has been unshouldering his musket, smashes its butt into the loose-tongued man's face and in the same smooth motion points it up at the gunwale of the Nau. His boat is rocking up and down, so he chooses a vertical line and as his boat's prow rises again, he makes his shot. It hits a Marine right between the clavicles and he tumbles, helmet first, into the sea. Surya, seeing the boarding party ready, signals to the gun captains of the galbats to use *gotis* next, and as the Kolis expertly swing their grappling hooks to ensnare the gunwale and gun ports, sacks full of thumbnail-sized iron ingots are loaded into the guns of the galbats. The gotis fired from the galbats momentarily clear the deck of musketeers till more emerge from the holds. The *haldi*-smeared Koli warriors dressed only in langots, now clench their meagre weapons between their teeth and clamber up the walls of the hull. Many in the first wave lose their heads at the gunwale or are stomped out trying to get into a porthole, but as many in the second wave make it all the way to the deck.

Soon the vessel is engulfed with hundreds of bare-chested Kolis swinging their weapons at everything in front of them. Kanhoji and Golu clamber up the ropes with their musketeers behind them.

David

As the stars shine through the dimming dusk, Kanhoji has his prisoners put on a galbat and taken to Gheria. Besides Manuel and Dom Alfonso, the only Europeans that remain are the gun captains—the rest of them have been put to the sword. The other prisoners are Topashis and Christianized Kolis that make up most of the Portuguese troops in the Estado, and like the gun captains, they are all possible recruits, being well trained in the ways of naval warfare. Manuel is well treated and kept with his Capitao Mor in a separate cell with a barred window that allows for light and fresh air. The grizzled Firangi had been seen sweeping a young Koli boy out of the way before clubbing a grown one's head in before he was taken. Manuel fought well, his jailers are told.

'How could you let this happen? What are they going to do to me?' the petrified Dom Alfonso asks his ward.

'Have you not read the Book, Senhor?' Manuel asks calmly. This has been an act of God.

'How is this possible?' shrills the terrified boy, crying and flailing his arms at the unperturbed Manuel who just holds him in an embrace and tries to calm him down. Manuel is not bothered about his situation. Undoubtedly it is a first: galbats have never boarded a vessel of this size and armament in the Konkan before. How indeed was it possible? What bothers him was how his ship was taken.

A great fear takes root in him when he realizes the efficiency of his captor's strategy. The guns on the Marathas' prow have a massive advantage to guns on the broadside. When a boat rocks as it does with every wave, the guns on the broadside move in an arc that muddles up the aim, whereas the guns in the prow move only straight up or down. When faced with a vertical target, the chances of hitting the mast somewhere along its length greatly increases.

'It is all your fault,' Dom Alfonso whines through his tears.

'Haven't you heard of David slaying Goliath?'

'How dare you call us Philistines?' the boy demands.

Manuel does not say anything in response, but he knows they have lost because they were too big and blind, and this Angria, an unlikely David, has just changed the game in the Konkan.

Dom Alfonso quietens down and is kneeling in fervent prayer. If Manuel returns to Goa, he will have to be the necessary scapegoat. Somebody has to have lost that ship and it can't be the Viceroy's pretty nephew. Manuel is not worried, after all, this is the Indies: business-minded people who have no interest in torture or conversion. They speak a more universal language, and he knows they have a goddess called Lakshmi to whom he has himself prayed. Manuel calls for his jailer in fluent Konkani and when the young Koli boy—an expert off-season fisherman—comes, he tells him that he would like to speak to Angria himself.

The guard goes to check with Surya and returns to take him up to the Sarnaubat.

'The boy in the cell with me,' Manuel continues, after introductions are made in Konkani, 'is our nawab's nephew.'

'So I have heard. But how close a nephew?' inquires Kanhoji.

'His own brother's son recently arrived to make his fortune under the auspices of his kaka.'

'That means he will pay very well for him. Thank you, and what about you? Is there anybody who will pay for you?'

'Probably only you. I cannot go back; I was charged with his safety. You have some of my best gun captains below and I think I can get some of them to join you, along with me. If you will have us?'

'Look Manuji, I have modelled my protectorate on the lines of our great king Chhatrapati Shivaji. Neither he nor I have ever looked upon a soldier's caste or creed. We only seek ability and talent. That is why all of you are still alive, unlike your gunners and lascars. You, I had no hope in joining us the way you conducted yourself, but yes, I need gun captains who can aim and conduct my gunners. But why do you wish to join me?'

'Saheb, not only will I be made the *bakra*, but unlike you, the Estado de India does look upon one's caste. I deserve to have been a Capitan Mor, but I know I will never rise above a first mate. It is simply the nature of my birth. I come from carpenters, not knights.'

'Such kingdoms will necessarily fail as the Mughal's is as we speak,' says Kanhoji in a genial tone.

'You picked the right place to surprise us. The sandbars at the Karli's mouth prevented the galleons from coming within attacking range.'

'What would you have done? If you had to attack me?'

'I would have chosen small galleys with musketeers and chased you down into the river. Your forts, like the Siddi's, are impregnable and there is no point in wasting artillery there. Or better still, put 10,000 *reals* on your head.'

'Easier said than done, Manuji. I had small guns on the southern bank of the river, in case you had chased us down. Tell me how you will be of use to me?'

'I can sail any ship, Saheb, and I can run guns faster than any gun captain. My father and his fathers before him were carpenters and that runs in my blood and what with the *saag, sal* and *shisham* here . . .'

'Well, let's see what I use you for, but you may definitely join me and bring as many gun captains as you can. Now, if you excuse me, let me arrange for better board and some food for His Excellency's nephew before the rats get to his toes and make a meal of him,' Kanhoji says chuckling.

Reputation

A pair of monsoons have dared to intervene since he took the *Nossa Senhora*. But even the monsoon will eventually let up once her bosomy clouds are wrung dry, and he will resume acquiring the rights to the coast's bounty. Mathurabai, however, is of an indefatigable breed of women whose bosom never runs dry nor needs his dastak.

'Piloji is making a fountain in their courtyard,' she screams from her kitchen at Kanhoji's ancestral house in Kulaba. Its tiled roofs slope to the ground over wide polished verandas.

'The marble was brought down from the Sawai Raja's quarry, same stone as the Taj Mahal,' she adds as she cuts the moringa into finger lengths. She has already visited the construction site twice, the second time hidden in a palanquin.

'And look at this place,' she says.

'What's wrong with my father's house?' Kanhoji shouts back incensed.

'It's still just a house,' she replies.

'Fountain, *ma chi . . .*' Kanhoji shouts suppressing an abusive word.

Mathurabai gets up from the kitchen floor and runs to the veranda, knife still in hand, where Kanhoji is oiling the barrels of some of his flintlock muskets.

'*Pha*,' she says gesticulating with the knife: 'Look at you? Do you look like a sarnaubat even? Does this look like the house of a sarnaubat? You haven't spent a *kowdi* on the place.'

'Why should I waste money unnecessarily? Does the roof leak? Are the walls broken?'

'How will people know who you are? You are a sarnaubat, live like one. Even Swamiji, who has taken *vanvas*, lives better than you, and talking of wasting money, I know where it goes, to low and diseased serpentine women, from Vasai to Vengurla,' Mathurabai hisses.

'*Chee*,' Kanhoji shouts, making a spitting gesture with his mouth.

'You spend your day with useless women, listening to their nonsense and rumours. The women you talk of are my informants. Brainless fool. You just try and cook food that can go down my throat,' Kanhoji says with finality and starts picking up his muskets and shouting for Golu to ready his horse and call for Surya.

'Where are you going?' she asks timidly, averting his flashing eyes.

'Sagargad,' he says perfunctorily and storms into an adjoining room. Due west and only four kos from his family estate in Kulaba, Sagargad had been a small fortress when Kanhoji had taken it over with the help of Bhivaji Gujar and Sarkhel Sidhoji Gujar from Siddi Kasim of Janjira. From Sagargad one has a vantage of the sea and can view both Undheri and Kanheri islands to the north-west and the sun setting over the roofs of Bhivaji's and Tukoji Sankhpal's houses in Kulaba.

He hears Mathurabai screaming again: 'Sagargad? Are the women in Sagargad also informants? I know what you and Bhivaji go there to do. Oh, Mother split open, swallow me up, Mother Earth . . .'

'You think you are Sita *Mai*?' he says and leaves.

In the year they had it in their possession, Kanhoji has slowly built it up into a simple and well-appointed hunting lodge with absolute privacy that can be used by his Sarkhel or his neighbour Bhivaji. Stone steps along its steep gradient make travel on horse or palanquin possible in any weather. The three of them support its garrison jointly and share all its other costs. Kanhoji has a team of five men posted there who can signal Kulaba with coloured Chinese *agniphul* rockets. Sagargad is on a ridge, in the midst of forests thick with tigers and their ample prey. The grassland is dotted with yellow *sonaki* flowers, and the trees are heavy with fat beehives dripping honey. The skies abound with kites and eagles, and partridges call from behind shrubs and quails sing of juicy worms. A gossamer-thin waterfall lies like a veil over a narrow gorge to the north, spraying a cooling mist on to the faces of leaves and sleeping leopards.

Kanhoji expects Sidhoji's absence as only a week ago he had fallen off a new horse. His granddaughter had scared the filly, running to him screaming with joy and a copper tumbler of milk for her *dadu*. The horse had reared up high in fear, and old Sidhoji had toppled off and broken his hip. Kanhoji hopes Bhivaji will not visit, he seeks solitude and freedom from the incessant chatter of the coast. When they get to Sagargad, its walls still wet with dew, they go to the pond for a swim and then have a hearty lunch of wild boar curry, boiled partridge eggs fried with rai and kadipatta served with a thin but hearty jungle fowl stew the killedar's wife has sent up. Kanhoji takes a rare nap before the evening hunt and wakes up at twilight in a dreamy haze that holds on to him all night.

The next morning as they are returning from the hunt, a messenger arrives from Kulaba: Sarkhel Sidhoji Gujjar has departed for the next life. Surya almost claps Kanhoji on his back before he turns it into a gesture of condolence by patting Kanhoji's shoulder. But it is nothing to hide as even the messenger cannot help but think of his master's inevitable promotion. They immediately leave for Kulaba to help their sarkhel's family with the funerary rites.

A few kos from home, a servant is waiting to inform them that a dignitary has been waiting for Kanhoji at his home in Kulaba. The Sar Subedar of Pune has come to meet him, says his retainer. That was quick, Kanhoji thinks. The Sar Subedar is obviously here to confirm him in the sarkhelship.

Entering his house, Kanhoji is pleasantly surprised, though he knows it is not the bearer of his promotion.

'Balaji, Balaji,' Kanhoji halloos in joy as he enters his father's courtyard to find Balaji sitting cross-legged on a charpai.

'You are the Sar Subedar?' he hugs his friend who has gotten up to greet him.

'My, my, Sarnaubat Saheb, look at you? You have become fat,' Balaji says teasing.

'And you have lost weight, if that is even possible,' counters Kanhoji.

'Are you back from Jinji?'

'Yes, but just recently. The siege at Jinji is hopeless and, unlike the Konkan, there are no forts to hop around to. Chhatrapati Rajaram may have to come back.'

'But he must. He is much safer here amongst us. Bring him to Gheria, there is no safer place on Earth.'

'If it weren't for the daily miracles that Santaji and Dhanaji have wrought, we would have been finished by now. Now Dhanaji has sent me to Pune.'

'Good, it's good to know you are closer to us. But tell Dhanaji to come back to the Konkan. I am truly ready to help. I'll show him what to do with Zulfiqar Khan.'

'Oh, how that infernal man perseveres. But you have already helped, Kanho. The money and materials you sent were greatly appreciated.'

'We took a Firangi nau, and then several other vessels that refused to carry our dastak.'

'We heard. With new tactics, that too.'

Kanhoji had disproved many of his detractors and demonstrated that the *Nossa Senhora* was not entirely luck and providence. But they also witnessed how luck had always kept in stride with his progress: an imp in battle that wet the enemy's charge or nipped at their cables and blinded their lookouts.

'Hope for the rudder but go for the mast, don't even bother with the hull or their cannons. Once they can't move, then I send entire villages on board and overwhelm them.'

'Dhanaji thanks you for the emeralds you sent. There seems to be no better currency to swing a Mughal's loyalties than egg-sized emeralds.'

'For those, you must thank the Firangi Nawab's nephew who was so kind to carry them all the way from the other side of the world.'

'And for the barud. He especially thanks you for the barud and asked me to quote him exactly in saying that a lot of our men owe their lives to the barud you sent.'

'Lokhande's boy has a factory up at Gopalgad. And I've got good Firangi gun captains now, and more Topikars are coming to see me, courtesy Ramaji Kamath.'

'I need to tell you something,' Balaji says, turning towards Kanhoji and his face set in exaggerated disappointment.

'What is it?'

'Don't expect to be made Sarkhel now that Sidhoji is gone.'

'Of course not, they will send someone in from the Desha as usual,' Kanhoji says as he visibly crumples into a slouch.

'No, it's not that. They don't have anybody to spare right now anyway. But let me tell you, Kanho, success does lead to fear and caution. Truthfully, they are a little worried about you.'

'Worried in what sense? Say what you mean—do they doubt my loyalty?'

'No, just your growing power and influence.'

'They talk of me in Jinji?'

'Everywhere, Kanho, everybody is talking of Angria. I intercepted a letter from the Firangi Viceroy complaining about you maiming your prisoners before returning them for good money.'

Even the Firangis, listening to the tall tales of their mixed-race Topashis, have come to fear Angria's destiny: he is most definitely beloved by his god and visibly by his silhedars, killedars and his band of Kolis. His share of the wealth he seizes, once dues to his king in Jinji are satisfied, flows over him like a river unto the sea of his people. Kanhoji values their loyalty and needs them to know that he can match anybody's offer.

'Just blinded gun captains who would not join me—that too only in one eye. It is foolish to return well-trained men to an ongoing conflict. Gunners, spies, navigators—they need to be taken out of the equation.'

'Just be careful about opening up too many fronts at the same time. That's just what we are doing to the Mughals,' says Balaji.

'Oh, don't worry. I am on excellent terms with the Firangis. Why, the Viceroy's own nephew is a dear friend. I sent him some of Bhawanji's *hafus* mangoes, and he has chosen rearing and eating them as the calling of his life. I got him land in Ratnagiri.'

'That's another thing, Kanho, your familiarity with some people also worries them and I am not just talking of the Firangis.'

'If you mean Siddi Khairiyat, it was your dearest Swamiji who introduced him to me. I am glad of it, and you should be too as it is one less front.'

'Relax, Kanho. These are things everybody was talking about, and I am letting you know what about you worries them. Do you understand that? Or do you consider me their agent?'

'Of course not, Balaji. But why are they wasting their time worrying about anything? I will take care of the Konkan; they need not worry about how. It's my responsibility and duty and I will perform it. Trying to look up my nostril from the Desha cannot work. I can only do it in my way—how else is it possible?'

'Well, Kanho, you just need to be aware that it is because of these worries they have, they are not going to make you Sarkhel.'

'I don't care what title anybody gives me.'

'Sorry, Kanho. I tried my best, but my opinion is not one they value in these matters,' and then after a pause, Balaji adds: 'yet.'

'So, what are they planning to do?'

'I have no idea; they haven't appointed anyone Sarkhel yet.'

'Well of course, it's a foregone conclusion who should be Sarkhel. It's just that they are obviously unable to come to terms with it.'

Surya comes in to call Kanhoji as the local dignitaries are trickling in to Kulaba to pay their respects to the family and the state.

'Sarkhel, we . . .'

'Don't call me Sarkhel,' Kanhoji shoots back, ruder than he wants to be and then says in a kinder tone: 'Don't call me Sarkhel yet,' as he and Bala get up.

Surya looks down, his eyes awash with disappointment and a feeling of shame and hurt. There are rumours being spread in the Desha, that Kanhoji is a Koli and not a Maratha. He thinks of the blood, Koli blood, that had dripped off the decks of the *Nossa*. They still can't get it off, the oak is dyed wine red.

Rajmata Tarabai

Barely a month after Sarkhel Sidhoji's death, Chhatrapati Rajaram has a narrow escape as he crawls out from under Jinji's crumbling walls, making his way down the boulder-strewn hillock, and escapes to Vellore. Zulfiqar Khan's besieging army finally succeeds in breaching the high granite walls of the formerly impregnable fort to find his quarry gone. With help from the Rani of Vellore, the Maratha king finally makes it back to Satara. Kanhoji goes to pay his respects to the Chhatrapati who is at Sinhagad Fort. He takes his finest horses and has two new kurtas stitched. The three queens are pleased with their gifts as is the Chhatrapati with the auspiciously marked piebald Arab stallion. But no one asks after his father nor is there mention of the vacant sarkhelship.

Early in the next year, just as the cool season ends, the last son of Shivaji Maharaj, Chhatrapati Rajaram who is just thirty years old, dies of a lung infection. The senior-most of his wives, the issueless Maharani Jankibai, joins him on his pyre as a Sati.

Maharani Tarabai throws herself on to the pyre of her husband's legacy. Shivaji Maharaj has a new avatar, as she proclaims his infant grandson, Shivaji II, as the next Chhatrapati. The mantle of governance upon her own shoulders, her husband's generals unite behind her. Tarabai's father, Hansoji Hambirao Mohite, had been the senapati of the Marathas in the time of Chhatrapati Shivaji Maharaj's reign. He is also his king's brother-in-law. Tarabai has grown up at the centre of Maratha power and her exposure and intelligence will now hold the Marathas together, helped by her extensive and notable family. She vests her faith in her father's old friend Ramchandra Bawdekar and makes him the Peshwa. An experienced strategist who has been her father-in-law's *amatya*—finance minister, and her husband's *hukumat panah*—imperial regent, Ramchandra Amatya Pant has, like his queen, spent his life at the core of the Maratha court.

Kanhoji goes to Satara, this time accompanied by Brahmendra Swami, and presents himself to the new Regent—again proffering her bushels of pearls and bales of silk he has purchased on credit. She is a few years younger than Kanho and isn't a day older than twenty-five. She is courteous and sophisticated and understands the protocols and intricacies of political life. But she is still young and impressionable, and in the nape of her neck he can see her need for control. This is a person he can work with and possibly even impress upon the existence of the Konkan.

'Can you please explain a mystery to us, Sarnaubat Saheb: When we left for Jinji almost a decade ago, the jungles of the Konkan were teeming with tiger. On our return we find them empty and have been accursed with unsuccessful hunts—day after day and night after night. Who is responsible for this?'

Kanhoji can extrapolate from her indulgent tone and eager posture that she is teasing him.

'Your Royal Highness, pardon my impudence, but a boar told me that they have all escaped across the Koyna on hearing of your esteemed return. They fear for their lives and are sheltering at Waghode under our inaccurate aim.'

'Waghode, is it?' the Queen Mother smiles: 'The deer must be lying then for they told me they have all gone to your love nest at Sagargad.'

Kanhoji blushes deeply and cannot counter the Queen Mother in any fashion without resorting to impudent lies.

'Rajmata, it is merely the headquarters of your signals battalion. The late Sidhoji Gujar took it. We have been trying to implement a system of coloured rockets to communicate emergencies to the sentry forts.'

'We are sure of that. But do take us hunting there when you can make the time from your busy schedule.'

'I am forever at your feet, Rajmata,' Kanhoji says, looking down at his own finely sandaled feet.

'Sarnaubat Saheb, I will be needing horses now, and guns and more of our fine barud. I hope you will not presume things based on my age and gender?'

'Not at all, Rajmata. A Maratha woman stirred can emasculate Narsimhan. Your Highness, after all, you are not only the daughter-in-law of Chhatrapati Maharaj and the niece of Maharani Soyarbai, but the blood of Hambiraoji Mohite runs through your veins.'

'It is our karma and the dharma of the House of Bhonsale,' the young Regent says imperiously.

'At your command, Rajmata,' Kanhoji says. He is elated, there are pleasant sensations in his chest. A vision flits across his mind's eye.

Angria makes gifts of the finest Portuguese and Dutch globes he has in his possession to the infant king, and taking the child's blessing, departs for Kulaba. Again, there has been no mention of the sarkhelship, and his hopes lie with Swamiji who has been requested by the Rajmata to stay back another day. Brahmendra Swami is proud of Angria's etiquette and sweet words and congratulates him when they meet in private in the evening.

That night he has a dream. He shouts for Gangadhar.

'A wall in the sea, half a kos off the Vijaydurg Fort,' he dictates to the perplexed Gangadhar. He cannot make out too many details from his dream, but Mathurabai's stone forehead is clear to him. He has seen its base of black basalt shoulders in the dream. He goes to take a bath. As the cold water pours over him, Kanhoji wonders what it is that is keeping him from being appointed the Sarkhel. He will drop by Anjanvel Fort to see how it is holding up under the command of Bhawanji Mohitay on his way to Gheria. On the way down the ghat, he explains the submerged barricade to Gangadhar.

Chaal

The once formidable fort at the mouth of the fertile and fecund Vashishti is in shambles. The fort's killedar is a drunken lout Kanhoji finds fast asleep at midday, drool running to his bare chest. The Killedar appears in a hastily put on kurta, unshaven and dishevelled. He is a sorry sight and not in the least ashamed. Kanhoji's instinct is to whip the crumpled indiscipline off the man, but he decides instead to probe him a bit.

'How many people do you have?'

'Two hundred and forty, Sarnaubat Saheb.'

'I could not count more than eighteen, including yourself. Where are the rest?'

'Some are unwell, and some have gone home for a break. Anyway, with yourself around who would dare attack us?' he chickers.

'The same people who would not think twice about attacking me at Kulaba. Anyway, I had just come to pay my respects to Bhawanji.'

'Sarnaubat Saheb is not here. It's been months since he has graced us with his presence. It's been a year, I'd say. He is at . . .'

'Bhawanji is a capable administrator. He can do from a distance what I cannot being there myself. I am my own munshi–mazumdar and need to keep running around like a headless chicken,' Kanhoji says prudently.

'The fort is well taken care of and secure, Sarnaubat Saheb has his full confidence in me. Please stay and eat something Saheb,' the Killedar offers.

'Some other time maybe, it seems your water may be polluted as so many of your men are sick.'

'Nothing like that, Saheb, actually indigestion, they eat too much.'

'Gluttons make terrible soldiers,' Kanhoji says as he whips down back to his galbat having seen everything he needs to.

Kanhoji is disgusted with the fort and its miserable commander. It stank of refuse and was littered with garbage. None of the garrison was at their posts and instead he had seen pockets of sipahis gambling with cowries and cards—their tumblers full of vile and cheap drinks. A single Portuguese galleon could take the fort or just one of his paltans. Bhawanji's men would be dead before they knew it and the fort would fall into whoever's hands that bothered to try. If Kasim or the Viceroy of Goa realized what the situation here was, they would pounce upon the opportunity.

But Bhawanji is prompt in sending his revenues up the ghat and that is all that matters. Since Chhatrapati Sambhaji, not a single king has bothered to tour the Konkan. Kanhoji very much doubts if Tarabai will show interest in these parts either. By the time Kanhoji arrives at Gheria, he is glad that the powers on the plateaus are blind to the coast: it will give him an opportunity to do what he wants and in his own way. But for that to happen, Anjanvel needs to be secure and protected by some competent authority. There is nothing but a whisper that separates the fort and its retinue of endless barges that float down the Vashishti, from the claws of the Siddi or the Viceroy. There is little he can do while the fort is with Bhawanji. Swamiji is a Mahapurush indeed—the height from which he can see into their future.

There were good reasons for Brahmendra Swami insisting on Gangadhar to be employed as his sachiv, Kanhoji is beginning to realize. Gangadhar has already sent a messenger to Babuji Kotla, the architect, to be present at Gheria, as Sarnaubat Saheb wants a wall built in the sea. Gangadhar could sense the impatience in his master's mood as they sailed back. Kanhoji is glad and meets the precise and diligent Babuji, who is waiting for him at the fort gate, immediately. Babuji spent his youth with Hiroji Indulkar, Shivaji Maharaj's chief architect. He carefully listens to Kanhoji's vision, his head bowed and slanted to the left. He feels like he is his guru Hiroji, and his current employer: Shivaji Maharaj. He appreciates the fact that his yajyman always knows exactly what he wants and trusts him enough to share his intentions and purposes.

'When the naus comes in to bombard the seaward side, they hit the underwater wall in the sea and get stuck on it. It should be at a distance where even their biggest cannons cannot hit us with any damage. It needs to be unseen and underwater during both high and low tide but still high enough to catch a Firangi vessel. I will let you know by tomorrow what its distance from the low tide mark needs to be,' Kanhoji explains, as Babuji nods his tilted head.

That night, Kanhoji is in his library, and all who enter it wonder at its curios and the man who collects them. Though in the eyes of many, it is a travesty: books in foreign tongues bound in the hides of unknown beasts; skulls of even lesser-known beasts and illustrations whose viewings could send your soul to *narg*. He spends the night looking at models and charts he has accumulated to determine the draughts of war dhows, carracks, galleons and East Indiamen—anything able to carry large guns that could do damage to the fort walls. Angria lacked access to large cannon that the Siddi had and could use to keep ships away from his walls. Till he gets those bores, this is the only way, and if he did get them, he would need them at Kulaba anyway.

The next morning, he leaves for Brahmendra Swami's ashram with an estimate from Babuji on the cost of building his wall. He finds the ashram much improved. The air is perfumed, and bowls of almonds and pistachio sit in silver bowls on clothed tables. When Vishnu hears Kanhoji tell him of the hazardous situation at Anjanvel, he realizes the time is right to declaw Siddi Kasim of his most able commander.

'Go north or go south, anywhere but far from Anjanvel and let Khairiyat take the fort while he can,' says the Swami.

'I will get you your cannons and loan you the money for your wall,' Brahmendra Swami promises, as Kanhoji tries to wrap his head around the proposal.

'Don't get stuck on the semantics. See the bigger picture here. We need Anjanvel safe and secure no matter how or who. If Bhawanji is a security lapse . . . and this way Kasim loses Khairiyat forever. Leave these matters to us. Trust me, it is not betrayal. Shouldn't you be the sarkhel and not have to rely on Khairiyat to secure the mouth of the Vashishti?'

'Swamiji, have you spoken to the Rajmata about the sarkheliyat. It lies vacant, to their detriment.'

'See, Kanho . . . Did Bala not tell you? They fear you up on the plateau. But you, like an obedient child, send the Chauth up, never delaying a day. It has become a joke—Angria's payment comes in like the full moon, always when it is expected. Then you come here to borrow money from me?'

'I do not understand what you are saying?'

Brahmendra Swami laughs at his innocence.

'Let the payments be late, miss one here and one there. If you are already giving them what they want, why would they give you anything in return?'

'Well, because that is my duty, I am bound to it, and I am good at it.'

'No, Kanhoji. They and anybody will only help themselves, twice over: their share and yours. Now grow up. I shouldn't have to tell you every little thing. Enjoy yourself. Live it up. Build a nice house for yourself in Kulaba: live like the prince you are. Remember: kings are forgetful, especially when it comes to paying.'

'Then don't forget the cannon. That's my price for looking the other way,' Kanhoji says.

'In four days then, on *amavas**, Khairiyat will move on Gopalgad. Be as far away as you can be.'

'I suggest next month, when it is the mango season. Why risk a battle? In one month, he is going to be camping in his orchards,' Kanhoji suggests.

'Actually, Bhawanji is already there now, keeping the parrots away from his precious mangoes, there is no better time,' says the uncannily informed Swami.

'One more thing Khairiyat would like to give you: he says Kasim has a spy within your establishment but does not know who. Find out who it is,' adds the Swami.

---

* Moonless night.

If Not by Name

Now that Kanhoji has as many vessels as Siddi Mistry had led into battle at Thana Creek, he will let Surat know. Leaving ten galbats in Kulaba, he takes all his ghurabs and the remaining galbats north, escorting several machuas, dhows and barges loaded with barud. They will deliver it to the Punjabi and Pakhtoon caravans that are waiting on the coasts of Sindh. On his way back, they will hug the coast eastwards and visit Surat and Daman, which is the ostensible purpose of the whole trip.

'We are at war with the *Turki*, and we can no longer let the Firangis think they have dominion over these waters,' Kanhoji reminds his men as they set out. Throughout the year, except for the monsoon, his patrols along the coast have been ceaseless: functioning as precious drills that keep the muscles of his men supple, and the hulls of his boats wet. Bhawanji Mohitay has a different take on his job as co-commander of the Konkan. His duty extends only so far as keeping the absolute minimum number of men at the forts that have fallen to his control and negligent care. The villages under each fort, whose revenue he is a shareholder of, go straight into his mango orchards or around his wives' necks. He had never asked for the job, and it had fallen to his family, and he needed to pick it up for the larger good of his clan. He doesn't have a martial bone in his body. He prefers cows to horses and ploughs to muskets. Nor is he expected to, as his true and accepted calling is the growing of the finest hafus mangoes in the universe. There have been sightings of Lord Khandoba visiting his orchards, and one summer Bal Krishna purportedly got more of the fruit than any parrot could: or so said his sling-armed troop of boys who guard the mango trees.

Khairiyat simply has his men climb over the walls with ladders that are propped up on the ramparts of the undermanned fort. The garrison is woken up at spear point and bundled out of the fort. Bhawanji's men do not know what has happened till they find themselves outside in their langots. Their commander will later claim that they thought they were being replaced by another Maratha garrison. As the story of Gopalgad's capture spreads from the town of Anjanvel, it arrives in the well-watered by-lanes of Satara as Siddi Khairiyat having spotted Angria heading north with what seemed to be his entire fleet, pouncing on the opportunity.

On their way back, the holds of the vessels Angria had escorted have been laden with almonds, walnuts, pine nuts and pistachio along with oak chests full of turquoise. Kanhoji takes some of each and pays his condolences to the unflappable Bhawanji Mohite. They meet at Bhawanji's orchard where he is sitting bare-chested under an umbrella, fondling mangoes that are being presented to him for inspection. One afternoon shower a month ago, has pitted a lot of the fruit, and Bhawanji is dismayed.

'I wish you would have brought me back some ice.'

'It is summer, Saheb, there was not a sherbet or kulfi to be found in the entirety of Surat. But when I go to Kashmir, I will definitely bring you back some ice.'

'Why are you going to Kashmir?'

'Tibet, actually—via Kashmir. To hunt the four-cocked mountain lion,' Kanhoji jokes.

'Marvellous. Bring some ice, even a handful. Mangoes taste so much better if they are chilled in cold water or saltpetre. I once had a *langda**** in Agra that could dare compete with our haphus only because it was served in ice. Imagine a haphus on ice!'

'I really can't. But Saheb, don't worry about Gopalgad, we will get it back one day.'

'Oh, do I look like I am worried? It was too much work as it was. Garrisons to pay. How much repair cost! I am not worried if you are there: our most diligent killedar: blessed by the gods themselves. I sleep peacefully knowing you are on our side,' says the inherently arrogant Bhawanji.

'As I will always remain. You needn't worry Mohiteji, we are wide awake at our posts. Neither the Siddis's rakshas-like face nor the height of a Firangi galleon scares us now.'

'Well, you may be a Sarnaubat, but you have taken on the responsibility of the Sarkhel after all, do what you have to do and keep my orchards safe from the Firangis and the Siddi.'

'With your blessings always,' Kanhoji says smarting at what Bhawanji has just said. Everyone seems to be aware of it and his competitor accepts it, except those in Satara, who matter the most: they are oblivious. The meeting goes as well as it can and Kanhoji feels a little less guilty about what he has done. It is not an emotion his swami ever indulges in but the letter he receives from Dhavaddshi makes him feel much better. Khairiyat has sent Angria cannon and has also agreed to enforce and share in the Maratha dastak for all vessels porting at Anjanvel or sailing out off the Vashishti.

---

* A variety of mango grown around Benares.

The Rising Sun

The dapper and immaculately groomed Rustomji Dorabji is waiting patiently in a sal-pillared veranda adjacent to a room allocated for meeting agents and traders at the Kulaba Fort. Rustomji Dorabji has arrived at Kulaba drenched in his voluminous white achkan and pagdi. He has been waiting for the rain to stop but it just isn't letting up. The rain is noisy and clamorous, a violent mob rushing up towards the ghats. He wouldn't risk the short journey across the mouth of the Thana River to Kulaba and had instead taken the land route and chosen to risk the streams and rivers that gush down the seaward slopes of the precipitous hills behind him. It has taken him three weeks to cover the distance that would have taken him half a day if he had risked sailing across the bay. But all vessels, from the smallest dugout to the largest galleon, are either beached hull up or anchored in a protected inlet.

An attendant escorts the Patel of Bombay Fort and his personal *jamadar*[*] to a room where the Patel may change before he meets the Sarnaubat. Rustomji knows that the success of his masters' business enterprise would be heavily dependent on peace with this rising star of the Konkan. He has been able to convince his boss, General John Gayer, that amity with the Marathas is essential for the growth of

---

[*] Groom.

trade. General Gayer is worried and concerned, for the Siddi at Janjira has made it clear to him that there is no other authority than himself and through him the Badshah Aurangzeb. In the end, General Gayer acquiesces to his Patel meeting the de facto Admiral of the beleaguered Maratha kingdom. Rustomji has his ears in the marketplace and all the seths are of one opinion: the Bhonsales are finished, and the Old Man is bound to take the Deccan; the Konkan, on the other hand, they opine will increasingly become the dominion of Angria who, having no master left alive, will eventually become the Badshah's Wazir himself, replacing the Siddi. The low settee Rustomji has been directed to sit on is spotless and well cushioned—each setting provisioned with a hookah, pandaan and a spittoon. As soon as he sits down, a pankhawala takes up position behind him and fans him with vigour.

The shame that had been brought down upon the entirety of Bhawanji's soldiery soon spurred the eager commander of Padmadurg to confiscate the crew and cargo of two salt barges on their way north. The barges belonged to the primary Angrezi Company that had their warehouses and docks south of Mazgaon at Palva Bandar and were the employers of Rustomji. This group of traders, in all ways exactly like any other group of traders to be found on the Konkan, made a great insistence on having not only their distant and irrelevant Raja's *firman** but one issued by the Badshah himself. But these topi-wearing traders were bereft of all loyalty as when the sun shone and they were within their warehouses, they traded in their raja's name, but when it set and they were without, they traded in their own names, always offering marginally better offers than they had offered during the day at their compound north of Palva Bandar. The commander of Padmadurg was demanding Rs 20,000 in return for the crew and the cargo along with the vessels. Built solely for the conquering of Janjira, like its *casus belli*, Padmadurg remained incomplete.

The elegant Rustomji enters and his nazrana of a pair of pistols is presented.

---

* Royal decree.

'Your seth has good taste. Do thank him for me,' Kanhoji says perfunctorily.

'He thanks you for so promptly and judiciously releasing the salt barges and their crew.'

'Think nothing of it. I have the safety of every trader in the Konkan in my heart. That is my dharma. We welcome all people. Let them come here and trade in peace, as that is what is best for the success of our people. We wish them success and great profits for taking our produce to their distant lands.'

Rustomji bows in namaskar.

'We would like to request your Seth for some land near your fort or within it to produce barud. It is the best barud available. I will give you a sample for the Seths.'

'I will take your request to His Excellency,' Rustomji replies in Marathi.

'Tell me, Patelji, these Angrez, how do their vanias take on martial titles? Our vanias do not go around calling themselves Sarnaubat or Sarkhel.'

'They trade in the name of their king, Your Excellency,' Rustomji explains.

'I heard the Angrezi king did not take on a Nederlandi wife? Did they have to fight it out?'

'It is a very complex situation in their lands, Your Excellency. There are many families, mostly related, constantly fighting each other. They have not had peace for many generations. I understand little of their politics.'

'But they need to have a better understanding of our politics and that it is politic to be at peace,' Kanhoji says.

'And they, Sarnaubat Saheb, or should I say Sarkhel?'

'Stick to Sarnaubat for the foreseeable future. Sarnaubat Bhawanji Mohite shares in my command. If anyone moves a finger at him, I am duty-bound to protect my cohort and friend.'

'Saheb, I am here to offer a treaty of peace between yourself and the Company at Bombay.'

'There already exists a treaty between the Swaraj and the Angrezi Company. There is no need for more. It is an affliction particularly amongst your community and dare I say amongst your employers. Constantly writing things down. Action, my friend, is what makes a treaty, not pieces of paper.'

'Of course, Sarnaubat Saheb. It's just that the General Saheb would like to have an ancillary treaty of friendship. The other treaties are between the House of Bhonsale and the Company.'

'So then, should you and I also have a treaty, Patelji? Any treaty between the Maharaj and anybody else—I am strictly bound to. Please understand that.'

'But Saheb, those are not ratified by you personally.'

'Who am I to ratify anything? How dare I?'

'Merely a treaty of friendship?'

'If you insist on writing it down. So be it, but we will hold you and the Company to your acts.'

'You must be well aware,' Kanhoji continues, 'that the Angrezi sell their right to trade to other traders or for themselves as private individuals on account of this treaty between your Seths and the Maharaj, essentially undermining that very same treaty and stealing revenue from us.'

'Indiscipline is rife, and I cannot deny that there are thieves amongst them. But Sahebji, truth be told, there is another company of the Angrez trying to consume us.'

'Companies? Dens. Dens of thieves. Thugs of the highest order,' Kanhoji says, sharply recalling Venko's abduction.

'Every Angrez is not one of us, Saheb,' Rustomji explains.

'That cannot be an excuse. It's like me saying that I am not to blame for my troops terrorizing every Angrezi vessel that crosses our waters. Have I not settled the matter with the salt barges?' Kanhoji continues.

'I truly appreciate your position, Sarnaubat Saheb. My employers are naive, but give them time to learn our ways.'

'Makes no difference to me, Patelji, who takes the yarn or the masala or the barud. But your words are as sweet as Ramaji Dubash's. It must run in your blood,' Kanhoji teases.

'Saheb, they say that 700 years ago, when we got to the coast of Gujrat fleeing the Arab's steel, the King of Gujrat sent our chief a glass of milk full to the brim . . .'

'Ah, I know that tale, and your chief put a spoonful of sugar in. But sugar is a cheap sweetener. A good gun is a sweeter addition, Patelji. And I will give you the barud at an excellent rate, the same rate we pay till we manufacture it at your fort.'

'Saheb, that is very kind of you. I will speak to the General about it. He has authority over all Company matters. I am merely an instrument of communication.'

'Don't be so humble, Patelji, you are much more than that and we appreciate your efforts. But tell me, will the Siddi be told of this treaty of ours? Or will you hide it from him in fear?'

Rustomji has not prepared for this question. It was the Mughal's favour his masters sought in Surat and Bengal and vainly at Agra or at the Padishah's ever-shifting campsite where they remain in some form of continuous presence and expectation. Fort George is not Surat, the Maratha is not the Mughal for them.

Rustomji is not a superstitious man and does not believe in the legends and stories whispered about Angria. He is convinced by the young man's perseverance that he may someday somersault to the top. Then again, there is nothing stopping him from breaking away from the Bhonsales, but he hasn't bothered. At last count, Rustomji has noted that Angria has twelve ghurabs and twenty-eight galbats— almost as many as his former king by whose name his employers still refer to the Marathas: Sevajees. The day might come, Rustomji fears, when they would be known as the Angarees.

'The Company's treaty pertains to Surat and Bengal, Sarnaubat Saheb, and it is in no way conflicting with our own separate treaty,' Rustomji tries.

'Go ahead and prepare a draft and I will have a look at it and revert with any changes if necessary.'

'That is all the Sethji requests,' Rustomji says relieved.

'Don't fear the Siddi. Let me tell you plainly that as a child so did I. Our mothers and aunts would tell us stories to scare us to sleep: the Siddi will do this, the Siddi will do that. But the first thing you learn when you grow up is that the Siddi is just like us, only a little darker and with curly hair. I learnt everything I know about the sea from Habshis. Of course, I improvised on it. There is no kind of vessel we cannot take—it does not matter how big it is or how many guns it has. I have Habshis, Topashis, Firangis, Mussalman, Kolis, Agaris and Bhandaris working for me. You know why? So that there isn't a festival or *muhurat* a garrison is not at their posts.'

Rustomji had guessed as much. He needs a treaty with this man who has entrenched himself across the bay at Kulaba. Angria truly isn't bothered about the Portuguese and the Dutch or themselves and is so obviously focused on the Siddi and the Padishah. 'He is going to concentrate on the Siddi's fleet and fortifications, and after subduing him, become the Padishah's new naval chief.' Rustom's theory is coloured by the fact that Angria hasn't retaliated against Khairiyat. It is also possible that he is widening the rift between Kasim and Khairiyat—either which way, this horse is in for the long run.

'Good tidings to your Seth, Patelji. Trade in peace and make sure your coin remains true,' Kanhoji says, dismissing Rustomji.

Samudra Manthan

Lord Varuna retreats—his wrath deflated and spent—back into the ocean. The moon grows bountifully on towards Nariyel Purnima, the festival marked to thank the respite-giving god of the sea and rain. The currents in the streams and rivers are still strong as they carry their dusky silt into the sea while the squelching earth is carpeted rock to rock in sprouting grass and procumbent vines. Below, pebbles and boulders shine after their annual bath while above, the canopy is an orchestra of buzzing flycatchers, chirping crickets and burping tree frogs. This is the festival Kanhoji eagerly awaits every year. They walk down from his estate at Hirakot, both his wives and their children in tow: Ladu astride his neck and Sekho and Tula walking by his side, carrying coconuts as offerings to the sea gods. First, he heads to the Koliwada where Suryavanshi and the other Koli families welcome him. For them he is yajyman and *annadaatta**—he is Annapoorna. From there, they all set out to the beach in merriment and the children dancing whilst Kanhoji leads the way, swaying to the hypnotic drumbeat: '*Dhada dhada dhad dhada dhad.*' Once they reach the beach, coconuts are offered to the sea and floated on her lapping waves along with other sweetmeats and flowers. Surya leads the fishermen to their freshly decorated boats

---

* Giver of nourishment and life.

with their recently tarred bottoms, the knots securing their planks tightened and their hulls painted in bright colours like the scales of tropical fish. The purohit says prayers over the boats and invokes the gods for safety and a bountiful harvest. The nakhwas then break a coconut on the prow of their fishing boats and then join their crews in dragging them out of the surf and into the awaiting and bountiful sea.

As the tide comes in, the young strapping men of the fort's garrison and the surrounding fishing villages take off their fine clothes and congregate around Kanhoji for a swimming race across the channel to the fort on Kulaba Island. Kanhoji is always glad that Surya chooses to take out the boats instead of joining him in the race where he is sure to beat him. Kanhoji's massive chest is a furious mill as it rotates his arms through the waves towards the island as the younger boys try to get to the island first—crossing him only to run out of breath a few gaj down. On this occasion, he is bested by a slim boy with skin as dark and smooth as polished basalt that has darted past him like a *bangdo**. Kanhoji is greatly impressed with the nervous boy who is now unsure if he has done the right thing as the other participants emerge covered with the seaweed of envy on their brows.

'What is your name, boy?' Kanhoji asks the dripping boy who is now trembling.

The boy whispers through his chattering teeth as little Sekho, who has participated for the first time, raises the winner's frail arm.

'What?' Kanhoji asks, unable to catch his name.

'Well, Bangdo, will you join up with me when you are a little older?' Kanhoji says, as he presses a minute gold *panam* coin into his wrinkled hand.

The newly christened Bangdo shuffles his feet and mutters something again.

'He says he is ready to join us this year, Baba,' Sekho who is right beside him volunteers.

---

* Mackerel.

Now, Bangdo speaks directly to Sekho who transmits his words for the benefit of his father: 'He says he can row just as fast and climb up ropes even faster.'

'Well, Sekho, if you speak for him, then he is your responsibility. He will be your second from now on. Take care to feed him well or an eagle is likely to pick him up and use him as a twig for her nest,' Kanhoji says smiling as those gathered around burst out laughing.

The custom at Nariyel Purnima is to return after a ceremonial boat ride and plant trees on the land. Kanhoji is so much enthused about this aspect of the day that last year he hurried a puja. This year, though, as Surya and the rest return from their decorated boats, Kanhoji leads them in an elaborate ceremony he has devised with the purohit, where they will plant the saplings of what will eventually become his galbats and ghurabs. He centres all the attention on to his young sons and their playmates, telling them that though he would not be here to reap the timber of these trees, they would— and this will be their greatest patrimony. All his garrisons and troops follow suit all the way down the coast. At Bankot, large tracts of land have been cleared during the monsoon and now are planted with teakwood saplings he got from Dindelli and the Karnatak. As the sun sinks into the horizon, the women set diyas made of cashew nut leaves on the retreating waves and the congregation proceeds to the temple within the fort for the arti.

The boats haven't been out a week when Sekho and Bangdo take a dhow returning from Basra. In the hold, hidden beneath bales of lion skins are several sacks of pearls, that to the untrained eye would have passed for rice, along with a pair of large chests that hold the finest and largest of the consignment. The dhow is dragged to Kulaba, and the bounty taken up to the Sarnaubat. Kanhoji lets the unarmed dhow and its Habshi crew off, imprisoning only Siddi Kasim's representative, who had been aboard the dhow with his pair of armed guards. The guards are stripped to their langots and let off too. The Siddi's man is sent south to Gheria to languish in the new prison Kanhoji has, in necessity, made there. There are invariably some people who, either due to their skills or knowledge, pose a threat to his plans, and these he feeds on his own account at his prison in Gheria. Kanhoji is deliberate in this matter, as he has seen his actions spread to his cohorts: the kinder he is, the kinder they are, and the crueller he is, the crueller they are. He needs more capable sailors, stronger oarsmen and as many musketeers as he can get a hold of and any with experience are already employed. No maiming, no cutting off of noses. Instead, pay for your transgressions with coin, Angria will not pay the *jallad*[*].

---

[*] Executioner.

Pearls

Seeing the seven baskets filled with pearls and after carefully examining some samples from each of the two ebony chests, Kanhoji feels the cooling breeze of grace blowing him gently forward. Whatever Swamiji wishes for seems to always come to pass. The *malamatdas* has barely completed the entries into his ledger when Kanhoji comes up to the *Toshkhana*[*] and commandeers a sack for Swamiji and the two chests for the Rajmata. A tall tumbler full or pearls is set aside for Khairiyat Khan and a similar one for Bhawanji Mohitay. These he dispatches immediately. He gives another tumbler worth each to Sekho and Bangdo, and another tumbler to be shared amongst their crew. Then hearing Mathurabai's voice grating against his peace, he takes a measure each for his wives. Taking no chances, Kanhoji takes an escort of three platoons and heads to Swamiji's ashram.

Gone are the bedraggled acolytes and in their place stands a bevy of apsaric *sadhvis* waiting to greet Kanhoji at the ashram. Vishnu meets him in his new durbar hall which has a high ceiling hung with a chandelier of diyas. Brahmendra Swami walks in as Kanhoji is admiring the fragmented rainbows that waft out from every crystal facade.

---

[*] Treasury.

'Your friend Ramaji has great taste,' says Brahmendra Swami.

'It runs in their family,' Kanhoji says as he bends to touch Swamiji's feet. They sit down as Kanhoji's attendants carry in the pearls and leave. A damsel in a tissue-thin white *malmal* blouse and churidar opens the sack and delicately lays out the pearls for Swamiji to see.

'Where did you get this from?' he asks, amazed.

'Khandoba himself. Sekho took a dhow. Kasim has become a jeweller, it seems. Well, this year, he must break his *bhaanda*.'

'You are beloved by Khandoba,' says Brahmendra Swami, blessing him with his raised hand.

'One of the Patels of the Angrez came to see me during the rains, to make a treaty,' Kanhoji says without wasting any time.

'I heard. Good you sent it up to Her Highness. See this is what I mean, they see you as the authority here, not Satara. That is why Satara fears you.'

'Will this help?' Kanho asks.

'If it doesn't, you can be sure her heart is made of harder things than these pearls.'

'Pearls are brittle, Swamiji, and I hope so is she, at least in this matter. I can buy Bhawanji out. His sons will be settled and he can retire to his mangoes.'

'*Dhairya*, my boy, dhairya. It will all come to pass,' Brahmendra Swami intones.

'But why the delay? If I wished to break away, I would not ask for the sarkhelship, I would not need to. But I am not a traitor. Do they not understand that? Have they not seen that?'

'*Tch tch*,' Vishnu clucks at Kanhoji.

'Your closeness with Khairiyat, your inability to help Bhawanji...'

'What? That was your idea!' says Kanhoji in disbelief.

'Of course, it was, but you were the one to do it. It was, is, the right thing to have done. That doesn't mean it will not be viewed in different ways by different people,' says Brahmendra Swami.

Smiling like a cat, he changes the subject: 'Your friend Panduraoji has an acquaintance amongst the Ashtapradhan . . .'

'I don't know what his problem is,' says Kanhoji before Swamiji can finish.

'He seems to have some deep-seated hatred of you. You are in no way competitors: he is just a dalal. I do not understand it either.'

'We all went to the same gurukul, Balaji, Venko and him. I pushed him while he was taking a shit one day. Maybe it's just that. Can't you talk to him?'

'I have heard that he openly calls me a fraud and a trickster. It will be hard. But I will try.'

'At Suvarnadurg, I treated him well. The ransom is just business. He would have done the same to me. Perhaps now I shouldn't meet him, give him the privilege. He's a worthless little bhadwa.'

'Come now, Kanhoji, don't let your pride get in the way.'

'It's not my pride. It's just that I have realized he is a poisonous snake and has always been so. Gotten worse in fact: malevolent.'

'Whatever you wish, but I would still advise you that your first instinct was correct, and you should end this matter. Sometimes a small scratch when not tended can lead to infection and amputation if not worse.'

'Forget it, Swamiji, I don't have the time.'

'Anyway, I want you to present this sack of pearls to the Rajmata. You don't have to repay me now. The interest will go up a little bit, but till the next dhow. Go straight from here.'

'I am obliged, Swamiji. But what of the cannons, Swamiji, everything hinges on the cannons?'

'Why don't you try to make them? It's hard getting cannons of the size you require, harder transporting them. I have heard that the Kalal Bangdi is made of rings that were forged together at Janjira.'

'That Hansu is very slow. He can fix the muskets. That's about it. I find it hard to believe he was a gun maker to kings in his homeland.'

'It will happen, Kanho, just keep your faith in me.'

A Chilling Wind

On riding into Satara, Kanhoji discovers that the Rajmata has left for Kolhapur. He follows them south and has caught up to the royal caravan by the time it arrives at a previously prepared camp on the banks of the Tarli River. The campsite is on a slightly raised hillock amongst a grove of *siras* trees that grow not far from the riverbank. While dozens of armed sentries encircle the camp in a tightly strung necklace of pickets, others roam the area defending it against a troop of stout and stubborn macaques that hiss at the royal party without fear.

Kanhoji immediately seeks an audience with the Rajmata as soon as her entourage has encamped. Though granted readily, on reaching the makeshift durbar tent, Kanhoji and his men are kept waiting outside it for a pointedly long time. The hexagonal tent is made of simple dun-coloured canvas but is well guarded. There is a cold evening breeze blowing over the river that after drying his sweaty clothes is now raising the hairs on his body. When he enters it, it is equally chilly and stiff within the durbar tent. The Rajmata does not bother to open the chests and waves them away into her personal quarters. Neither does she make any eye contact with Kanhoji and instead is signing firmans that lie on a low folding table in front of her. The elderly Peshwa Ramchandra Bawdekar, who has been the amatya for so many years that despite being both the Imperial Regent and the Peshwa, is still called Amatya Pant, stands by her side, and he is the first to speak to Kanhoji.

'Sarnaubat Kanhoji Angre, the Rajmata thanks you for carrying her possessions to her. But they could have well been left at Satara, where they would have been guarded. Yet you carry them to the countryside.'

'They are Basra pearls we just acquired from the Siddi,' he says, looking at Tarabai to catch her expression. She tries to control herself but her eyes dart towards Kanhoji.

'And I thought it best I relay them immediately to Her Highness.'

'Most fortunate. Her Highness has written a letter to the Viceroy at Goa, and she wishes you present it to the Viceroy personally,' Amatya Pant continues.

'At your command,' Kanhoji says, bowing his head as he steps forward towards the raised platform upon which the Rajmata's bolstered makeshift throne stands.

'It is already sealed?' Kanhoji asks as he receives the sealed cloth packet.

'Is that a problem?' inquires the Prime Minister.

'Not at all, I just thought if the Firangi Nawab responds I would have a reference for his reactions,' explains Kanhoji politely.

'There are appropriate channels for His Excellency the Viceroy to respond through. You needn't worry about it,' the ancient Prime Minister says, watching Kanhoji intently.

They have turned him into a dakwala, but he does not let the insult show.

Then the Rajmata speaks for the first time, still looking at a document in front of her: 'Sarnaubat Kanhoji, it merely tells them to desist from terrorizing our people or face destruction and to not think we are so busy with the Mughals that we do not have the time to teach them a lesson too. It also asks them to abide by their treaty and assist us against the Mughals. Lastly, it says that if they have any complaints about the excesses of our own sardars I will not hesitate to take punitive action against them.'

Kanhoji wonders if she is referring to him or if this is nothing but a ruse to get him out of the way and be rid of him once and for all? But how will that ever benefit her or the other sardars?

'At your feet, Rajmata. I will take this letter and hasten to Firangistan,' Kanhoji says.

'Take care to present yourself to the Firangi Nawab in a better state than you bother to present yourself to your own queen,' Tarabai quips.

Kanhoji blushes in embarrassment and he chides himself for not changing before meeting her. Amatya Pant looks down his starched dhoti at Kanhoji and sneers at him from under his cold black eyes. The youthful Rajmata then turns to her minister and whispers.

Kanhoji bows lower than his station accords and steps back towards the exit and leaves ignored and undismissed. 'If they treat me like a dakwala, I better behave as one,' he thinks. He finds his men with his horse, and they all mount their rides and head towards Gheria, leaving the cart to work her way down. He does not even treat his own killedars in such a fashion. A light rain has commenced, and it stings his face with the same intensity as the fresh insult still does. He wipes his face with the back of his hand and ignores both the stings. It does not matter to him in the least; he will go into the red bear's cave and deliver the letter no matter what lies ahead. But he will not go as a dakwala but as an ambassador of the Maratha state. He also decides that from now on, no matter where he travels, his *hajaam* and *jamadar* will accompany him along with his usual retinue that consists of Gangadhar, Surya, Golu and his sais. Mathura is right, he needs to look the part.

Firangistan

A ruthless sun has baked the season's rain out of the soil and a fine dust has risen to settle on the thick vegetation surrounding the washed Palacio. Two men are standing on the turret, eyeglasses in hand. Like wiser travellers of the Konkan, both have fine muslin veils over their faces to shield them from the dust and the blinding sun.

'Those, *Vossa Excelencia*, are Khairiyat of Anjanvel's dhows that have dropped anchor across Aguada,' Pandurao points north across the mouth of the Mandovi.

'He brings the negro for his protection? He fears to come alone?' asks Frei Agostinho de Anunciacao.

'He no longer fears anything, Vossa Excelencia. That is the problem,' says Pandurao.

'It is naught but the fear of God that separates man from beast,' says the Archbishop crossing himself.

'They are docking. Vossa Excelencia. That man there, on the dappled Arab, is Kanho Sankhpal,' Pandurao points to a docking ghurab ahead of a fleet of Maratha galbats.

Kanhoji is astride Neelkanth, a statuesque Arabian stallion, dappled grey with a black temple and throat. His mane and tail match his muscled neck creeping with a lattice of veins that support a finely cast head that stands well above all others in the stable. His hind legs are muscular, and his rump well curved from swimming the channels.

'A truly Konkani horse, born to the water,' Surya had once remarked to Kanhoji.

The Archbishop watches as Kanhoji's mount confidently steps on to the jetty followed by his mounted bodyguard. Surya wears Prince Akbar's dagger at his waist and his iron talisman now hangs around his neck in a thick gold chain. Golu wears a necklace of monkey skulls and his chin is red like his pan-stained tongue. As headgear, a lion's head, courtesy the Siddi's confiscated cargo from Basra. Piloji and Nirakant Javle are dressed in silk pants embroidered in gold with matching shawls and muslin kurtas. Their pagdis are tied as large as possible. Surya had requested Piloji to restrain himself in this regard, so as not to outshine their Sarnaubat. Every weapon is gleaming.

Kanhoji's crew are in indigo-dyed *sheershukker* kurtas and turbans while his infantry in saffron-dyed ones, and they now follow his bodyguard off the ghurab. They consist of the most physically impressive specimens in his employ.

'His wives' jewels, Vossa Excelencia,' Pandurao says to the visibly impressed Archbishop.

Manuji Castro, looking every bit a Maratha, from his pagdi to his upturned moustache, takes his place as Dubash amongst Kanhoji's closest coterie.

'And who is that?' the Archbishop asks, pointing at a tanned Firangi with a tilak on his forehead.

'The capitan that betrayed the *Nossa Senhora*, Vossa Excelencia, he is to translate for Kanho,' Pandurao replies with fealty.

'A traitor to his God and his king, see how he dresses like one of you monkeys, sporting blasphemous markings,' the Archbishop says vehemently. How can his mission succeed if his own abandon him? This is the worst kind of apostasy.

'He dares to return?' spits the Archbishop.

The Archbishop and Pandurao watch with their eyeglasses as Kanhoji's bodyguard, followed by eight silhadars on their mounts and finally a platoon each of musketeers and lancers on foot, make their way up to the palacio's gate. Gangadhar is on a horse to the left of Kanhoji sitting behind a rider holding an umbrella over Kanhoji. Surya is at Kanhoji's right, holding a rope to which two Firangis are bound.

'Maria, what is that?' the Archbishop gasps, pointing at Golu.

'A demon, borne to a mermaid, Vossa Excelencia, always at his side,' Pandurao confirms.

Kanhoji and his retinue ride past the gate and on through the rising gardens to the palacio's arched entryway on top of a plateau. Here Kanhoji and Surya dismount in front of two guards with their lances crossed in front of an arched stone gateway. Piloji, Javle, Gangadhar, Golu and Manuji are already on foot, followed by the attendants carrying the gifts, when they are met by the Viceroy's adjunct. Surya hands the leash holding the two prisoners to the caparisoned adjunct, who accepts it with a bow and then immediately lets it drop to the ground. He then leads them through a verdant courtyard ringed with giant Nilotic warriors and ancient Greek pots both standing akimbo, into a large hall where Dom Antonio, in an engraved golden *plastron*, is seated at the centre of an ebony table as long as a galbat. Replacing Dom Pedro at the helm of the Portuguese Estado is Dom Antonio Luis Gonsalves da Camara Coutinho. Through an intermediary, Kanhoji has been able to contract a respectable amount of trade. The former Viceroy's initially unfortunate nephew, Dom Alfonso, is now settled in Morjim growing mangoes but has not been averse to buying muzzleloaders and small cannon from his uncle's replacement and forwarding them on to Kanhoji, his former captor.

The Archbishop hurries down the steps to a window from which he can further watch the proceedings.

Dom Antonio in his pompous chestnut wig remains seated, but the two equally resplendent gentlemen in silver plastrons who have been sitting on either side of the Viceroy, stand up as Kanhoji is ushered in. Kanhoji takes the only chair—a stool in the roman style—that has been placed on the opposite side of the gargantuan table. Manuji stands behind Kanhoji to his right and Gangadhar is to his left, while Piloji and Javle stand behind them. Surya and Golu have been unable to move beyond the entrance door and now giddily eye the immense chandelier that hangs ephemeral and impossibly high over the entire hall.

After the adjunct introduces the bejowled Viceroy, Manuji introduces Kanhoji who immediately hands over the sealed letter to the Viceroy. The Viceroy turns his large head to the young gentleman on his left who accepts the letter on his behalf. The *Senhor* breaks the seal, unfolds the letter and begins to read it aloud in Portuguese.

'The Vice Admiral comes as a messenger?' Dom Antonio asks, 'or because he finds himself mentioned in it?' he says in Portuguese once the letter has been read.

The Archbishop, unable to hear from his hiding place, abandons it.

'He comes as a friend and as a partner in the safety of our shared coastline. Her Highness has heard complaints against her sardars and has sent the Sarnaubat here to ascertain directly whether these accusations are truly just,' Kanhoji replies in Marathi after Manuji has translated the Viceroy's question.

'Senhor Angria, I am honoured to meet the man who took the *Nossa Senhora*, but I must insist it was unjust,' Dom Antonio says, breaking a smile.

'I merely led Saheb, my thousand boarders, surprising her as she was on her way to attack us in conjunction with the Siddi,' says Kanhoji, looking into the Viceroy's tired and swollen eyes.

'Impressive, indeed. I hope there will be no further cause. We will respect each other's custom houses and I will write to Her Majesty that while I am Viceroy, there will be no breaking of temples and killing of farmers and pilgrims,' Dom Antonio says.

'We will not board or detain any vessel without cause, Your Excellency,' says Kanhoji.

The large, polished rosewood doors of the audience hall burst inwards as the Archbishop, in his billowing white dress and a buttoned red cape pushes past Golu and Surya and strides towards the Viceroy unimpeded by any of the several guards that line the walls of the hall.

'Why was I not informed of this meeting?' he shouts agitatedly.

'It's Angria, our neighbour in Chaul. He brings me a letter,' responds the red-faced Viceroy.

'Written by whom?' the indignant Archbishop asks rather rudely again.

'Not ecclesiastical business, Vossa Excelencia, merely by a minister of the Satara King,' answers the Viceroy.

'Heathens, shit-coloured heathens,' the Archbishop roars, sneering at the Maratha contingent.

'And know this, Dom Antonio, here in India, all business is ecclesiastical,' he continues as steam rises off his body.

The Viceroy, too, fumes under his wig. The fumes condense on his forehead and roll down his beet-tinged face.

'In the future, please make sure I am in attendance as their benighted souls are under my purview, and we here in the Estado, whether you are aware of it or not, are on a mission—a mission from God,' the Archbishop says, crossing himself. In his opinion, Antonio Luis is the worst kind of man they send out from Iberia: not caring for the naked millions but lusting only after the rich merchants and zamindars to pillage or trade with. Such men never teach the heathens about the True Way nor bother for the millions of souls that are to be had; millions of benighted souls—a hundred lifetimes wouldn't be enough for him to convert them to the truth and dress their shameless naked bodies. He will let Lisbon know of the Viceroy's corrupt and pagan friends post-haste, and he will also let Rome know.

Kanhoji, apprised by Manuel Castro as to who it is, stands up from his chair and greets the chief acharya of the Firangi God with a respectful namaskar.

The Archbishop looks at him with disdain and then at Manuji.

'Apostate, traitor, you are hereby excommunicated,' the Archbishop shouts at Manuji.

Kanhoji gently slaps his own cheek and then turns the other towards the Archbishop. Manuji bows low in namaskar.

The Archbishop, visibly rattling in his vestments, turns his back on them and storms out with the same zealous urgency he had barged in with.

The Lion at Rest

In all the years Kasim has been the Yakut Khan of Janjira he has not once ventured out of his citadel, and he congratulates himself on his prescience. Now, without Khairiyat at his command, he debates with himself on what he should do. If this Angria is left unchecked, he will grow to become unbeatable. If for some foolish reason the woman at Satara makes him Sarkhel, Angria and the Firangis will between them have a stranglehold on the entire coast. Of what use would he be at Janjira then? Return to the privateering of his youth? He knows he is much too old, nor can he retreat to Surat if he is of no use to the Badshah. The Badshah does not have the reputation of protecting failed fighters. Now a lame and lowly kafir is drawing him out of his basalt cocoon. Is it a trap? In whose charge will he leave his beloved Janjira? With the confusion comes the indigestion, though on this occasion, the nausea is brought on by this vile creature that stands before him stinking up his court. Commanding the presence of Seth Pandurao Phangaskar, Kasim seeks solace with a masseuse at his ostentatious hammam.

Pandurao, who had let the functionaries at the Janjira court know that he was across the channel at Rajpura, is immediately found and presented to Kasim's chamberlain at the durbar hall. The room is bustling with its usual citizenry of soothsayers and slavers but the *gaddi** is empty. In a dark corner, the heavily pockmarked lame creature stands, his eyes lustily bulging out of their sockets as they drink in the glistening curves of the bare-bodied Habshi Amazons who stand with large scallop-shaped fans made of ostrich feathers and gently fan the humid durbar. The Chamberlain directs the lame man and Pandurao to follow him as he makes his way through a guarded passageway. As the Chamberlain walks briskly ahead, Pandurao drops his pace momentarily and lets the lame man catch up.

The Chamberlain leads the two men down a steep flight of stairs into a large hammam. The walls of the hammam are tiled with flesh-coloured marble and pink onyx over which water continually slides down through a system of fountains and gutters. Shells of mother-of-pearl filled with camphor oil holding burning wicks of cotton are strung about from the ceiling, puncturing the darkness with orbs of gentle light. Kasim's immense naked torso is lying on a marble slab, each limb attended to by a naked muscled boy. A young Caucasian girl is at his head, massaging his grinding jaw, creased forehead and his pink gums. They continue as the chamberlain announces the spy and Pandurao into his presence.

'This *langda* says he works for Angria, at Kulaba,' Kasim's voice drawls out from the pentagonal ring of masseuses.

'Tell me again,' the voice rings out after a long pause.

The Chamberlain strikes the lame man who is fixated on the naked bottom of the girl massaging Kasim's melon-sized head.

Kasim hears the man slurp before speaking: 'The Sarnaubat has been in Suvarnadurg for the past few weeks. He is going to be there for another month at least. This year, the Nariyel Purnima puja is to be held there. All his horses, sardars and family are at Suvarnadurg. Every year now, on the last full moon of Shravan, there is nothing but merriment. This year, he has left Kulaba empty.'

Before Kasim can muster the energy to form any words, Pandurao barks at the lame man: 'Why should we trust you? You are Kanho's man. For all we know, it is a trap.'

---

* Throne.

'Saheb, you can go and see for yourself, Kulaba is empty but for a handful of Mussalman and Topikar sipahis who are manning the garrison and a few guns.'

'Well, I will ascertain the truth of that for myself,' Pandurao says, striking the man on the side of his head with a short baton that is suddenly in his hands.

'Why are you betraying him? Why should we trust you?' Pandurao prompts the lame man.

'Saheb, look at me. Lost my leg to a Firangi's bullet. What did he do? Invited my young son for service. Where is my son now? Dead. In a war? No: while practising horse riding. Trampled to death. For what reason? My family is finished. What can I do now? He will eat up every Konkani child to feed his own ambition.'

Pandurao is impressed: the lame man is much smarter than he looks, not that he has been chosen for his intelligence, he has been chosen for his desperation and lust.

'Wazir Saheb, in this matter this creature speaks the truth. The jungle around Bankot has been felled and is being prepared as a plantation, and felling has started in the jungle behind Hirakot,' Pandurao says.

'Is he personally planting the trees? How do we know if his sardars are with him?' Kasim shouts with surprising and sudden vigour.

'His pack of fishermen will definitely be with him. I will find out about Piloji from the goldsmith—they meet almost every day. Anyway, Surya Koli is the one to watch out for.'

'Yet, if this Angria would have submitted to the only true God, he could have been one of my sardars or a killedar of a fort,' Kasim says between moans.

'He is doing very well for himself, after all, he is amongst his own kind: what with him having lost his caste as a child. He would eat with the cowherds and potters. On one occasion I saw him accepting a packet of food behind the gurukul, *jhinga* no doubt, from the scavenger's son. Can you imagine that? The scavenger's son,' Pandurao scoffs.

'All men are equal in the eyes of Allah,' Kasim proclaims lazily and then, realizing the nature of the hands massaging him, adds: 'except for slaves of course, whom Allah commands to dutifully serve.'

'This is your chance, Wazir Saheb, willed by Allah himself, if I dare say so. Once you take Kulaba, Kanho will be at your feet, begging to be circumcised and turned to your true God,' Pandurao says.

'I would wear it around my neck and give him a daughter and make him a sardar,' Kasim says, sinking into a fantasy.

'Then I shall see to the whereabouts of Piloji and his other sardars,' Pandurao says, satisfied with his day's labour.

'Do that, while I decide what needs to be done,' Kasim says as his meaty hand grabs a posterior.

The lame man almost slips off his rudimentary crutch before replacing it in his armpit and hobbles off behind Pandurao Phangaskar.

The Lion Attacks

It is the night of Purnima in the month of Shravan. A throng of dark clouds crowds the night sky, and the moon is nowhere to be seen. After the evening prayer, Kasim, the Yakut Khan, proceeds from his unimpeachable fort; he takes his ambitious sons with him and leaves the dullest one behind. Who can one trust in this ephemeral life? And to what lie their loyalties? Though covered from his neck to his toes in a billowing white tunic, a thick crimson silk sash at his waist and a matching turban, Kasim feels naked outside Janjira's walls. His northbound dhow is painted black and covered with yellow spots to emulate the hide of a leopard and match those worn by his Habshi bodyguard. From the bow of his dhow, he can see the vessels of his commander Amabat Khan approaching from Mazgaon and heading to Sarjekot Fort on the northern tip of the rock that houses Kulaba Fort.

The tide is high and Kasim directs his fleet to the eastern side of the rock where the Mahadarwaza and the entrance to the fort lies. Mistaking the lame man's information for a prophecy on the auspicious outcome of the battle, Kasim waits for the hunter's moon to show itself. Startled by the fleet of dhows, the fisherfolk on the mainland, who have come out to venerate the sea by floating their diyas on it and make their oblations, run, escaping to the safety of the jungles behind their homes as the garrison at Hirakot Fort shuts its main doors. Fire signals and messages race south to Suvarnadurg. The short-handed killedars of Kulaba, Sarjekot and Khanderi shut their gates and race to ready the garrison and the gunners.

As the moon pops out from behind a low cloud, Kasim's massive fist falls and the gunners on his dhow light the charges to their 20-lb and 30-lb cannons. As the dhow jerks with the simultaneous kick of ten gun carriages, Kasim steadies himself by hugging a mast. A pair of attendants rush to his aid but he brushes them off. Then he makes his way portside and seats himself on a cushioned chair. A woman with a large ostrich feather fan cools his back as a slave boy massages his feet.

'Make sure,' he commands his Chief Gun Captain, 'to not harm the dargah of Haji Kamaludin.'

The Gun Captain is perplexed. He hasn't a clue as to where the dargah is situated. He thinks of asking the Wazir but instead takes refuge in prudence and issues orders for the cannons to be knocked a few degrees lower.

The Siddi is offered two wads of cotton wool topped with plugs of wax and he sticks them into his ear canals. His gunners are still swabbing their cannons when another attendant brings him a small china cup of coffee spiced with cardamom and cinnamon. He eggs his gunners on with bilious threats and sweet inducements as they run up the carriages and load their second shots. The rusted iron shot thunders out towards the eastern walls of Kulaba Fort to barely pox their basalt surface. Strengthened at the orders of Chhatrapati Shivaji himself, the walls of Kulaba are made with interlocking basalt stones with such precision that it did not require the use of any lime mortar. Kasim immediately sees that this fort is kin of his own ancient fort and settles down with a second cup, this time filled with rumbullion, a truly martial spirit. For three watches, Kasim drinks cup after cup as he watches in vain and growing frustration. His sanguine elements are diluted and replaced with bile and wrath as he realizes that breaching the Mahadarwaza or the walls of Kulaba is impossible. The gunners on the ramparts of Kulaba Fort have not bothered with his dhows and instead concentrate their infrequent but accurate firing on any attempts by the Wazir's troops to land on the island. Frustrated, Kasim commands his dhows to head to the town of Alibag on the mainland.

As his troops disembark on the mainland, those residents of Alibag that have the time to reach it and the status to be afforded entry, seek refuge behind the robust sloping walls of Hirakot. Unable to find sufficient inhabitants to vent his fury and frustration upon, Kasim orders his troops to attack the most loyal sentinels of the coast: the coconut trees and the fruit trees farther inland. Their scimitars and swords join the axes already at work and chop away at the slim towering coconut trees. Many of his men are crushed and mangled by crashing trees their confederates have cut down nearby. Many of the trees smash into the nearby huts, some of which burst into flames sparked by kitchen fires that had been hurriedly abandoned inside them. Kasim then turns the cannon that had been unable to breach the walls or the gate of Hirakot on to the orchards of mango, cashew nut and jackfruit that surround it. The cannonballs explode out thundering and then whistle through the orchards, splintering the old trees with crashing groans and crushing thumps.

All around there is carnage and cacophonic chaos: donkeys braying, goats bleating, cows and buffaloes mooing while riderless horses run terrified through the pockets of fire and swathes of smoke. As each shot rings out, Kasim's mind racks up the cost of dressed stone and cast-iron shot that is failing to bring him any return. In the darkness, Kasim raises his palm and a feather-liveried boy with a drum strapped to his waist and a kudu horn dangling by his side, raises the horn and blows a mournful note into it. As the note is relayed by a series of similarly avian boys, the firing comes to an end.

'All of you, gunners and captains included: go into the jungle and find some saleable specimens and take what cattle and livestock you can. Go earn your keep,' Kasim commands.

'Masons and carpenters,' he shouts behind them, 'we need masons and carpenters.'

The skilled and nimble hands of stone and wood workers are a valuable and rare commodity, and an Omani client of Kasim's, a chief and veritable king of his people, is planning to make a haveli on the island of Zanzibar. Kasim and his sons head to the Datta Mandir to denude it of its accumulated wealth and find favour with their iconoclastic and invisible God.

Pillage

The moment the first report of the attack flutters into Kanhoji's hands, he immediately sails north for Kulaba. But he knows it is too late. Kasim has by then already returned to the safe confines of Janjira but leaves a sizeable portion of his fleet with Amabat Khan, who having failed with Sarjekot, is now attacking the rocky outpost of Khanderi supported by their guns at the twin island of Undheri. Kanhoji's pennant still flies atop the bastion at Kulaba, and he is glad to see her walls barely marked.

Arriving back at Hirakot only by morning, he is shocked to see all the coconuts and large fruit-bearing trees have also been destroyed. Some seemed trampled by elephants and others were burnt at their roots. Cannon had been turned on the orchards and doubly decimated. Branches and trunks litter every yard and footpath. It looks like a tidal wave of fire and stone has laid waste to the shore.

Gangadhar solemnly informs Kanhoji that more than 800 coconut trees have been destroyed.

'*Kalpas* of growth eradicated,' Gangadhar says in dismay.

'What is done is done,' Kanhoji says, his eyes welling up.

'Gangadhar, I want you to appoint one of your boys to liaison with the *talati*. All the trees are to be replanted and those that have lost them, compensated fairly,' he says.

'From where, Saheb?' Gangadhar wonders aloud, then bites his lip to halt his regrettable question in its tracks.

Kanhoji glares at Gangadhar as he removes the gold rings from his ears, and hands them over to him saying: 'The silver in my kitchen.'

Gangadhar knows better than to trifle with Mathurabai's wrath, he will approach the Mahapurush and suffer the interest instead.

To attack on a festival day is a cheap and desperate attempt by Kasim and it does not tender mercy.

Distrust

Tarabai is rarely at Satara. She makes her way from one allied fortress to the next in screened howdahs, making sure the loyalties of the sardars are on her side. Her vigour and virility is noted. It has become prudent to pay the Old Man's commanders to betray their side or leave the field at the opportune time. The *tijoris** are dry: drained by horse, shot and powder. Back at her palace in Satara, Rani Tarabai holds court as Ramchandra Pant hovers over her in his stiff and spotless pagdi. She has dealt with the petitioners and ambassadors for the day and is waiting for Dhanaji's envoy Balaji, to arrive in Satara from the Karnatak with news and payments for the treasury.

'Kaka Saheb, what do we do with this Angre? I was gone for a week, and we have four complaints against him. I should call him to Satara or maybe go down to Kulaba myself.'

'No, Rani Sahiba, you should command him to come when you wish to, but there is no need for it.'

'No need? He will jeopardize all the treaties we have with these traders. Who will we get the guns and cannon from then? He is needlessly antagonizing them. Why did he take the Angrezi ship?'

'The duties of the Konkan are rightfully ours, and he has been collecting them for the first time with any real effect. We need it,

---

* Coffer.

Rani Sahiba, there is no tax to be collected from the Desha, as things stand.'

'But what of the treaty? Does it not exempt them? And what of the other ship he took?'

'That belonged to the Firangi traders. They are not exempt. And Rani Sahiba, it was a ship of thirty bronze cannon. Ten of which he immediately sent up to us. No doubt he should have sent more but let's not forget that he is a steady source of revenue.'

'They will stop selling us guns and cannon, Amatya Saheb, mark my words.'

'Angre is rightfully confiscating all the weapons he finds on the foreign ships and supplying them to us. He has a factory supplying us the best barud. Anyway, Rani Sahiba, there are two or maybe more Angrezi companies and who knows which one has the treaty?' Amatya Pant says, relaying Kanhoji's confusion.

'All barud is rightfully our property anyway. I wonder how much he keeps for himself? He may become a danger,' Tarabai worries.

'Dangerous he is, but also naive: childlike. It's all guns, horses and women for him. He doesn't understand politics.'

'What if he is led astray and betrays us?'

'That is a risk you run with every sardar. I know he is a bhakt of Chhatrapati Shivaji Maharaj and that is what will always work in your favour with him,' the Amatya Pant assures her.

'But he made a treaty with Siddi Khairiyat on his own, and was conveniently unavailable when we lost Gopalgad,' the Rajmata adds.

'We cannot micromanage the Konkan from here, leave him to his own devices. But you are right, he is becoming much too rich, and we never truly know how much he sends up and what he keeps for himself or gives Dhanaji without our knowledge.'

'What can we do?' the Rajmata asks sincerely.

'I will send a mazumdar to audit him. It will give us some idea as to what he is up to.'

'Yes, but it must not look like we don't trust him. I am scared he will strike out on his own and we will be left dry.'

'Then make him the Sarkhel, after all, it is the role he is successfully managing. He will be indebted to you forever. It's what he wants more than anything.'

'No, this is not the time to give him even more power. I can't imagine the jewellery his wives wear.'

'They fight to be as well kept as his killedars' wives, Rani Sahiba. He still lives poorly and if not for his mount or his demeanour, one would not . . .' Amatya Pant trails off.

'It's the demeanour that troubles me,' she says pursing her lips.

'Don't worry, there is not much he can do on land. Leave him to his *chowpatty**.'

The chamberlain announces that Dhanaji Jadhav's son Chandrasen has arrived. He is asked to be presented and is immediately ushered in. He bows in namaskar to Tarabai and touches the Amatya's feet.

'Where is Balaji Vishwanath?' Bawdekar asks Chandrasen.

'With Baba, whose new pastime is to rear snakes,' Chandrasen says sullenly.

'Chandrasen,' Amatya Pant admonishes his friend's son: 'Balaji is a competent and diligent employee of your father's. He is not your replacement.'

'Kaka, tell Baba that. He reposes all his trust in Balaji and none in me.'

'Anyway, not in front of Rajmata,' the Amatya says as he directs Chandrasen to stand below Tarabai's throne and address her directly.

'Rajmata, my father sends his salutations to you and wishes you a long life,' Chandrasen says sulkily.

'I am honoured, how is he faring in the Karnatak?'

'We are always on the move, picking on them constantly and striking them when they least expect it. A network of spies informs us of their movements, and we are always a step ahead of their armies.'

'What does your father send to the treasury?'

'What we could take from the Mughals.'

---

* Beach.

'And by way of Chauth?'

'Nothing, Your Majesty. The countryside is ablaze. The peasants have run away, their fields trampled by the elephants of the Mughal army. There is no Chauth to be had in the time of war.'

'It is the collection of Chauth that truly indicates that you have won a victory. Swaraj cannot survive on looted enemy convoys alone. We must have the Chauth.'

'We are trying, Rajmata, but their forces are limitless, and they have better cannons and muskets. Father has requested heavier cannon. Bronze not iron.'

'So has every other sardar. They take the Rajmata's palace for a foundry and her ministers for blacksmiths. There is no cannon to be had: bronze or iron,' Bawdekar interrupts.

It's all that everybody wants and needs and though he understands, he is helpless to do anything about it.

'We will all have to be responsible for acquiring our own artillery pieces by taking them from the Mughals,' he continues.

'Well, maybe you can request Kanhoji Angre to spare some from his stockpile. He takes them from the Topikars and wastes them on his fishing boats.'

'Has he sent nothing to your father?' asks Amatya Pant.

'Not for years now. Will you request him?'

'We are,' Tarabai snaps, irritated by the oafish son of her foremost sardar. She still prefers him to Dhanaji's usual agent, Balaji Vishwanath. She finds him haughty and too sure of himself and does not trust his face and his cat eyes.

'Anyway, you better hurry back to your father before he adopts that grey-eyed snake for a son,' Tarabai smirks and almost laughs at Chandrasen's dropped jaw. Bawdekar gives her a look demanding restraint and decorum. Chandrasen takes his leave and Bawdekar again approaches the foot of the throne.

'By saying such things, you plant a seed of rivalry between Chandrasen and Balaji. Balaji is a very intelligent and industrious man, it would do Chandrasen good to have him by his side.'

'Kaka, that man is far more ambitious than you think. Chandrasen will be better served watching his back.'

'As a queen, you cannot let whims and personal prejudices get in the way of efficiency. Your duty is to keep everybody united.'

'He just gives me an uncomfortable feeling. I don't know why.'

'It is just a whim. He is a sharp boy and loyal. He should rise through the ranks to the level where he can do the utmost for the rule and success of your son, the Maharaj.'

'And for himself too. Kaka, write to all the Topikars: Firangi Angrezi and every other one. We need muskets and light cannon—as many as they can sell to us. And to Angre, too, tell him we need more muskets.'

A Fishing Trip

Trimbukji Meghji and four of his sweat-drenched partners from Rajapuri are at Kulaba. They have hurriedly dashed south demanding to meet Angre immediately. It is an emergency they say in unison. One of their paus, over 400 tons, has been detained on its way back from Aden despite having a Maratha dastak. The Angrez have taken the vessel and moored it at their docks at Palva Bandar, on the eastern side of the archipelago.

Surya leads the distraught Trimbukji and his associates up to Kanhoji who has been disposing of a captured Angrezi ship called the *Success* to a consortium of Javan traders. As the Javans leave to take possession of their frigate, Kanhoji turns to Trimbukji's delegation.

'I have already heard about it. They took it on the high seas. Don't worry, Trimbukji. I will get your ship back.'

'We heard you have been detaining every vessel that carries their flag. What chance is there of them returning the ship, Saheb? Your cargo is also on that ship.'

'Trimbukji. I am hurt at how little you trust my word or have faith in me,' says Kanhoji, twirling the ends of his moustache.

'It's not that, Saheb,' Trimbukji says embarrassed.

'Please understand that the most valuable article they have detained is my dastak, my guarantee. We will have what is ours back. Give me some time and you will have your pau back, unmolested.'

'We will pray for your success,' Trimbukji says, as he leads his distraught and disheartened partners away.

'We should strike at their warehouses. We can distract them with a naval attack and then come in from the north from Parel, flatten their warehouses and burn Palva Bandar. Or we can just land at Walkeshwar. They are defenceless and exposed from all sides,' Piloji suggests as the traders leave.

'No, no, Piloji. We don't want to frighten them away—much less get rid of them. We just need to remind them where they are, like we did with the Firangis of Goa and the Topikars of Vengurla.'

'How?' wonders Piloji in a lemon-coloured pagdi.

'Let's go fishing. We haven't since we were children. Let's all go fishing. Take all the galbats and ghurabs we have here,' he tells Surya.

'Should I call for more from Gheria?' asks Piloji.

'No need for that, I think we have a sufficient number here. But take food stores for a week, rice and oil. We are going to have a week-long sojourn in the sea.'

'Saheb, this command you need to communicate yourself as I have no idea what you are thinking about. Let me assemble all the men and you tell them yourself because they will not take me seriously,' Surya says perplexed.

Kanhoji and Piloji return to their game of *Shatranj** as Surya leaves to assemble the captains.

* * *

A cool breeze blows over a languid sea. The sun is restrained in his splendour. At dusk, he wears a cape of pink that darkens to purple at the hemmed horizon. Piloji has tied a matching turban and climbs aboard Kanhoji's ghurab with his checkered board and wooden pieces in hand. The fleet of several galbats and four ghurabs leaves Kulaba, with every fishing boat in the vicinity following them eagerly.

---

* Chess.

As Piloji jumps his horse in front of a *paidah**, Kanhoji instructs the fishing boats to form a chain on the eastern side of the archipelago reaching all the way to the mouth of the Ulhas River. Piloji's chariot is taken off the board as Kanhoji is told that the ghurabs have been anchored on the road to Palva Bandar and linked with chains and the galbats positioned at suitable intervals behind the fishing boats.

Pausing the game, Piloji accompanies Kanhoji to the prow where they cast a fishing net into the bay. Every Maratha vessel follows suit. The Sarnaubat Kanhoji Angre is fishing, the nets cannot be crossed. They return to their game and sacrificing his elephant, Kanhoji sends Surya with a detachment of vessels to similarly block the traffic of all vessels sailing south past Bandora and Mahim Island.

Kanhoji and Piloji play from dawn to dusk. Stopping only to shoot at the sea birds flying overhead or to spear turtles for shark stew. The daily feasts include sweet estuary crustaceans fried with chilli powder, pomfret poached in coconut milk, gelatinous bombils battered in rice flour, consumed around fires made in large cauldrons, drinking and making randy jokes. Piloji accompanies Kanhoji every afternoon to a different vessel to a share a meal with his people. Of course, Piloji will not tell his wife that he ate with Topashis and Agaris, Pathans and Bhandaris, Kolis and Habshis.

As Piloji loses the second game, the coastal vessels that bring the goods in from the Desha to Palva Bandar languish at nearby mainland ports, while some seek southern ports. The large East Indiamen the Angrez have, wait empty at Palva Bander, not having any cargo to take on. The third game, which Piloji is winning, is interrupted by a letter from Seth Ramaji Kamath.

'Ramaji says there is panic in the town and the Angrez are worried sick,' Piloji summarizes Ramaji's letter to his sardar.

'Why? Does Kamadhenu not graze on their rocks? Tell them to grow their cotton on the sand, pluck their cloves and cardamom from the *saru* trees. At Walkeshwar they can pan salt and saltpetre.

---

* Pawn.

Their ships, they can fix with wood from mangrove forests. Why are they complaining?' Kanhoji asks.

'Is that what you want me to write?' Piloji asks, laughing.

'Of course, exactly what I have said. He will, I am sure, get the message across to them.'

They are tied now at two games each. Kanhoji gives the command for the fishing fleet and his own galbats to leisurely withdraw whilst approaching all the jetties around the archipelago in a gentle feint. Rustomji Dorabji arrives wet in a rowboat flying a white flag. He says Gayer has lost his senses in fear. He is made to play Piloji as Kanhoji watches.

'Trimbukji's pau must be returned forthwith before any dialogue can be initiated,' the Sarnaubat says as Rustomji loses his first *piadah*. Rustomji pleads that a rift within the Company has messed up their affairs and put their Surat faction at loggerheads with the rightful one in Bombay. Rustomji begs Kanhoji to give an audience to their General as he loses his first elephant.

The Company of Merchants

The damp castle, amidst overgrown lawns, suffocates in thuggish weeds. Within the tallow-lit offices of the general of the Company, Rustomji is having a difficult time convincing General Gayer to meet the Maratha Sarnaubat. It was easier convincing him to return Trimbukji's pau.

'They can have their bleeding boat but why do you want me to meet Cornerjee!' Gayer says horrified.

'It will be wise and prudent, Your Honour,' Rustomji advises.

'What if . . .' Gayer, searches for an excuse.

'General Gayer, it is not the question of ending the blockade, which he has already done unilaterally for the pau. He is making a point and it would behoove the future success of the Company if you would meet him at Kulaba and straighten things out.'

'I don't think that is a prudent course of action—to descend into the mouth of a muggermachch*. I think not, dear fellow, I think not.'

'I will be with you, sir, and there is no danger at all. The Sarnaubat is an honourable man. He will never harm you while you are a guest of his. It is just not done here, and it is definitely not his style—you have nothing to worry about.'

'Can he not come here to the castle?'

---

* Crocodile.

'Sir, he is the Sarnaubat of the Marathas, having independent charge of the North Konkan—there is no way he will come to you. You must go to him. Please understand that Bombay is undefended. He can attack us from any direction.'

'Sonnerbats are nothing. I outrank him for am I not equivalent to a Sennerpotty? He must either come here . . .' Gayer trailed off pretending to look for something on his desk.

'That is a matter of contention, Mr President, and he definitely does not see it that way. The problem is that he is more than just a sarnaubat: he takes his duty very seriously, sir. Here, they,' correcting himself, 'we, call it Dharma, righteous duty.'

'Reynolds, then. On behalf of the directors, I shall send Reynolds. I personally should not leave Fort George. It would be most unbecoming.'

'Honoured sir, I still advise it should be you.'

'Your advice is goodly noted, Patel, but William speaks some of their tongue and has better knowledge of their customs and protocols, he has been in the Indies much longer than I have.'

'Sir, I know all the protocols and can guide you as far as customs go and will be your personal translator. Please understand that he will not take a person of middling authority seriously.'

'Reynolds is not of middling authority; he is my number two. As it is, Sir Nicolas Waite at Surat has ludicrously accused me of privateering! I dare leave Bombay or be seen calling on the Sevajees.'

Rustomji can see his General's childlike fear on his face.

'As the head of a trading concern, Your Excellency, you do not have any more influence or authority than any of the Seths as far as Angria is concerned. Anyone less than the man at the top would be insulting to Angria.'

'Reynolds, Rustom, Reynolds will go with you. Call Reynolds.'

William Reynolds is called in.

'You are to meet Cornerjee Angrayer on our behalf,' says Gayer.

'Why me, Your Excellency?' says Reynolds, equally horrified.

'A poltroon is you, Reynolds?'

'Not at all, sir.'

'Then go and meet him. Rustomji Patel will go with you. Just remind Cornerjee of our Treaty of 1698 between the former Sevajee king and ourselves.'

'Chhatrapati Sambhaji, Your Excellency,' corrects Mr Reynolds.

'See, he is well qualified to meet Cornerjee,' says Gayer with the profoundest relief and bundles them out of his dimly lit office.

Aukat

Rustomji Dorabji and Mr William Reynolds leave Palva Bandar the very next day for Kulaba with Trimbukji's pau in tow. Rustomji is dressed in a billowing white tunic that is fastened at the waist with a vermilion cummerbund and a matching pagdi. Reynolds is garbed in the cleanest and least mended vestments he can muster. His woollen pants are alive with scrambling nits itching his thighs to distraction. In the local style, he has worn his sapphire earrings, a gold *vadiyanam* necklace he had acquired from the Coromandel and as many rings as his fingers can accommodate. On reaching Kulaba, they are made to wait overnight—lodged at a clean guest house within the fort.

They are summoned in the late afternoon when the day is at its hottest. They are escorted into an airless vault for the meeting. Even before the Sarnaubat arrives, Reynolds' coat is drenched with sweat, his eyes sting and his entire body itches. When the Sarnaubat arrives, Rustomji and Reynolds formally present Kanhoji with a pair of English-made wheellocks that have unfortunately seen some use. Kanhoji dismisses them with a look of disdain. Reynolds is as courtier-like as Rustomji and makes a deep bowing namaste before he reads out the six-year-old treaty.

'Thank you for reminding yourself of our treaty as you Angrez seem to never remember it or intentionally never keep your word,' the Sarnaubat replies immediately.

'But we endeavour to, Your Lordship . . .' Reynolds begins before he is cut off.

'Who is this man? Where is your Seth?' Kanhoji demands, looking at the blushing Rustomji.

'Saheb, this is Mr William Reynolds, sachiv to our Seth and his confidant. Gayer Saheb has an upset stomach and could not make it and sends his apologies. He has deputed Mr William Reynolds as his ears and his mouth,' Rustomji says, looking embarrassed.

'Red waxy ears he sends me, your Seth,' Kanhoji says to Rustomji as he stares at Reynolds in amusement.

Rustomji bows from the waist in an exaggerated manner and keeps his gaze lowered when he resumes his stance.

'We are at peace with the Firangi, and they can use any of our ports. But we are at war with the Turk, and we will seize and search every vessel that does not carry my dastak. You Angrez may do as you please,' Kanhoji says while looking at Rustomji.

'We do not wish to displease you in any way, Your Lordship,' Reynolds says in Konkani.

'Then do not take me for a fool. You are selling your flag to every trader on the coast and if you continue to do so, I will give you cause to remember my name,' Kanhoji says in a firm tone.

With that the audience is over, and Mr Reynolds and Rustomji are escorted out of the kiln-like room and to their machua docked at the fort's jetty. The cool sea breeze dries Mr Reynolds' sweat-stained cravat and proceeds to choke his sinuses and enphlegm his chest.

'Rustom, he means business, that boy,' Reynolds says as soon as they are well out of earshot.

'I hope you can relay your emotion to His Excellency the President.'

'I will try, but by St Crispin, do we have something on our backs now.'

'He is very serious and not a boy. And it isn't about money and when it isn't about money, it is most dangerous,' Rustomji says.

Reynolds is shivering in a fever by the time they reach the jetty at Palva Bandar and make to General Gayer's office where its incumbent is eagerly waiting for his envoy. By the end of their meeting, Gayer has a cold too and he struggles through the next day as he writes a letter to Kanhoji besieging peace, cordiality and increased trade. He promises that while he is at Bombay, he will ensure that there is no abuse of their permit or flag.

In a few days, Gayer receives a gentle request from Kanhoji: make half a dozen bronze twenty-pounder cannons available for purchase, and he also asks the Company of Merchants of London to reconsider his previous demand for a gunpowder workshop near their compound.

Aurangzeb Is Dead

The next year, unbeknownst to Kanhoji, Balaji goes to meet Chhatrapati Sambhaji's son, Shahu. Dhanaji Jadhav has been grating against the youthful Rajmata's constant demands on him and is looking for an alternative. He assigns Balaji to a secret mission to meet Shahu. A prisoner along with his mother Yesubai, he had also been captured by the Mughals when they had captured and brutally killed his father. For the past fourteen years, he has been living the life of a Mughal nobleman at Agra where he is much favoured by Shahzadi Jahanara. The Padishah's sister felt that with the right education and cultural conditioning, the boy could one day grow up to be the Mughal Subedar his grandfather had refused to become. Dressed as a pilgrim, Balaji takes a longer and safer route as he makes his way north, accompanying caravans of traders going to Jaipur from Surat, entirely avoiding war-torn Malwa.

He arrives at Mathura, one of the Sapta-puris. Keshava Deva Mandir has been replaced by the Old Man's Shahi Eidgah, but he takes a darshan of the land underneath and spends a few days in that holy city staying at Vishram Ghat. He takes a river barge south to the imperial capital where a teardrop reflects on the still waters of the Jamna. Arriving at Agra, Balaji switches to urbane attire and heads straight to Shahu's apartments. He spends a week with the young prince, first trying to ascertain whether he is indeed the son of Chhatrapati Sambhaji and next as to where his loyalties lie. Undoubtedly, he resembles not only his father, but his grandfather too, not that Balaji has seen either, though his skin seems much lighter and his jawline softer than the stories. The prince is fluent in Marathi and speaks it to his native retainers and is surprisingly well informed about what was happening in the Dhakkan—in fact, it seems to be his only obsession along with an admiration of his grandfather whom he reveres and deifies. Convinced that Shahu is bona fide, Balaji takes his leave from Agra after meeting Rajmata Yesubai and proceeds back to Dhanaji's camp in the Dhakkan.

After briefing Dhanaji, Balaji takes personal leave and proceeds to meet Brahmendra Swami in whom he confides the details of his latest mission. Swamiji is pleased to hear that the prince has grown up to be an urbane and sophisticated man and is still very much in love with his people and country. Before Balaji can leave the next day, Swamiji dispatches four disciples of his to Agra with a *jeneu*[*] and a silk langot for the prince and a letter addressed to Shahu in which he writes: 'You will overcome all opposition and rule in peace.'

* * *

At the ashram, it is evening, and his closest acolytes and most influential devotees assemble to hear the Mahapurush speak. Brahmendra Swami is smiling, there is a calm to his features and a mettle in his voice. His will is coming to pass.

'Did you feel the earth shake a few days ago?' he asks his coterie. The hall is sparkling with chandeliers and the upholstery is cream-coloured silk filigreed with gold thread.

'It was not an earthquake, but the fall of a titan, for never again will any of that house match him in might.'

He reminds his audience to sip the offered sherbets.

---

[*] Sacred thread worn by twice-born Hindus.

'The House of Chagatai, through much experience, readies for the civil war that will now surely render the family apart, as the three remaining shahzadas will fight for that magnificently bejewelled throne, cleaving court and trampling over fields for it. Each fratricidal shahzada will divide the empire into different factions, each noble gambling the lives of his kin and their fortune to the shahzada they have chosen to bet on. Reprisals and revenge will come later with high positions and power redistributed to the winning son's faction. Castes will rise and banking dynasties fall, ancient forts will be abandoned to tigers and their fields will fall fallow. In other backwaters, dense jungles will be felled to build new palaces for the promoted. This is the legacy of a family cursed, when on the frigid steppes of the north—many, many hundreds of years ago—a young boy called Temujin shot his brother dead with an arrow.'

An acolyte, previously instructed to enter at the word arrow, arrives with a letter.

Thrones

Aurangzeb's eldest son Azam is declared the Padishah, and the Friday prayer at Dilli and Agra is said in his name. In Kabul, where his brother Muazzam is governor, the prayer is said in his own name as he mobilizes for war. The Governor of the Dhakkan, their younger brother Kam Baksh, whose mother Udaipuri Bai they know to be their father's favourite, mints coins in his own name declaring himself Shahenshah. Dhanaji Jadhav is focused on acquiring these *mohurs** as he waits for Balaji to return from Ahmednagar with Shahu Raje. Balaji has been sent with a company of Silhadars and told to meet Shahu and his retinue and guide them back to Dhanaji's camp.

An ochre sun of chaos and confusion bathes the days. Unsurety grows like weeds, and the farmer pays his tax to as many groups of armed collectors as accost him till at last, he is forced to give away his cattle, wife, child and then his own body like Raja Harishchandra of yore. Pindaris roam the countryside, and everywhere death and ruination are but a hoof beat away. The mornings and evenings are still cool, but the days are starting to get hotter. Shahu Raje and his retinue are disguised in the robes of mendicants but make for a curious sight riding on the Arab mares gifted by Zeenat un-nissa.

---

* Gold coin.

Balaji has a palkhi for his own use, though he prefers to walk beside Shahu Raje's milk-coloured mare.

They have ridden for three days, heading east to Beed and then they turn south towards Latur. The news of Chhatrapati Shahu's return spreads ahead of their convoy, disseminated by Balaji and he is encouraged by the response their king is getting. Shahu Raje is initially excited, but his discussions with Balaji now leave him with an equal amount of anxiety.

Walking in the dust, his head at his mounted master's feet, Balaji apprises Shahu on the situation back home.

'Rani Tarabai is an ambitious woman, and she has Ramchandra Pant by her side. She has drunk from the cup of power and the liquid it holds is stronger than blood or even duty. We cannot just yet walk back into Satara,' he says to Shahu on his wondering why they were not headed straight back.

'What about Raigad?'

'Raigad is in ruins, and it is not the question of a fort or a palace for your use, but acceptance by all the sardars that you are the true claimant for the throne.'

'But We are. Are We not? And as beloved Tai's regency is no longer required, should she not retire with my cousin with my gratitude and in dignity and peace?'

'Her dignity is her power, and she is not going to just give it away, Raje. You will have to force her hand.'

'How?'

'By making sure all the right people support you. You already have Dhanaji's support, but it is Amatya Pant whose support you most need.'

'We will receive it,' Shahu Raje says confidently as he silently prays for it to pass.

'The Mohites may always support her, but you need to convince the Ghorpades, the Pingales, Khando Ballal and the Chitres, the Shirkes, the Ghatges and lest I forget: Kanhoji Angre.'

'Kanhoji who? I have never heard of the man,' Shahu replies.

'A sarnaubat in the Konkan, he holds Kulaba, Suvarnadurg and Sagargad for the Marathas and a true devotee of your revered grandfather.'

'Well, then he is on our side,' smiles Shahu Raje.

'Therein lies the problem, my king: you have a cousin, and he too is the grandchild of Shivaji Maharaj. Pardon me, but it's why the Badshah let you go.'

Shahu turns around to look at Balaji who is begrimed in sweat and dust and nods pensively.

'I know, Balaji, I know it only too well. I will not allow it because it's not about fighting each other or even the Turk but working together in service of the Empire.'

Balaji shoots a nervous glance at his sovereign.

'A Maratha Empire, my lord, under thee,' Balaji says solemnly.

Shahuji laughs, replying: 'Go now to your palkhi before you leave your feet on the stones.'

Civil Wars

In Satara, Amatya Pant hears of Shahu's release and proceeds to the Rajmata's apartments to inform her. The Regent Queen fingers a chain of Basra pearls as she hears the news.

'The Old Man persecutes us from his grave. It is another ruse, and this boy is a pretender and an impostor,' Tarabai responds immediately.

'We cannot tell for sure, Rajmata, we will have to wait and see,' responds Amatya Pant, having expected the response. The addiction to power trumps all else.

'How dare you? That is treason,' Tarabai screams, tearing the pearls from her neck and flinging them aside.

'There is nothing to see. Shahuji died years ago: slowly poisoned by opium. This is a Mughal trick to divide our sardars and destroy the Swarajya. You are my Peshwa and the Hukumat Panah to my son. How can you even entertain the thought? You know better, Amatya Saheb.'

'I am the Peshwa of all Marathas,' Amatya Pant thinks to himself.

'Dhanaji Jadhav is convinced that this is the real Shahuji,' the Pant says.

'I doubt he's even Maratha. This Mughal usurper is nothing but a ploy to destroy us, destroy the Swarajya.'

'Rajmata, we have to wait and see how the sardars react,' he advises.

'I will not wait. Call them all to Satara. I want to meet them and have their assurances that they will not abandon the true Bhonsale, their Chhatrapati.'

'I will see to that, Rajmata, but please do not forget that both you and I are at the service to the Rajya, and it is our duty to keep it secure. The Mughals are in a civil war and are trying to send us in the same direction when they are vulnerable.'

'Exactly, we should be attacking them instead of giving any weight to this ploy of theirs. Shahu or not, any other claimant to the throne is our biggest enemy right now. So, forget about this man and carry on with the work of statehood.'

'I do not disagree with you there, Rajmata,' the Amatya Pant concurs.

'One more thing, issue a firman. Kanhoji Angre is from this day forward the Sarkhel of the entire Maratha Navy. Do it now and send it off to him before it is too late and Dhanaji's man gets to him,' Tarabai says suddenly.

'A wise decision, Rajmata,' the Pant says, hearing the first good news of the day.

'I am told that it is Balaji Bhat who is escorting Shahu back,' he adds.

'That grey-eyed snake. Did I not tell you that he could not be trusted to do any good? I will have his head when the impostor is put in his place along with Dhanaji Jadhav.'

'Rajmata, I humbly beg you, only negotiations must suffice. We cannot afford to attack or antagonize our own sardars, especially Jadhav.'

'Not if they are treasonous, and disclaiming my son is treason of the highest order.'

Amatya Pant, pleading patience and restraint, leaves to do his sovereign's bidding. He makes a mental list of all the sardars and the probabilities of their loyalty as he walks towards his offices. What would the Ghorpades do? Did things always go the way the Ghorpades went? Or did the Ghorpades go the way things went?

He too has been at this game for a long time, from the very beginning. There is no more senior minister than him, no one who has been unstintingly loyal to the House of Bhonsale for this long. He is a high-born Deshashtha Brahmin, he is the first minister and first amongst all ministers. There are no claimants to his position, regardless of it being Tarabai or Shahu, he will still be the Amatya Pant. He is Ramchandra Neelkanth Bawadekar, a man who has breathed the same air as Chhatrapati Shivaji Bhonsale. Now, more than anything, but only in his deepest heart, he wants to hold the grandsons of his king, one in each arm. Suddenly, thoughts of his friend Hambirao flash across his mind, and he goes to find one of his sons, brothers to his Rajmata and undisputed allies in the matter at hand.

Not many kos away, the fields and hamlets burn. The new Badshah Azam Shah is already dead, and his younger brother Muazzam teeters on the throne as Bahadur Shah. While this Badshah's grandfather had been called the king of the world and his father the conqueror of the universe, Muazzam is content with just being brave in this unsure and confusing time. If he, the Pant, cannot find a solution, Shahu Raje will drive Tarabai out of Satara and establish himself here. The Rajmata must leave before Shahu arrives. Go to her family seat in Kolhapur. But she will not listen to him. First, he must write to Kanhoji and tell him of his promotion. For the ports of the Konkan are ever busy as the demand for horses, muskets and silver, like the tides, never abate. The vessels from Chin, Java and Persia sail in every day and those from the west have increased greatly in number. Gold and silver pour into the tijoris of all the traders from Surat down to Calicut and up the other side to Bangal. Even the Siddi at Janjira is subdued, as he lies forgotten by his overlords who are too busy trying to survive themselves.

As the Pant enters his office, his sachiv informs him of Dhanaji Jadhav's death.

'Oh, foul and inauspicious day,' he says massaging his creased forehead. What is that saying about bad news? He mulls to himself as he begins dictating Kanhoji's appointment.

Sarkhel

Surya cuts the second cheek of the mango Dom Alfonso has sent for Saheb. After two successive failures, the sweetness of this year's crop has been unprecedented. For at last, Kanhoji Raje is Sarkhel, and Surya finds the word sweeter than the golden fruit. Raje is attracting every adventurer in the Konkan and beyond as he is not only the most generous employer but also the one with the brightest future. But some are rotten, rude and uncivilized.

One such mercenary, an Angrez called James Plantain, has been appointed by Raje as the captain of all gunnery captains and charged with devising more efficient systems of artillery.

'Surya, enough stomach exercise,' Sarkhel Saheb's voice booms merrily.

They are at Hirakot. Having finished his hatha yoga, Saheb commences with his weightlifting exercises in a grass-covered courtyard with his personal bodyguard. Gangadhar is in attendance with his charcoal pencil and a pad of paper. It is Saheb's practice to meet his men and hold court during his exercises and the subsequent sesame-oil massage. Sarkhel Saheb is rotating a heavy weight around the trunk of his body when Plantain comes forward with two men carrying metals objects.

'Paltanji, I am concerned about the accuracy of our gunners,' Sarkhel Saheb says, putting down the weight.

'Circle Saheb, we are working on that but beyond a point, trying to increase accuracy is meaningless because the galleys and grabs rock on the waves. We need new ordinance like these,' Plantain says pointing to the samples of chained shots. Unlike the usual round lead cannonballs, some have serrated edges, and some are a conglomeration of several shots chained together.

'These are better at dismasting and damaging the sails of a ship than the usual balls. We will train with these once you have had them fabricated,' the captain of gun captains rudely replies.

'Give these samples to Hansuji. Tell him to coordinate with Gangadhar on the moulds and finances,' Sarkhel Saheb says unbothered.

'Yes, Circle Saheb,' Plantain says and takes his leave.

'Ramoji is waiting, Sarkhel Saheb,' Surya reminds Kanhoji of his next order of business.

'Ask Manuji to join us.'

'Yes, Sarkhel Saheb,' Surya says, relishing the sweetness of the sound.

Surya sends a footman to summon Ramoji Pawar and Manuji Castro.

Kanhoji drops the dumb-bells and falls forward on his palms and is horizontal to the ground with his toes supporting his legs. He commences another set of push-ups. Once Castro and Ramoji approach him, he gets up and returns their greetings.

'You have an early start here, Sarkhel Saheb,' Ramoji says.

'Yes, earlier the better and it does not end till late into the night. This is going to be nothing like your life with Bhawanji.'

'Not a moment too soon, Sarkhel Saheb, even if you wouldn't have been given full command, I was planning to come to you.'

'Now you are here without making anyone uncomfortable. See how Khandoba works?'

Ramoji nods in agreement.

'We are going to create a battalion of silhadars. A force of 1000 horses with its own detachment of 500 artillerymen.'

'How many do we have now, Saheb?'

'Only a few hundred. We will need to recruit them from outside. Not from my navy.'

'Are we expecting trouble from the Siddi?' Castro wonders.

'These are troubled times, Manuji, we must be prepared. We need to be as capable on land as we are at sea. Train them thoroughly like you have our snipers and gunners. Paltan will take over the naval arm. Let him work on the ghurabs and galbats.'

'Yes, Sarkhel Saheb, it will be done.'

'Also, find a competent Topikar to head the artillery, and find some burly Pathans to work the guns. Speak to Paltan if you need any help.'

'We will if we need to, Sarkhel Saheb,' Castro says as his eyes meet Surya's. They have seen Plantain trying to impress Angria and take on a larger role than he deserves. Besides being a mutineer, Plantain is Angrezi, and neither trusts him. Ramoji and Castro take their leave as Kanhoji dips into another set of push-ups.

Surya spots a slight man in a dazzling white *angarkha* and a black pagdi enter the courtyard and walk towards the exercising Sarkhel. Seeing Surya, he puts a finger to his lips. He winks at Gangadhar and him as he crosses them and proceeds to sit on Kanhoji's back. Kanhoji turns his head to see who it is and then bucks the man off his back and stands up laughing. The man is flung into the air and caught by the prescient Surya.

'Sarkhel Kanhoji Angria,' the man says once Surya has righted him on his feet.

'Balaji Vishwanath Bhat,' Kanhoji responds and hugs his old friend, wetting his spotless clothes with sweat and sesame oil. Balaji does not shirk and instead hugs him back tightly.

Sarkhel Saheb removes to a bath as Surya escorts Balaji to the residence.

'Why are your eyes grey?' Ladubai asks Balaji as Kanhoji walks in. Surya is laughing by the wall.

'Because when he was young, the Siddi blinded him, so your kaka caught a cat and took its eyes,' Saheb tells his daughter, and her eyes widen in fear as she runs into her father's lap.

'I have joined Shahu Raje, and he has made me the Subedar of Daulatabad,' Balaji blurts out.

'Are you joking? Why?'

'What do you mean why? He is the eldest son of the eldest son.'

'Or a Mughal plant. Have you seen his dingle? Are you sure it's not cut?'

'What are you saying, Kanhoji? The blood of Maharaj runs in his veins as surely as the Narbada flows.'

'I am sorry about Dhanaji Saheb. You must be indispensable to his son.'

'I have had a fallout with Chandrasen. The bastard tied a feedbag full of ashes to my head. I barely escaped with my life.'

The Sarkhel and Surya burst out laughing.

'That bastard. I will kill him the next time I see him,' Kanhoji says.

'No, no. It was providence and because of it, I am now with Shahu Raje as Saheb wanted.'

'Balaji, even if this man claiming to be Shahu is not an impostor, he is compromised because his mother is still with the Mughals. But what happened with that oaf Chandrasen?'

'We were out hunting deer.'

'You and hunting deer?'

'Baba: I want a deer,' Ladubai interjects with the hope of getting one immediately.

'Of course, my sweetheart. I will get you a fawn the next time I go hunting,' Kanhoji promises his daughter.

'If you can believe it. He is always out hunting, and I would have to accompany him. He was just looking for an excuse, the first opportunity to insult me and drive me away. It is my stupidity. I should have left the day Dhanaji Saheb passed. Anyway, Sarkhel Saheb: congratulations on achieving your life's dream.'

'No, no, no, Balaji, it has just begun. Why did you not go to Tarabai?'

'As Sambhaji Raje's son, Shahu Raje is the rightful heir.'

'Let's not get into this argument now Balaji, first eat something and let me show you around.'

'Of course, that's why I am here: to see what new tricks you have come up with, my brother.'

'You are the trickster. Your advice is what I need. Truly, I miss it.'

'Sarkhel Saheb misses you dearly Bhat Saheb,' Surya tells Balaji.

'From what I hear, your Sarkhel doesn't need anybody's advice.'

'Actually, I need your advice on one matter,' says Kanhoji.

'What matter?'

'Tarabai has given me Rajmachi Fort. Just received the firman day before yesterday.'

'But Rajmachi is with Shinde. And he is Shahu Raje's man. It is not hers to give.'

'Exactly. What should I do?'

'See, Kanhoji: even when you don't want to talk about it—it forces itself upon us. We cannot run away from this.'

'I can't betray Rani Sahiba. She has been good to me. She made me Sarkhel.'

'Baba is Sarkhel,' Ladubai says, pulling at Kanhoji's earrings. He removes one and gives it to her.

'I understand your loyalties, Kanho, but do understand you will be called upon to take a side and you will have to not only pick one but stand behind one—actually in between them and in the thick of battle.'

'I don't want to pick a side. This has nothing to do with me. The Bhonsales must work this out between them. Bala, the Old Man is dead, and his sons are killing each other. Now is the time to fix the Siddi and take Janjira once and for all. This is all Aurangzeb's doing. Why would they release him then or at all?'

'Just ignore it then. Forget about Rajmachi.'

'She doesn't let one forget things, Balaji. You know her as well as I do. But you need to keep Shahu Raje off my back at least. This has nothing to do with me.'

'Don't worry about that.'

'I will just delay taking over Rajmachi. That is all I can do. But knowing her, she will ride down from Kolhapur one day and insist I get her in.'

'Her ambitions override her loyalty to the cause, Kanho.'

'She is Hambirao's daughter after all, and she rides and shoots better than you, Balaji.'

'You won't have to worry about this mess for too long. Amatya Pant has also recognized Shahu Raje.'

Then lowering his voice and looking at Surya, Balaji says: 'This does not leave the room, but her days are numbered, Rani Rajasbai has also started to wonder why her son isn't Chhatrapati as he is as much a grandson of Shivaji Maharaj's as Tarabai's is.'

'I hope they all come to an understanding and then get on with fighting the Mughals,' Surya says.

'From your lips to the ears of Khandoba,' Kanhoji tells Surya.

'Kanho, the power is no longer with the Badshah. Those days are gone. The old man's sons aren't even a fraction of their father. Now the Sayyid brothers and Qilich Khan are the centres of power, and they decide which shahzada sits on the throne,' Balaji explains.

The Sarkhel and his shadow shrug.

'I don't give a rat's ass about the damn throne. All I care about is the Konkan. Remember Balaji—*Dilli ast door**. Come; let me show you what I have done here. Nothing compared to what I have at Vijaydurg, but I am very proud of Kulaba too.'

Surya picks his master's daughter up and puts her on his shoulders.

'Baba, Kaka has not eaten yet,' Ladubai reminds her father.

'It's okay, I am not hungry, we will eat later.'

'No, you have to eat now. Ai has made so many things for you.'

They accede to Ladubai's demands and sit down again to find the servants coming in with trays of food. Balaji turns around to

---

* Delhi is yet far.

separate himself from his friend so that his caste will not be broken. Ladubai joins Balaji immediately, spooning more rice on to his banana leaf.

'*Dharambrasht*,' Kanhoji calls out, and the three men laugh to Ladubai's amazement.

'Bhat Saheb, you must come and be with the Sarkhel, none can pay better,' Surya says, having stationed himself outside the room's entrance.

'I'm sure, Surya, as your belly is ample proof,' Balaji retorts and Surya curdles in embarrassment.

Innovations

A grey monsoon has transformed the countryside into a patchwork of glistening black rocks and sparkling emerald leaves. Blinding white salt pans, the dhobi ghats of giant Rakshasas punctuate the coastline interspersed amongst bright dun-coloured beaches and dank mangrove forests. The Count of Sabugosa, incumbent Viceroy of Firangistan follows in the footsteps of his predecessors and readies his native fleet for their transoceanic carracks and galleons to arrive swollen with gold, silver and emeralds from the mountainous jungles on the other side of the planet. They will be escorted up the coast to Chaul, Bassein and then on to Daman and Diu. It is an annual event that coincides with Diwali, and this year Kanhoji is waiting at Gheria. He has freshly retrained gunners and new-fangled artillery. At his command are forty galbats armed with pairs of 12-pounder and 18-pounder cannons at their prow and twelve ghurabs bristling with 20-pounders along their broadsides.

He has used the discord within the House of Bhonsale prudently. Instead of sending their share up to the Desha, he has allocated those funds for the strengthening of his forts' defences, dredging docks and for building roads, water tanks, bridges, *dharamshalas* and temples. With the best pay in the Konkan, he has been able to attract not only the surest horsemen and gunners but also the most skilled masons, carpenters and shipwrights. And when there are no crops to be harvested, or salt to be panned, the sons of farmers and fishermen flock to his forts in search of glory and small coin.

The tide is high and Kanhoji's fleet waits hidden in the creeks and crannies of the Vagothan's estuary. Bound by rock cliffs that hang over unseen inlets, Kanhoji and his men are silent and still. The only sounds that punctuate the repetition of the waves are the frequent slaps against pesky mosquitoes. Ahead, in the sea, the Portuguese armada passes by unaware of their presence. One after another, a fleet of caravels and carracks confidently sails up the Konkan coast. The setting sun witnesses a towering nau from the convoy lurking towards the shallows. Its captain spotting red and yellow eyes shining amongst the mangroves—the possibility of game—has come closer towards the shore at the lip of the estuary to hopefully spot the legendary tiger. Kanhoji, squints back through his eyeglass and catches the dull glint of bronze in the moonlight and then another one a few moments later at the same height: an array of cannon. He signals Plantain to move on it. Plantain sets out with twenty galbats silently rowing to the stern of the lone ship. As they approach the newly constructed carrack, they take up the dreaded U-shaped formation and proceed to fire at the mast of the ship with their recently manufactured chain shots. Kanhoji can hear their unholy whistling in the darkness.

He can hear the yardarms crash on to the deck and the ship is dismasted within the watch. The galbats in reserve with their decks packed tight with Koli boarders, their bodies painted in haldi, and lighter infantry armed with swords and sickles now speed to the stranded nau. Like thousands of ants on a mound of jaggery, the boarding party clamber up the high walls of the ship with grappling hooks and single-pole bamboo ladders. Some men push the cannons on the lower decks in and climb in through the portholes and slash their way up past the unarmed gunners. Overwhelmed by the massive force, the captain surrenders his ship and her thirty-four guns, when his men have no space to swing their swords or raise their muskets.

Plantain presents himself proudly to Kanhoji. Viroji Katkar, who has led the boarding of the ship and had accepted the Portuguese captain's surrender, joins Plantain in accepting Kanhoji's generous rewards. Viroji has brought a few men along with him whom he commends for their bravery and Kanhoji rewards them in turn.

'I am pleased how smoothly and quick that went,' Kanhoji says impressed.

Got the mizzenmast in the second shot and had the main mast cut in half,' Plantain says.

'That you did, Paltanji, but how many men have you lost?' Kanhoji asks.

'Over a hundred, Sarkhel Saheb,' Viroji says

'Spread these around to those who you think did well last night,' Kanhoji says as he gives him rolls of coins in canvas socks.

'We can well surprise them in the dark or while they are near the coast. Now Paltanji, I want to see what you can do a little farther out at sea,' Kanhoji challenges Plantain.

'Sure, Cornerji, that's where all the fat ships are, fresh from Blackwall and Lisbon, not expecting anything but singing mermaids,' he says in English.

'Well, you have nothing to hide behind out there and they will see you coming many kos away,' Kanhoji reminds him.

'They will think we are fishing boats, nothing else,' Plantain says.

'Well, I want some results soon, the sea about the Konkan is under the jurisdiction of the Maratha Chhatrapati, not just the shore and the estuaries. I want you to venture out a little. Get some ships coming in from your homeland so that they understand where they have come to. These waters are not the property of the king of Angrezistan.'

'And we will, sir,' says Plantain.

'What is this sar-sar, Sardar or say Sarkhel Saheb and no khanuji khanuji,' Surya shouts at Plantain who raises his hand in apology.

'Also, Paltanji, try to minimize the loss of life. My men are very important to me so don't be hasty or imprudent with their safety,' Kanhoji says.

'I will take care to do that, Sarkhel Saheb,' Plantain says as he leaves.

Kanhoji calls for the prisoners taken and gives them the option of joining him. Those who don't are sent to the darkest bowels of Vijaydurg. He relieves the ship of its cannon and artillery material and has it dragged to Keki's dry dock upriver.

Viroji and Plantain take an armada of galbats and tow the ghurabs out to sea towards the south-west till they are on the route ships coming in from Socotra take. There they slip out their stone anchors and wait. They take the Angrezi *Grantham* that is on her way to Surat first and drag her back to Gheria. Then return to the same spot in a week to board the *Somers* that has been on her way in from Portsmouth. Kanhoji leads eight galbats and three ghurabs south towards Vengurla. Men willing to board for him are waiting eagerly in the south.

The Season

'Tis the season. The Governor of Bombay's armed yacht, the *HMS Algerine*, departs from Karwar sailing north to Bombay. It is escorting and providing a flag for a fleet of barges carrying a cargo of nutmeg, mace, clove and black pepper. Standing on the bow of the teak deck are the newly married Thomas and Katherine Chown, ecstatic with the luxury of being allowed to journey on the Governor's yacht and the use of his cabin. They watch the dolphins swimming beside their yacht as they hold each other in the happiness that new beginnings always bring. Thomas is an employee of the English trading company and posted at their warehouses in Karwar. Freckled and pug nosed, his flaxen hair mingles with her lighter tresses in the tropical wind.

'Oh Thomas, I feel as if the curse that had bound me has been broken,' says the recently widowed bride.

'Dear Kate, what curse do you speak of? And why speak of curses at all. It is nothing but superstition.'

'Oh, you do not know, Thomas. To be widowed at fourteen in a foreign land, away from all family. To be married again and then to lose my second husband in horrible violence just a few months on?'

'That's all in the past now, dearest Kat. You needn't worry any more. I am with thee now,' Thomas says, kissing his wife on the temple.

Katherine hugs her husband who is fortunately much younger than either of her first two husbands and much closer to herself in age.

'Well, here's hoping the third time's a charm,' she hopes and then curses herself for jinxing it.

'You will be happy, mine love; I will make thee and keep thee. Happy and rich and we'll head home to Kent, a lord 'n' lady.'

'Oh Thomas, I love you.'

'And I thee, Mrs Chown,' Tom says proudly.

Their loving reverie is broken by a whirring sound that culminates in a terrifyingly close smashing and cracking of wood. Thomas looks up to see the top of the foremast crash into the sea. Thomas grabs Elizabeth and they run to the aft of the yacht—every step of theirs, accompanied by distant explosions and the loud and prevalent sound of ripped rigging and tearing of sails and shrouds.

'What is happening?' Katherine whispers to Thomas lest the Grecian gods hear her again.

'Pirates. We are being attacked. Stay below decks till I fetch thee,' he says to his wife as he sends her below deck.

Thomas runs towards the bow of the yacht. Three steps and the top mast comes swinging down like a pendulum and smashes into his head and upper body. The captain of the yacht needn't pull his colours down, they are in tatters on the water around the yacht with her sails. The captain runs aft with a patch of white cloth and waves it at the Maratha galbats that are lined up behind his stern. Kanhoji sends a galbat to the yacht with instructions for taking on board the commander of the vessel along with his officers and bringing them to him. Once the yacht's red-bearded and orange-skinned captain is safe in the Maratha galbat with his Parsi translator and men, Kanhoji gives the order to board the low-slung vessel and search it.

The captain and four of his top officers are taken on to the ghurab Kanhoji has been directing the attack from.

'This is General William Aislabie's yacht, sir, and you have destroyed it without cause.'

The Parsi translator, correctly presuming whom he is standing in front of, is more circumspect.

'Yes, though the cause will be determined. Do you have the dastaks for these barges? Because according to the nakhwas of these barges, either you have them on your person, or they will be found on this vessel,' Kanhoji states.

'A dastak? For the Governor of Bombay's own yacht? We are in treaty with the Sevajees, if that is what you are,' the captain says. The dubash merely informs Kanhoji that it is indeed the yacht of the head Angrezi Seth.

'Did I ask you for a permit for this vessel? I am asking you about these barges that you accompany?'

The Dubash is silent for a moment and then translates it for the captain of the yacht.

'General Aislabie's yacht,' the captain repeats.

'Does that treaty give you permission to undercut us by providing your flag to local merchants?' Kanhoji asks the captain.

'Captain Saheb, the person in front of us is Kanhoji Angria. He is the commander of the Maratha Navy and the Chief in the Konkan. I think you may have heard of him. Sir, he can have Bombay by the end of the day, I would pray caution and deference,' the young Dubash says, dreading a stint in the infamous Vijaydurg prison.

'The pirate,' the captain mumbles back to the Dubash.

'Tell Lord Connajee that these are the goods and cargo of the Company of English Merchants, we have a Royal Charter and a treaty with his queen,' the captain says to the Dubash.

'From whom? From what royal authority? And which queen? Is it from Rani Tarabai or from Rani Rajasbai? As of now, I will even accept one from that impostor called Shahu,' Kanhoji now tells the Dubash.

As the captain turns to open his mouth, the Dubash sternly tells him to shut up. When he tries again, the Dubash shoves the captain and puts a finger to his own lips begging silence. The captain slaps the Dubash.

'Dubash, you may apply for service at the fort, if you wish,' Kanhoji says and then orders his men to arrest the crew and imprison them at Vijaydurg.

Just then, Kanhoji's men arrive with a young woman who is crying.

'Look what we found, Sarkhel Saheb, one of their women.'

'Where is Thomas?' she keeps repeating through her bosom-heaving sobs.

'Who is she?' Kanhoji asks the Dubash.

'She is Katherine Chown, married to one of our factors at Karwar and on her way to Bombay,' the Dubash replies.

'I think he is lying, Saheb, we found her in the owner's quarters,' one of the men says.

'Are you sure she isn't anybody important—the Seth's daughter, perhaps? Why is she on his vessel in his quarters?' Kanhoji asks again.

'It was just the kindness of the General, a gift to young Thomas. She is not General Aislabie's daughter, Saheb.'

'Find her husband and take them with the captain and the other prisoners. She needn't be kept in the jail with the other men. Make her comfortable and make sure she doesn't die.'

Several guards take the English prisoners away to another ghurab as Kanhoji proceeds to board the yacht and give it a look over.

'It is a beautiful boat, isn't it, Surya?'

'That it is, Sarkhel Saheb, and also nimble and swift.'

'But too many riggings and sails, if you ask me, to escape from our mast-busting ordnance.'

'We got lucky the captain did not know it was us. Had he an inkling before we attacked, we wouldn't have been able to catch them.'

'What is that on the hull of that galbat?' Kanhoji points to a galbat that has a black and white banded curving line on the hull just about the waterline.

'Just a design. A snake. I can ask the nakhwa of that galbat why he put it there.'

'Don't bother. It's nice and it is a little confusing, isn't it, Surya, with the sun reflecting off the sea?'

'Yes, it does look like it is the sea level.'

'I want all our vessels to have that black snake painted on to the hull, just above the waterline and thicker.'

'At your command, Sarkhel Saheb, it will be done,' Surya responds.

Kanhoji inspects the yacht and confiscates all her logs and maps. She is lashed to a quartet of galbats that tow her back to the dry dock at Vijaydurg where her ordnance, telescopes and other nautical instruments will be removed along with her exquisite bronze cannons. She will be sold, either back to the Angrez or to a more appreciative buyer.

The House Divided

Rajasbai knows the will, ambition and talent of her co-wife well enough to prevent her from either writing to or meeting any of her supporters. Tarabai is under constant guard within the palace at Kolhapur and not allowed to leave the wing she and her coterie have been assigned. The newly empowered Rajasbai has been too busy negotiating her son's continued existence as the Raja of Kolhapur to bother Kanhoji with any demands. Instead, Kanhoji has received a letter from Amatya Pant who has joined Shahu Raje as his finance minister. In it he makes two requests of Kanhoji: the first is to send the Chauth to Satara and the second is to come and meet him in person, as he wants to discuss naval strategy and the status and interaction with the foreign traders in the Konkan. Kanhoji writes back that he would be delighted to discuss naval tactics that he has been developing for the Maratha Swarajya in the Konkan. He completely ignores the call for paying up any revenues and signs himself as servant to the sons of Chhatrapati Sambhaji.

Instead, he sends confiscated logbooks and cargo manifests, which he has had copied for himself, of European ships they have taken to the Amatya Pant. These documents will better demonstrate the true nature of the quantum of trade in these parts carried on by the various Topikar traders and apprise the Amatya of the stupendous profits the traders are making, even along the coast.

As he has the last of the documents packed in trunks for the Amatya Pant dispatched, he calls in his next appointment.

Sukhdeo has been asked to present himself to Kanhoji. They haven't met for nearly a year, and Angria mistakes him for Lokhande Seth himself.

'I thought your father had taken on a regimen of exercise,' Kanhoji tells the boy.

'It's been two years, Sarkhel Saheb,' Sukhdeo says apprehensively.

'You have never given me any reasons to keep you away from the excellent work you are doing. But now, I have another project for you.'

'At your command, Sarkhel Saheb,' Sukhdeo says relieved.

'People from all over the world come to Vijaydurg now—if not to take a dastak, then to fix their boats, or even sometimes just to meet me,' Kanhoji laughs.

'Yes, Sarkhel Saheb, Vijaydurg has become famous even beyond the Konkan.'

'That it has, with the blessing of Khandoba. We have been able to make it entirely self-sufficient—well almost. All we need now is a facility to make gunpowder.'

Sukhdeo nods in silent understanding.

'I want you to set up a facility for the production of barud within the fort itself.'

'Of course, Sarkhel Saheb. When do you want me to start?'

'Now is as good a time as any other. Come, let me show you the places I have been thinking about,' Kanhoji says as he steps out of his office with Sukhdeo, Gangadhar and Golu in tow. Kanhoji leads them past what looks like a bazaar. But in the wooden structures that would have normally housed shops are offices of translators, money changers, jewellers who can assess the value of any stone or metal, workshops of gold and silversmiths, an office that deals exclusively with timber and his teak forestry projects, and another which is dedicated to metalsmiths and carpenters. They pass Babuji Kotla's large shed, teeming with his apprentice masons and head stonecutters. Next are the blacksmiths and Hansuji's forge and opposite them, the non-marine carpenters. The now wealthy shipwright Kekibhau, lives in Rameshwar—half a kos up the Vagothan River—and works at the dry docks there. Most of his family have moved south to join him there.

The laterite-cobbled street ends at a gravelled path that has stores made with bricks and mortar on either side. They walk south towards the water tank and then turn east to an open area overgrown with bamboo and mustard-coloured weeds.

'What do you think of this place?' Kanhoji says as he points to the unused plot of land he hopes to designate as the gunpowder mills.

'It is as distant a place to the sea and enemy fire that I can find for you,' Kanhoji adds.

'Yes, we can do it here, there . . .' and then Sukhdeo stops speaking and turns around as he hears someone running up to them.

It is Surya, with a scrawny boy in a white langot and two soldiers guarding the boy.

'Sarkhel Saheb, this boy says he has a message for you from Balaji Vishwanath Pant.'

'What is it, boy?' Kanhoji says to the panting bald boy from whose forehead the vibhuti paste marks are now running down into his eyes in ashy rivulets of sweat.

The boy stands on his toes and whispers into Kanhoji's bent ear.

Once Kanhoji has heard him once, he asks the boy to repeat the message. Then, after hearing him a second time, he slips a thin gold ring off his middle finger and palms it to the boy.

'Give him some food and let him rest and then send him on his way when he is ready,' Kanhoji commands one of the guards, and then he addresses Sukhdeo.

'Sorry son, something has come up. But you needn't waste any time or wait for any further orders from me. You can start immediately,' confirming it with a nod to Gangadhar, who like Golu, is always by Kanhoji's side.

Sukhdeo bows in namaskar and takes his leave too.

'All well, Saheb?' Surya asks, reading Kanhoji's face.

'I was dreading this and now they are pulling me into it when I don't want to be a part of it,' replies Kanhoji cryptically.

'Balaji says that Shahu Raje is going to send his senakarte, Bhairoji Pant Pingale, against us.'

'When?'

'Within the week.'

'But Bhairoji Pant isn't a fighter. What made Shahu choose him as senakarte?'

'Hopefully, Balaji. But must they attack us now?'

'But weren't you expecting Shahu to move against us at some point?'

'Yes, but not now. We are being forced to play our hand, Surya. I never wanted to be a part of this family dispute. They need to figure out amongst themselves who I send the revenue up to. This is going to undermine my authority here, will it not?'

'Not if we win,' says Surya smiling.

'Even if we win. It opens up our internal dissensions for others to witness and abuse, and they will rightfully perceive us to be weak and disunited. This is why that *khadoos* Aurangzeb let Shahu free.'

'Well, it looks like you have no choice now, do you?'

'At least we have been informed and won't have our backs to the sea.'

'What is your plan, Sarkhel Saheb?'

'We need to meet them on the way down. We can't leave them to attack our forts one by one.'

'They are bound to come down through Lonavala.'

'Then they will rest at Lohgad: it is close to Kulaba, and it is held by one of Shahu's men—let's meet them there.'

'Gangadhar, take this message for all killedars and send it out immediately: sparing only those garrisons required for maintaining the fort, bring all fighting men and available horses to Kulaba immediately.'

'Surya, get Ramoji Pawar to Kulaba. The time has come for his cavalry to prove its cost and his skill.'

The Senakarte

Bhairoji Pant Pingale isn't a fighting man. His father, like Amatya Pant, has been one of the eight ministers of Chhatrapati Shivaji's original Ashta Pradhan, and Bhairoji has grown up with a pen in his hand. Balaji suggested that it was vital to send someone of reckoning, someone from an old family with impeccable loyalty to the House of Bhonsale, to deal with Kanhoji. Bhairoji is honoured. Nor is he worried. He has heard of Kanhoji's peculiar and impressive ability to attack and board the largest of Firangi ships. But that is on the chowpatty. He will lead soldiers hardened by Mughal battles.

Bhairoji leaves Satara with 1000 mounted Bargis carrying muskets, 2000 light horsemen with lances, 1000 artillerymen wielding heavier guns and another 3000 light infantry. It is a large battle group in the Mughal style: an army of reckoning. He is sure that Kanhoji will surrender upon seeing the massive force at the gates of Kulaba. It is going to be a presentation and display of power and statecraft, and Bhairoji is well versed in these crafts. It takes him a fortnight to reach their camp at the foot of a Y-shaped massif, in the shadows of Lohgad. Here they will re-form before the trek down the ghat.

The commander of Lohgad comes down on his horse with a troop of servants carrying refreshments, mats and entertainers to welcome Bhairoji Pant. Bhairoji complains of the leeches. They are everywhere he says, sitting cross-legged on a charpai—its four legs in thaals of salt. His attendants can't fan him fast enough and the water tastes salty. The Killedar apologizes for the bad water but lists all the foods that have been arranged, by a Brahmin cook, of course.

'I shall rest here today and then tomorrow we shall go to Tungi Gad,' he informs his host.

'Saheb, I shall join you with my men and accompany you to Kulaba,' the Killedar of Lohgad says.

'Be my guest, the more the merrier,' Bhairoji says.

'Saheb, your dhoti, if you don't mind, it is unbelievable,' the Killedar says, looking at the cloud on the charpai Bhairoji Pant is floating on.

'*Dhakai malmal, hajaar dhaaga**,' Bhairoji says proudly.

'It must be very expensive?' the killedar wonders.

'300 rupees for this dhoti length,' Bhairoji says.

The killedar's mandible drops to his chest and his eyes pop out of their sockets. He has nothing to say. It is incomprehensible to him. He does not make that in a year. He swallows and imagines the wealth of some people.

'Saheb, the *vanvasi* here have a very pleasing dance. There is a troupe, if you wish to see them perform,' the killedar offers.

'Absolutely, above all, I am a rasik,' Bhairoji Pant says, and an area is cleared for the forest-dwelling children the Killedar has mustered up to dance. A cowherd, herding a male calf in the fields beyond, ambles over to watch the performance. Bored with the performance, he panhandles his way through the entire camp. The Senakarte, a man of taste, enjoys the performance which is accompanied by a lengthy meal. It is followed by a ballad, *Afjal Khanacha Vadh*, and the Bagris fire their muskets into the air. War is not that unpleasurable, after all, Bhairoji thinks as he goes to sleep on his salt-footed charpai, fanned by four footmen.

Bhairoji is in an Indralok of his own imagining when that heaven bursts asunder into darkness. Noise all around: noise that

---

* Dhakka muslin, 1000 thread count.

can shake the body and the ground beneath his cot. The ground shakes as something immensely heavy crashes outside his tent. It must be a dream he thinks, rubbing his eyes. Then Manuji Castro's second salvo of boulders assures him it isn't. Bhairoji's throat constricts as nausea spreads through his chest. He makes to move but cannot. His footmen and jamadars are around his bed waiting for him to do something or to say something. Noisy, thundering and terrific moments pass. They begin to dress him up in another diaphanous dhoti, three *khaandi* in length. They put on his sandals and lift him up.

The flap of Bhairoji Pant's tent is parted: hell, and pandemonium. The Mughals? The ghost of Afzal Khan?

He feels the thunder of horses charging towards them and can hear the battle cry of *Har Har Mahadev*. Ramoji Pawar's Bargis are charging down towards the camp firing their muskets as his guards disperse in every direction save the one the onslaught is coming from.

Bhairoji retreats into his tent to put on his armour and is just fastening the strap of a highly polished and unused bronze helmet filigreed in soft gold, when the first of Ramoji's men slashes his way into the tent, the footmen gutted at his feet.

'Are you the Senakarte?' asks a wild-looking man.

'Yes, yes I am,' he mumbles back in hope.

Several sword-wielding silhadars grab him by his arms and lift him out.

They face him towards a young Maratha, mounted on his steed. Simply dressed but of a haughty demeanour. Could this be Kanhoji?

'Ay, be careful with the Senakarte, treat him properly and give him a horse,' shouts the man. They lighten their grip and put his feet back on the ground. He is then lifted on to a fine Rajasthani Bay.

'Saheb, if you wished to meet me, you should have merely asked, and I would have come to you in Satara. Why did you bother coming all the way down the ghat?' the man asks him.

'Kanhoji Angria?' Bhairoji asks.

'At your command, Senakarteji,' Kanhoji says, folding his hands.

The captured Senakarte looks down at his mount's neck in embarrassment. He is still shocked and unsure of what is transpiring.

Weren't we just leaving for Kulaba? Bhairoji wonders to himself.

'How are you here?' Bhairoji Pant asks.

'Saheb, like I said, I would have come, the road is the same. It does not behoove a senakarte to visit a sarkhel. So, I have come.'

Bhairoji is numb and cannot feel his legs any more.

A dark, muscled man without a pagdi rides in with the captured killedar of Lohgad.

'Piloji, the Senakarte is dizzy, arrange a palkhi for him,' Kanhoji tells a courteous and finely dressed gentleman.

'I am Kusumji Marve's second son,' Piloji says in introduction.

The Senakarte knows the family.

'Santaji Ghorpade would be proud of the management skills *Sat* Sarkhel Kanhoji Angre displayed in getting his army here. Don't you agree, Senakarte Saheb?' Piloji asks Bhairoji as he helps him off his horse and into a respectable palkhi.

'You were expecting us? That means we have been betrayed,' Bhairoji asks him.

'Not at all, Pant Saheb, Sarkhel Saheb has scouts and spies all over the Konkan, and he heard of your plans the second you left Satara,' Piloji assures him.

From within the palkhi, the Senakarte hears orders being shouted by the young Sarkhel.

'Surya, let's occupy the fort first, we can use it to hold all these prisoners.'

'Take the guns, leave no guns behind.'

His palkhi halts and its curtains are parted.

'Pant Saheb, I am afraid you must accompany us to Kulaba till this mess between Rani Rajasbai, Rani Tarabai and this Shahu is sorted out.'

'You are a traitor, Kanhoji, Chhatrapati Shahu is the only legitimate sovereign,' Bhairoji screams suddenly.

'Well then, it is for him to recognize who the legitimate Sarkhel of the Armada is and who the rightful Subedar of the Konkan is.'

'Is that what you imagine yourself to be, Kanhoji?'

'What did you imagine, Pant Saheb—that I cannot access these areas because my boats couldn't reach here? Were you planning to fight us on the chowpatties? Isn't that what you call me? Beach boy?'

'Let me go. I have come here as an ambassador of Chhatrapati Shahu!'

'How convenient. You lose and you are suddenly an ambassador? You will be my prisoner till this entire issue is sorted out. Don't worry, Pant Saheb, you will be a guest in my house and be well taken care of.'

'How much do you want to let me go? My family will pay you what you want.'

'Nothing, Pant Saheb, I want nothing from you at all. All I want is for this mess to end. For it is doing me much damage. I beg your pardon in advance, but for a few days I will need to display you so people can be sure of my total and absolute victory over you. But don't worry, I will make sure you are not harshly treated.'

Bhairoji Pant Pingale is now visibly trembling and Kanhoji has a shawl brought for him and rides away saying: 'Now that we have Lohgad, we will always have a good view of anybody trying to enter the Konkan,' to the dark pagdi-less man that follows him like a shadow.

Mrs Chown

Katherine Chown has been captive at Vijaydurg for half a year when she is informed that her release is imminent. Practice has ensured a shorter period of grief. Once she heard the tales about her captor, she endeavoured in every way to come to his attention and to speak to him. Plantain would translate for her whenever she was given the opportunity to meet the Rajhah. She is with child, possibly Plantain's. She has had the freedom to move as she pleases within the fort complex and is quartered in her own little shack which Plantain often visits. Today, she spots the Rajhah with Plantain at the jetty as he returns victorious from another battle.

'Oh Cornerjee, the butter of my youth has been pressed out of me. My joy, my energy all expended,' she says bowing low and easy.

'You will soon be free to return to your people,' the handsome Rajhah assures her. His arms are thicker than her last husband's thighs.

'I have a problem, Your Lordship. You see, I have quite a fortune. Inherited from my first husband and then some from my second. But the Company does not want to release it to me before all the accounts are settled and they are taking their own sweet time to do that.'

Paltanji translates as best he can.

'Kathribai, I cannot dictate your personal terms in any treaty my king concludes with the Company.'

'Not terms, Your Lordship. If you could ask for a ransom worthy of me and then perhaps loan me some of it till I can repay you from my dues from the Company?'

'You are neither the Governor's daughter nor a shahzadi. What could your ransom be worth and who would pay it?'

'But they will, Your Lordship. As I told you, they need me to settle both my late husbands' accounts. It's just not the Company that's involved, but a few private lenders at Bombay Castle.'

'How much ransom will they pay for you?'

'If you ask for thirty and loan me fifteen?'

'That is ridiculous. Who would pay Rs 30,000 for you?'

She squeezes her bosom together but the Rajhah bursts out in laughter.

Katherine is hurt.

'Kathribai, you are no doubt comely but unless you have a lover down at Mumbachi . . .'

'Please try. What is the harm in asking them?'

'All right, I will. It will have nothing to do with the treaty they wish to sign. Please be aware, they have not singled out your return yet and have mentioned you only once in all their communications.'

'Either which way, I think given the transactions that are to be made, I am well worth Rs 30,000.'

'Well, I don't want this to be mixed up with the upcoming treaty. If you are so confident, I will make the demand now. Why wait?'

'And if they refuse to pay, will you keep me?' she asks coyly.

'No, I will release you when we sign the treaty as a measure of good faith as I am not in the habit of ransoming off women, especially those with child.'

Kanhoji sends the reluctant Plantain to meet the Governor at Bombay Castle to make a demand for Katherine's ransom. For three whole days, Plantain waits while he stays in accommodations provided by Ramaji Kamath. After their accountants have gone back and forth through the accounts of her first two husbands, Misters Harvey and

Gyfford, they conclude that Rs 30,000 is an acceptable sum for her release. The very next month, Kanhoji receives thirty thousand silver rupees for Katherine Cooke-Gyfford-Harvey-Chown. He gives her Rs 15,000 and has her escorted to Bombay Castle in the best health the young woman has been in since she arrived on these shores. Plied with coconut water and bananas, the teenaged girl has recovered to her espousing beauty.

Treaties and Entreaties

But with Plantain returns Rustomji, pressing for the new treaty. The English Company in Bombay has come to realize that a new treaty with Kanhoji will ensure the continuation of their efforts in Bombay. Kanhoji, on the other hand, does not want to lose the lucrative revenue the Angrezi trading boats are bringing his way through non-compliance. Governor William Aislabie wishes to pay his respects to the Sarkhel and is willing to cross the bay to Kulaba to discuss a treaty and sign it. Since the release of Katherine Chown, Rustomji Patel has been travelling north to south with draft in hand. Kanhoji travels farther south, and Rustomji follows him. Till at last they are at the doorstep of agreement.

Rustomji escorts Governor Aislabie to Kulaba when at last Kanhoji returns home. A well-lit room has been chosen for the meeting and special furniture constructed for it. Kanhoji on his bolster rung mattress and the Angrez on the uncomfortable and undignified chairs they prefer. The mattress has been raised on a platform to the level of a table's top, which separates the two parties. The table chosen is an old Firangi one. Kanhoji acquired it for the very purpose. It is made of ebony and filigreed with ivory inlay along the borders and on the legs. It is a heavy and dense piece, much like the walls of his forts. Gangadhar stands besides Kanhoji, and a pair of his assistants sit on the floor with their low sloped desks in front of them.

Aislabie sits in the middle chair flanked by his secretary on one side and Rustomji, preferring to stand, on the right. After the announcement and introductions, Kanhoji asks what happened to Reynolds, and Rustomji tells him he passed on to the next life, surprised the Sarkhel remembers the name. Rustomji congratulates Kanhoji on his victory over Bhairoji Pant Pingale. A retinue of servants, groomed by Mathurabai, in matching yellow pagdis carry in silver thaals filled with *farsaan* and an array of beverages from solkadi to Porto wine.

Kanhoji urges his guests to partake as he watches them.

'The Siddi of Janjira is the vassal of the Mughal with whom we are at war, yet you provide them refuge in your harbours, water their ships, sell them your best muskets and cannon,' Kanhoji opens.

'Your Lordship, the Siddi accuses us of the very same thing. He accuses us of being his enemy by favouring his enemies. He attacked Bombay, I will have you know, for the same reason—claiming that we have been supporting you in your war against them.'

'The exigencies of the local politics you find yourself having to deal with I leave unto you, but the Siddi's fleet can no longer be allowed to dock at your jetties—for if I find them there, I will be forced to destroy them along with the port.'

Aislabie merely nods his head. If he must acquiesce to this demand to enable the treaty, he well knows that he will never be able to abide by it.

'There being discord in the House of Bhonsale, between Rajaram of Kolhapur and the Sow Raja, whom you recently defeated, may we have the treaty in your name, My Lordship?' Aislabie asks. This is what he wants more than anything. Rustomji translates.

'Yes, you may, if it is a treaty between me and yourself, not your company but in your personal name,' Kanhoji replies.

'My Lordship, I am but a temporary servant of the Company, it's my Lords in London . . .'

'The same is true for me, Asalbiji, here today gone tomorrow. I too am a servant to the Chhatrapati,' Kanhoji says.

'And which one will that be?' Aislabie wants to know.

'The one who sits in Kolhapur,' Kanhoji retorts.

Rustomji wants to know which one exactly but waits for his master to initiate the question.

'Patelji, I must return south, so please read the salient points out and then we can conclude this matter,' Kanhoji adds, noticing the Patel's eyes cajoling Aislabie.

'The Company of Merchants of London Trading to the East Indies agrees to pay an annual sum of Rs 50,000 as duties for ships coming in from England. Further, all English coastal ships will pay for their dastaks based on the cargo. The same will be charged at two and a half per hundred of the worth of the cargo. Sarkhel Kanhoji Angria will ensure the safety of these cargoes. A further one-time reparation for the loss of lives incurred in the taking of the Governor's yacht, the *Grantham* and the *Somers*, will be Rs 1 lakh, all of which is to be paid in our English silver. Kanhoji will return the aforementioned vessels and release all the English prisoners he has in a gesture of goodwill. The Maratha state and the English traders will be allies and interact with peace and amiability from now on,' Rustomji reads out first in Marathi and then in English.

'You have forgotten to mention that your coastal vessels are not to carry cannon. They must pull oars or drop sails when approached by us,' Kanhoji tells Rustomji.

'My Lordship, how would we know it is not the Sow Raja's force?' asks Aislabie at last.

'I am the only authority in the Konkan and my sails are the colour of the Chhatrapati's flag. Do you see anybody else's galbats in the sea? You do not, so do not confuse yourself in a maze of misunderstanding: pay your fair dues and carry on your good work,' Kanhoji says with a finality. From outside the room, there are sounds of musket practice and hard drilling, and every so often, a cannon goes off on a bastion.

The Walls of Satara

The Angrias, as the folk beseeching their force have been calling them, have camped for the night by a clean spring, three days' march from the gates of Satara. Behind the gates, they are called traitors. After capturing the senakarte, Kanhoji Angria has turned his army towards the sons of Maharaj. Behind the gates, they said it was a matter of time. Kanhoji surveys the camped army with his younger son Sambhaji, as they stroll through the well-spaced tents and paddocks. They approach a band of silhadars who are recleaning their wheel-lock muskets and arranging their charges. Golu stands behind Kanhoji with a mashaal in his hand and Surya is beside him. The silhadars stop what they were doing, stand up and bow to Kanhoji as he approaches them.

'Son, what is your name?' Kanhoji asks the leader of the platoon.

'I am Jagu Bhandari, Sarkhel Saheb. I am in Ramoji Pawar's battalion, and these are my men.'

'Ramoji has spoken of you. Where do you hail from?'

'We are from Chondhi, Sarkhel Saheb.'

'Why are all of you so glum? Have you not eaten or are you missing your wives and children already?'

'No, no, Sarkhel Saheb,' they protest in unison.

'I hope you are not worried or fearful of what lies ahead?'

Again, the troop dismiss these charges with vociferous denials and their nodding heads perk up their limbs.

'Then why so glum?'

'Aren't we attacking our own people?' a boy from the back pipes up.

'No, Khandoba wants the Konkani to decide who is the true Chhatrapati.'

The boy's doubts fade away. A great metallic weight rises from the camp and disappears into the dark sky above.

'Remember that you have fought against the Topikars and their superb cannons and muskets and yet prevailed. These warriors in the Desha are not fighters, they just mull around as their sardars are bribed this way and the other. They don't fight. Whereas we Konkani have to continuously defend against threats on a weekly basis.'

The silhadars are excited with the praise and get more animated. Groups of men camping nearby come to join the silhadars.

'This is a Konkan army that is going to teach the rest of the world a very important lesson: don't take the Konkani for granted.'

'*Swarajya cha amar rahe, Sarkhel cha amar rahe,*[*] Surya shouts and the silhadars respond in kind.

'There is nothing to fear when we are prepared, and we are destined to overcome.'

The gathered crowd of soldiers cheer Kanhoji as he speaks to them. He is interrupted by a platoon of infantrymen who approach Kanhoji. They are escorting an unarmed man and four soldiers who had been accompanying the young man.

'Sarkhel Saheb, we caught these men approaching the camp. The boy wants to speak to you. He says he has been sent by the Peshwa.'

'Bring him here,' Kanhoji commands the men holding the Peshwa's man.

'Whose Peshwa? And who is this Peshwa, may I ask?" Kanhoji demands of the messenger.

---

[*] May the Swaraj remain eternal; May the Sarkhel live long.

'The Peshwa of Chhatrapati Shahu Maharaj, Sarkhel Saheb, and the Peshwa in question is Balaji Vishwanath Bhat.'

'Then what is the password?' Kanhoji asks and the man whispers it into his ears, and it confirms that the messenger is indeed Balaji's.

'What is your message?' Kanhoji asks, not entirely surprised.

'The Peshwa wishes to meet you at Valvan—two kos from here, tomorrow morning.'

'Tell him I will come, but I will bring my entire army with me.'

'Peshwa Sahib has specified that you must come with your army, and he will enter your camp at Valvan tomorrow once you are encamped there.'

He dismisses Balaji's messenger and his guard.

'Surya, send scouts out with some guards and check the area around Valvan. Send them now so if this is a trap, we will know for sure before we get there,' he decides.

'Do you think Balaji will try to trap you?'

'Maybe he's under duress. I don't know but why be surprised when you can be sure.'

The scouts are back by dawn. They report that there is a small camp set up in Valvan with not more than 100 horse and twice as many infantrymen. There seem to be an equal number of palkhiwalas and attendants as there are soldiers. Kanhoji's army decamps, while platoons of silhadars keep guard over the main body of the army. With Kanhoji at its head on a piebald grey, they make their way north to Valvan along the winding road to Lonavala.

At Valvan they see the camp the messenger has referred to and stop at a safe distance from it. As soon as the camp guards spot the army, a large palanquin heads out towards them. The palanquin bearers stop before Kanhoji and an elegantly dressed man steps out of their slight burden.

'Balaji, is that really you?' Kanhoji says as he recognizes his angular-featured friend.

'Are you really the Peshwa?'

'Can't you believe it? Look at my palkhi.' It is much festooned with silver.

Kanhoji dismounts from his stallion.

Kanhoji and Balaji crisply bow to each other with folded hands before Balaji hugs his old friend.

'Actually, I am not yet the Peshwa,' Balaji whispers to Kanhoji in his ear.

'What, but I . . .'

'Let's talk privately, away from all ears.'

Kanhoji has a large canvas tent set up with mattresses on charpais for them to sit on. A platoon of soldiers forms a ring around the tent, standing with their backs to the tent. Balaji and Kanhoji enter the square tent and sit down close to each other.

'Why did Shahu Raje send Pingale against me?'

'Other minds prevailed. The documents you sent Amatya Pant gave us a fairly good idea about your finances. Chandrasen felt you were getting too rich and independent. They were and still are terrified of you.'

'You did not intervene?'

'I tried at first, but then realized it was exactly what we needed. I knew you would overcome Pingale, he is not a man of war. Now, I am the only man who can negotiate with the enemy at the gate. It has given both of us leverage.'

'Then what do you mean you are not yet the Peshwa?'

'It all depends on the outcome of this talk.'

'How do you mean?'

'If I succeed in pacifying the terrible Angre, I will be made Peshwa.'

'And what of the terrible Angre?'

'He will be made Sarkhel of the entire Maratha Armada.'

'But I already am Sarkhel.'

'But not for life and not of a united navy. Shahu Raje will give you full command of the Konkan and invest you with new and increased *watan** lands. The Konkan will be your subah, to run as you wish: subedar of the Konkan for life.'

---

* Hereditary estate.

'What of Kolhapur?'

'Kolhapur will come under the aegis of Satara.'

'Then why didn't all you great strategists sign the treaty with Kolhapur instead of getting me involved.'

'Because Kolhapur had you. Now with you on our side, they do not have an option but to accept Shahu Raje's supremacy.'

'You are sure he isn't an impostor?'

'Come now, Kanho, all that talk is ridiculous gossip. You have met his father, meet Shahu Raje and judge for yourself.'

'He is compromised, though; his mother and wife are still hostage in Delhi.'

'No, no. It is not that simple. Things are going to change for us as we have new allies in Dilli, and we are a force to reckon with—if we are united.'

'Don't tell me that I was the cause of any disunity.'

'That's not at all what I meant. But look, Kanhoji, Mahapurush Brahmendra Swami was right. Look how destiny and fate has got us together and taken us to such heights.'

'It is the grace of Khandoba, but I want one more thing,' Kanhoji says.

'What more do you want?'

'A joint attack on the Siddi first and then the Firangis. We need Janjira and Bassein, and I can't do it on my own. I need artillery and infantry and I need cannons.'

'You will get them, and we will take both Janjira and Bassein and who knows, one day Goa. Kanho, when you meet Chhatrapati Shahu Raje, you will know him for the prince he is.'

'I look forward to it. How are Radhabai and the boys?'

'With the grace of Swamiji, all is well.'

'Well, I hope you have taught Baji and Chimmaji how to ride?'

'I made sure that like their Kaka Kanhoji, they rode before they could walk.'

The Mouse and the Lion

Behind the mighty basalt walls of the Janjira Fort, Siddi Rasool Surur Yakut Khan is holding his saline court. The death of his badshah has left him an orphan, hungry for the succour of relevance he had become accustomed to. The aged sons of Aurangzeb are following their family's pattern of succession: *takth ya takhta**— and are unconcerned with the Konkan and its politics. The fight for the Peacock Throne has extended to the next generation, and Farukhshiyar has become Padishah after killing his brother, Mirza Jahandar Khan. The calibre of people who are coming to meet the Siddi Wazir has fallen drastically, and his durbar has become the refuge of gossip mongers and mischief-makers. In the dim light of the durbar hall, ancient kilims and tapestries suffer humid flattery along with their master. Pandurao Phangaskar has brought a stunning specimen of womanhood as a gift for the Yakut Khan, who accepts her happily in these listless times he is boiling in.

'It seems that fortune has been smiling on you, Panduraoji. Where on earth did you acquire her?'

'Wazir Saheb, she is the daughter of a chieftain in the hinterlands of Persia. Her uncle killed her father and her brothers and sold her away into slavery. My agent bought her in Basra without ever asking

---

* Throne or coffin.

me but when I saw her and realized how much he paid for her, I thought only you deserve such a creature.'

'I thank you again for thinking of me.'

'You are always in my mind and in my prayers.'

'How is business, though?'

'What can I say, Wazir Saheb? On one hand, Laxmi Devi has been most generous, but with all the taxes, customs and these new dastaks, it has become difficult to make ends meet or run a profitable trade.'

'But what duties do you pay for women?'

'No, I mean on the other goods I trade. This is not my business, it's only for your . . .'

'I know your business well enough, Panduraoji, and there are no duties charged on either women or rumours. I don't think even Angria requires a dastak for your kind of cargo.'

'Huzoor, who is it that can afford to not take a dastak from Angria? I think even your vessels are subject to his dastak when they are away from Janjira or Surat.'

'Absolute nonsense: I will have any captain of mine who takes a dastak from Angria hung on his mast. No one would dare.'

'I merely heard that some of Your Excellency's ships pay for the dastak when they venture south.'

'Nonsense, utter nonsense.'

'Well, everybody in the Konkan is scared of him.'

'Not me. I need not fear anybody.'

'Wazir Saheb, have you not heard what happened in Satara this month?'

'If you were there, then tell me. Otherwise, I am not interested.'

'Wazir Saheb, I was very much there. Over Holi, Shahu Raje confirmed a former slave of your predecessors as the Peshwa, and Angria was made the Sarkhel of the entire Maratha armada and the Subedar of the Konkan. He was given charge of twenty-six forts: many of which are in your possession.'

'How is that possible? To give away what is not theirs?'

'Rajapuri, Chaul, Thal, Khanderi and Undheri have all been given to Angria.'

'Chaul is Firangi. It makes no difference; he will have to wrest them from my hands. This is nonsense.'

'I am just telling you what I have witnessed. But it cannot be denied that Angria is the most powerful force in the Konkan.'

'Nonsense, there is no greater power than that of the Badshah in Dilli and no greater sailor and warrior than his Wazir at Janjira. It would be best you know that, Pandyo.'

'Huzoor, since the death of Badshah Alamgir and the year you became the Yakut Khan, we have already had a handful of badshahs. The days of Shah Jehan and Aurangzeb are long gone: the turkic moon wanes.'

Siddi Rasool snorts in derision: 'I do not need Dilli, Dilli needs me. I am the only true subedar of the Konkan. All others are impostors.'

'Huzoor, there is only one more thing I would like to warn you about. Angre has in his treaty with the Chhatrapati included a clause that calls for the extinction of you and your office.'

'Let them come, many have tried before, and all have failed, and no one will ever succeed on my watch.'

'Inshallah, Wazir Saheb. They are calling him the Samudra Saranga and even Samudratala Shivaji. He has an annual income of Rs 36 lakh . . .'

'Yes, yes,' Siddi Rasool says, dismissing Panduraoji with a shake of his fingers. He has been so looking forward to spending some time with his comely gift when this pimp ruins his mood with talks of Angria. Panduraoji prattles and provokes as expected, but he is also right: Angria has become dangerously powerful. The Topikars no longer called the Maratha forces in the Konkan Sevajees; they were now calling them the Angrians, and it pains him to realize that a lot of his commanders fear them too.

Sanyaas

Ramchandra Bawdekar has come down the winding forested road from Satara. He was thoroughly impressed with Angre when he met him at Satara at his investiture as Sarkhel. The sagacious Pant has wanted to retire to his estates in Gaganbavada after having faithfully served five Chhatrapatis. Reluctant to let him and his invaluable experience leave his court, Shahu Raje has commissioned him to write a code of military and civil administration. It is in this regard that he comes to Kulaba to meet and learn from Kanhoji. Humbled and glad for the privilege, Kanhoji has his four sons attend to the Amatya Pant on his visit. After showing him Kulaba, they sail south to Suvarnadurg and then take him to Vijaydurg. Kanhoji's son seats the aged man on a litter carried by four stout palkhiwalas to save his knees from the undulating geography of the fort. Amatya Pant has known many subedars and *deshmukhs** in his time and visited the courts of the Adil Shahis and the Golkondans when they still existed, and still this man has left him astounded.

'How many guns do you have on your walls and bastions?'

'A little over two hund . . .'

'Two hundred and fifty-eight cannons, Shriman,' Sekhoji corrects his father.

---

*Hereditary head of a district.

'I need to take notes, there is so much here that I am scared I will forget some point or the other,' Amatya Pant says to Kanhoji.

Kanhoji directs Tulaji to do the needful for the Pant.

'Where did you get the shipwrights from?'

'Surat, Bharuch, Kutch, even Keral. Wherever we could find good men who would work here. Of course, one must make it worth their while, then they come on their own.'

'But why do you have so many Topikars here?'

'I have 200-odd Firangis here, including a few Angrez. I have a laskar from Chin and another from Java in my employ. We have Habshis as nakhwas and Pathan gunners. I only look for one thing and that is skill and talent: It does not matter to me where they are from or what god they believe in. *Gunaah pujaasthaanam gunishu n cha lingam na cha vayah.** '

'That was the policy of Chhatrapati Shivaji, and it is good that you are following it, but I still do not know if these Topikars can be trusted.'

'They are mercenaries, no doubt, but what skills they possess, especially in blacksmithing and as gunners, has greatly helped our cause.'

'But we invented steel. What of spies?'

'Spies need to be dealt with severely and publicly, but there is no way to ensure that none of your people will betray you. I have learnt to only give commanding positions to men I trust and only share information that is necessary. What would you suggest?'

'There is little I can suggest to you, Kanhoji, and I only wonder at your loyalty to the House of Bhonsale for it has been a boon unto them.'

'It is on my seal, Pant Saheb: I am forever at the feet of the Chhatrapati.'

'You are like Hanuman was to Lord Ram.'

---

* Good qualities are appreciated in whomsoever they are found, regardless of sex or age.

'I fear to accept the compliment, Pant Saheb, but please do know that what revenues people claimed I was keeping for myself was all used in public and defence works, not on the vainglory of me or my family.'

This Amatya Pant can well see, as there is little ostentation in the Subedar of Konkan's life. Except for his vast and immaculately maintained stables, the likes of which the experienced Amatya Pant had only seen in Bijapur.

The next day they take Amatya Pant upriver to the dry docks, and then they get him up again to show him the gunpowder factory and Hansuji's workshop.

'Another Topikar?' the disgusted Pant asks after seeing Hansuji, who is begrimed and sweating.

'He is from another country, the enemy of the Firangis and Angrez. He has been with me a long time and fixes all our guns and makes our shot.'

'Why can't some of our blacksmiths learn this?'

'They are, Pant Saheb, he has only local apprentices and he directs them and teaches them.'

'Shriman Amatya Pantji, talking of learning from the Topikars: Wouldn't it be wise to make ships like they have and sail to their lands to trade?' asks Sambhaji excitedly.

'Who will sail these ships?'

'Our Habshis and Mussalmans. Imagine the profit the Topikars make—it could be ours. With such vessels, we could control the seas up to Yaman and Oman. The Firangis don't have any gold or silver in their own country, but get it from mines in another land they conquered. We could go straight to that land.'

'What your father is doing is good enough, my son. Why bother with these people? Let them come and take what they need and make what profit they do. Why get involved with every little backwater in the world? They are seafaring *banjaras*[*]: casteless, uncultured and

---

[*] Nomads, ancestors of the gypsies.

uncivilized. We are the bountiful centre of the world, flanked by Chin and Pars and beyond that there is nothing,' the Amatya Pant explains to the ignorant child.

'Forget the rest of the world, Shambhu, we still have to deal with the Siddis and throw the Firangis out of Bassein and Daman. It would behoove you to ask Shriman Amatya Pant for his advice rather than giving it,' Sekho tells his younger brother.

'And to also make sure that the Angrez or some other species of Topikar not take the same advantages the Firangis took,' Amatya Pant warns, looking directly at Kanhoji. It is no secret that the Amatya distrusts people with overly fair skin, be it the Firangis or the Chitpavan Brahmins, who are proliferating in the court these days.

'Not as long as the Angres are around,' says Tulaji proudly.

'Shriman Amatya Pantji, we would also like a copy of the code you are writing,' Manaji chimes in.

'Listen well to your father, boy, and follow what he sets out, for he practises what I am laying out.'

'Any advice you can give us, Amatya Pantji?' Manaji asks obediently.

'Always be loyal to the House of Bhonsale,' the Amatya Pant replies, nodding his head gravely at the profundity of the advice.

Hawa Ghar

It is the day after Chaitra Purnima. Kanhoji is in the newly constructed Hawa Ghar, where Babuji Kotla and his team are still installing the last of the latticed marble screens. Babuji sent his sons to the mines in Makrana to choose the finest stone. The Hawa Ghar had been conceived the previous year when sweat trickling off Kanhoji's wide forehead had drenched drawings of a dry dock that Babuji had been presenting. Raised to the level of Kulaba Fort's ramparts to allow for the sea breeze, the Hawa Ghar's roof is shaded by a thick canopy thatched with immense bundles of straw reeds. Above and around, curtains of white muslin and silk nets protect against insects and mosquitoes. A system of pulleys and wicker fans has been engineered on to a network of beams. The walls are a double layer of the honeycombed marble screens that to Babuji's granite-cutting masons from the south felt like *maska**.

Kanhoji sits on a raised platform cushioned with mattresses and bolsters drinking a glass of buttermilk spiced with fennel, *khus* and kokum as he deals with the business of the torrid day.

'Who do you think I am? Seth Mangatram?' Kanhoji quips.

'Forgive me, Shriman,' the turbaned man replies.

---

*Butter.

'There has to be some alternative to *kesar**, it is not a kurta you are dyeing, Dinuji,' Kanhoji says.

'Shriman, I have tried haldi and *lal-matti*, but you did not like the shades,' Dinuji the dyer replies.

'I cannot afford kesar, it is sails we are talking of, Dinuji. Think of a solution. The colour of our sails should exactly match the bhagwa of Maharaj's pennant. We have to show ourselves; every trader, every nakhwa and every oarsman must know it is our vessel,' Kanhoji explains.

'Give me till Amavas, Shriman, and I will have a solution,' Dinuji says and excuses himself.

'Raje,' Gangadhar whispers in Kanhoji's ear: 'Manaji has arrived.'

'Arrived, indeed,' Kanhoji says irritably.

Manaji enters the Hawa Ghar and pranams his father, almost falling over on his face. His eyes are bloodshot, and his face is creased and swollen both with sleep and the lack of it.

'Where were you yesterday? Your mother and your sisters were looking for you,' Kanhoji asks sternly.

'Yesterday was *chutti***, Baba, so I went out with some friends,' Manaji says.

'*Chutti* from me, not from your family and your traditions,' Kanhoji corrects his son.

'It won't happen again, Baba,' Manaji says, looking embarrassed.

'You are to go to Khanderi and take charge. Clean the place up and keep the watch tight. Everything that you see is to be immediately relayed to Kulaba. Figure that out too. I want constant communication.'

'Baba, can I go to Manuji instead. I want to hunt the Siddi's vessels with him,' Manaji says eagerly.

'He does not need you, Khanderi does,' Kanhoji says and dismisses his son with the wave of his hand.

---

* Saffron.

** Leave.

'Raje, the first fire signal from Rajmachi has arrived,' Gangadhar says excitedly.

'What does it say?' Kanhoji asks.

'It's from Tulaji Raje. It says: "Baba at your feet at Sunrise."'

'How long did it take?' Kanhoji asks Gangadhar.

'Three and a half *muhuratas**,' Gangadhar replies, smiling, and then notices one of his assistants vying for his attention. He makes his way to the man who is the last link in a chain of whispers.

'Raje, Seth Ramaji Kamath is at the gate, he has not made an appointment,' Gangadhar tells Kanhoji, making the whisper audible at last.

'Bring him up immediately, Gangadhar, and keep in mind that Ramaji Seth never needs an appointment to see me. Always bring him into my presence immediately, unless matters of state or war are being discussed, in that case, host him like my kin,' Kanhoji says.

Gangadhar nods and then tells his assistant to escort the Sethji up.

'*Lakshmipriya*** Ramaji; what brings Laxmi Devi's most favoured son to a poor soldier's doorstep?' Kanhoji says as he warmly welcomes the suave banker. Ramaji bows deeply in pranam.

'A soldier? You can fool everybody else, Kanhoji Raje, but I see you for what you are: the king of the Konkan.'

'Don't say that; you will get me in trouble,' Kanhoji says, clicking his tongue.

'If one serves his people as a king does, then he is definitely a king.'

'I am just another Subedar of the Chhatrapati, Ramaji—you know me to have no other ambitions.'

'You have left your ambition far behind you, Sarkhel Saheb, and only Saraswati knows if it can even catch up with you in this lifetime.'

Kanhoji laughs to hide his embarrassment and parries, as is his instinct.

---

* Unit of measurement of time equal to 1/15th of a day.

** Beloved of the Goddess of Wealth.

'But tell me one thing, Sethji: you live on that little island with the Angrez, in spite of having *karkhanas** and godowns in Kalyan, Thana, Bassein and down to Vengurla, forgive me for not listing them all, but is there enough space on that little rock to store all your wealth?' Kanhoji says.

'None of it is mine, Kanhoji Raje, it belongs to the community,' Ramaji laughs in reply.

'Where are the princes?' asks Ramaji, not letting up.

'Sekhoji and Sambhaji are at Birwadi Fort, keeping an eye on the Siddi,' he says. 'Tulaji just sent me a signal from Rajmachi in under three muhuratas,' he proudly adds, deciding to let news of Manaji pass.

'So heartening to see you in each of them,' Ramaji adds.

'So, how can I be of assistance?' Kanhoji inquires.

'Raje, there is a ship you took. It was a cargo of horses coming in from Oman. I have a large investment in it along with Siddi Suleman of Rajapuri.'

'It must have been under the protection of the Wazir,' Kanhoji replies.

'Well, they were not flying his colours but were in a convoy along with the Wazir's dhows.'

'Well, I hope this one deal will not break you because there is nothing I can do. The horses are all already deployed. There was a beautiful grey stallion that Sekhoji now rides. It's too late, Ramaji. I am sorry.'

'Is there nothing you can do?'

'Please excuse me this time, Ramaji, but anything under the Nawab's shadow is welcome picking. I hope you understand I need to choke them out of their dammed fortress and dry up his revenue. When I take Janjira, I will definitely reimburse you then.'

'Is that going to happen in the foreseeable future?' Ramaji wonders aloud.

---

*Workshops.

'I am no jyothshi. I have been taught to plant the tree and tend to it and not bother about the fruits.'

'And the pearls?' wonders Ramaji about his secret cargo.

'Disbursed, up the ghat as always. As you can see,' Kanhoji says pointing to his chest: 'none have ever touched me.'

'I do hope you succeed sooner than later,' replies Ramaji.

'I will. It is just a matter of time. How is business?' asks Kanhoji.

'As good as it can be, provided we don't get crushed between two larger wheels.'

'You will have to suffer a bit along with us, but once this rumbling is over, the Konkan will be administered by one authority and there will be peace and trade will flourish like never before.'

'There is a new seth in Bombay,' Ramaji informs Kanhoji.

'Another one?'

'Yes, his predecessor just lasted two months.'

'How is this one?'

'He was in the Tamil Desha before this. Fancies himself a warrior. He immediately attacked the Topikars of Vengurla and Karwar. But it led nowhere. He is building fortifications around the warehouses, and he is planning to build a little navy to protect their trade.'

'Protect them from what?'

'Dacoits, I assume—of the sea-faring type.'

'They needn't bother with such things, that's why they pay for the dastak. Tell me, have you ever been looted after that first time?'

'Never, if I don't count the horses and pearls,' Ramaji says cheekily.

'Hah, forget about those horses, Ramaji, we still have a life ahead of us.'

'I am sorry I brought it up, it was a bad joke.'

'Forget it. Tell me: what kind of work are they doing at the Angrezi warehouse?'

'Walling their warehouses and residences all the way from Dongri to the tip of the island; he plans to build bastions by Palva Bandar.'

'What good would a wall do? Last time I just choked their coastal trade—didn't let any vessels through to their ships.'

'Well, if you ever attack, just remember to spare our homes, warehouses and bazaars.'

'Don't worry about that. I have nothing against them, though the same can't be said of Amatya Pant. Anyway, he has retired.'

'We need them, Kanhoji. The Angrez buy everything regardless of the quality. They aren't the Chini, always bickering and picking apart our goods. And they pay in the best silver there is to be had.'

'I am not trying to stop any trade. Haven't I always welcomed it? But it must be on our terms—there can be no compromise there. I have compromised enough with everybody and given too many chances and free passes.'

'You have always been generous, Kanhoji, no one can fault you that.'

'Tell me, how is your relationship with the Angrez?'

'I had the previous Governor's ear, Asalvi. Then one Stuts came in for a few months, hardly got a chance to meet him. Now it's one Boone.'

'Bhoon?'

'Yes. I have donated over 10,000 rupaiya towards the *girija** they are making.'

Kanhoji whistles at the sum.

'It's the cost of doing business,' Ramaji smiles wryly.

'You are wise. If you get the opportunity, ask whether the new Governor would be amenable to us putting up a gunpowder factory, maybe in Parel or thereabouts.'

'Sure, I can do that. I am meeting him later this week. Let's see if Boone will see the wisdom and profit in it.'

'Thank you,' Kanhoji says, knowing that Ramaji is not the kind of man to make empty promises. Kanhoji would have liked to return the cargo, but it would set a precedent that would lead half the merchants of the Konkan to his doorstep.

---

* Christian place of worship.

'I must take my leave now, Kanhoji, and best of luck against the Wazir.'

Kanhoji gets up to bid Ramaji farewell and then calls for Surya once his guest has departed.

'Ji, Raje?' Surya says, finding his Sarkhel by a window looking out at the sea.

'Surya, I think it's time we lay siege to Janjira and Danda-Rajapuri—nothing in and nothing out. Let's see how long that bastard lasts.'

Surya smiles, his white teeth mirroring the marble of the Hawa Ghar.

'Gangadhar, take this message down for Peshwa Balaji: send me artillery and infantry, we are taking Janjira and will attack on the night of Amavas, ten days from now.'

Casa de Orta

A humid air conducts the smell of thousands of drying *bombils** through the dank interiors of the castle. Built on the gardens around the manor of Garcia da Orta, the Portuguese horticulturist to whom the island had been leased by its former masters, it is a modest affair. The English, when they got possession of the island, built its only defensive structure, a wall around the rehabilitated manor that now functions as the Governor's residence. Only a sundial survives from the times of its previous occupants, and the famous eclectic garden that existed there has long perished.

The latest resident of the castle has been sent by the directors of the East India Company, headquartered at Leadenhall Street in London, with the express purpose of reducing the massive overheads that plague their trading enterprise in the Konkan. They have chosen the Surrey-born man for his prudence and pig-headedness as much for his indefatigable energy. Charles Boone is a god-fearing man and he carries his copy of the King James Bible in his left hand. It had lately become drenched by the sweating fever that plagued its reader at his arrival to this vermin-ridden archipelago. A bout of dysentery had left him with a raw and inflamed rectum and a debilitating weakness in the entire corpus.

---

* A fish, Bombay duck.

The kindly Mr Pando Row had been most helpful during the illness by sending the Governor's retainer coconuts and lichi bananas to feed his new boss. Mr Pando Row often pops by with some *churan** disguised as medicine and a packet of basil seeds for the Governor to consume. Panduraoji is also gracious enough to share the gossip from the bazaar and is generous with his reviews of the personalities and people the Governor must deal with.

The much-recovered Governor is at his office when Pandurao Phangaskar comes in that day. The Governor has been going through his drawings and plans for the fortification of the island. The smell of tallow candles lighting the offices makes Pandurao gag.

'So how is your good health progressing, Your Excellency?' Phangaskar says, offering him a packet full of different kinds of *imli*** and *hing*** churan he has purchased outside the gate.

'I am much better now. Thank you,' Boone says, accepting his miraculous though tart medicines.

'And the fortifications, sir?'

'Not as well. They are too slow, and the contractors don't seem to understand the simplest of drawings. I think they are putting me on.'

'These Konkani people are not to be trusted, sir: sticky fingers and stickier tongues. Especially the dark ones.'

'Shouldn't that include you too?'

'I am not dark,' Phangaskar shoots back flustered.

'But you are Corn-Corny.'

'Not at all, sir. My ancestors came from the north and I am hailing from the south. My native place is on the border with Firangistan. Also, I am of the highest Brahmin caste, which itself is the highest caste in all these lands.'

'I know Brahmin, Iyer, Iyengar. Your father was a priest then?'

'Very much so, sir, and so am I,' Panduraoji replies.

---

* A digestive made of spices often eaten by children as a candy.

** Tamarind.

*** Asafoetida.

'My sire too was a man of the cloth, though they wear but a little here. Dressed or nude, men of God can always be trusted,' Charles Boone says.

'But you have to be careful here. There are many who claim to be men of God but are nothing but charlatans.'

'Fear not, Mr Pandoraji, even I know the difference between a snake charmer and a man of God. Have you ever read the Bible?'

'Many times, sir, and I know the Kristapurana by heart: the story of your God and his almighty son in our own language.'

'Well, you are a man of diverse parts: physician, priest, trader and a linguist for good measure: good on you.'

'Indeed, sir, indeed.'

'Well, you might as well have a seat,' says Governor Boone pointing to a trio of chairs lined up on the other side of his massive oak desk. Pandurao closes the door behind him and jumps into the nearest chair and then very visibly looks around the office to see if they are alone.

'What is it?' Boone wonders at his guest's sudden desire for privacy.

'Your Excellency is new to this office, and I must warn you that these old walls have sharper ears than most.'

'How do you mean?'

'Well, Governor Saheb, isn't everybody interested in what you and your Company are up to? The Dutch are as keen to know what you have in your warehouses, as every other trader in the bazaar. The Portuguese in Goa are envious of and curious about your status with the Mughals, both here and in Surat. The Habshi Wazir at Janjira feels he is owed all information coming in and out of here. And then there is Kanhoji Angre, the Konkani Crocodile who ravishes the entire coast. He has his spies everywhere and in the most unexpected forms: children playing in the street to old, trusted retainers who serve others while secretly serving him.'

'But isn't Angrier the Sow Raja's delegate.'

'Delegate? Saheb, he marched on the Raja of Satara but last year. Turning his entire army against his overlord and extorted the

most profitable outcome. You can ascertain from your predecessors'
records. His ambition knows no bounds and he is definitely far from
considering his king or yours.'

'But we have a treaty with him.'

'Treaty? Sir, not two years ago he kidnapped a defenceless
English widow and returned her fully pregnant and naked.'

'Ah, you mean Mrs Chown.'

'I mean the very same, Your Excellency,' Panduraoji says as he
keenly scans all the papers and documents lying on the desk.

'But that matter was resolved and a treaty entered into by
Aislabie.'

'Sir, I mean no offence to your august office, but few men
have been worthy of it. I am sorry to say but Governor Aislabie
feared Angria and possibly compromised. Angria first captured
then returned the Governor's personal yacht at the time of the
negotiations.'

'You are sure of this?'

'Sir, you can check with General Aislabie himself.'

'Well, he is halfway around the world Mr Pandora, it will take two
years to receive a reply from him.'

'Then you should trust me, sir, my interests are only your
interests. I have no agenda but the increase of your trade, on which
I am dependent.'

'Heaven forbid, Mr Pandora, I am not so uncouth as to call you
a liar, I was just pointing out our predicament.'

'Well, Your Excellency, it also works to increase your
independence from your masters.'

'I am in no need of independence from the directors,
Mr Pandora, I am their true and loyal representative, sent to
accomplish their tasks.'

'Of course, Your Excellency. I just hope so distant from them,
you too do not come to fear Angria.'

'A poltroon I am not. I do not fear anything but Our Lord,
especially not an overambitious extortionist from the backwaters
of Bombay.'

'I am sorry to say, sir, but Bombay itself is the backwaters. He is from the backwaters of the backwaters,' says Pandurao, grinning and assigning a totally different and scatological meaning to the word.

'Well, not by the time I am done with this place. Tell me more about Angrier.'

'A villain and shifter, sir, as you will learn soon enough. He has taken the right to board all vessels that cross these waters. Earlier, I used to purchase a pass from the Company itself and he has stopped that practice, causing great harm to your revenues and to my profits.'

'How did he achieve that? Why did Aislabie agree?'

'Fear: he was poltroon as you are not.'

'Well, I am Charles Boone, and such emotions are not in my habit: I do not care to cower. Except these damn mosquitoes,' the Governor says, trying to crush one feeding in the red jungles of his forearm.

'A handsome and strong-looking man like yourself, Governor Saheb, I should definitely think not. I will get you some neem leaves. You can crush them and apply the juice on your skin—it is the only remedy.'

'You are a kind man yourself, Mr Pandora, and I hope I will be able to count on your godliness.'

'Absolutely, Your Excellency, you can trust me. But I must take my leave, I have already imposed myself on your precious time.'

'Not at all, dear man. Do drop by when you can. You have been most helpful. Mr Patel is obviously still indebted to Aislabie—he never thought to apprise me of this aspect of the office's history,' Boone says of the long-serving revenue administrator.

'Rustomji is a Parsi, Your Excellency. They avoid the bitter truth. But tomorrow I will send a servant to you. A woman. To help you bathe and press your feet,' he says deciding it is still too early to wink. The woman will let him know.

Siege

Initially, the bird catchers cursed their luck as the booming cannons startled their quarries. Now their luck has changed as the exhausted kingfishers and the frazzled hummingbirds collapse into their gossamer nets. The cattle remain skittish, the dogs howl in fear at the unending explosions and infants cry through the night. The farmers are scared to work their fields and the Bhandaris hesitate to climb the coconut trees as they have for generations. Sarkhel Kanhoji's artillery is pitched, smoke-belching panthers against the elephantine walls of the Siddi's fortresses. Their respective infantry and cavalry raid each other's unmarked dominions, trampling fully ripened vegetables and fat stalks of millet underfoot. The coastal trading boats remain at their jetties, scared of being caught in the crossfire between the Subedar's galbats and the Siddi's war dhows. Kanhoji moves from skirmish to siege, seeking the battle that will end the war and inflating his men with the hope of success.

A sea-drenched wind blows against Kanhoji's face as he looks up at the sun blotched out by distant clouds black against the orb's fire. He stands on the deck of *Mandar*, a tri-masted ghurab armed with nine 20-pounders on each side. She gently rolls at anchor in the bay north of Janjira. He returns the letter he has just received from Balaji to Gangadhar. Balaji, in spite of his earlier assurance, hasn't been able to send any artillery garrisons and can only offer

319

some infantry troops who, Kanhoji knows, will be recalled to the
Desha as soon as they arrive in the Konkan. The saffron-coloured
sails of his ghurabs blockading the Rajapuri Creek to the south,
pick up the light of the evening sun and shine like the spires of
conch shells on the inky sea. His ghurabs are arrayed in a siege
formation with new cannon lined up broadside on new and sturdy
teak decks along the western walls of Janjira. But the war-winning
battle eludes Kanhoji as the Wazir sits cocooned in Janjira. The
Siddi has been judicious in this matter, as his family and cohorts
know they are fighting for their very existence. Hansuji's foundry,
though flowing with streams of molten lead, hasn't been able to
satiate the demand the artillery captains make for shots that barely
scratch the walls of Janjira. Nor can Babuji Kotla and his masons
chisel as many spherical balls of laterite and basalt as Kanhoji's
largest siege cannons need. His heart grows heavy as he realizes
that the rains will soon force an end to the siege. Kanhoji has been
pacing the deck the entire evening and though he is not tired, he
can feel a frustration growing in his thighs. Maybe if he looks at the
fort long enough, he can figure a way out. He orders a cessation of
the firing to let his enemy pray, as the azan for the dusk prayer rings
out from the minaret of the mosque in Janjira Fort.

Kanhoji lies down on a charpai on the deck as Golu massages
his calves and feet. Kanhoji closes his eyes and wills his knotted brow
to relax with every exhalation, sinking into the rocking charpai. In
a moment his dreams come and take him on a tiger hunt with his
sons. They stand in the bows of their galbats, muskets in hand, flying
through dense jungles. A giant barasingha leaps across their path.
They spot a tiger. It turns and smiles at Kanhoji. It has a wound on
its face. They stalk the injured tiger through the dark shrub. A bear
jumps out of the brush . . .

'Baba, baba,' Sambhaji's voice warns him, and he opens his eyes
to see his son looking at him. Sambhaji, rarely having witnessed his
father resting or asleep, is worried by the sight: Is he unwell or God
forbid, ageing?

'Are you feeling well, Baba?' Sambhaji inquires in worry.

'Yes, of course. What are you doing here? Why have you left Vijaydurg?'

'Vijaydurg is well protected, it's unassailable. They haven't been able to scratch the walls. They lost several large dhows on the sea wall. They just can't get close enough to be of any harm to us.'

'Why are you here?' Kanhoji says anxiously.

'I have come with my galbats to be by your side when you take Janjira.'

'Well, actually I am in the same situation here that the Siddi finds himself in Vijaydurg. We haven't been able to make a dent here either.'

'Nobody amenable inside?' Sambhaji wonders hopefully.

'I offered Rs 7,86,000 and not one taker,' Kanhoji says smiling.

'Do we have that much money?' Sambhaji asks, shocked.

'Not in coin, but yes, it can be made available. For Janjira it is a pittance,' Kanhoji says.

'Baba, there is this horse in Kalyan. If you have that kind of money, just buy this one.'

'How much is it?'

'Twenty-five thousand, negotiable,'

'A live horse or a statue in gold?'

'Worth ten times more than gold, Baba. Are the troops coming from Satara?'

'I just received the letter: none are available currently.'

'Kaka has really let us down this time. I cannot believe that he would do this to you.'

'Kaka is doing more important things with his troops, son.'

'Is helping the Mughals more important than taking Janjira?'

'Well, when you are helping them against themselves—maybe?'

'He has forgotten us after taking your help and making himself Peshwa.'

'Son, mind your tone when you speak of your elders and the friends of your father.'

'I mean no disrespect, Baba, but this is absolutely unfair. We should have first finished off the Siddi and then he could do what he wants in Dilli.'

'He hasn't sent any troops, though. You do know that, don't you?' Kanhoji reminds him.

'Not yet, but he is itching to, and he has forgotten all about the Konkan. Kaka, like every other royal minister, too has relegated the Konkan to a secondary status. The battles fought on the Desha will always seem more important to those in Satara or Kolhapur, and now after Dilli has entered his horizon, the Konkan seems even more distant and unimportant to them.'

Sambhaji has mouthed his innermost thoughts, but they sear his ears with pain when he hears them spoken aloud.

'Son, my career began with Janjira, and it will end with it, but maybe just not this year. The rains will be upon us soon. It is far from easy, and some think it impossible.'

'You have taught me that if one acts against any challenge with full vigour, then nothing is impossible.'

'Within the laws of nature, my son: the waves will always crash on the rocks and the rains come every year and we must retreat in their face. But you and your brothers have done well in taking the villages that support this fortress. Next year they will be weaker still.'

'I think that they don't want you to defeat the Siddi. It would make you too powerful, wouldn't it?'

'And who is this they that you talk of?'

'You know very well, Baba: Kaka and Swamiji and especially the Chhatrapati. If you think about it, not one of the sardars of the Desha wants you to succeed.'

'Is that what you think?'

'I do.'

'We are the Subedars of the Konkan, the Sarkhel of the navy, and we are the servants of the Bhonsales, the family of Shivaji Maharaj himself.'

'Let's see, Baba, which family survives the vagaries of time and who is whose Subedar,' Sambhaji says bitterly.

Kanhoji is irritated at his son's inability to control his emotions.

'It would behoove you not to say treasonous things against Shahu Raje in front of his loyal Sarkhel. Temper your ambition with decency and limitations,' Kanhoji admonishes his son.

'Forgive me,' Sambhaji says as he turns away, equally disappointed. He has never been able to understand his father's loyalty to people who give him neither importance nor treat him in the way he deserves to be treated. Why wasn't his father made peshwa? Why does he even remain a subedar when he can be a raja. It makes no sense to him.

'What do you think we should do now?' Kanhoji asks his son, hearing the clamouring inside him.

'Forget Janjira. It is too late already. Let's go back and destroy every dhow that flies his flag.'

'That's my son,' Kanhoji says with excessive cheer. 'Let's do what we can and leave what is not in our hands to Khandoba.'

They are all his sons, yet each so different, Kanhoji thinks, and thankfully Sekho is the eldest.

The Company's Man

Every vessel on the coast, small and large, is dragged on to the beach or anchored within protective inlets. This happens annually when clouds high enough to smear the sun's aura darken houses and workshops with lazy grey shadows. South-westerly winds then begin to gale and incensed waves chop violently against the shore with frothy axe heads. Amongst the last to be pulled ashore are two galbats that, patrolling the sea off Bassein, spot four *shibars*[*] that are trying to pass off as ships of the Angrezi Company. The ships and their cargo, as the Sarkhel's inspectors realize, belong to Seth Gordhan Das of Surat. There is no cause to believe that the Company itself is complicit in this deception and it is possible that the Seth has tried this ruse on his own accord. The inspectors send the shibars to Kulaba and have the bales of cotton offloaded and stored at the warehouses that hold confiscated goods. Kanhoji, waiting for carpenters he has requested of Governor Boone, hurries to the jetty thinking they have arrived at last, for the Governor had said he would send them before the monsoon began.

Across the bay, the new Angrezi governor hates the rains as much as Angria does. The quarries stop producing their stones and the labourers find it impossible to work in the squelching mud. The

---

[*] A large coasting vessel.

season begins with the body of his factors and writers shivering and laid down with aching joints. Boone despises the darkness and delays the rain brings and is appalled at the vicious and unhindered way it beats down—nothing like sweet Albion where the rain is but a gentle inconvenience. Here on this rocky outpost, even the paper refuses to cooperate, as it lies damp enough to fudge the finest line of ink into bulbous and incomprehensible pythons.

Boone is in a room that adjoins his personal office. It is a large room with a series of bay windows that are now letting in the diminishing light. The room is connected to a corridor that opens to the smaller private offices of the Revenue Administrator, the Chief Accountant, the Chief of Stores and the Patel. Boone prefers meeting his subordinates in this office, where he has a desk and bureau assigned to each task or department. Most of the desks are given over to the creation of a coastal naval force and the fortification of the port and warehouses. Boone's secretary Chittlesworth is seated by a desk, looking through a massive ledger. Boone is speaking to Rustomji when Pandurao Phangaskar walks in.

'What of the carpenters that Angria has requested, Governor Saheb? How many do you want to send?' asks Rustomji.

'You can send four and a master. I am sure we can spare five of our men?'

'Yes, Saheb, four and a master then,' says the Patel.

'Good day to you, Governor Saheb,' Phangaskar says as he steps in to shake Boone's hand.

'If it isn't my favourite Corn-Corny, Mr Pando Row,' Boone says, pumping Pandurao's hands.

Rustomji does a namaskar to Pandurao, who deliberately ignores it.

'Oh, you haven't met. This is Mr Rustomji, the Patel of Bombay as his father was before him.'

'Of course, who does not know Rustomji,' Pandurao smiles mechanically.

Age has melted away from the Patel and he stands straight and broad-chested. His skin is no longer wrinkled, and his beard is black and much shorter than earlier.

'His Excellency the Wazir sends his regards to your honourable self,' Pandurao says to Boone.

'Thank you, Mr Pando Row. I have a letter and some bills for His Excellency, if you would be willing.'

'Of course, I would be for I well know that none of the other Seths or even your emissaries would be willing in the coming days,' Pandurao says, glancing at Rustomji.

'The blasted monsoon,' Boone exclaims as he sends Chittlesworth to get the pending invoices for the Siddi.

'It is a time for rest and for staying at home with the family,' Rustomji says.

'Blood to rest, Rustom! We shall rest when we are dead,' Boone says energetically.

'Well said, Governor Saheb, we will rest only when we are dead. Meanwhile Rustomji can rest—as there will be no fishing boats from which to take a fish each,' Pandurao says, alluding to the customary right Rustomji holds as the tax collector of the villages surrounding Bombay.

Irritated, Rustomji excuses himself from the room, citing the census Boone has demanded. He has counted 16,000 souls, saved and doomed, that live on the archipelago of Bombay under the Company's jurisdiction. He goes to his office, in the adjacent room, separated by a wooden partition, and puts his ear to the wood. The conversation, though muffled, is audible.

'I don't want to intervene, but did I hear the Patel mention Angria?'

'Ah, yes. Cornerji was requesting some carpenters.'

'Of course, he would. It's how he always does it. Has he sent you the mangoes and the gunpowder?'

'Yes, and both of the greatest quality, I might add. But how do you know?'

'It's his way. It's how he got to Aislabie before you. Gifts and other little exchanges: carpenters for gunsmiths, saltpetre for cannon shot.'

'I think not, Mr Pando Row, he isn't all that bad a person. Rummerji says he is a man of his word.'

'Well, it is in Ramaji's interests to sell him to you unalloyed.'

'Come now, Rummerji is as honest a shroff as I have had the opportunity to work with. He has donated Rs 20,000 towards the cathedral we are building.'

'There is a saying in these lands: *daam saam dand**. Which means . . .'

'Spare me the local pithies, but I must presume, Mr Pando Row, that you have a personal animosity towards Cornerji.'

'Seths like myself cannot afford to have personal whims getting in the way of commerce, Governor Saheb. It is nothing like that. I have studied at the same school as he and the current Peshwa did, under the most reputed teacher of our time. My teacher accepted students only from the most distinguished families of the Konkan. How Kanhoji was accepted, I do not know. But I have known him for a long time and I know how he thinks and is apt to behave. You can say I am an expert on Kanhoji. Anyway, as they say: live and learn.'

'Can I come in?' chimes a gentle voice at the door of the office. The arrival of Govindji, Ramaji Kamath's clerk saves Boone any response to Pandurao.

'I have some work with Rummerji's man, Mr Pando Row, we will discuss this at some other time.'

'Of course, Saheb, I had just come to look into your health. I will just take His Excellency's bills and be on my way to Janjira before the storm sets in.'

'Yes, thank you,' Boone says as he turns his attention to the matter Govindji has brought up regarding exchange rates. After Pandurao has left, Boone sends a clerk to Rustomji with a message to hold off on sending the carpenters to Kanhoji for now. It starts to drizzle.

---

* Money, negotiations, then a stick.

Monsoon

Ye re ye re pausa / Tula deto paisa
*Paisa jhala khota / Paus ala motha**

The rains begin and the brown-skinned landscape explodes with silver veins: streams and rivulets gushing back to the raging sea. Mahapurush Brahmendra Swami is increasingly hailed as a prophet and a seer without parallel. He crossed the River Savitri on a lotus leaf. He has witnesses to his prophecy on the rise of Balaji to the highest office in the land, touted to all who have ears. His blessings have always been with Balaji and with Kanhoji, and they have risen to great prominence and wealth, well beyond all others in the Konkan. Reed mats tremble and clatter on the windows, trying to keep the rain out. Diyas flicker hesitantly through these dimly lit days that teach patience.

'Pralaya,' Mahapurush Brahmendra Swami says ominously.

'It is all with my grace,' Swamiji explains to the Wazir's son Siddi Abdul Rahman Khan who has come in his father's stead, on why Angre has brought the Siddi to his knees.

'Bless our family, too, Swamiji, so that we may prosper.'

---

* Marathi nursery rhyme: 'Rain, rain come / I will give you a penny // the penny was fake / yet it rained a lot'.

'Son, my grace has never abandoned you. But what do the stars foretell?' Swamiji says, smiling serenely.

'It is your family's survival that most worries me. Your father has taken too much pride in himself. The Navagrahas are misaligned, Varuna unpropitiated and Allah is ashamed with his servant's ways,' he says, the tempo and his tone more urgent.

Siddi Abdul Rahman bends his head and closes his eyes as he raises his folded palms to the sky in forgiveness.

'My father was blinded by the arrogance of the Turkis in Dilli, Swamiji,' Abdul Rahman pleads.

'Anyway, what is most important now is that you are negotiating for your father. Know that I requested for you,' Swamiji says surreptitiously.

'The Peshwa is coming here and so is the Sarkhel-Subedar. We will all four sit down and work some compromise out. But if your father cannot ratify it afterwards, then neither I nor Prajapati can do anything,' he adds.

'Rest assured, Swamiji, I speak for my father. Did I not show you his letter?' Abdul says confidently.

He takes the letter from his clerk and gives it to Swamiji's secretary.

'Keep it as his word. Whatever decision you come to, we will, and he will, abide by it.'

'Good, that is good. We don't want to further antagonize them. Balaji already feels that my heart is kinder to your father than to him, and Kanhoji openly says that I favour your father in all things.'

The Wazir's son bows to Brahmendra Swami and takes his leave.

'I have made arrangements for your stay at the ashram. I will call you once Bala and Kanho have arrived,' Swamiji tells the Siddi of Janjira's son.

The ashram has been transformed into a miniature town and banking centre. Both Balaji and Kanhoji have built themselves dharmshalas, for their stays at the ashram. Swamiji has sold them plots close to his own limestone residence that are nestled amongst gardens and shallow pools at one end of the ashram compound. Balaji arrives from Satara and Kanhoji from Suvarnadurg on the same day. Though they have constructed lavish little cottages at the ashram, neither has spent much time in them. They have never been used for more than a bath or for changing clothes by either of its donors.

Balaji is the first to arrive and he brings his elder son Baji with him, along with an expanded retinue and bodyguard that suits his position as Peshwa. As soon as they arrive, they head to their private dharamshala to get bathed and dressed. They then go to see Brahmendra Swami and offer their dakshina.

'You will reach heights greater than your father even and you will live a long life and have many sons,' Brahmendra Swami says when the young Baji prostrates himself at his feet. Baji stays down and lets the prophecy sink in before he slowly gets up with his palms clasped in a namaskar.

'He has the body of a warrior,' Brahmendra Swami says to Balaji.

'And he can ride like a Rajput prince,' adds the proud father.

'Where is your friend?' Brahmendra Swami inquires of Balaji.

'I haven't the faintest idea, but I can well presume an animal got in his way,' the Peshwa says.

'You know, I always tell him no hunting before coming to the ashram, but I know he never listens,' Swamiji says indulgently.

'Or maybe he is not willing to come, Swamiji. He feels we have betrayed him in this matter,' Balaji voices Kanhoji's concern.

'He is wrong to think like that, Balaji. Don't worry, I will explain it to him.'

'I think we should have done that before calling the Siddi here.'

'What are you worried about? The Wazir is not here; his eldest is here on his behalf. He is my own child. Don't worry about anything.'

'What of Kanhoji?'

'He too is as much a child, mine own child. But he is obsessed with taking Janjira. The Habshis need order too. What do you say, Baji?' asks Mahapurush of the Peshwa's eldest son.

'Guruji, I think one must always seek a balance. Did Astika not stop the *Sarpa Satra**?' Baji replies.

'See, even your adolescent son has more sense than your friend. Not that it's Kanho's fault. He has a fire burning in his chest. We must cool it first, no?'

'Well, then let him hunt himself to some peace before he arrives,' suggests Balaji.

'That will only whet his appetite, Bala. He eats too much meat.'

'Perhaps only you have the power to make him give up prawns, wild boar and deer.'

'Prawns and all are permissible, but the pig and deer, he must stay away from. Even the Wazir's son has been on a purely *shakahari*** diet the past few days and I never hear him complain to anyone.'

'By the power of Your Grace, Guruji.'

'Anyway Bala, tell me what progress you have made with the Turkis?'

Bala narrates at length his efforts to get the Mughals to ratify the Maratha right to impose Chauth on all the areas that had been held by Chhatrapati Shivaji. Baji listens intently as the Mahapurush smiles at him and pats his shoulders avuncularly.

By late morning, Kanhoji arrives at the ashram with Golu, Gangadhar, Surya and his sons Sekhoji and Tulaji, having fed entire villages on the way. They wash off the grime and gunpowder smoke from their bodies before Kanhoji takes his sons to meet Brahmendra Swami who is at his durbar hall with Balaji, Baji and an assortment of clerks and secretaries.

'I hear that Janjira's son is here. Is it true?' Kanhoji asks Balaji.

'Yes, he is, as my honoured guest,' says Swamiji as he takes Kanho by his arm and leads him towards a window at the end of the durbar hall. The rain has ceased momentarily.

---

* A sacrifice undertaken by Emperor Janamejaya to annihilate all snakes.

** Vegetarian.

'What have you achieved this year?' Swamiji asks, his forehead smudged with condensation and vibhuti.

'I would have succeeded had I been given the promised troops and artillery. But even then, we have achieved a lot,' Kanhoji says.

'Why do you keep harping on about Janjira? When neither Shivaji Maharaj nor Sambhaji could take it, what chance do we have?'

'Janjira is not Gheria, Swamiji, I could well have taken it. Let the rains end. This coming season, Janjira will be mine. Regardless of anybody's help.'

'What are you? An ant? Always moving in the same old line, next season, next month, next fort and next war. Hari, Hari, Hari,' Swamiji says, smiling.

'I am not going to enter into any treaty with Siddi Rasool. I knew he would come running to you. Even if we did not take Janjira, I have demolished his navy and taken his villages.'

'This treaty has nothing to do with you or with Siddi Rasool. It is between Shahu Maharaj and the Turk, and the both of you will have to toe the line. You are putting your friend Balaji in a precarious position and undoing all the success he has achieved.'

'Shriman Peshwa,' Swami shouts across the durbar hall and motions to Balaji to join them.

The Peshwa walks over to the white marble jharoka the two men are standing beside. It begins to rain.

'Kanhoji, I know you are disappointed with me,' Balaji says.

'What disappointed? I just can't believe that I cannot trust you any more. You have become just like any other sardar in the Desha: wary of my success.'

'No Kanho, no. Understand what this is about. All that I have been trying to do is get back Maharaj's old sardeshmukhi and the rights of Chauth.'

'And we need the permission of the Mughal to do this? If we already collect the tax, then we are the rightful sardeshmukhs, are we not?'

'Kanhoji, there are more men than you can imagine who are willing to fight us over this right. What is stopping Dilli from giving these rights to some Rajput or Persian general? The Nizam Saheb wishes to carve a kingdom out for himself in the Dhakkan. Now he needs to be back under the shadow of the throne, lest other proxies mount it, and it leaves us minding the Dhakkan for them.'

'Then why have you even bothered to call me? If this treaty is between Shahu Raje and the Mughal, why do you need me here?'

'Because you are the index finger of the Maratha hand, and you need to understand what we are doing. It has nothing to do with frustrating you. This treaty is going to end Siddi domination slowly but surely. You will be invited into Janjira soon, trust me. But now, this treaty needs to go through, and you need to adhere to it.'

'What are the terms of the treaty? What do we get?'

'Their fort at Padmadurg and eleven villages.'

'You can't be serious. We already have possession of their outpost on Padmadurg and more than eleven of their villages. Do you want me to return some?'

'Having possession and having hereditary rights are two different things. Kanho, everybody is just trying to work towards a settlement that ensures peace in all the villages and fields. Only when the farmers can harvest their crops in peace and the boats sail unmolested with their cargoes can we ever hope to harvest taxes.'

'Siddi Rasool also wants your personal assurance to any treaty,' Swami Brahmendra chimes in.

'I want the Kalal Bangdi then.'

'We will see what we can do,' Balaji says quickly.

'Now, don't scare the boy when you meet him,' Swamiji says mirthfully to Kanhoji and pats his arm to console him.

The three of them walk back to the boys who have been having their own discussion.

'Send for the *Wazirzada*,' Swamiji says as they take their seats on the impeccable white mattresses.

A Gift from Khandoba

Kanhoji is at Vijaydurg, personally overseeing the vast refurbishment of the wooden town within the fortress. Though he has not been spending as much time as he would have liked to, he is sure that when he is older, he would like to live at Gheria. The fort is his pride and joy, and he knows it to be the best-defended fort in the Konkan. What nature has not given it he has taken care to afford it. He had always felt an affinity with the place and the little village of Gheria that nestles beside the isthmus the fort is on. He considers the fort perfect and a much better fortified position than Janjira, which is still intact despite the much-diminished sway of Siddi Rasool. On the other hand, his old ally Siddi Khairiyat is wealthiest and most powerful of all the Siddi Warlords.

Kanhoji is short of timber for his project and the sawyers wait silently for more wood to arrive. His own shipment has been delayed and he is tempted to turn to the stocks he has at his shipyards. But he will not do that. Amatya Pant was kind enough to send his treatise, the Adnyapatra, composed for the benefit of Shahu Maharaj, to Kanhoji too with a letter of thanks and blessings for future success. In response Kanhoji had sent a box of large pearls and a sack of lesser ones to Amatya Pant who has retired to a neighbourhood at the top of the ghats not far from Vijaydurg, where the hard-working and loyal minister was gifted his *jagir*. In his treatise, Amatya Pant has drawn attention to the necessity of maintaining a fully functional and well-stocked and manned ship repairing and building yard. It is from Kanhoji's own example, and it also suggests the plantation of teak for timber. However, the treatise has no direction on how to hasten time or conjure up shipments of wood.

Sambhaji is atop a bastion with his father in the open air they both prefer. Kanhoji is sitting on a charpai rubbing his eyes when one of his men comes up to him with some pleasant news: a Company ship out of Surat is laden with timber and on its way south. Kanhoji has the supercargo of the ship brought up to him once its captain is made to dock at Vijaydurg.

'You are heaven-sent, my man. I hear you have wood on board.'

'Yes, Saheb,' says the young English supercargo, 'we do have timber on board and are on our way to Karwar to sell it.'

'Aren't you going the wrong way? Taking wood to the forest?'

'Planks of red sal, Saheb, from Rattanpore and a few bundles of *agar* wood from the east,' the boyish supercargo says excitedly.

'Heaven-sent, indeed, it's exactly what I need. If you don't mind, I will purchase your cargo of timber immediately. Just tell me the price and I will give you ten *takka*[*] more,' Kanhoji generously offers.

'Of course, Saheb,' the man says, glad to have been able to help the powerful and generous Admiral.

'I don't require the Agar, but if it saves you the journey, I will buy it too,' Kanhoji adds, and the factor readily agrees.

As Gangadhar arranges for the sum in silver for the young man and his captain, Kanhoji suggests: 'If I were you, I would put this money to good use and buy some gunpowder from us.'

'I will from the gratuity you have given me, if you don't mind, sir, the Company's coin I will leave for the Company,' the young pony-tailed factor replies gratefully.

'As you wish,' Kanhoji says happily as the matter is concluded.

---

[*] Per cent.

Kanhoji is about to accompany the boy to the jetty to look at the wood Lord Khandoba has so kindly sent for him, when Sambhaji stops him.

'Baba, why do you do these things? Let us,' Sambhaji says and goes down to the jetty.

Alone, on the bastion, looking out into a disappearing horizon that is indistinguishable from the haze on the sea, Kanhoji takes stock of the year. Thank Khandoba for small mercies as the great ambitions of life yet elude him. Maybe, Balaji is right: balances and checks exist naturally and maybe are even good. But how can a check against him be natural? Or why would Balaji accept it? As things stand, after the treaty between the Mughal and Shahu Maharaj, the Siddis of Janjira are finished as a force, and yet Balaji does not want them annihilated. As a child, Kanhoji had never been a victim of the Siddis as Balaji had been: enslaved and orphaned. Yet.

Khandoba must be thanked for the most important things. The boys are all fine men, untouched by greed or lust and none have a cruel streak. Only Tula is still worrisome. Most importantly they are respectful of their elders and accord the correct respect to his eldest Sekhoji. He worries now, what if the curse that infects the Timurids has come down with the old man and may one day infect his own sons.

Sambhaji returns to break his reverie.

'Baba, what if we were to make ships like the Firangis and Angrez?'

'They are only for deep-sea voyaging.'

'Exactly. We can send our traders out to Persia, Chin and even the homeland of the Firangis. You have no idea at what price simple spices and cotton cloth are sold compared to what they pay for it here.'

'Are you planning to become a vania?'

'We don't have to do it, we become part owners. We just provide the ships and the security. Traders like Kaka Ramaji, they decide what to buy and sell and they pay for the goods. They give us a percentage of what they make for providing the gunships with artillery, men and sailors.'

'The Siddis have been doing this for centuries. It is nothing new.'

'But they don't have ships like the Firangis do. They trade with Malindi and Yaman, where there is limited profit and no desire to pay for our products like the Firangis do. What about the New Land they get their gold and emeralds from? We can go there directly.'

'Where are you getting these ideas from?'

'We were discussing it.'

'Who are we?'

'Kaka Ramaji's son.'

'Had to be,' Kanhoji says.

'Are you upset? Will you tell Ai?'

'Forget your Ai. The business at hand, my son, is far from done. Leave this nonsense to the vanias—it is not becoming of any son of a subedar. And as long as the Firangis have Chaul and Bassein and the Siddi Janjira, our work is not complete.'

The Insult

A fortnight later, Kanhoji is still at Vijaydurg, pushing Babuji Kotla and his team of carpenters to work the heaven-sent red Sal into door and window frames for his new bazaar. Rustomji Patel is announced and Kanhoji has him called in immediately. The young Patel, not as resilient as his father, is looking the worse for wear and Kanhoji insists he sit on a chair. Rustomji delivers his missive hesitantly to Gangadhar. Gangadhar begins to read it aloud, and then stops and wisely returns it to Rustomji and asks him to read it out instead. Rustomji creaks out of the chair and stands to read the letter written by his Governor in Fort George. When he finishes, his body is trembling because his knee joints have lost their strength and can't keep his body straight.

Kanhoji's jaw has clenched upon itself and an estuary of veins in his forehead has ballooned up in anger.

Kanhoji gestures for the distraught man to take his seat.

'He is accusing me of robbery,' he says to Rustomji who puts his hands up in apology, though more as a plea for restraint.

Gangadhar stands at the ready to compose his master's response to the English Governor's letter as Rustomji mills around uncomfortably.

'As I had great necessity for timber when the vessel came from Surat, I brought her in, in a friendly manner, believing we observed a friendship without scruples. And what of a little timber? Had I written to you, you would have given it to me, but then maybe somebody would have stopped it? So, I took it and paid you the price. In this there is no cause for difference.*

Turning to Rustomji, Kanhoji asks: 'Satisfied? Is that a conciliatory response enough for you, Patelji? You are witness to the gracious pardon I have made to this most insulting act,' Kanhoji says incensed.

'Is there not much to worry about in their business or is there no trade to be had, Patelji? To send you here—to have the time and energy to write this: it is truly unbelievable. I would be upset, if I did not find the entire incident humorous and ridiculous,' he lies. He does not find it to be either.

'Sarkhel Saheb, there are people whose eyes get pinched with salt when they gaze upon you. You must know this,' Rustomji hints.

'And what kind of adviser are you, Patelji, to these small, petty and unwashed men?'

'Do we all not listen to what we want to hear and only see what we wish to see? My father and I have always spoken for that which is true and righteous,' Rustomji replies.

'I do not doubt you, Rustomji, but you must make sense prevail for if they are to quibble over every little thing, we will miss the opportunity to work on greater things together. You promised me carpenters and did not send them. Did I take offence? What of the passes that you sell to every local merchant? Passing off their goods as yours and robbing me of my rightful revenue?' Kanhoji asks him.

'Saheb, this new one is *kaan cha kacha***, I beg patience and forgiveness on your part,' Rustomji says.

'You call the Sarkhel a thug, Patel,' Surya says suddenly, 'people have died for thinking less,' he ominously adds.

Kanhoji raises his palm to rein Surya in and adds: 'It is not Rustomji's fault, he has always tried his best to maintain peace and

---

* From an original letter of Kanhoji Angre.

** Easily given to hearsay.

amity. What can he do if they keep changing the fool in charge and we have to demonstrate the ground realities to each one in turn?'

Rustomji smoothes his beard in embarrassment and receives the sealed reply in silence from Gangadhar.

Surya escorts the shaken Patel down to the jetty where his little tender is tied. He takes the opportunity to ask what his masters do to clean themselves after defecation. As Rustomji is getting into his tottering boat, Surya warns him in the crudest Konkani: 'Tell Bhoon I will shove an oar up his ass and *bhuno*[*] him if he ever shows disrespect to Saheb again.'

Rustomji wobbles on to the boat, trembling.

---

[*] Roast.

Bills

The sun has just climbed up over the ghats and tallow candles light the passageways and offices of the castle. Boone is sitting at his table under a candlelit chandelier. In the distance, an arrhythmic beat of hammers marks the progress of time. He is writing an entreaty for more funds back to his employers in London when Phangaskar knocks on Boone's door.

'Ah, Mr Pando Row, you are up early,' Boone greets the Seth.

'Up? Kind sir, sleep is for babies and women. I never sleep. I just can't get myself to sleep,' Pandurao explains.

'That's a little unlikely, don't you think?' Boone insists.

'Not at all. *Dhyana*, yoga; with the correct diet and lifestyle, one rarely needs to sleep. I myself nod off for a few watches a week, just to rest my eyelids.'

Boone looks at the man incredulously.

'If you insist. Anyway, how can I help you?'

'Governor Saheb, I just wanted to present you with the bills for the timber that I have supplied so far.'

'*Kasu illa, kasu illa*,' Boone says cheerfully, waving his left hand as he continues to write with the other.

'Please pardon me,' Pandurao replies perplexed.

'Oh, you don't speak the Tamilly here. I meant I wouldn't be reimbursing you now. I was quite clear on that,' Boone says.

'Of course, Saheb, just for your reference. I will update the accounts as we go along,' Pandurao says.

'Thanks be to you. As you well know, we are still waiting for the funds to come in from Leadenhall. A trifle delayed. Must be stuck in the doldrums,' Boone explains.

'Right you are as always, Governor Saheb,' Pandurao says.

'I was just writing how we need to protect ourselves out here,' Boone says, pleased with his supplier.

'From what, Saheb?'

'These waters are beset by pirates: Sanganian Goozeratis that Hamilton encountered, the Muscat Arabs who strike where they please and even Javans around the coast on the other side.'

'You have forgotten your main problem,' Pandurao adds.

'He's a pirate, all right. Just helped himself to my wood like it was nothing,' Boone adds bitterly.

'This is just the start. This is how he does it. Give him a finger and he'll pull you in to your armpit. He is nothing but a glorified bandit.'

'I had offered my hand in friendship, but he twisted it. All these black fellows are the same. They are blacker back in Madras, though,' Boone says scornfully.

'None blacker than Angre, Governor Saheb.'

'Is he blacker than you? He acts like someone with the blackest skin. You are less black, more like a Spaniard or a Portugal,' Boone wonders.

'It is because I am a Brahmin, of the highest caste. Dear sir, lightened by the most ancient and supreme knowledge,' Pandurao explains.

'What is he?' Boone asks.

'*Aenh*, they say they are Kshatriya, the princely warrior class, but they are not. The true warriors were annihilated by a Brahmin sage many years ago. Not far from here,' Pandurao says.

'And Rummerji? He is much fairer than you, almost as fair as an Englishman and has Irish eyes?'

'Washed up, shipwrecked Yavanas, Sire. After my ancestor Rishi Parshuram, the Brahmin sage, killed all the warriors; he needed somebody to perform a purification ritual. He found Yavana corpses washed up on the shore and resurrected them as Brahmins to cleanse him. Much like your Jesus himself.'

'Dear man, you cannot compare the resurrection of the Son of God by God himself to some necromancy,' Boone says horrified.

'I meant no offence, Governor Saheb. But let me tell you something. This Angria cuts off people's noses and ears.'

Boone learns something new every day and transmits his newly gained knowledge back home. The western coast is very different from the eastern one. Everything is different: the people, the languages, the food, and the diseases. And regardless of the coast, the Christians here are essentially Pagan or worse: Catholic.

'Well, it soon will not matter. Once I have my fleet ready. I don't want any delays in your teak shipments, Pando Row,' Boone says, returning to his work.

'Don't worry about your wood, Governor Saheb, it will always come in on time. I am supplying you with only the best seasoned wood, Saheb.'

'I do hope so. Is there anything else?'

'Nothing, Saheb, I will have Chitalwar acknowledge my receipts and be on my way,' Pandurao says, leaving the impatient Governor. Boone dips his quill in the ink bottle and returns to his letter: 'None dispossess us as much as the pirate Cornerji Angria, who makes tall claims of authority from the Sow Raja, whom he recently attacked.'

Outside, in the swamps that surround every island, the firmament is buzzing with the deadliest and most insidious kind of mosquitoes: the ones that bring lifelong chills, growing infirmity and eventual death.

The Jaatris

Ballu Nakhwa has taken a shibar along with all his men to the Dargah at Mahim. It has saffron-hued sails and a pattern on its waterline. The Dargah is the grave of a man of learning, a magician, a granter of wishes who is hailed as Qutb-e-Konkan and draws believers from all faiths. Unarmed and returning in a joyful hum, a pair of armed barges flying the English Company's red striped flag halts them off the rocks at Varli. Their protests of being in the service of Sarkhel Kanhoji Angre do not let them through, and the entire crew is arrested, and their boat towed off to Palva Bandar. Ballu and the eight men from his village are imprisoned in an airless underground cellar that has existed from the Portuguese days. The next day, the same Bhandari guards they had mingled with at the Dargah come to guard them.

Rustomji races to the Governor's apartment as soon as he finds out about the debacle. Angre's men can be released, and the incident smoothed over as a case of mistaken identity. But it has not been a mistake and the barges have taken the Maratha ship deliberately.

'He is a pirate and will be treated as one,' Boone snaps at Rustomji.

'President Saheb, calling him a thief as you have done will undo all the goodwill we have with the Marathas. They have never acted against us unjustly and there is no cause for this. They have always had use of our ports as we theirs. I besiege you, sir, please at least let his people go.'

'Go where—return to piracy? Confuse me not with earlier incumbents of this august post. I give as good as I get and am not cowed by this black Lothario.'

'Sir, Kanhoji paid for the wood he took. It would be highly imprudent and costly to move against him on that account.'

'Don't teach me my job, young man,' Boone says and dismisses Rustom who makes his way to the cellar. He bribes the guards to ensure that no harm will come to Angre's men till this business is sorted out.

Rustomji then hurries to meet Ramaji Kamath whom he knows to have ready access to Kanhoji. As he is trundled down the bazaar in his palkhi, he realizes that the traders already know what has transpired and are bracing for an immediate response by shutting shop. Rumours and questions swirl around him like the loo[*]:

'Very bad timing. Angre is at peace with the Siddi.'

'Angre is going to sack the place and put it to the torch.'

'As if these walls and his little boats can keep Angre at bay.'

'Friends, just keep your godowns empty and your heads low.'

'What will happen to the trade?'

'Just when everything was going so well.'

'Let's go back to Thana.'

Rustomji pushes through the crowds to Ramaji's daftar.

'What do you want me to do?' asks Ramaji.

'Meet with Subedar Saheb. Tell him to be patient. I will resolve this soon. He is bound to find out soon, it would be better if you tell him.'

'If he does not already know? Do you think he has to wait to find them missing? He definitely has people here who keep him updated.'

'Either way, Kamath Seth. We all stand to lose if the relations between the Company and Angre deteriorate.'

---

[*] Hot summer wind.

'You are telling me? I have business dealings with both of you.'

'Exactly, you are the one man who can do it. Then you must come back and talk to Boone. Maybe he will listen to you.'

'My man told me that he heard Pandurao talking to Boone about Angre in the upstairs office.'

'That man has his own axes to grind. He has greatly ingratiated himself to the Governor.'

'Cured his *julaab*[*], I heard.'

'This is no time for jokes, Sethji. If you could make your way to Kulaba.'

'He may not be at Kulaba currently. You must search him out and follow him to wherever he is. He is always on the move,' Ramaji explains.

'This is very important, Kamathji. As a favour to me, as a kindness to this; your settlement and your community,' Rustomji pleads.

---

[*] Diarrhoea.

Embassy

Ramaji sails on his newly polished boat with its immaculate white sails to Kulaba to find that the Sarkhel-Subedar is still at Vijaydurg. Ramaji sails south to Vijaydurg, arriving just in time to find Kanhoji at the jetty and about to leave.

'Ramaji, my friend, what brings you here?'

'I was sent to talk to you.'

'Talk to me? By whom?'

'Rustomji Patel.'

Kanhoji shakes his head.

'Come with me, we are going to Suvarnadurg,' Kanhoji says suddenly.

Ramaji gets into Kanhoji's ghurab as the entire fleet departs and his own nakhwa follows them.

'The Angrez have taken my shibar with all men on board being held prisoner. They had gone to the mela in Mahim.'

'You already know?'

'Of course, Ramaji. Opportunity doesn't travel on sails, my friend, it flashes like lightning. What does Rustom want?'

'Patience on your part. He assures me that your men are fine, and they will be returned as soon as possible.'

'By Rustomji? He is nothing but a munshi. He has no power to return them.'

'He says he is trying his best. What are you going to do?'

'What is there to do? I will just be. From this day forward, my friendship with them is over. When Khandoba gives, one must take; and what Khandoba gives, I will take.'

'But the Angrez need you to be their friend. The bazaar is worried. As am I.'

'It is the nature of the world, Ramaji, that bad decisions of important men behind walls must be suffered by the entire land. But if I were you or any other trader, I would think twice before moving anything on an Angrezi ship,' Kanhoji says as he pats Ramaji on his shoulder to comfort him.

'If the Siddi behaves and keeps to his slaves, I have to keep off him as I have given my word to Swamiji. There is not much else to do and the Angrez continue to sell their flags to every trader they can and cheat me out of my revenue. They need to be fixed. Every new governor needs to be fixed as soon as they take charge. It is going to be my policy from now on.'

'Good riddance then. We can make our own ships and sail them out west,' Ramaji says.

'That's the nonsense you have been filling your sons' heads with.'

'What is so nonsensical about it? I know shipwrights and carpenters that can make one of their sea sailing vessels.'

'And who would go? You?'

'Obviously not. But we can get any Topikar captain, Mussalman or Habshi sailor. That is the least of our problems.'

'And the trading, negotiating? Who is going to do that? Well, it is between the boys and you, fanciful as it is.'

'You do not support the idea?'

'Is it not taboo? Are we permitted? Does anybody know why? It is different for you, a trader and a businessman. It is different for my sons. So, I must see their reason in it and challenge their assumptions,' Kanhoji says.

'The logic is sound. There is no reason why we should not trade farther, take the risk of the open sea and make those massive margins,' Ramaji wonders.

'Well for now they are occupied, now the boys will be busy with those things that have been brought to hand.'

'Maybe I should move south,' wonders Ramaji.

'Come on, Ramaji. Why should you stop working with them? Don't you worry; you will come to no harm. Aren't you their biggest *saraf*? I am not against them being here and doing what they do best—but under the rules of the Swarajya.'

'They are the greatest source of silver and gold, Kanhoji, we cannot forget that.'

'I know it only too well. But the Firangis and your Dutch Topikars are also there. Don't forget about them. Speaking of the Dutch: Bhoon attacked them and the Raja of Karwar.'

'All these Topikars are militarizing like the Firangis. If we are not careful, they too will have their Goas with their mandovis all over the coast.'

'There is no chance of that, Ramaji. They are not jagirdars. The Firangi took what he did from the Bijapurkar's, let the Angrez try that now,' Kanho says with finality.

Kalyana

Kulaba and Hirakot are abuzz. Literally, with flies and bees attracted to the meadow of flowers that adorn the bride's home. One can hear the hum from Shiroda in the south to Udwada in the north. Kanhoji is at the helm, directing an armada of pandits, cooks, flower arrangers, carpenters, jewellers, musicians and entertainers. Maunds of rice, flour, dal, vegetables, jaggery, butter, ghee and oil daily arrive and are deposited in temporary storage tents beside the makeshift outdoor kitchens. Musicians arrive from the Karnatak, as do troupes of actors, acrobats, magicians and animal wranglers from all parts of the Desha. Since the best dancers are from the Konkan, the very best are commanded from the local towns and cities.

'I want all my people here, enjoying the festivities with us,' Kanhoji has commanded Surya: 'Make sure they all get to come.'

'We can't leave the forts empty, Raje,' Surya counters in surprise.

'Sure, you can, just keep them locked,' Kanhoji says. Surya is unsure if he means it as a jest. Surya knows that it is impossible. He also realizes that every single garrison's guard and every oarsman would want to be associated with the festivities. He will get them to draw lots and leave a minimal number of men to guard the forts. It will be sufficient, after all the one man who would not hesitate to move against us at a time like this is defanged and sits nestled behind the high walls of Janjira.

For the first time in many years, his and Mathurabai's hearts are aligned: if they could have invited the entire Konkan, they would have. Long as Mathurabai's list is, it isn't the census. They do, however, try to feed the entire population of the Konkan. Every family member and friend is personally invited, and every employee and acquaintance invited by running messengers and town criers who bang on a drum and proclaim: 'Sarkhel Subedar Kanhoji Angre's daughter, Ladubai Raje, is to get betrothed and you are invited to come and bless the couple and take part in the festivities.'

Though Kanhoji is proud of all his sons and loves them too, the sweetest mangoes have always been kept aside for Ladubai. A good rider and as good a shot as any of her brothers, Kanhoji's darling is being prepared for her betrothal. If one asks her, she does not say anything, but she is neither happy nor ready to move out from under the cooling shade and security her father provides her. Ladubai's husband is from a good Maratha family, chosen by Mathurabai herself. He is still a young boy, not much older than Ladubai, who has recently become much irritated with the constant teasing and attention. The boy is related to the Rajas of Kudal, and Kanhoji too is very pleased with his wife's choice. Kanhoji has never been extravagant, except perhaps with horses and guns as is the nature of such a beast, but this time he has let Mathurabai do as she pleases. He too wants to share his happiness with his people, and expense is no longer an object.

Pandurao Phangaskar has been invited too, along with his entire extended family, many of whom are known to the Angres. Once Phangaskar has the dates, he rushes to Governor Boone with the news. He insists they meet alone and behind closed doors and Boone too is excited with the secrecy shown.

'I know Angre very well. He loves showing off his fraternity with his common sailors and will well insist that all those in his employ be present at the wedding.'

'You think he would leave his forts undefended?'

'He would insist that everybody be there in Kulaba for the wedding. The other forts will be empty.'

Boone thinks about it and does not say anything further, just keeping in mind the dates Pandurao has mentioned. Pandurao leaves the pensive governor with his mind seeded and steps out to find himself an elephant to hire for the wedding. He prays that he will be able to see the expression on Angre's face when he hears of Vijaydurg or Suvarnadurg being taken, and it will be so delicious in the happy milieu of the wedding.

Mantap

The air grows hotter every day and the ground drier—the leaves have turned the colour of dust and are caked in bird droppings. But one cannot choose the auspicious day based on comfort, and one must obey the stars. The wealthy denizens of the Konkan are out in their finest clothes and jewellery as they make their way to Alibag. They pass fields of Brahmins being fed and tents dedicated to the feeding of different castes and communities that are in attendance. Musicians with giant *tutaris** announce every dignitary while drums beat rhythmically behind mellifluous *shehnais* and *sitars*. The air is sweet with the smell of jaggery and fried maida and amorous with the aroma of *mogras*** and *rajnigandhas*. The blessings of Mahapurush Brahmendra Swami are doled out wholesale after he has blessed the young couple.

'Where is your Sarkhel Saheb's friend?' the Rani of Kudal asks Mathurabai, echoing the crescendo of 'Where is the Peshwa?' and 'How come Balaji Bhat is not here?' that swirls under the music.

Gangadhar leaves his master's side to create distance between Kanhoji and the continuous and never-ending work of subedari and sarkhelship and teams up with Surya to keep all at bay. Surya has

---

* Horned instrument like a cornet.

** Jasmine.

never been this harried, not even in battle. Currently, he is dealing with the accommodation and feeding of elephants, oxen and horses and their mahouts or drivers that have ferried the guests in. Nearby he hears the palkhiwalas complain that they haven't got any food yet. Nothing can go wrong during this wedding, Surya feels, as it would directly impact his Sarkhel's prestige. It is then that the Killedar of Vijaydurg pushes through the throng of people.

'What now, Shirke?' Surya snaps.

'Saheb, the Angrez have attacked us at Vijaydurg, I just received a signal message.'

'Angrez? To what effect?' he says incredulously.

'They are at Vijaydurg, attacking the walls with a few small vessels they have. I had told my men to pretend like there are many of them still at the fort. The Angrez had not been able to break through when I received the message, but I must leave with my men immediately.'

'Go quietly and take Ramoji and Manuji with you. Don't let the news spread and I will have your head if Raje hears about it within the day.'

'No, Saheb, we shall slip away unseen and unheard.'

'Keep me updated,' Surya says as he watches Piloji and Kanhoji laugh at something the Raja of Kudal has just said.

'Saheb,' Killedar Shirke confirms as he turns around and whisks through the bodies of revellers that loom in every direction. Surya will not tell Kanhoji anything, at least not till tomorrow. But what if tomorrow is too late? Then he will pay with his own head, but today Raje shall not be disturbed.

Pandurao Phangaskar cannot make his way through to Kanhoji as all paths to him are blocked by fattened coteries of the most important Konkani. The recently harassed Raja of Karwar is present and so is an envoy of the Firangis. There can be no better time to greet the Sarkhel and to let him know of their loyalty. Rustomji has come of his own accord, and Boone was glad to be rid of him. Boone has obviously not taken his bait, Pandurao thinks, when he sees Rustomji and is disheartened to be robbed of his drama.

Vanaprastha

Large umbrellas with canvas canopies dyed dark with *neel*[*] have been set up at the ramparts beneath the flagpole. In their shade, charpais with thin cotton mattresses covered in white sheets have been placed with low tables alongside. Kanhoji is with Sambhaji and Sekhoji at their daily group sessions where they exercise and train with their personal bodyguard whose job is less to protect the two young men and more to keep pace with them when fighting. After getting a soothing massage, the three men bathe and then proceed to the bastions at the flagpole. Only the most trusted servants are in attendance as the three men each take a charpai: Kanhoji lies down while his sons sit close by on the edges of their diwans.

'I have reached an age where a little bit of relaxing does one good.'

'Indeed, Baba, you have carried the fortunes of our family on your shoulder and now it is our time to help you.'

'We are ready,' chimes in the younger.

'When have I ever told you that you are not ready? Haven't I given all of you responsibility and charge?'

'That's not what we meant.'

'Should I take sanyas or become a *vanaprashth*[**]?'

---

[*] Indigo.

[**] Renounce the world.

'No, Father, but as your sons—let us follow your command while you pursue your pleasure.'

'Being myself and doing my duty gives me pleasure.'

'Though we still want you to lead us and teach us. There is so much we still need to learn from you.'

'Then learn this: never fear and never think when you have to act.'

'But Kaka Balaji says that . . .'

'Kaka Balaji's words are enforced by the swords of people like me and our willingness to act and put our lives on the line. Though you must know when to act, and in that, there is no better person to advise you then your dear kaka.'

'Baba, right now the biggest problem is that we don't have money.'

'What nonsense, the treasury is full. It's bursting at the seams.'

'Exactly, Baba. It's either in a treasury here or with Swamiji. But there aren't enough coins in the bazaars. I was speaking to Ramaji Kaka about this. We have a lot of gold and silver in the treasury, but when it comes to paying someone, there is no coin.'

'We need our own siccas. There are so many transactions but there isn't enough of a trusted coin to transact in.'

'What does he suggest? What do you suggest?' he says, emphasizing his son's input.

'That we mint coins, Baba. A rupaiya, a silver sicca.'

'I don't think Shahu Raje would take too kindly to that.'

'Well, you send trunks of silver up every month, what would it hurt if it was in your fashion and based upon the trust and integrity you stand for.'

'The Sankhpal family stands for.'

'Now everybody knows us as Angria.'

'It does not matter what they call us, what matters is that we perform our duties as the custodians of the Konkan. Now tell me about the coins.'

'I have a man. He came to me some months ago. He used to work at the Bijapuri mint. He can help us with copper, silver or gold coins.'

'Let's meet him then and look into this further. We will mint it in the name of the sovereign Chhatrapati of the Swarajya.'

'I will get him up tomorrow, Baba. I had him put up in Kulaba till we could discuss this.'

The attendants serve flavoured buttermilk with basil seeds and retreat to a respectable distance.

'This mint idea is a good one. But I want to discuss something important with the both of you.'

'Yes, Baba,' say the boys in unison.

'I have got news that the Angrez Sardar met the Sardar of Bassein secretly. Having failed as miserably as he did with his attack on Gheria during Ladu's wedding, I think he is looking for an alliance against us.'

'Maybe we should crush them. Annihilate them once and for all.'

'Never make that mistake, Sekho, they are where the silver and gold come from.'

'Not if we build and send ships out to their ports. In fact, we don't even need to go to Angrezistan, just to the lands where they get their gold and silver from.'

'That is not our business as I keep reminding you. Let them bring their gold, wherever they got it from, to our doorsteps.'

'But, Baba . . .'

'I am talking of an impending attack, forget about the other side of the world for a moment,' Kanhoji says impatiently.

'Yes, Shriman, I am ashamed.'

'We have to expect something, but we haven't been able to determine where they will strike.'

'We will put all the forts on ready.'

'Shambhu, I want you to take over the systems of spies I have put into place.'

'I will, Baba. Should I stay back tomorrow?'

'Yes. Sekho, you carry on to Kulaba, but first notify Suvarnadurg and Khanderi to be ready for action.'

'Okay, Baba, I will leave today.'

'All right. Remember me to your mother and tell her I will be with her shortly.'

'She never believes you any more, Baba. Ai says that even you don't know where you are going next.'

'She speaks the truth as always. You know she likes beautiful bowls and plates more than anything though she never uses them or when she does, she breaks them after being used as is our custom.'

'The Firangis just wash the dishes and use them again. Chee,' says Sambhaji.

'Well, even the Chini do, and they are the ones making them. There must be something to it.'

'They have bowls that change to the colour of blood when there is poison in them.'

'Anyway, I have a whole collection put aside for her, take them,' Kanhoji instructs his son.

'What about Angrezi ships?' asks Sekho.

'Don't spare a vessel, if you see one. Did I not send you both copies of the letter I wrote?'

'Yes, Baba, you did,' they say in unison, and it gives immense joy to Kanhoji when he hears both his boys speak in one voice.

'So, how is it going with your brothers? Do they follow your lead?'

'Yes, they do, Baba, all of them. But . . .' Sekhoji hesitates.

'Say it,' Kanhoji says impatiently.

'Tula is always at loggerheads with Shambhu. Always vying for my attention and before that yours. It's a very old story. They have been like this since they were children.'

'How is Tula with you?'

'He is fine. It's Shambhu he has a problem with.'

'You know how much I regret not having a brother by my side. You boys are lucky to have each other. It's like having one body in four places,' he says to his son.

And each with his own mind, Sekhoji thinks to himself. He knows his father considers them extensions of his own body. That's how he has always treated the four of them, as limbs.

'Look, I do not have more than ten years left, if I am lucky. We Sankhpals have large hearts, we use them a lot and run them down, like your grandfather has done and his before him. I am not going to be around in my old age to guide you boys.'

'Don't speak such inauspicious things, Baba,' Sambhaji says.

'You are a grown man now, Shambhu, and not acknowledging one's own mortality is an inexcusable vice. There is no guarantee of a tomorrow, and we can die any time. Accepting this is what transforms us into warriors. It gives us rights and privileges that others do not have.'

Two against One

Khanderi is a bean-shaped rock jutting out of the sea. Its killedars have a bane of mortal enemies always nipping at their heels. It is the rodent population they share quarters with on this blisteringly hot rock. It is the least preferred posting in the Konkan, though each one of Kanhoji's sons has done their stint on the little island. A pair of islands north of Kulaba, Undheri is the much smaller twin, closer to shore, and has an even bigger rat problem. It is again in the possession of the Siddi who repaired the small fort there after Kanhoji had destroyed it some years ago. Khanderi's current commander is a young Koli man called Sakaram who has risen through the ranks to become commander of the fort. A position he has held for two years after taking over from Manaji Angre. The island is two kos out at sea and on the northern approach to Kulaba Fort. A fleet of galbats and a ghurab or two are always berthed at Khanderi to venture out to the busy sea roads to Palva Bandar, Mazgaon, Thana and Bassein.

A brief dawn is dissipated by the majesty of the sun as it rises ferociously to look at itself in the sea. As he has these past few days, Sakaram takes the eyeglass up to the bastion at the northern end of the fort and peers through it at the glimmering sea. Sakaram can tell that it is going to be a hot day. He flexes his taut arms and does a few squats to dispel some of the energy he has wound up in his legs. He walks up to the edge of the rampart and peers through the eyeglass again. There isn't any wind, and the tide has receded to its lowest.

As Sakaram looks through the brass eyeglass one last time before heading down, he sees a lone seagull turn right towards the coast. It must be some vessel, maybe a fishing boat, he thinks as he leaves the ramparts and heads to check on the lines of men that will carry the gunpowder to the cannons. As he reaches the bottom of the stairs he hears the clanging of a bell, which grows to a shrill metallic cacophony. Sakaram turns around and runs back up the stairs to the ramparts of the bastion and whips out his eyeglass. He can see the square red cross of the Firangis on the masts of massive carracks and caravels heading towards him. He counts four large ships that are Firangi and sees another fleet behind them. As the second fleet comes into focus, he sees that it flies the familiar red striped flag of the Angrezi traders, often found flying on every coastal trading vessel that is intercepted. He counts two massive three-masted vessels and six smaller vessels that include an odd-looking barge. Sakaram mounts a horse and rides south on the ramparts, shouting warnings to the teams of gunners he crosses and heads to the signals team at the south end of the fort. He still does not know whether they are headed for him, or they will continue farther south to Kulaba, so he signals their approach and position to Kulaba. As Sakaram relays the information, the signals man shoots out a flare that reaches high into the sky before bursting into a ball of bright orange dust that then falls in a slow curtain of colour. He then shoots out a red flare that bursts into six orbs. As Sakaram leaves, the signals team relays another more detailed message using a highly polished brass mirror to another set up on the mainland to the south of the island.

By the time Sakaram reaches the northern tip of the fort, he is sure that the fleet is headed for him and is not going to bypass him from the west. Sakaram's drummer is waiting for him with five boys who will dart around with his commands and instructions.

'Prepare for attack,' Sakaram shouts and the drummer beats out the message on the drum that is fastened to his belly.

Other drummers posted around the fort pick up the beat and relay it to every crevice of the island. The pujari in the Vitthal Mandir blows on his conch. All the rats stop for a second and arch their necks high and take a few sniffs before scurrying away into the closest hole they can find. Sakaram is intermittently laughing as he is wont to do when he is nervous. His compatriots do not know this, and they look at him queerly as he makes his way around the fort barking orders and laughing.

The Portuguese fleet sails to the western side of the fort and assumes a line position with their broadsides facing the walls of the fort. The smaller Angrezi ships sail east and present their broadsides to the north-eastern tip of the island, south of which lie the gates to the fortress. As platoons of Maratha musketeers file up the stairs and on to the ramparts of the fort, the massive and awe-inspiring Firangi Man o' War lets loose its first volley in a thundering crescendo. While most of the shots fall harmlessly short, some from the uppermost gun deck find the base of the fort's walls. After every salvo, the Firangi gunners adjust their cannon behind a screen of smoke.

Sakaram has already given the order to fire, and Maratha cannons start their bombardment. After each shot, they too adjust the angle of their gun: hammering at a wedged piece of iron below the cannon's barrel to raise it. The English fleet has also started its firing but finds itself too far away to hit the fort's walls. The Angrezi ships raise their anchors and tack to get closer and present their starboard broadsides. Sakaram orders the gunners on the northern side of the fort to fire on the Angrezi vessels as they seek to replace themselves beyond the Maratha range. On the western front, the teams of gunners are firing continuously on the Portuguese as they fire back on the fort. Unable to harm the thick oak walls of the hulls of the Firangi ships at that distance, Sakaram commands his gunners to change their ordnance. He has them switch to the chained shots he is familiar with and goes for the masts of the ships. He has pots of rotting rats brought up and fired at the vessels. If nothing else, the stench will drive them crazy.

Sakaram gets word that twelve rowboats have left the Angrezi vessels and are making for the fort. As much as he would have liked to watch the attack on the Firangi ships, he makes his way to the northern tip, taking a body of musketeers that have assembled on the ramparts. Sakaram watches the Angrezi rowboats strike east and then south. They make for landfall in the navel of the bean, as it is the only spot that is not protected by the black basalt rocks that this island is composed of. Unmindful of the death that faces them, the Angrez jump out of their boats carrying ladders and run to the walls of the fort. As one infantryman drops with a Maratha shot, another comes up to take his place and move forward. Sakaram's musketeers are firing from the bastions as the Angrezi landing party reaches the walls. The ladders that have been put up at much cost of life are too short and are soon abandoned on the walls themselves. Instead, the Company's infantrymen move to the gate of the castle where their artillery unit has set up a pair of small mortars.

As the sun dips towards the western horizon, the call of conches tears through the impending dusk. Sakaram sees the fleet first: the sea to the south of Khanderi is dotted with saffron-dyed sails moving north on a warm sea breeze. The Firangis see it next and as soon as they spot it, they raise anchor and head north back to Bassein on the same wind that has carried the Marathas to them. Tulaji's fleet makes for the confused English Company's line of vessels that is just witnessing their allies abandon them. Sakaram watches as Tulaji's galbats blow up a barge that has been converted into a floating artillery base. They manage to dismast and board another locally made ship with forty guns as the rest of the Angrezi fleet turns around and escapes to Bombay. The surrounding sea and the beach at Khanderi are littered with corpses and it smells of rotting rats and sulphur everywhere.

The Response

The very next day, Kanhoji attacks Chaul and destroys all Portuguese vessels his men come across. Sekhoji goes up to Bassein and bombards the jetty, burning as many vessels as he can. Tulaji regrets not pursuing them when they retreated from Khanderi and the thought pokes at him like a shard. The unresolvable pain of regret he transfers upon anything Portuguese his men come across till the combined tip of these efforts finally pokes the Viceroy in Goa.

As the monsoon rages, Luis Carlos de Meneses, the Viceroy of the Estado Portuguesa, sits in his darkened seaside palace, writing a smudged letter to Angre: 'Dom Carvalho has been seduced by the English traders; Goa had neither any knowledge of the attack, nor did it commend it.' He prays for peace between the two states and calls for a stop to attacks on Portuguese property and offers reparation to Angre for losses incurred. Angre writes back letting the Firangis know that their estimation of losses is on the lower side and that he will return all the prisoners taken once a more respectable amount is agreed upon. The Viceroy is amenable to Angre's demands and a suspicion-laced peace is resumed between the two parties.

Pirate

Did he not just shut his eyes?

Boone wonders at the gentle voice of his native groom requesting him to rouse. The man announces Rustomji Patel as he dresses him.

'At this devilish time, Rustomji? Could it not wait till sunup?' he asks.

'Sire, it's the *HMS Charlotte*,' the Patel answers.

'Is she in? At last, our funds have arrived,' the President says gaily, his mood altered and his body energized.

'Sire, she was taken off Rajapuri but a few hours ago,' the worried Patel says.

'Impossible, the devil himself,' Boone explodes in red-eared anger as all hope is extinguished within him.

'Are you sure?' he asks before turning around towards his bed. His shirt is spotted with blood and pus from the boils on his back.

'Yes, sire. It was Tulaji Angre. Dismasted her as the Siddi watched from the ramparts of Janjira. He has taken her to Kulaba.'

'We are lost. This settlement is doomed. She carried our funds for the Bombay Marine, the walls,' he says as he collapses on to his bed fully clothed.

Now, the shipwrights and carpenters will have to work without pay and the timber traders will be paid in promissory notes. What should have been a glorious day has been upended before dawn.

He was hoping to finish the design for his latest artillery barge before leaving for the inauguration, but it does not matter now. He had named her the Phram and when she would have been ready, she would have been the end of the Angrians. Her low draught would have allowed her to enter shallow waters and blow the walls of his forts to smithereens.

President Boone sleeps through the middle of the day, fanned by two sweating boys in a shaded room, while the sun is at its zenith outside. Putting on the fourth new shirt of the day, President Boone proceeds to the inauguration. Every Anglo-Saxon person, whether employed by the Company or a private trader, is eager to attend the function. The most respected local merchants are invited too, and they all are glad to attend. Ramaji Kamath has personally donated Rs 20,000 towards the construction of the cathedral and took up a collection from his merchant friends that equalled his own contribution. The Hayastani merchants are in attendance as are the Yehudi oil magnates, who too have contributed generously to the persistent Chaplain Cobbe. Pandurao has bought an invitation with a contribution of Rs 501. His eyes are pierced with envy when he sees the Chaplain stride across the room to Ramaji and welcome him with a gushing handshake and a head full of smiles.

Once everybody has taken their seats, Boone is invited to say a few words before the service. He makes his way to a raised platform besides the pulpit. The small choir that is standing behind him is half made of boys from the Indo-Portuguese community that live near Mazgaon. They may be papists, but they can sing. The distraction has removed the pain from his back and replaced it with a feeling of victory. He can see from the crowd in attendance that the denizens of this small port fully support its administrators. Everybody is in attendance. Boone welcomes the congregation and thanks it. He congratulates Chaplain Cobbe on his success and reads a passage from his own Bible: 'Philippians three seventeen, verse four. Brothers,' he says and then pauses as he surveys the congregation, 'join in imitating me and keep your eyes on those who walk according to the example you have in us. For many of whom I have often told you about and now tell you even with tears in mine eyes, walk,' he pauses again, 'as enemies of the cross of Christ. Their end is destruction, and their god is their belly, and they glory in their shame with their minds set on earthly things. But our citizenship is in heaven and from it we await a Saviour our Lord Jesus Christ, who will transform our lowly body to be like his glorious body by the power that enables him even to subject all things to himself. Therefore, my dear brothers, whom I love and long for, my joy and crown stand firm thus in the beloved Lord.'

'Hallelujah,' the Saxons respond.

Boone clears his throat and looks out at the audience.

'Presently this evil, sent to test us and to make us strong has taken the body of the Angrians and its head Cornerjee. An extortionist, a predator and a pirate, he is the very epitome of devilry. It is his greed that has become the greatest subversion of our cause. Now that this holy cathedral has been completed and soon a bishop will be appointed, we must look at this evil that threatens not only the sanctity of this hallowed ground but the very existence of our little port. I shall expect the same cooperation we had in making this edifice as we shall have in keeping it extant and successful.'

Many in the congregation stir uncomfortably in their seats, others will when it is translated for them. As wisps of hope fall from Rustomji's beard, Pandurao Phangaskar, seated several pews behind him, smiles with profound satisfaction.

Ramaji is left horrified.

The Games of Low Men

Pandurao is on foot. A black scarf is tied over his head and across the lower half of his face. He pushes through a mob headed in the opposite direction. The mob are carrying sticks and mashaals. From their excited cries he can make out they are heading out to chase away a female leopard that has got too close to their tenements by the fields. He spots two Bhandaris amongst them carrying spears, obviously sent out by the Patel to not only assist them in this endeavour, but also give the mob the legality to form. The Patel does not want any mobs ever forming without his acquiescence and participation.

'*Sala Parsi,*' Pandurao mutters to himself, their dominance of the office of Patel grating against his sentiments as much as their inability to accept a bribe.

'Indeed, fire-worshipping Pharisees,' says a voice right behind him and Pandurao almost jumps out of his skin.

Pandurao makes to turn, when a cold white hand, veined and cracked like a vulture's claw, squeezes his shoulder. He recognizes the vile touch of his contact and carries on walking without turning.

They enter the low walls of the fort through the Bazaar Gate and turn left towards the Mandvi Bastion. They move at a discreet pace, sticking to the shadows and keeping their covered heads down. They stop at a wooden cloister that has been built abutting the stairs going up to the bastion. There is somebody waiting for them inside in the darkness.

They can barely distinguish each other's features, but they recognize each other's voices. Pandurao wrinkles his nose as the detestable stench of alcoholic sweat and sweet port assault him. He takes a step back before the other man can open his mouth.

'You're late. You've kept me waiting like a crippled coolie.'

'My apologies, dear sir. I was waiting for it to become a little darker,' Pandurao says.

'Gets any darker and I won't be able to *shee* you,' the man mumbles, chuckling.

'This is Seth Pandurao,' the other man whispers hoarsely.

'Pandora, is it?' the drunk Englishman says.

'Please, let us discuss what we need to. I have to leave before they close the gates,' the priest says.

'What is your plan for Ramaji?' Pandurao asks them both.

'I say, just clobber that bugger on the head,' Cox growls. Perpetually red in the face and soft in the stomach, Cox is the standard of factors employed at the fort and throughout the Company. He is a man whose career has been myopic in all ways.

'That is infantile and not as easy as you make it out to be. What is the point of simply murdering the man? His son will inherit,' the other man says.

'Well, I want him out, that miser. He has refused to cut me in and says that the next time I suggest any such thing he will tattle me out to Boone,' Cox says vehemently.

'He has always been like that, never wanting to share his success or his profits. It was I who introduced him to Boone. We need to destroy him and his establishment. If we kill him, his son will step in. We need to eradicate his name and his influence,' Pandurao says.

'What do ye propose?' Cox the clerk says, offering Pandurao a swig from his bottle of port.

Pandurao shrinks back, covering his face with the crook of his elbow.

Cox offers his bottle to the priest.

'No thank you, Senhor. Look, he is a very close friend of Kanhoji Angre. It is not possible that his loyalties lie with anyone other than Angre. In truth, he is a deceiver and a traitor to your Company,' the priest says.

'He is not an employee of the Company,' Pandurao corrects him.

'He needn't be employed by them to betray their goodwill. He is a spy: Kanhoji's spy. Passing information from here to there. He is bound to have done this in the past and continues to do it presently,' the priest explains.

'What proof do you have of this?' Cox asks.

'The proof exists, we just don't have it with us because he is a cunning man,' the other man replies.

'Then how do we get the proof? As far as his dealings go, there is nothing we can touch. He is thorough and methodical with every transaction and there are ledgers of multiple copies he keeps,' says Cox the clerk.

'You will get the proof. Nothing to do with his business but the information he passes on to Kanhoji,' the priest says.

'From whence in my deep desires do you expect me to extract this proof?' says Cox the clerk.

'From your offices and from the Governor's desk. Anything sensitive. Anything that pertains to Kanhoji—plans of the ships being built for the Marine. Fort defences, anything like that,' the priest explains.

'That is possible. Then what next?'

'Leave that to me. Just get me everything you can, and we'll meet again next week. But not here, not within the walls of the fort,' Pandurao says, looking knowingly at the priest.

'Bugger that; same time and right here. I am not risking trying to take any official documents outside the fort,' Cox says, taking another swig of the saccharine port.

'Ye need not fear, but I will come here anyway,' Pandurao says. It is a risk Pandurao is well willing to take given the reward.

'Wait for some time after we leave,' Pandurao says as they depart and make their ways back separately to the Bazaar Gate, which is always the last to be shut.

Saswad

The days have started to lengthen and grow hot. A messenger comes down to Vijaydurg just as the sun is setting into a roiling sea. From one guarded gate to the next, he is directed closer towards Kanhoji till Sekhoji finally meets him and receives the news on his father's behalf. Sekhoji makes his way to the bastion called Durga where he knows his father is watching the setting sun. Sekhoji finds his father staring out as the orange arc slips into the horizon like a large gold coin falling into a slotted tijori. Sekhoji waits for the sun to disappear completely before he coughs to get his father's attention. Kanhoji turns around slowly and smiles at his son.

'Baba, a messenger has come from Saswad.'

'Oh. Are we expecting your kaka, then? I was missing him just now. What a long life he has.'

Sekhoji is silent for a few moments as he reforms the sentence he was hoping to speak. But instead, he just blurts out: 'Kaka is gone.'

'Back to Delhi, to get poisoned again.'

'No, Baba: he is no more. He is gone.'

Kanhoji's eyes narrow and his lips jut out as he shoots back a 'How?'

'He was ill, Baba; he had been for some time. It was in his own bed.'

When Bala came back from Dilli he was ill, and Kanho had suspected that he had been poisoned at the Mughal court. It would have been a slow poison that would have eaten him up from inside. Now he is gone. Bala never needed a sword or the ability to wield it, for his mind was his greatest weapon. 'While I was the brute,' Kanho thinks to himself. But now, the warrior that I am, I need to be by the side of Bala's sons. He prays that Balaji's two sons are united and without any animosity towards each other.

Kanho and Sekho leave Vijaydurg immediately, heading north to Kulaba on a swift galbat with their personal retinues. Sambha is waiting for them along with Mana and Tula. It is a large party that heads west and up the ghats to the estate of the dead Peshwa. As they approach Saswad, the word is out: Angria has come himself. Young boys slip out of workshop windows and abandon their goats and cattle to the fields, running towards the path the Angres are taking. On seeing the party, they gawk at the chargers and at their shining lances and polished muskets. Many of the older children ask if they can join their ranks and are sent away with good humour and gentle rebukes on their size or lack of facial hair.

The departed Peshwa has already been cremated by the time Kanhoji and his retinue march into Saswad. When he finds out that Brahmendra Swami is present, he first seeks him out. Balaji's boys are with their father's spiritual adviser when Kanho meets them all. They are standing at the entrance to the new residence Balaji had recently built. It is imposing and spacious though not splendid by any measure, just as its builder had intended. It is airy with a large courtyard and has the largest windows Kanho has ever seen.

'See, here comes the Konkan Yudhishthira, the epitome of loyalty. I knew he would come,' Brahmendra Swami says to Baji as Kanhoji strides up to them.

Kanho prostrates to the Swami as the two boys prostrate to Kanho, and then Kanho's sons seek the guru's blessings. As the six boys talk amongst themselves, Brahmendra Swami draws Kanho aside.

'Good you came so soon.'

'We left as soon as we found out.'

'The confirmation from Satara has yet to come in,' Swamiji says, wringing his hands in an obvious show of feigned worry.

'How did he die?'

'What do you mean? He was sick,' Swamiji says, eyeing Kanho quizzically.

'Yes, but what sickness? Why? How did it begin?'

'None of us are young any more, Kanho. What are you getting at?'

'I think they must have poisoned him in Dilli.'

'Who and why?'

'Somebody; maybe the Sayyid Brothers? Aren't there always reasons enough in politics? Poison is after all the weapon of choice when it comes to the durbar and the *kacheri*.* That or a knife in the back.'

Swamiji squeezes Kanho's upper arm: 'You can't believe he is gone. You can't believe he was taken from you. And Kanho, you can't believe he died in his bed.'

Swamiji's grey eyes have dulled around the edges of the cornea, but they are still full of life, when he wants them to be. They will flash green in an infinitesimal burst of anger or be dark and still as a pond at dawn. Now they look lovingly, though curiously at Kanhoji.

'Do you realize that we are getting older? I don't even know how we have made it this far. From where Balaji came, this is not a bad death: in his own palace on a comfortable bed, as the Prime Minister of the kingdom. Not bad? His life has been miraculous.'

'But it has been cut short. His boys are still young. They need him, the Chhatrapati needs him.'

'Kanho, the world goes on perfectly without even the best of us. The travails of our youth come to haunt us as we grow old. The aches you have in your shoulders and knees came from abusing them when you were younger. None of us can escape it.'

---

* Court.

'Except the *chiranjeevis*.'[*]

'Yes, except them. But you do know that the name of your friend will always be immortal?'

Then in a louder tone, one which will attract the attention of Baji and Chimma, Swamiji says: 'He rose to the highest position in the land a person of his rank could, and I predicted it when he was just another impoverished and orphaned Brahmin boy.'

---

[*] Immortals.

Kaala Paani

Sambhaji Angre is, at the best of times, a simply dressed man, much to the chagrin of his family and friends, but most of all to his old retainer Bhimaji, for he never wears any jewellery besides simple gold earrings and a silver bangle on his right bicep. Sambhaji has an inconspicuous and very dark-green turban on his head, and he disappears into the crowd around Pydhonie where they washed their feet after they had squelched through the harbour muck like common loaders and traders, the fringes of their hitched dhotis blackened with the pasty filth that settles by the docks. They make their way to one of Ramaji's several warehouses. This one is situated beyond the newly built northern walls of the Angrezi Fort. Hardly defensible against any determined enemy, they might not be very high or thick, but they have cannons to spare. Short fat culverins and longer barrelled iron pieces bristle along the top of the walls. Their dusty black noses poke out of square embrasures at regular distances along the length of the fort.

Sambhaji knows the warehouse well as he does the environs around the English Fort. He moves everywhere, as very few people know what he looks like. He well knows that if one does not make a show of it, no one ever gives you a second glance. No one ever looks at your face or even remembers it, they only see the elephants, chargers, hear the drum beaters or count the attendant retinue.

Tulaji, you can spot at a distance, as a son of Angre, just from his gait. Ramaji's assistant meets them at the gate of the warehouse, and they are taken through a maze of goods piled high on each side. First, bales of canvas and cotton, then barrels all sealed, sacks of spices that sting the eyes and tickle the nose, and then through endless shelves of glazed pottery stacked blue and white.

As Sambhaji is announced, Narain, Ramaji's son gets up and approaches Sambhaji, his hands folded in a namaskar. Sambhaji greets the seated Seth Ramaji, bending towards his feet.

Ramaji stops him and stands up.

'Kaka,' Sambhaji says in the most familial greeting.

'*Bodyo*, you are looking more and more like your father every day. You need to be more careful with the way you travel around so openly. Not many may know you, but the fame of your features precedes you by a generation. Be careful.'

'I am, Kaka. I do. You are looking well.'

'I look better than I feel these days and that is why I am going to excuse myself from our discussions today.'

'Oh Kaka, not you too? That is what Baba has said.'

'Look, both of us have too many responsibilities and worries as it is. This is something for Naro and you and your brothers to figure out. Our blessings are with you, and I have told Naro everything I know on the matter. I have even found you a nakhwa.'

Bhimaji follows them with one of Sethji's clerks carrying large *potlis* of documents and maps behind him. They enter a well-lit room with large windows, and the subdued evening light filters in comfortably. Narain's clerk opens the potli and with practised ease unrolls a crisp and springy map drawn on a stiff and thick parchment that is obviously foreign in origin and could well be the hide of an animal.

'This is a map of the world as described by the Topikars. My father acquired it from the traders at Vengurla.'

Pointing to a spot on the western coast of the peninsular Indies, he continues: 'This is where we are.'

'Naroji, I have seen the maps before. This is where the Topikars of Vengurla come from,' Sambhaji says, pointing to the Netherlands on the map.

'Definitely, and right here, not but a few kos away is where the Angrez come from. This little island,' Naro says, pointing very close to where Sambhaji has his finger.

'But it does not matter where they come from. They have nothing. Some sheep, with which they make all the wool they have been trying to offload to us these many years. Otherwise, within their lands they have nothing.' Narain's finger slides south and west across the Atlantic, passes where on the map there is a representation of a massive sea snake in the middle of the sea. Sambhaji points to it and wonders aloud if it could be a representation of Vasuki.

Narain's finger reaches Brazil.

'This is where the Firangi get their gold from. Their gold and their emeralds, and this is where we need to go. Baba is very clear on that. He says we must go to the source of the gold directly. There is no need to go to here,' Naro says, and his finger slides back north-east to Europe.

'So how do we get there?'

'They come east and south till they reach the southern tip of the Habshidesha, here,' he says pointing to the Cape, 'and then north, blown in by the monsoon.'

Pointing to Europe on the map, he slides his finger down the Atlantic again going south and west: 'They start up here and then go south and west and then south again. If they go west far enough, they get here. Musa or Muso. Emeralds as thick as your thumbs are to be found like groundnuts. Then to get east, they go farther south. Here are winds constantly blowing and they take them still farther east to Chin. They can stop here, as I said earlier, or go east all the way and then north to the Konkan.'

Sambhaji has seen all this since he was a child.

'Here,' he says pointing to a vast open sea to the south, 'are mountains of ice floating in the sea. Sometimes when they run out of water when they are going east all the way, instead of reprovisioning here, they break off chunks of these floating pieces of ice and melt it and drink the water.'

'What are the dangers? What of these creatures shown here? And what of these snakes and squids attacking this ship? Maybe there is a reason we are not allowed to cross the oceans. Yet others do and survive.'

'I do not know, and the stories keep changing. Like stories of ghosts and ghouls, never have two people witnessed any of these creatures together. But possible, is it not? Just look at the ocean, it is endless. What is of constant danger are dead winds here and mountains of ice here, and rocks all over the ocean where the ships wreck themselves, losing one's sail, one's rudder; running out of food and water; rebellion of the crew, sometimes madness and more often sickness.'

Narain, with a look of absolute wonderment continues: 'There is this sickness the sailors get, because there are no fresh vegetables available to them, where all their old wounds, wounds they had received and were healed in childhood, open up. Their teeth and hair fall out.'

'Then how do we do it? You are making it sound impossible.'

'Not at all, Sambha. If they can do it, and do it drunk out of their minds as they seem to, so can we. My father has found a pilot. He has been here,' Narain points to the easternmost extremity of the South American continent. 'It is called Hesife. This land to the west of it is nothing but jungles and gold mines.'

'I heard that the gold has already been mined into utensils and such. Who rules the place?'

'The Firangis. Their own kings and chiefs are no more. Beaten by the Firangis some hundred years ago. Lain low by sickness but blessed with gold and silver. If we did not have such bizarre laws, maybe we would have found them first. But are we allowed to explore anything? I do not understand this stricture against travel. The Mussalmans can do it, and they have been profiting from it for centuries. The Mussalman captains of Keral have already travelled the world and have been visiting Malindi, Muscat, Aden, Java, Bali and Chin these many thousand years.'

'Are you planning to go?'

'Either me,' Narain stops speaking and turns over his shoulder and looks at Bhimaji and his clerk before continuing, 'I know you or your brothers can't, but we need to send someone we trust. More than that, I just want to see what is out there.'

Narain dismisses his clerk with dire threats and a promise of silence, and gives the maps and other documents to Bhimaji to carry. As they make their way down the staircase, Bhimaji muses to Sambhaji: 'Imagine, running out of drinking water in the middle of the sea surrounded with all that water.'

Budgets

Sitting in his office, Boone frets as his left leg jerks up and down on his toes. His hands are clasped together in front of his face and his index fingers are extended to his nostrils. His thoughts about Angria have transformed into a spectre that consumes his days and distracts him from his work. Boone has been spending all his effort and most of his budget on the expansion of his Marine force and fantasizing about attacking Vijaydurg with it again. The trade he manages has become too intricately entwined with the Maratha Sealord. Passing off local vessels as Company ships for a fee has long been a sure and steady source of income. Now not only is it lost but he is losing his own ships which Angria takes with increasing frequency. Boone is losing his ability to negotiate with the Konkan Subedar as all his protestations sent to Satara are redirected to Angria with the instructions that they should deal directly with their representative at Kulaba.

Gilberts, sallow and smooth-cheeked, brings in a sheaf of papers and a pair of large registers, one bound in dark-green leather and the other in a maroon.

'You had wanted to see the shipyard's accounts, President Sir.'

A quick wave of the hand tells the boyish clerk to leave the accounts and exit without further intrusion. The might of the Siddi seems to have dissipated these past few years and with it the wonderful animosity the Abyssinian held for Angria. He sorely misses the complaints he used to receive from both sides on the Company supporting the other faction. If only there was some way of rousing Janjira to some common cause against Angria. Was there something he could do to instigate the one against the other? His mind is blank with frustration. Boone also knows that he will not be in Bombay forever and he needs to do something, anything to strike at Angria before his time here lapses. He pays heed to the heat and is irritated by it. A prickling sensation spreads through his back and buttocks. He can't do anything to Angria or hope to involve the Siddi. The days of the Company are numbered on this little outpost. It will be eventually abandoned like so many other outposts, spread all over the tropics. Madras was hotter, he remembers, but Bombay is more fatal. In Madras, there was a buffer of flat innocuous fields that separated the fort and the little town around it from the inland. Here he feels cornered by Cornerji, pushed up against the ghats, scrabbling at the edge of the high tide, and the dark unknown jungles of the inland tumble down and over his clutch of little islands— which are little more than rocks rung with mangrove swamps. Leopards and mosquitoes are everywhere. The Portuguese princess had brought a poor dowry indeed to the king with whom he shares a name. But now, exactly one more than fifty years since that day, how good and diligent Protestants like himself have built that swampy archipelago into a beacon of trade. It is not yet Surat, nor Kalyan, Thana, Rajapuri or Chaul, but if not for the infernal meddling and policing of Angria, it could well become an equal to any great and ancient port to the north. His experience in the Company has taught him that the path to increase his own financial wealth is through the commissioning of building works, whether of walls or of boats. The allocation of revenue opens so many avenues that lead down to compounds of pagodas. The board has financed his little navy, and for it to continue, they will need to believe that Angria is a pirate trying to extort them.

'I am going to hurt the man. I don't know how, and I don't know when. But I am going to hurt him as the Lord is my witness,' he mumbles.

Boone shakes himself out of his nervous reverie and removes himself to a small writing table that is against the wall behind his desk. The least he can do is continue and increase in his efforts at painting Angria as distinct from the heirs of Sivajee. If the Sow Raja will not condescend to take up our concerns against his Admiral, it is time to treat the Admiral as an entity unto himself, uncontrollable by his own king. With his goose feather quill, Boone paints Angria in the red-hot colours of a pirate once again in his journalled letter back to the directors at Leadenhall Street. He will not waste a moment.

There is a knock at the door and Boone turns around irritated and snaps out a who-is-it. His tone and mood soften when he realizes that it is the serene and efficient Patel.

'Yes, Mr Patel, what brings you here? Away from your incessant responsibilities?'

'I thought Your Excellency would like to know that the Honourable Sarkhel Kanhoji Angre's son was seen just outside the fort's walls a few days ago. He then proceeded to Mahim on a pleasure cruise. There were dancing girls on board from what I was told.'

'Which one?'

'That is yet to be determined. But my informant, who has had the privilege of laying his own eyes upon the father once, says it but has to be.'

Boone now bristles at the man's incorrigible formality and him calling his nemesis honourable has rendered him almost senseless.

'Well catch him and have him shackled the next time you hear of their presence around here. How dare he? The gall, the rotten red liver of the man and his progeny.'

Boone has spit at the corners of his mouth and his lips are pursed constipatively.

'And who may I ask was his host here?'

'Seth Narainji Kamath, the Honourable Seth Ramaji's youngest son.'

The Patel looks down at his feet before he continues.

'However, Your Excellency, I would like to qualify the rumours that even if the man looked exactly like the Sarkhel, he is known to have many natural issues right down the entire coast.'

'The sins of the father, my dear man. Legal or natural, if they have a drop of his blood, I want them apprehended. It would also be gallant of you, Mr Patel, to tell the Seth Rummerji that one of his sons has been consorting with a seed of the Angria.'

'Your Excellency, but the honourable Seth Ramaji is well known to the Sarkhel and is also received well at the court of the Maharaja at Satara. In fact, I would be hard-pressed to point out a family that the Sethji does not know well. He is famous for having the most amiable of relations with all the great houses of the coast. He is a pillar of his community and has been our constant friend and partner.'

'Exactly, my dear Mr Patel. The Sethji is a pillar not only to his community, but also to my presidency and to this entire port. It is our duty to let him know if his son is debauching with one of Angria's seed.'

The Patel, like his father and grandfather in Surat before him, has been a loyal employee of the Angrezi Company. The educated and competent amongst their community have been greatly sought after as translators and revenue agents as they have been born into a religion that greatly emphasizes righteousness and honesty. Also, like the Angrez, the Parsis do not have restrictions on beef, pork and untouchability or sharing of dining spaces. Seth Ramaji, too, has many Parsis in his employ, though they eat separately, and it will not be impossible to relay information to him through them. The governorship of the archipelago has changed many times in the three generations the Rustomji Dorabjis have been working at first Surat and now Bombay. The incumbent tends to disappoint and disgust the Patel, as he had his father, and he wonders when Boone will be removed for wasting the Company's resources.

'I will have the information passed on to the honourable Sethji,' Rustomji Dorabji says and leaves. He has felt a bit like a common informer, but as the security of the tenants of the Company lie to him and his loyalty to his prescribed duties, he had felt it was imperative that Boone should be told. The Patel's own fear rises from the fact that he knows the defences and the geographical realities of the archipelago well. He also has a fair understanding of the Maratha Admiral's capabilities on sea and by land. The people on the coast call him the Shivaji of the Seas but he is also known as the muggermachch and is equally lethal on land.

The Forger

How long had he been nursing this plan in the depths of his bosom? No, he must not be proud. This has been divine grace. He is merely the instrument. It is the inexorable law of karma. It is the triumph of right against wrong. It has fallen from the open palm of the Devi, and it has fallen slowly and piece by piece. He has been patient and he has waited and now Lakshmi Devi will reward him. Had that vile Kanhoji not made the gods themselves party to his falsehoods and lies? Bala, too, has been complicit, and see how the gods struck him down at the height of his glory. It will not be long before the other Maratha sardars chewed up his two young sons—he could not even live long enough to protect them. What a waste, a life wasted. Ramaji is part of the same clique. They are the fingers of one hand, a greedy grasping claw that grabs at others' destinies. Each digit needs to be broken and crushed, and if that is not possible, he could at least pull out a nail from each one of them. Pandurao has found this goldsmith after a protracted and meticulous search assisted by the unholy priest whom he had met years ago at the Siddi's court in Janjira.

Tinku Soni is worth the effort, as he is a particularly talented craftsman, not as a goldsmith but as a forger. The Firangi priest counts the lowest dregs of humanity that can be found in the Konkan as associates and is in that way very resourceful. When the moon waxes, the priest is filled with the spirit of Soma, and seeks out young men. It does not bother Pandurao; such things are common amongst all castes that live in the Konkan, though the Angrez and the Firangis hide the inclination the most. Pandurao makes his way gingerly through the muddy street's many potholes, each brimming with its own concoction of excreta and garbage. The Soni's establishment is at the very edge of the tanners' street in Kalyan, where it slopes off towards a creek. He can no longer eat or drink with his own community. It is a wooden shop in a narrow lane of similar wooden shacks that bear testament to their inflammatory properties with charred pillars that stand out at intervals along the lane. It is a lane inhabited by people cast out by their own kind who cannot even have water given to them by their families.

He turns into the third doorway as he was directed, to find a small man in a dirty little loincloth sitting on a low wooden plank. It takes a moment for Pandurao to register that both the man's legs end above the knees as rounded stumps. The man is etching into something that may be a seal or stamp of some sort. He looks up at Pandurao and peers at him through squinting eyes.

'Sathe sent me. He is a friend of mine,' Pandurao tells the man as directed by the priest.

The Soni waves him in and Pandurao searches for a clean spot to sit, and not finding one, decides against it.

Tinku Soni asks him to sit down, and pulls his little plank forward. It has little wooden wheels at the bottom, and he creaks his way to a pile of wax chunks and clears a space by pushing them all to one side. Pandurao bends down and sits on his haunches.

'Look, I can pay you very well, but I must have absolute secrecy here. This does not leave the room,' Pandurao tells Soni who is just an arm's length away from his face.

'Saheb, I am not a famous physician that cures the incurable and needs to announce what great deeds I have done. For what work you have come to me, I am sure there are those who would have us both decapitated for it. I do not wish to lose my only head. I am very good at what I do, and I am discreet and that is why I charge what I do.'

'How much do you charge?'

'Well, it depends on what you want made.'

'Letters, just letters. With lists and other written documents. Nothing complicated.'

'Saheb, letters require seals, signatures, stamps. Everything is complicated. I will need something to work with, of course. I need something for reference.'

'Yes, I have quite a few items for reference,' Pandurao says and reaches into his kurta and pulls out a roll of papers from a pocket under his shoulders. He gives a thin paper letter to the Soni. It is an original of the first agreement of a deal that Ramaji had given him so many decades ago only because he was his younger brother's schoolmate. The agreement is for the purchase of seventy maunds of rice and it has been signed by the young and steady hand of Ramaji Kamath, himself. The Soni takes the letter and peers at it. Then he suddenly turns to Pandurao and shakes his head.

'What is wrong?' Pandurao asks anxiously.

'This is going to cost you extra. He is a big man, a very big man. Big men are dangerous, and I have seen that they have the ability to survive such attacks and then their predilection for seeking out their attackers.'

'He will not survive if you do your job well. You may not know me, but I am a very big man myself.'

'What is your name?'

'What does my name matter? I have the money for your service.'

'Don't tell me your name, it's unlikely I would have heard of you, but I have heard the name of your mark.'

'You need not have heard of me,' Pandurao says, his bile rising, 'I am known by those that matter. I am a very important shroff and contractor; I do a lot of trading with the Firangis, and I have warehouses in Surat,' he says, ending with a blatant lie.

'Well, Sethji, I meant no offence. If you have enough to pay me, with half in advance, you are Jagat Seth as far as I am concerned.'

'I will pay you 10 per cent as advance and the rest once I am satisfied with the quality of the job.'

'I am sorry, Sethji, but I am sure Sathe Saheb told you what my terms are. I am busy as it is. Maybe you can find someone else to suit your terms.'

'Alright,' Pandurao says, accepting that he is already in too deep having revealed his mark's name.

'You will have your advance. I will need at least fifteen documents; seemingly written over the years. It must look perfect. I already have the drafts of the letters.'

Then he remembers the last document. He looks at the crippled goldsmith, wondering how he should best present it. He unties his kurta and reaches into an inner pocket where his coins are safely kept. He feels around and pulls out a fat and gleaming gold rei which he holds out in one hand and with the other he gives the troublesome document to the goldsmith.

'This is for just this one letter. A full advance with faith that you will not run away, or . . .' he looks at Tinku awkwardly and stops speaking.

Tinku's eyes scan the document Pandurao has given him. It is a letter to the Seth and when he gets to the bottom of it, he startles, and the paper drops from his fingers.

Pandurao's thick lower lip hangs out trembling and from its wavering Tinku deduces that he is good for another 100 rupaiyas at least. He might as well retire for good. Buy a woman and live in bliss.

'Sethji, I ply my trade so I can feed my family and I hope to work for as long as I can, as long as my eyes can see, and my hands are steady. But what you are asking me to do will leave my family orphaned and destitute. This letter,' Tinku says to Pandurao, just pointing to it, 'will cost you another two hundred rupaiyas, two hundred silver Alibagi rupaiyas.'

Pandurao looks as if he had been stabbed and his nostrils flare and his eyes widen in unison. Where has Sathe sent him? Again, he knows he must follow this through to the end or kill the Soni right now. A chill comes over Pandurao, and for the first time, he knows he is in the game for his life. He smiles a little more and agrees to the goldsmith's demand, pulling out a dastak that has the seal of Kanhoji Angre upon it for reference.

Time

The omnipotent sun is silent in its oppressive stride across the firmament. Every trace of moisture has been sucked dry from the soil, and the liberated dust blows, crusting the darkened leaves. The black and grey rocks and the craggy patches of rusty laterite reach feverish pitches of heat. It warps the air, and twisting plumes of mirages swirl like dervishes over the surface of the Konkan. First hot winds blow towards the land and then a cooler high wind whistles, gently and seductively. Its rising pitch presages a stampede of muscular Gaur like clouds that trample the land with their foamy white ankles.

Kanhoji suffers it, more unbearable than the last year. But he does not want the monsoon to break. He hates it. It steals his men away to their fields. The stone mining and construction work stops. His galbats and ghurabs are hauled in and laid on their sides or hull-up. Life slows down and often it just stops. It gets dark, and dry riverbeds turn to impassable torrents of water. Trading vessels and fishing boats disappear, and the angry sea is a desolate expanse.

Sitting by the pool at Hirakot, watching a dappled filly nursing from its statuesque grey mother grazing on the lawn that surrounds it, Kanhoji wipes the sweat off his forehead with the back of his palm, as a nervous attendant rushes to him with a bowl of cool water and a soft muslin towel. Kanhoji removes his turban and splashes his face with the saltpetre-chilled water. He wets his fingers and runs

them through his hair which though still thick is creeping with grey
and white strands. Kanhoji can still feel the immense strength in
his chest and shoulders, but he has also come to accept the layer of
fat he has accumulated all over his body, especially his stomach. It
does not bother him too much either, though he flirts with the idea
of increasing the duration of his morning rides. Now he rides at a
leisurely pace, merely for the pleasure of having a steed below him.
He rarely puts the horse or himself through the paces any more.
Such beautiful and elegant creatures, he is loath to risk an accident
that could damage their sculpted legs. He does not bother putting his
turban on again. There is no one there but Sekho and it would take
an earth-shattering calamity for him to be called upon now. Systems
have been put in place, and he has his sons and his sardars running
around for him and making sure that their Sarkhel, the *Samudratala
Shivaji*, never need be disturbed.

Kanhoji looks at Sekho, his eldest, and from the moment he
heard of Bala's death, his decided heir. Sekhoji, called Jaisinghrao
by his subjects, has his mother's large eyes and his grandfather's thin
lips. Sekho never removes his turban as he has already begun to lose
his hair unlike his father and younger brothers who are blessed with
thick manes. Sambha looks the most like Kanhoji, and those who
had known the father in his youth swear that he is the very image
of his young father. He loves all his sons, but he is glad that it is his
eldest who is engendered with the courage and patience a leader will
require. His son has a calm and unflappable manner he himself was
never able to acquire. This boy grew up gentle and compassionate
and remains so except when it comes to attacking or boarding ships.
The moment Sekho is on deck of his ghurab, he is a transformed
creature. His smile disappears and his eyes grow cold, all emotion is
erased from his face. He still prefers his position behind the gunners
manning the cannon on the fore of a galbat chasing down a ship,
and he will have the nakhwa of that galbat break formation to join
the first boarders of a dismasted vessel. This he gets from Surya
who has been deputed to always remain by Sekho's side, teaching

and guiding him at every instance. And in Bangdo, he has his Surya. A Javan called Sumitro, who wears a garland of shrunken heads like Devi Durga, carries his gun for him, making rude gestures with every appendage is his Golu. But no more galbats and boarding. Sekho is the heir now.

'Baba, maybe you should swim in this pool occasionally. You only stay by it and never get in. It will do your knee good.'

'My knees are perfectly well. What's wrong with my knees? I go riding every morning.'

'You could hardly bend them yesterday,' Sekho says.

'Ah, that was yesterday. Just a little stiffness, it's nothing: old wounds reminding me of a happy and exciting past with a creak here or there. Tell me, what news of Baji and Chimma?' Kanho asks, deftly changing the subject.

'They are well but much harassed. A lot of the other sardars feel that he is much too young and inexperienced to be the Peshwa.'

'Of course, they will. I have been receiving feelers from Sumant, Naro Ram and even the Pant Prathinidhi.'

'What are they asking for?'

'Well, not as forward as to ask, but they want to know if there is anything that could change my mind, might change my mind.'

'Have you responded?' Sekho asks anxiously. He is fond of Baji and the feeling is mutual, though they have not had the opportunity to spend enough time in each other's company.

Kanhoji laughs and looks at his son with renewed joy. Sekho still has a simplistic naivety about him that is born of humility.

'It is I who press the coin. I will buy them twice over.'

'At the rate Ai is throwing it on daan and pujas . . .'

'Let her be, she is the Subedar's wife, after all. Poor thing, I made her suffer for too long. Don't worry about money. Khandoba gives. You know why he gives it to me? Because he wants me to breed the best horses, here in the Konkan. So, I may make the best cannon and muskets, here in the Konkan. The best gunpowder. Build ships and forts.'

'Like Maharaj,' says Sekho, recalling the founder.

'And one never knows how and when one goes. Look at Bala, survived through the toughest tribulations and then suddenly gone in the security of a grand and comfortable home, surrounded by servants and supported by a large estate. After me, you will lead your brothers. You will keep them united, and you will take our legacy forward.'

'I will try my best, Baba,' is all Sekho can truthfully say.

'I very well know how important it is to personally lead your men, it is vital, but there comes a time when one must step back on to the deck of a ghurab or take a high point on the rocks and direct the battle from there. A lot has gone into you and your brothers. Do you realize that your lives are worth more than those of the uneducated men you pension off for two hundred rupaiyas?'

'I understand, Baba. I will not lead any more boarding parties.'

'Or man the deck of a galbat in chase?'

Sekho takes a long breath. There is nothing he delights in more than dismasting a large sailing ship; a passion that has cost him half his hearing already. It is a fine science with him, and he tries to make every attempt smoother, more efficient and safer for his people.

'The next season will be my last. I will train officers and teach them the skills required to direct an attack.'

'So be it, son. After all we are Sankhpal, it is our karma to risk our lives and our dharma to stay alive to serve.'

Sekho nods his head and remains silent as his father lies back on the divan. It is not the best time to tell his father about the pain he is having in his sides. It comes in spells and then disappears. It isn't severe enough to immobilize him or for anyone but his young wife to notice. It has been bothering Sekho because he cannot understand its cause. He has broken his ribs many times, but this sharp pain is more towards his back, under his shoulder blades.

Kings and Generals

Governor Charles Boone has spent the day arguing with a trifecta of shipwrights. He has explained to the three men his design of a hull that would have a draught of half a fathom. It is essentially a thick plank ringed with a short gunwale. All three shipwrights look at each other in amazement and tell the chief administrator of their port that it is improbable, but if the Saheb can envision it, they will build it for him. The shipwrights are already off to their colleagues and carpenters, relishing the thought of sharing the insane ideas of the Gavnar Saheb. Even a child would know better. Has he never floated a leaf down a stream of water? The Saheb wants a flat surface to support cannon, no hull! They laugh as they have these many years. The purpose and need for such a craft are well known to the shipwrights and they find it even more ludicrous and bizarre. Here is this chit of an Angrezi vania, working for a pathetic little company that cannot match one well-heeled Surti trader, out to take on Angria. Has the man not heard that the one called Shivaji, albeit of the seas, is not of the House of Bhonsale, but of Kulaba, ten kos dead south? The king of the Konkan sits there, in his least defensible fort watching the traffic pass by him. But there is money to be made so they say they will build him something, anything at all. They only must build the craft and test it, so they leave him with estimates and return home knowing that while this man runs the settlement, their children will eat meat dhansak every day.

After they leave, Boone removes his thick black jacket and hangs it on a coat stand and then takes off his lice-ridden baked-wool wig, powdered with lemon-scented starch. Boone likes to appear in what he considers his working uniform. He feels undressed without his wig or his coat, though this is not the weather for such sartorial choices. But what can one do? One must represent the board and its directors and shareholders, amongst whom is His Protestant and Germanic Majesty: King George of Hanover, England, the Scots and Ireland.

Gilberts knocks on the door and announces Seth Pando Row. Boone rolls up his eyes at the man in response. He is not in the mood for any remedies or gossip though the itching on his back and buttocks has crawled into his ear. He sticks his little finger into his ear and shakes it rapidly.

'He says it is very important,' says Gilberts, who had accepted a dam to disturb His Excellency. If Pandora gets called in, he is owed another.

'It always is, send him in,' Boone says as he gets up to put on his coat and wig again.

Pandurao comes in and greets Boone in his usual effusive way. The man is looking obviously bereft and Boone shudders at what new complaint the Seth is going to voice.

'What is it, Sethji? I have a lot of work to do.'

'Itching, is it? Tonight is the full moon. Irritation waxes too. Oil of fresh coconut, Your Excellency.'

'Indeed, this mortal vessel itches in this infernal weather: neither fit for man nor steed,' the Governor replies.

'Your Excellency, I am torn asunder, truly asunder. I do not know what to do so I am doing my duty to you. We must do our dharma; however bitter it is. But before you decide on anything, let me bear witness to my friend.'

'Well, then go ahead, do your derma, or whatever it is,' Boone says impatiently.

'It concerns your *phairit*, Kanhoji Angre,' Pandurao whispers loudly, and Boone's attention is pricked in its navel.

Pandurao crosses the desk and comes to the side of the still-seated and now surprised Governor.

'I have heard the most unfortunate rumours and I cannot believe them to be true. But you are bound to hear them soon yourself.'

'What of Cornerji?'

'I do not know if you are aware of this, but Kanhoji and Ramaji's dear departed brother were close friends, studying in the same gurukul.'

'A what?'

'A school, as you say, where children go to get educated by wise teachers. I was there myself.'

'But of course, isn't it how you know he's a swine?' asks Boone exasperated.

Pandurao remains standing, not saying another word.

Boone stands up and directs Pandurao to a chair on the other side of the desk before he returns to his high-backed rosewood chair in the style of William and Mary. He has had it recently commissioned with a cane back and seat to cool his own a little, and the carpenter has done a fine job of it. Pandurao now leans across the table as Boone struggles to control another buzzing itch in his right ear.

'It beggars belief, Your Excellency, but though we all know that Seth Ramaji has long been in league with Kanhoji, there are indications that Sethji has been sharing the most sensitive information regarding the settlement, its defences, shipping and garrison with Kanhoji. All of it with the intent of scuttling your factory here and ending your trade with the coast.'

'It is a very grave accusation you make, Mr Pandora, against a beacon of your people and a friend to this town of ours.'

'I would not have said it if I did not have proof.'

'Proof, you say?' Boone says, imminently surprised.

'Why would he do that? A lot of his business is dependent on us, and we are on good terms,' he continues.

Boone now recalls what the Patel had told him just recently about the Angrian visiting the fort and then making merry with Rummerji's son. But this could just well have been debauched gentleman at play.

'It is Angria's intention to rid the coast of the Angrezi Company and the Portuguese. Has he not repeatedly said that traders need not and should not carry guns on their vessel? He feels your walls are illegal and you should revert to that position you enjoyed in Surat before the sacking.'

'Surat is the Mughal's but this rock we sit on is King George's and he has rented it out to the traders of the City of London.'

'Angria does not endure the sovereignty of the House of Bhonsale,' he lies, 'do you think he recognizes your King *Joz*? And what are the vanias of London to him? I intimately know his ambition: it is to be a king himself, and he has always believed that you are trespassing on his kingdom.'

'If this is so, what is stopping Angria right now? Why hasn't he moved?'

Now it is the turn of Pandurao to surprise the agitated Governor.

'Angria is waiting for some developments in Satara. Between you and me: he and his pawn, the new young Peshwa, are planning to overthrow the Bhonsales. Baji will get the lands east of the ghats and Kanhoji the entire coast.'

Boone digests the information as the itching in his ear comes home.

'Where is this proof against Rummerji you speak of?'

'Within the very walls of this fort, Your Excellency. At his warehouse by the docks.'

'His is a large establishment indeed. And what should we expect to find there?' he asks, fighting to maintain calm.

'It must be searched thoroughly of course, but it is a bundle of documents. The information he passes on to Kanhoji and possibly instructions to him from Kanhoji.'

'How do you know it is there? Do you understand my predicament? What if we don't find anything? How could I ever explain myself to Rummerji?'

'You will find it. It is on the upper floor towards the rear.'

'How do you have such exact knowledge of it?'

'An employee of Ramaji's: disgruntled. It was he who told me the whole thing,' Pandurao says smugly.

'May I interview this man?'

'He just died yesterday. He was ill. It was why I waited, so his family would be safe against any recriminations.'

'Very convenient indeed,' Boone says, his suspicions rising.

'A strike against Ramaji is a strike against Kanhoji, Your Excellency. Ramaji must hang for treason and his property be confiscated. People must see what happens to those who stand with Kanhoji.'

'That will be decided at his trial, if any proof is to be found.'

'It will be found but you must move on it immediately. Before the documents are removed to another place. I only request you to not send the Patel, or any other native persons. It would be best if English clerks were to conduct the search and the arrest.'

'You exceed your authority, Mr Pandora, as always.'

'Just a suggestion, Your Excellency, as they are such intimate friends.'

'Is that another accusation?'

'Oh no. Never would I even allude to the most honourable Patel in such a manner. Rustomji is the most loyal employee you have at your service. Merely to save his family the embarrassment, Your Excellency.'

Boone looks at Pandurao and wonders at the man. He knows him to be jealous of Rummerji Sett and they do share a visceral hatred of Cornerji, but would he go so far? Or maybe just that his prayers have been answered in the Lord's mysterious ways. Before Boone can ask anything else, Pandurao excuses himself, leaving Boone on a precipice.

The Arrest

It will be the night of Amavas: no light to hunt by. The Sarkhel-Subedar is in the middle of dictating a sensitive letter to his financially savvy guru, requesting him to return Rs 2 lakh he had given to Swamiji on 3 per cent interest. Brahmendra Swami has just lent an equivalent amount to the Yakut Khan, Rasool Siddi, and the Sarkhel hasn't been able to digest the information. He accepts Brahmendra Swami's indulgence of Siddi Rasool as a devotee and benefactor, but he cannot get his head around the Swami lending money to his enemy.

'As you had written in your last letter,' he dictates to Damodar. Gangadhar is dead from the pox.

Sekhoji strides in through the Durbar doors unannounced followed by Surya and Bangdo and everybody turns to look at them.

'Baba, Ramaji Kaka has been arrested by the Angrezi Seth. They have clasped him in chains and thrown him into a dungeon filled with common criminals. They have accused him of treachery against their Company and that he was in connivance with you to destroy their settlement.'

'What nonsense!' Kanhoji shouts back, shocked at this unbelievable news.

'On the basis of what? There is no truth in it at all. This Bhunji is mad, absolutely mad,' Kanhoji exclaims.

'They found letters. Even one from you to him, describing your plan.'

'Really? Describing my plan? Which asshole fool writes out their plans? This is ridiculous. They must be forgeries.'

'They have sealed all his warehouses and are considering confiscating all his property.'

'What jurisdiction do they have over him? Maybe over his property in their fort, but not him. And what of evidence? They need evidence. They cannot do this to him. He has supported their cause his entire life, the swine.'

'It is a conspiracy against him, most definitely. But we do not yet know who is behind it,' Surya says in a measured tone.

'What do the seths say? They cannot let this stand. Call Chota Rustomji. I want to speak to Rustomji.'

'I will get him to answer to you. Some of the seths wait like vultures to take what they can from the corpse of his enterprise,' Sekhoji says.

'Tell him he need not answer to me. But I hope he has some explanation for this madness or Bhun will answer to me.'

'He has let me know that he was not informed of the search or the subsequent arrest. Angrezi clerks went down to his warehouse, one within their fort, and found incriminating documents. Also, a letter from you and documents that he was going to send to you.'

'I wish to see this letter detailing my supposed plans. It is my right, as they say I have sent it, and presumably it bears my signature and seal. Tell Rustomji to bring it with him.'

'What do you want to do, Baba?'

'Get twenty men, intelligent ones. They are to take up employment with the Company and within the fort. Some labourers and a few clerks.'

'We already have people there.'

'No, leave them. Form this new team and their only purpose in life is to find out what happened and equally to get close to Bhun. Clean his pot or wipe his ass, they need to get as close to him as possible. Keep their eyes and ears open and be ready to act when the time comes. Form the team, get a leader and he will have a conduit to me directly.'

Everybody bows in acquiescence: silently and sombrely.

'And I want to speak to Chota Rustom now,' reverberates between the durbar walls.

Targets

The increasingly arthritic Babuji Kotla and his carpenters have constructed a target emulating the size of an East Indiaman by lashing two condemned ghurabs stern to bow and erecting three thick poles to play at masts. Yardarms and other spars have been tied to masts and there are a lot of old ropes hung about to imitate the shrouds and clewlines of a sailing ship. The contraption is towed out to sea and anchored lightly so that it still moves with the current and waves. Kanhoji is on the ramparts of Kulaba Fort watching the exercise with a large brass telescope that stands on a wooden tripod. A large blue umbrella held behind him shades him from the pervasive sunlight. Kanho can see both his sons, Sekhoji and Sambhaji, on the deck of a ghurab with spyglasses in their hands and their signalmen by their side. On the mainland to their north are the Siddi possessions of Thal and Rewas. Directly to the south is Chaul, under control of the Firangis, his only remaining rival.

The dark mood returns to Kanhoji. Rustomji has not made himself available. He excuses his presence at Kulaba with long letters that talk of shame. He hints he cannot be seen with the Subedar. A hive of suspicion flies amidst the settlement around Fort George, and it is evident from the fact that the Patel has had his letter transcribed and omits signing it. As Ramaji's son himself has told Kanhoji, the wizened and ageing Sethji has been tried by a tribunal and convicted for treason. All his property has been confiscated, the warehouses sealed, and his moneys seized, or whatever they can get a hold of. His distraught family has left for Kalyan. Rustomji writes that he had tried his utmost with Boone but to no avail. He further apologizes that he will not be able to deliver the proofs so rightly demanded by the Subedar but has had the opportunity of seeing them, and implicitly believing the Subedar, can only conclude that the documents are forgeries of great skill as the seals are identical and the signatures look indistinguishable from the originals to which he is privy. As to who could have masterminded the conspiracy, Rustomji is at a loss. As to who benefits from the downfall of the wealthy Sethji—the list is long. In the sealing and confiscation of the warehouses, Rustomji admits that he knows, though as always has no proof, that a lot of goods, money and valuable items have not even made it to the inventory list. He is trying his best to keep the incarcerated Seth comfortable. There is also no possibility of a ransom as Ramaji is considered a treasonous criminal. He also does not dare to hide the fact that Seth Ramaji is devastated. Brought upon by the sheer insanity of the charges and the subsequently bizarre proceedings at which he is helpless to defend himself, Seth Ramaji has lost his health and his composure. He is broken and unable to continue in the abominably filthy conditions he finds himself in. Kanhoji sorrowfully realizes that it is in all ways the physical manifestation of the Seth's personal hell. Rustomji ends his latest letter with an exhortation for patience on the Sarkhel's part: Boone is to be replaced soon; he is spending too much of the Company's money on infrastructure that brings no returns. The directors in London, he heard from his father, never tolerate spenders, and Boone has been profligate. Nor has Boone made any friends on the coast. He has just driven out some Portuguese missionaries, earning the ire of the Viceroy in Goa, and his relations with the Siddi are almost non-existent. Boone is singularly frugal in his gifts of nazrana, a concept that is unnatural to someone of his class—his gifts are considered mean and insulting by those potentates who receive them. Kanhoji knows this through experience.

Kanhoji will not wait for Bhun to escape. If he were the sole problem, as Rustomji makes him out to be, and not the Company, then he will tackle the problem directly. They will have to send out a new governor sooner than they are planning to.

Powerless

Poornima. The monsoon is no more than a week away, and heavy and wet winds from the south and west have begun to blow. Overhead, bow-shaped kites survey a pair of new frigates, built of Dindelli teak, at the Ribeira das Naus dockyard in Goa, and follow them up to Bassein where they join Commander Antonio Cardim Froes' northern fleet. It seems the Sarkhel has resigned himself to the end of the season. They watch his garrisons leave, and the rats emerge to haunt the remaining guards. His ghurabs are being hauled ashore for repair or being safely moored in inlets at Gheria, Bankot, Suvarnadurg and Purnagad. The first rains of the season break and as the kites take shelter in large rain trees, the crows from the crematorium tell them that a large fleet of Firangi ships is moving north. Inquiries made of the gulls at Chaul indicate that the Viceroy is moving against the Angrez in retaliation to the expulsion of Catholic missionaries from the settlement.

That evening brings thirteen Firangi ships into view at Kulaba where they remain anchored through most of the night and are gone before dawn breaks. During the night, the perplexed and slightly eager vultures, with only 140 guards of the garrison left and half the gunners gone, wonder if they were positioned there to merely prevent the Sarkhel's own fleet from assisting the Angrez. The night passes and they are robbed of their breakfast feast.

By dawn it has begun to rain again, and the clouds come down in fast-moving sheets of water. A sparrow finds refuge on the rafters of the durbar hall at Hirakot. The Sarkhel enters the hall after an abridged exercise regimen. Requesting an immediate audience is Frey Verississimo, Kanhoji's chief Firangi translator, envoy and adviser on all things Firangi. His news is flabbergasting, and the court erupts into a murmur that drowns the sounds of both the waves and the rain.

'Seventy-six vessels, My Lord, from Goa, Daman and Bassein. The thirteen we saw last night were the only ones that could make it through the rain. It was Antonio Froes who anchored by us.'

'And their plan was to attack us?'

'Yes, Sarkhel Saheb. They wanted to surprise us at the end of the season.'

The Sarkhel closes his eyes in relief and throws his hands up in the air and thanks Khandoba.

'Khandoba has brought confusion to his enemies, but it will be imprudent and impious for us to relegate him to such offices. Well, never again are we going to disband or pull our boats in before the rest of them do. That cunning snake,' he says, referring to Froes. The sparrow startles at the mention of the serpent.

'It is Antonio Cardim, he has been tasked with regaining Portuguese supremacy over the coast again,' voices Piloji, the peacock amongst the Sarkhel's sardars.

'Well, it is good to know that the Firangis have the humility to accept that they have lost the north at least.'

'Sarkhel Saheb, Bassein should be our focus. Maybe with the help of the Peshwa, we can take it. It will give you absolute supremacy over the northern coast, and the Portuguese will be restricted to Goa,' says another sardar the sparrow recognizes well.

'I will be glad if we can accomplish it in my lifetime. If only I could see the fall of Bassein and,' pausing, the Sarkhel adds: 'Janjira.'

'Raje, let Janjira wait. I have heard rumours of another treaty soon to be enjoined between the Viceroy and the Angrez,' Frey says as a wet sunbird flies in and shakes itself dry.

'Freji, you must go south to Goa and do all you can to prevent it. I also want to know the pretext they would have used to excuse the attack, had it been successful. Tell them we were prepared and will remain so, and ask His Excellency what bothers him so to plan such devious attacks on his friend and brother. Buy me some time while I deal with this Angrez.'

As Freji takes the letter addressed to the Viceroy along with a requisition for gifts to be presented from Damodar, Chimmaji Bhat is announced to the surprise of the court. Sekhoji gets up from his place beside his father and goes to receive the Peshwa's fourteen-year-old brother. Chimmaji enters energetically and rushes to the foot of Kanhoji's raised platform and prostrates himself.

'Sarkhel Saheb, the Peshwa Baji Rao sends his salutations.'

'I would welcome you to the Konkan, Chimmaji, but there are those I still cannot speak for, so I welcome you heartily to my home,' Kanhoji says, blessing the boy with a raised palm.

'Jaisinghrao, take him to Bagh Haveli and make him comfortable there,' the Sarkhel commands his eldest son.

To Chimmaji he says: 'Eat something and rest. Tonight, I am taking all of you hunting.' The sunbird shakes the last of the rain from its plumage.

Chimmaji is about to protest, but Kanhoji continues: 'And you are going to spend some time with your brothers here, don't say you have to leave because I am not going to let you.'

Chimmaji smiles back happily. He has been instructed by his brother to return as soon as he can, but he cannot deny his host and his father's elderly friend. Chimmaji winks at Sekho as they make their way out. There will be new swords and fascinating guns and there will be horses and hunting. Chimmaji is in heaven for he knows his host to be an Indra of the age. The sparrow follows the two young men through the cloistered town.

Ice

Summer comes again. Eyes squint against a scorching sun, glaring on the wide flat sea. Throats grow parched and thirst rages. The nagging pain in Sekho's upper back has birthed a fear in his mind: he is to predecease his father and upend his plans. What would happen then? There is blood in his piss, and it terrifies him.

Sekho contacts a merchant come in from Dilli who has previously supplied the House of Bhonsale. Shahu Raje's years at the Mughal court have given him expensive tastes, and the coolness of ice for those who have experienced it can never be satisfied by the saltpetre-cooled drinks of the Konkan. The speed at which the blocks of consistently melting ice travel and the care that goes into delaying the melt, make it an embarrassingly expensive venture. Sekho finances the indulgence from his own personal account. The massive blocks of ice have sailed down the Sindhu till they reach Thatta at half their initial mass. They are repacked in sawdust, hay and canvas and rushed south in the dark holds of the swiftest vessels available. When Sekho has news that the ice has crossed Diu, he prepares for a party at the Hirakot pool. The best Hafus mangoes of his father's extensive orchards are individually identified and marked as they wait on their trees for the ice to arrive.

On the banks of the Hirakot pond, his father has constructed a pool built with dressed stones and lined with glazed turquoise tiles from Persia. Granite pillars carved in the Karnatak in the shape of apsaras bedecked in foliage support a series of trellises that ring the pool. A well with a Persian watermill powered by two oxen drives the fresh water into the pool. A narrow stone-lined channel connects the pool to a large pond where the clear fresh water debouches. Sekho has carpets and rugs, also from the Safavid Empire, laid around the pool and channel. Low diwans are set about them and shipwrights and sailmakers are commandeered from the shipyard to construct large fans that can cool the area beneath them. Sherbets, buttermilk and solkadi are prepared to await their cooling. The acrobats and magicians who have come for the entertainment of the children are setting up their acts as the musicians and dancers get ready for their performances. Various types of incense are lit to clear the area of bugs and insects

Under the glaucoma-ridden eyes of Surya, the boat carrying the ice is beached on the stretch of sand nearest the pond. Of the two massive blocks that had been carved out of a glacier in the Dhauladars, only their frozen hearts remain. The blocks further shrink once they are cleaned. Sekhoji is the only person there who knows how much these two pieces of frozen water have cost him, and the quantity of the remaining ice makes him gag inside.

It does not bear, he consoles himself, Baba deserves it. The off-coloured and dirty ice on the top is used to cool the ripe saffron mangoes and the clear ice in the middle goes into the array of drinks spiked with kokum, khus, rose petals, anise and mint.

Baba and his wives, surrounded by their grandchildren, are led to the cool and beautifully decorated pavilion strung up with white mogra flowers and bedecked with potted champas in florescence. As they take their places, silver salvers filled with sliced mango on beds of ice are placed before them. The children pick up the slivers of ice and play with them for a moment before they melt into their wails. Kanhoji picks up a small piece and studies it intensely and then pops it into his mouth. The chilled mangoes are delicious beyond belief, the deep rich flavours bursting from their juices like they never have. Bhawanji sitting in his orchard appears in his mind's eye.

Small glasses of buttermilk, solkadi and mulberry juice are served to the gathering of family and close friends. Kanhoji calls Sekho to sit by his side and the visitors come to greet them.

'I thought I would have to go to Rishikesh to experience ice, Jaisinghrao. You have made it possible in my own home,' says Baba proudly.

'That is all very well, son, but how much did it cost?' asks his mother.

'Let that be. He can afford it. Enjoy it, Sekho's mother, and don't talk of money in front of our guests,' Baba gently admonishes his wife.

'Ai, I thought just once, just to experience it. Wasn't it worth it?'

'I don't know what the big deal is. And such a small amount of ice,' Ai replies.

'Ah, it has brought out the taste of the mango like nothing else,' the younger Ai consoles the stepson in turn.

'The water tastes of Amrit,' pipes in Sekho's youngest son.

'What do you know of Amrit?' Mathurabai asks, and ruffles her grandson's hair.

* * *

Dusk comes and the ice has all melted away. The revelries at the poolside pavilion continue as the more serious men talk business and politics away from the din of the music. Maloji Salvi is impatiently waiting at the canopied entrance to the pool area. He does not dare disturb the Sarkhel's rare leisure but is anxious that his news reach his master immediately. Maloji is pacing up and down the narrow mud path when a horse comes thundering down it. As he moves to the side to let the rider pass, he recognizes the rider as one of his own men. Maloji is suddenly less keen on reporting to Kanhoji. The mashaalwalas come in teams and light the rows of mashaals that are stuck into the ground, lighting the way to the pool. Soon, one of the family's personal attendants comes running out and orders the palkhiwalas to get ready. The grandchildren come running out, followed by Kanhoji. He sees Maloji waiting for him and goes over to him.

'Is everything all right?'

Maloji looks down at his dusty goatskin boots as he speaks.

'Saheb, I have found the forger. I am very sure he is the man responsible. But as I was waiting here for you, one of my messengers just came in with some bad news.'

'What is it? Don't be scared. Have I ever held the bearer responsible?'

'Saheb,' Maloji murmurs, 'Seth Ramaji passed away, either last night or early this morning.'

'He should have been here with us,' Kanhoji says to Sekho. The ice has left a bitter aftertaste through no fault of its own.

The interrogation is short and not at all bloody. When the guard left to watch over the culprit greets the Sarkhel at his arrival at the cell, the Soni loses control of his bowels and immediately collapses in a faint. When he comes to, he blurts out whatever he knows, and not knowing his client's name, bursts into tears again. He describes the Seth and tells them how much he was paid. He says he knew he would get caught and his life would be forfeit. Oh, how he knew it the second that cursed rat-like Seth had walked into his shop. A team of four men is immediately sent to Kalyan to find a man called Sathe.

Evening Ride

The ample beach at Gheria, south of Vijaydurg Fort, has been cleared of any hoof spiking shells and stones by the boys of the village. It's what they do for Raje. The beach provides the best footing for his horses, and the surf to cool their ankles in. Kanhoji's deep and abiding respect of the equine species combined with the possibility of washed sand under hoof and the beauty of the setting sun has crystallized into a daily habit. Every evening, after the sun slips into its descent towards the ocean's farthest edge, Kanhoji takes his favourite steeds out to the beach and exercises them. He knows he needs the workout far more than his horses. Beginning with his digestion, his body has discreetly begun to slow down. His eyesight is getting fuzzier every season and he is practically blind at night. His ears and his lower back hurt, his knees creak and jam, and his afternoons are spent in slumber.

Accompanied by their grooms, each horse waits its turn as Kanhoji canters them on the firm wet sand, waves incessantly clawing at hooves. A cool breeze blows in from the west and the pink sky swirls and deepens to a dark purple. The attention he pays to his horses is a wall that keeps away the day's anxieties and the mind's niggling problems. The evening ride always brings him calm and peace and ensures a good night's sleep. Banished temporarily, is the pain he feels at Ramaji's death—at his inability to prevent it—and hazy thoughts of the young Venkoji Kamath. The Siddi of Janjira matters no longer, nor his cannons or impregnable fortress. Even the bewilderment he felt when Sathe revealed that Pandurao was the perpetrator of Ramaji's fall or the impotence he felt when he could not hunt him down.

As he rides in the evenings, the clamorous din of war and the insidious whispers of politics disappear, and only the vast sea and the regal horse remain. Kanhoji is putting a Marwari mare by the name of Tara through her paces when Sekho arrives with Surya, the former's personal guard thundering around them. They dismount in the thickening purple dusk and wait for Kanhoji to bring the sleek mare back to their end of the beach. As Kanho sees them approaching, his sublime solitude is breached and the world comes back to him with the sound of the rambunctious waves.

'What could not wait?' asks the Sarkhel as he dismounts.

'Saheb, first some good news. Bhunji has been replaced at Mumbachi,' Surya interjects. His dark handsome face has a crop of silver white hair that makes him look striking and distinguished. Yet, the spectre of age is upon him.

'Bilyaam Fif,' Surya says, whistling through the gaps in his teeth.

'So? Is he amenable? Or a brute like Bhun?' Kanhoji inquires.

'He has sent six cannons and a trunk of knick-knacks. He wishes to call on you at your convenience,' Surya adds as he glances at an increasingly agitated Sekhoji.

'Good, good, I shall meet him. Call him after Chaitra Purnima. Isn't that when the Firangis celebrate the birth of their god from an egg?'

'Hao, Saheb, it will be a new beginning for both of us: trader and ruler. Rustomji has said that he will bring up the Kamath family matter with Fifiji,' Surya says, further placating Kanhoji.

'My brothers, Baba. Sambha and Tula. I have arrested them both along with some of their bodyguards,' quickly blurts out Sekhoji.

Kanhoji looks at his son incredulously, seeking an explanation.

'Raje,' Surya says apologetically, 'it is a very small matter. Just brothers . . .'

'It is not a small matter. They have stolen from you. They have misbehaved publicly.'

'What happened?' Kanho asks patiently.

'These two fools,' Sekho begins as Surya shoots a look of disapproval at Sekho.

'Raje, Tulaji apprehended a red and white flagged Topikar ship that was escaping from the Firangis . . .'

'Fransisi,' Sekho shoots in.

'Yes Fansi,' Surya continues, 'north of the Terekhol River. The ship did not have a dastak, nor did it want to be issued one and they threw our inspector off the ship. Tulaji saheb attacked and boarded it. They towed it to Sindhudurg where Dajisaheb was present on inspection. There were some muskets in the cargo, and Tulaji saheb and Dajisaheb had an argument about them and their men each tried to take the cargo of muskets.'

'No, both commanded their men to pick up the crates and keep them for themselves. Their men had a full-blown fight and two of them were killed and several seriously injured.'

'You did the right thing, Jaisinghrao, continue as you will,' Kanhoji says, patting his son's arm.

Sekho mounts a chestnut Arab mare. She is rumoured to have cost forty thousand Alibagi rupaiyas. He back trots her a few paces before gracefully turning her to his right and trotting away.

'Surya, I want you to stay back with me. I want this Pandurao. He was always a shit and there was a time I felt bad for letting him know it. But now when I think back, maybe I should have killed him at the gurukul. Bad has grown to worse, a festering wound. Look what he has gone and done: senseless and purposeless,' Kanhoji says, visibly upset.

'Raje, some say he has killed himself, others say he has gone to Kashi, others Malindi, Yaman or Bangal. We don't know for sure.

He could be using any name. But I don't think he is in the Konkan. Fear would have made him flee.'

'Find him in Kashi or Malindi then. For if he feared me, he wouldn't have done this in the first place. Find me a *chitari*: someone who can draw a realistic portrait of a man from description. We will have several copies made of his visage and hunt him down. It is the only way.'

Kanhoji does not want to think of his sons' misbehaviour yet; it was immaturity as Surya had said, but now it is beginning to prick him. He focuses his mind on Pandurao instead and wonders what or whom the man was avenging. Even after all these years, with all the power he has at his disposal, he has been unable to protect his closest friends.

The Elephant

This year, too, the beaches darken as thousands of little turtles scrabble into the waves. The ever-vigilant hawks and opportunistic kites swoop down and feast on the rare bounty. Dolphins play behind fishing boats casting out different-sized nets, each according to its season. Now, the large-holed nets are out, ready for badamundi that stalk the estuaries for anchovies. Jungle fowl, partridges and peacocks peck on the overflow of grains that have fallen on the mud-tracked paths that connect each hamlet to the larger villages and towns. With silver coins in their hands, some villages have taken to extending their temples, while others have sunk wells, built water tanks, bunds and reclaimed swamps or cleared forests. The plantations of teak Kanhoji had laid out around his shipyards now soar as cool deciduous forests harbouring chital and barking deer. A tigress has recently alarmed some villagers foraging in the teak grove behind Gheria, and Kanhoji is keen to corner her. As Kanho is leaving for the forest behind Rameshwar, he receives news that Brahmendra Swami is on his way to meet him.

Kanhoji knows why the Mahapurush Parmahans is taking the trouble. Shortly before Mahashivratri, his soldiers stationed at the check post at Makhjan—north of Sangmeshwar—had demanded the dastak for an elephant that was crossing over to the Siddi's territory. The elephant was accompanied by a troop of ten Pathans who were in the employ of the Raja of Savnur but did not possess any dastak. Little did the Maratha guards know that Mahapurush Brahmendra Swami was escorting the elephant—a gift from the Raja of Savnur—to Siddi Saad, Faujdar of Anjanvel. Saad had been trying to devise a way of getting the elephant to Gowalkat from Savnur for the past three years. The pachyderm needed to cross several territories including Vishalgad and those of Baji Rao and Angria. This year, Swamiji had decided to escort the gift to the Konkan on his way back from a southern pilgrimage. Tired from his extended return, Swamiji had stayed back at an ardent disciple's house and sent the elephant and the Pathans ahead. At the check post the Pathans tried to take the elephant through anyway and the outnumbered guards signalled to the killedar at Jaygad, Bikaji Mahadik, for help. Bikaji sent a platoon to Makhjan, and it chased away the Pathans and captured the elephant, taking it back to Jaygad. Siddi Saad, though a devotee of Swamiji, had always suspected that Kanhoji was unduly favoured and presumed that the Mahapurush had intentionally let the elephant be taken away by Angria. In a fit of rage, Siddi Saad marched on Parshuram Temple on the day of Mahashivratri, scaring away all the pilgrims and vandalizing the temple and looting the very lands he had given Swamiji for the temple's sustenance.

Kanhoji receives Brahmendra Swami with all due deference at Vijaydurg and makes suitable arrangements for his ever-growing retinue's accommodation. Swamiji is in an exacerbated mood and greets Kanhoji in a petulant sulk.

'I am leaving the Konkan forever. There is nobody here who cares enough to keep me safe,' he says accusingly.

Kanhoji bows low and encourages Swamiji to sit.

'No, I am not welcome here. You have forgotten me now that you have become a big man. You have forgotten whose blessing was the source of your success.'

'Never, Swamiji. How can you say that? This was a minor misunderstanding.'

'Minor? That *daitya*. He desecrated the temple; they tortured Chimnaji Bhagwat, Tambe and Lakhmaji. Stole even the *nagaras* and carried away the rosewood door frame. Utensils even: all the grain gone. The bell. Three medallions of precious stones—all worth Rs 12,000.' Swamiji's ears are the colour of wine and his face that of solkadi.

'These things are nothing, nobody lost their life. We can replace these things.'

'Someone will. But what about the desecration of the idols?' he asks Kanho, his eyeballs straining against their sockets.

'Saad,' Swamiji shouts, looking up at the mirrored ceiling and clenching his fists, 'you have ravaged sacred idols and violated Brahmins. You yourself will be subjected to that very fate.'

'Swamiji, I have already reinforced Bikaji and directed him to keep Shamal Saad in check.'

'That bastard Nilo Patki Chiplunkar was in on it. Vulture.'

'I will look into that too. But please do not be so distraught. These are temporal things, and you are a sant. I will deal with it.'

'No,' he shouts again, shaking his head from side to side, 'I just came to tell you that I am leaving. I am going to Dhavaddshi. Baji will protect me. Now I am off to Janjira to let that useless impotent Surur know what his vile servant has done.'

'Yakut Khan will redress all your problems, Swamiji. Isn't he your ardent devotee? He will make sure every grain is returned.'

'He can keep it: everything has been sullied by their yavana hands—it's of no use to me. You are the cause of this problem. It was your people who stopped the elephant. You have directly caused me the loss of Rs 25,000.'

'I thought it was twelve thousand.'

'Twenty-five thousand, twenty-five.'

'Whatever you wish, Swamiji. I have given you my junior wife Ahilya to care for you and attend to your needs, what is this little money.'

'She needs as many servants as I do. She is useless,' Brahmendra Swami strikes back.

'You, Surur, nobody can protect me here; nobody cares. You people just want my blessings and my power. I am going, leaving the Konkan forever.'

Kanhoji falls on to Brahmendra Swami's feet and grabbing the swami's hand, places it on his own head.

'Swamiji, just give me one year. I swear an oath: if you do not stay for a year, then I will die. Just give me one year.'

Brahmendra Swami tries to extricate his hand and remove it from the pate of Kanho's head but cannot, and Kanho repeats: 'I swear to it with Khandoba and Parshuram as witness.'

'I will stay for one more year from today and then I will leave.'

'As you wish, Swamiji,' Kanhoji says, getting back up on his feet.

'You must also return the capital you have borrowed. Some of your old loans are still pending. You should pay me back before loaning it to Baji Rao. Technically, that is my money that you have given him.'

'Swamiji, everything I have is yours, all this is yours. But give me some time. There are repairs in every fort this year and I have to replace a lot of my boats.'

'You always have some excuse or the other,' Brahmendra Swami says testily.

'Mathurabai and Lakshmibai have been eagerly waiting to serve you,' Kanhoji replies, trying to placate the Mahapurush, and leads him to the newly completed guest house.

'I will bless them, but then I need to be off to Janjira. Surur has to teach Saad a lesson for what he has done,' Brahmendra Swami says as he struggles to bring some calm to his face and a smile to his lips.

'So, have you taken any interesting ships lately? Anything special?' Swamiji asks eagerly.

'Yes, Swamiji. Tortoises, the largest you would have ever seen,' Kanhoji replies.

'Chee, what will I do with a giant tortoise? No pearls?' he asks, disheartened.

Empty Promises

It is Dassehra again. The Mahapurush has left the Konkan and is closer to Satara now. Kanhoji's patience has finally run out. The Royal Gaze has never deigned to look down the ghat these many years. Without Chhatrapati Shahu's and Baji Rao's support, the consolidation of the coast is near impossible. Not impossible, but it would be long, disastrous and ruinous to the Konkan. With them, he could do it between Meena Sankranti and the coming of the rains. Vasai and Janjira. In response to a letter last year, Baji Rao has written back: 'Shriman, do not worry about Vasai, soon I will give you Surat itself.' Kanhoji is not amused. Now it is taking Kanhoji inordinately long to get to Satara. He is frustrated but keeps a beneficent grin on his face and asks after each of the supplicants that has come out to meet him. It is the habit of the dusty *bhistis*[*] delegated to water the path ahead of Kanhoji to boast to curious onlookers, whom they were doing it for. When people hear it is the Sarkhel Subedar of the Konkan, they rush out in droves: perfumed Patils, bent sharecroppers, rambunctious naked children and shy brides hiding behind trees to spot the legend from afar.

'*Kashe chala sagle?*'[**] Kanhoji will ask.

---

[*] Water-carriers.

[**] How is it going with you?

419

'*Tuja kripa*,'* in various versions, depending upon the education and elocution of the respondent, is the only reply.

Sekhoji and Sambhaji, who are accompanying their father along with a spectacular grey Andalusian mare with black dapples and her mane and tail braided with white mogras, are beaming.

As they pass on their giant chestnut Arab mares, cheers of 'Jaisinghrao and Dajisaheb' rent the air, accompanied by the frequent cheers of 'Samudratala Shivaji'. Behind them, surrounded by hawkeyed silhadars mounted on Marwari geldings, is the nazrana packed on to six bullock carts. Platoons of infantry have taken the rear so as to not raise too much dust, and a battery of artillery follows mounted on two elephants, which bump along with a short cannon strapped to each of their sides. At the end, guarded by its own specialist men trained by the younger Lokhande, are twenty carts carrying the finest quality gunpowder.

They finally reach Satara well after sunset and must have the city gates opened. They are for Sarkhel-Subedar Kanhoji Angre. They make for Baji Rao's guest house that has been made available to them through Chimmaji. The next day, the nazrana is presented with an *aapta* leaf tied to the forehead of the dappled Raza Pura. The gracious Chhatrapati, relieved from his immediate fiduciary problems, can give Kanhoji and his sons both time and attention. They perform the *Ayudha* puja together on Khande Navami, presenting the most resplendent swords and muskets for the puja. Amidst a profusion of marigold flowers, the Chhatrapati hears out Kanhoji and nods in agreement with him.

'It is true, the Firangis are prone to persecute the common people,' Chhatrapati Shahu says in his quiet and dignified way. He moves gently, never with any sudden actions. Every gesture is controlled and balanced. Kanhoji finds it delightful to watch and tells his sons to learn: 'That's how a king ought to move—unhurried and

---

* Well with your grace.

unbothered', and then realizes that very characteristic is the cause of his own frustration.

'But Janjira falls under Nasiruddin's jurisdiction,' Shahu says, referring to Muhammad Shah.

'Maharaj: What subedar of his badshah steals from his master? Pays no heed to his duty. Does naught but aggrandize his own family?' Kanhoji attempts boldly.

'Every single one, Subedar Saheb, it is the nature of the beast. It just needs to be done with a little bit of finesse. The Persians taught it to the Mughals and they to us,' responds His Majesty.

'Maharaj, there is also their habit of stealing good men, carpenters and masons, and selling them, stealing from undefended temples and desecrating them.'

'I will write to Nasiruddin myself on the matter and he will set it right. He is *shareef*,' Shahu says.

'The Firangis then? If the Shriman Peshwa and Shriman Senakarte attack from the landward side supported by my silhadars and our navy from the sea, we will succeed: Vasai, Shaisti, Chaul.'

'Subedar Saheb, as of now all the other sardars are occupied keeping peace with the Nizam or our dear cousin Kolhapur,' His Majesty says temperately.

'And our young Peshwa, it seems, is beset with his own . . .' Shahu searches for the word in Marathi and then says: '*Junoon**.'

'We just need a few men, to push on the walls and prevent assistance from down south,' Kanhoji says, before realizing he has become too casual.

The Chhatrapati does not respond.

'Forgive me, Maharaj, I entirely understand,' he says smiling.

'The horse is from near the Firangi lands. They are reputed to run ten kos in eight watches, through rugged terrain. Her hooves would be best kept dry,' Kanhoji says, changing the subject. He needs

---

* Passion.

to control his breath. He controls it, taking long silent draughts to prop himself up.

'Patience, my most loyal Subedar, and I mean present company excepted, when I made that remark earlier. I meant it was the Mughal practice. When the stars align, then Lord Ganesh himself will clear our path,' His Majesty says.

'Indeed Maharaj, indeed,' Kanhoji replies.

'Subedar Saheb, Dilli is not far any more. Especially on this beautiful mare you have given me. Please do know, that it has not escaped my attention that it is a mare you have given me. Most give you stallions and keep the breeding stock to themselves,' His Majesty adds.

'I pray that you have the finest stable in the land, My Lord,' Kanhoji says bowing.

'Meet Mahapurush and do not fear the Siddi like a child,' His Majesty says, and it makes Kanhoji bristle with shame.

'I have a gift for you, I know you are a keen sportsman,' his Majesty says, snapping his fingers.

Attendants immediately bring in four cheetahs on iron chains, and Kanhoji makes a great show of his appreciation.

The Chhatrapati puts his hand on Kanhoji's shoulder saying, 'What is the hurry? It will come to pass. I assure you, when the time is right, I will come down myself, leading my troops and Baji by my side.'

The promise does nothing to lighten the sinking heaviness that pulls him down and darkens his mood like a rain cloud as he leaves the durbar hall. He has been too generous with his gifts and now, without the infantry and cavalry it was to have brought in, he regrets the extravagance.

The Stars

The jyothshis say that as each dark night passes, the stars have begun to align themselves towards increasingly favourable positions and the gloom that haunts the Sarkhel will surely dissipate. The *vaids** attribute the lightening of his mood to the control of his diet and massages they minister. Surya knows it is the fact that this year only a handful of ships have dared to smuggle anything and almost all have paid their duties. Kanhoji throws himself into his work and his appetite first returns, and then grows insatiable. Indeed, the Houses of Bhonsale, Bhatt and Angre are on the ascendant again. Early last year, Baji Rao cornered the Nizam at Palkhed and just a few months ago, he drove Khan Bangash out of Bundelkhand. In the Konkan, from Kutch to Kanara, the indefatigable discipline and effort of Jaisinghrao keeps the coast from getting infected by the chaos in the Desha. A string of thirty coastal forts within telescopic sight of each other marks the Subedari of the Konkan. The greatly expanded dry docks at Rameshwar have birthed a new fleet of sturdy galbats, several ghurabs and two large pals. Hundreds of masons chip away at basalt rocks to fashion perfectly spherical cannonballs, the rust-prone iron is used exclusively for chain, bar and extending shots. Each killedar has in his garrison a mix of Mussalman, Habshi, Topashi

---

* Doctors of medicine.

and Topikar soldiers supporting his Koli and Maratha garrisons. Never does a holy day pass that leaves any of his forts undermanned. The system of signals using differently coloured fireworks connects each fort to the next, and swift riders carry the most discreet missives between them. There has been an influx of people into the safety of the northern Konkan: some escaping the Firangi zeal head north across the Terekhol and others straggle in from the war-torn areas in the Dhakkan and Malwa. Lakshmibai has found a Telugu chef who arrived in the Konkan with his entire clan and makes the spongiest and softest little rice cakes. She sends him on to Kanhoji at Gheria. Mathurabai has found a jyothshi of great repute who has come south from ancient Ujjain: the navel of the earth and the home of great astronomers. At Ujjain, the jyothshi had had the opportunity to be amongst the first to use the new observatory built there by the Mughal Governor and Chief of the Kachchawa clan. Now the two wives and the jyothshi are on their way to Gheria and his third wife Gahinabai, nervously prepares for the arrival of her seniors.

Kanhoji is resting on a mattress in only his dhoti.

'*Haila*, Manaji's mother, look at your husband,' Mathurabai says as soon as they enter Kanhoji's presence, 'his face is fatter than a pumpkin,' she says to Lakshmibai.

'No, no, he is looking even more handsome,' says Lakshmibai, embarrassed, bending to touch Kanhoji's feet.

'Now we must as kings: flick our fingers, talk sweet things, eat sweet things; *resham ani aaraam*,*' Kanhoji says sarcastically.

'My, my Yessji's mother, his breasts have become bigger than yours,' Mathurabai continues turning Gahinabai red with shame.

'Well, Yessji's mother, now that Jaisinghrao's mother is here, you need not curdle the milk, it will turn on its own,' Kanhoji chuckles.

Mathurabai clucks her tongue and Gahinabai runs to the kitchen, leaving her seniors.

---

* Silk and leisure.

'Hiding in Gheria with his sudra playmates, overeating god knows what. If he doesn't care about his children's future, we do. I have brought a great pundit from Ujjain. Listen to what he has to say to you,' she says acerbically.

Before Kanhoji can say anything, his other wives intervene cajolingly and the jyothshi is brought in.

'My stars were read when I was born and then again when I was married, what new calculations have you done that those other greats could not?' he inquires sceptically. He has always found such people clambering over each other to confirm his good fortune—for a coin, of course.

'If you are aware of the new observatory at Ujjain built by Sawai Raja Jai Singh, its great size has allowed for greater precision of observations,' the jyothshi says.

'Raja Jai Singh: Who has not heard of the Subedar of Malwa? He who is worth a fourth more than any other man.'

The jyothshi bows, missing the sarcasm.

'So, tell me my fortune or is it my future?' Kanhoji asks bluntly.

The jyothshi makes to his little bundle of documents on various kinds of mediums, some rolled, some strung together while others bound.

'The Zij Muhammadshahi, the star chart,' he mumbles, picking a bound book.

'You have the time, date and meridian already, now tell me,' Kanhoji commands.

'Saheb, you have but twelve years to fulfil your destiny here, but your sons will rule as kings and the glory of the Angrias will be remembered to the end of the yug,' he says.

'Indeed, indeed. Nothing bad? Nothing requiring reparative pujas and sacrifices to cure and purify?' he wonders.

'Panditji, he consorts with chamars, mahars and the like. He even eats with them. He eats meat every day, drinks. He is in need of purification,' Mathurabai shoots in.

Kanhoji glares at her insolence.

'Yes of course, Rani Sahiba,' the jyothshi says.

'*Oye*, she is not a rani, don't address her as such. You are from Ujjain, so I'll excuse you this once. This is the Swarajya of Chhatrapati Shahu Bhonsale, who rules from Satara. Understood?'

'Ji, Saheb,' the jyothshi says, quivering.

'Say that to Kashibai,' Mathura says recalling Baji Rao's wife.

'Now go back to Ujjain,' Kanhoji says and the jyothshi shuffles away with his *jhola* of charts and calculations.

'How dare you speak of me like that in front of some *bidesi* pundit?' Kanhoji shouts at Mathurabai.

'He is not a foreigner, he is a learned priest and cares for our family,' she says equally loudly.

'Is this the future you say I don't care about? You push your sons to treason: especially the younger one. Woman, know this: you will never be the mother of a king, like your dear friends. You married a sarnaubat and you will die the wife of a subedar,' Kanhoji says, raising the baritone of his voice.

'Raja Chatrasal has offered his daughter to Baji Rao—do you know? He is your friend's son; the friend who became peshwa because of you. He goes around like a king, greater than Chhatrapati even. And look at you? The great Subedar of Konkan,' Mathurabai tells him.

'Shut up, you fool. What do you know? Can't cook to save your life, can't fart unless a parrot or a pundit tells her too,' Kanhoji chuckles.

Mathurabai storms away and Lakshmibai rushes after her.

The Comet

The heat daily grows, and the verdant coastline is suffused with a layer of fine dust. Gardens, streets and the forest floor are covered with the sticky purple jam of countless jamun fruit that have dropped to the ground. The loo swirls with the fragrant musk of ripe and rotting fruits. Swarms of minute flies thicken the sweet air of the mango orchards, bursting again with their bright succulent offerings. A battle is raging between paltans of young boys, fortified by Karvanda and Jamun and armed with slingshots and drums against invading droves of parrots.

Late one night Parma Prasad Ujjaini, Mathurabai's astrologer, runs to the Subedar with spectacular news. He has sighted a comet, one never recorded before, slowly moving across the sky near Brihaspati. The comet is very far away and that is why it seems to be moving so slowly across the firmament. Kanhoji asks him what the comet means, and Parma Prasad says that it is the harbinger of a new age. The comet has come to add the final impetus in Kanhoji's rise and as long as it will be visible in the sky, it will ensure his success, no matter what the endeavour is.

Kanhoji calls his sons to Gheria and asks his most trusted sardars and faujdars to join them immediately. Sekho brings his younger brother Yessji—apprenticed to him by their father—and Sardar Sambhaji Shinde from Suvarnadurg. Dhondoji, the youngest of his sons, comes with Sambhaji. Piloji, Maloji Salvi, Pratapji Kolgude, Bikaji Mahadik and Bawaji Mhaske arrive with eager anticipation. Manaji and Tulaji have an inkling that it has something to do with their stepmother's Ujjaini jyothshi. Though no one, including Sekho, knows the reason for this sudden assembly so close to the end of the season. All Sekho can deduce is that it will be an informal meeting as his father has called them to his private library at the Vijaydurg Fort.

This large room, panelled in rosewood, has a glass skylight. Mirrors from Arunmula strategically panel the walls to better direct the light. Under the square skylight is a mastodon's curling tusk that has been chained across the ceiling. It is immense and awesome, and he likes to tell his grandchildren it belonged to Ashwatthama. These shelves hold only his personal documents, his collection of maps and his most treasured curiosities from around the world. Scattered around are models of different kinds of nautical vessels, including those sailed by the Chinese, Javanese and the Firangis. A narwhal horn is propped up in an upturned turtle shell as big as a cauldron. His favourite guns and most priceless swords hang on the walls along with exquisite miniatures of horses done in the Agra style. Today, for the first time, the room feels crowded, and those crowded within it feel especially close and privileged. The meeting begins.

'I was reminded recently, when speaking to a very competent jyothshi, that I have completed my fifth twelve-year cycle on this earth. That is much longer than either my father or my grandfather lived,' Kanhoji begins. Tulaji and Manaji smile inwardly feeling triumphant as Sekhoji, a passive face hiding arrhythmic flutters coursing through his body, wonders at his own mortality. All eyes remain on Kanhoji anxiously.

The oceanic Shivaji's voice picks up volume and a deep tenor rises from his chest.

'We have been patient for so long, but now we cannot wait any longer.'

There is a murmur within the room that ceases when Kanhoji begins again.

'And I have waited: season after season, Dassehra after Dassehra. I cannot afford to wait any longer, so I am going to go it alone.'

'You are not alone, we are with you,' the room answers him back in all the variations. Some just vigorously shake their heads.

'Then we must accomplish it unaided, for both my dear friend's son the peshwa and our king, Chhatrapati Shahuji Maharaj, are much too busy with the affairs of the Desha and Dilli. So, we will match the Peshwa in his exploits and make a gift of it to the Chhatrapati.'

'Jai Samudratala Shivaji!' shouts out Sarnaubat Sakaram.

The room responds that they do not require the Peshwa or the Chhatrapati's assistance and it sounds like 9 lakh bees are buzzing in the skylight. It is already dark outside as a sky full of dense clouds blocks the sun and every particle of its light is suffused into itself.

'Kanhoji Angre,' shouts out Manaji, and Tulaji follows it with a '*Konkan cha Raja.*'

'Beware of pride,' Kanhoji says, 'just because we do this by ourselves does not mean we do it for ourselves. This is for Shivaji Maharaj; have you forgotten his dream?' he exhorts.

'Never,' the assembled reply in unison.

'Samudratala,' Sakaram hails again.

'Shivaji,' comes the resounding reply.

'Though we will take charge of the revenue and repay ourselves with interest what we are investing in silver and blood,' Kanhoji says chuckling.

His sons and his sardars clap and cheer at the prospect.

'The Firangis must be pushed out of Chaul, Vasai and Shashti; all areas north of the Terekhol.'

The room is crackling with electricity, and everyone's moustaches and the hair on their arms is standing up straight.

'Janjira must fall,' he says, and the room erupts.

Kanhoji raises a hand and silence descends like a downpour from a heavy black rain cloud bursting.

'For the next few days, we will meet and plan our strategy and till we have done so, not a word of this is to be spoken to anybody outside this chamber. Not to your commanders nor to your sons nor to your lovers. Is that understood by each one of you?'

The room responds with a single 'Hao Raje' that reverberates through the chest bones of all those who have spoken.

'It's not going to be pleasant. You need to press as many hands as you can and open your hearts and your purses,' he reminds them.

'Hao, Raje, we are with you along with our sons and horses,' proclaims the young Mhaske, who has but a three-year-old daughter.

'I pledge you my wife's jewellery,' says Piloji earnestly, and a ripple of laughter runs through the sardars.

'Yours would be better serving,' someone shouts out and there is laughter all around.

'We are with you, Raje,' the sombre in the crowd echo in unison.

'I am honoured and will be further this evening if each one of you would join me as my guests. We are going to have a feast together and we will all eat together as one, sitting down as one. Then, from tomorrow as one we shall clear a path so that the chariot of our destiny may flow unhindered towards its success.'

The room erupts in 'Jai Malhar' and 'Har Har Mahadev' interspersed with a spattering of salutations to other gods.

A 'Jai Konkan, Jai Swaraj' emanates from the depths of Kanhoji's wide chest, that is then echoed by the assembled till the ancient mastodon's trunk sways on its metal chains. Moments later, a loud grumble in the sky ends with a snappy crack and is soon followed by a flash that fills the chambers with bright squares through the apertures on the western wall.

'As you can hear,' says Kanhoji, 'we have very little time. So set your minds on what we have to do and be ready with ideas and suggestions for the coming discussions.'

The murmur re-enters the room as some moths and flying ants find their way in through the windows, seeking shelter from the rain they sense coming. Kanhoji leaves with his entourage of secretaries. His sons and commanders are left wondering if their sarkhel means to act before, during or after the rains. But they don't care. They will drive their horses through floods and climb wet walls or they will ready and wait.

The Serpent

The ocean overwhelms its banks and gropes at the land. The rain batters, it hammers against the ancient black rocks. Winds blow furiously, decimating any tree with roots too shallow to anchor it. The sky is dark all day long and mould grows on the walls. The hay goes grey with fungus and the fields have transformed into leech-ridden swamps. Snakes and scorpions take refuge in kitchens and by warm sleeping babes. The fleet is hull up; their planks fixed or replaced are getting snugly retied into place. The cannons are being polished and powder is being kept dry. The pigeons are reluctant to bear their messages but the brave boys hugging gourds and goatskins cross the torrential streams to their destinations. Damodar was taken in the hot season to join the litany of children that had predeceased him. Yashodar now studiously stands in his stead and answers to 'Ganga'.

The waves are unrelenting and loud, gasping away from the rocks to crash against the fort's walls. Sambhaji is asleep where he is sitting. There is a warm yellow light from the abundance of diya-filled chandeliers in Kanhoji's library.

'Has Khairiyat's son Hassan written back?' Kanhoji asks Sekho.

'No, we have not received any reply as of yet,' Sekho replies and then asks if his father has spoken to the Raja of Kudal.

'I know what his answer will be, though I am sure he will help in his way,' Kanhoji says.

Shambhu is sleeping on a diwan. Kanhoji covers him with a quilted cotton sheet.

'This year, after Nariyel Purnima, we will attack Chaul and Vasai, and next year Janjira, and what we take unaided we keep as our watan,' Kanhoji says decidedly to Sekho.

'Hao, Baba. We will control all the horse trading ports then.'

'Horses, Jaisinghrao, horses. Never forget the horses. Keep the finest stable in the land and keep their hooves dry with *chuuna*.'[*]

Other than the sentries posted at the door, everybody else has been dismissed or have excused themselves, including Yashodar who had been awake for the entire previous night working with Kanhoji.

'Well now that everybody is gone,' Kanhoji says quietly, 'you know your mother is crazy?' Kanhoji inquires of Sekho in all earnestness.

'Yes, Baba, she is just going on and on about it,' Sekho says.

'And what do you think I should do?'

'Baba, I don't think we need to rock the boat. We must stay loyal to Shahu Maharaj. What is in a title but trouble and expenses?'

'Well said. And who will bestow it upon us? Saying you are a king—even though you may control the lives of your subjects and tax the land and keep it all for yourself—doesn't make you a king; it makes you a traitorous rebel. And it does not matter anyway: Where is Chandrarao Jhavli now?'

'Well, Baba, you have been a kingmaker. It was because of you the Kolhapur dispute was settled.'

'Is it settled? It will never be settled. But yes, I played my part.'

'What do you think Baji will do? They say he is dismissive of Maharaj and makes all decisions unilaterally,' Sekho says apprehensively.

'You should know his mind better. All of us sardars need to be decisive. We can't wait for permissions and directions from our kings only because there is never any time on the ground. You must act,

---

[*] Limestone.

but one needs to always act towards increasing the fortune of your king,' Kanhoji reminds Sekhoji.

'Chatrasal Bundela has offered him his daughter and a third of his kingdom—won't that be a part of his watan then?'

'Of course, that would be his personal property to do as he pleases,' Kanhoji says.

'Almost a king then,' Sekho replies.

'Almost, but my boy, if it does not come from Heaven itself, or from the degenerate sitting on the Peacock Throne, then you are as much a Pindari as you are a king.'

'But Baba, haven't you been blessed by Heaven itself. Your sign, when you were a child?' Sekhoji asks proudly.

Something grabs him inside his neck and Kanhoji's heart falls into his stomach. He lowers his head and looks down at his lap in silence.

Sekho waits for a little time, and not understanding what has happened, changes the subject.

'The question is, Baba, do we attack the Siddi first or the Firangis? Or together?'

'Together and a sustained campaign till they both capitulate. Any news from Bala? Has he taken up the Nizam's offer?'

'You mean Baji and Chatrasal? He is currently busy in Malwa, but he has said yes to Chatrasal's proposal. He writes he has crossed the Rewa as many times as the local ferryman,' says Sekho, a yawn escaping from his clenched jaw.

'Why don't you go to sleep and take Yessa with you?' Kanhoji tells his son.

'I think I shall, Baba, why don't you call it a night too?'

'I shall, first I want to go out and enjoy the storm for a bit,' Kanhoji stutters.

'Please take someone with you,' Sekho says as he pranams his father and taps his brother awake.

Sambhaji opens his eyes and then after looking around stretches himself out on the low diwan he has been lying on and curls back to sleep.

Kanho wants to say something, but words escape him. He gestures to his eldest son to let the boy be and Sekho leaves. Kanhoji wraps himself in a fine shawl and heads out to the ramparts on the western side of the fort.

Kanhoji makes his way on to the wide ramparts of the outer battlements. The cannons are covered in waxed cotton and their gunners asleep in their quarters. A sentry on each bastion is huddled up in a cloistered picket and they do not hear or see their master. It is dark and the crescendo of the roaring sea is deafening. The spray from the smashed waves is indistinguishable from the fine and constant drizzle. Lightning strikes: a fiery metallic snake rises from the ground and splits the firmament with five crackling heads that light up the dark sky. Kanhoji is blinded and the image of a snake floats in front of his eyes. A few moments later, a thunderous guduk gadaak pulverizes the heavens. Kanhoji hears a deep voice grumbling for his blood: 'Little Kanho still awake, for the Siddi's hunger to sate.' Kanhoji sits down on the wet stone rampart and rests his back on the parapet. His mind is swirling with chaos, his mind is numb; he can't feel his tongue any more, his left arm and leg are leaving him, and his left eye closes in on itself.

Light flashes on Sambhaji's eyes and as they open, he hears thunder crashing over his head. It takes him a moment to realize that he is in his father's library. Ashwatthama's massive tusk is swaying on its brass chains. The rain is now louder than the sea. The room is empty. He searches for his father and comes across the freshly bathed Yashodar with vibhuti on his forehead and smelling of sandalwood. They look for Kanhoji. He is not in his bed. They wake Sekho.

He wanted to go outside. He was calling you, Yessa.

They go to the main bastion. They walk from one bastion to the next. They find him drenched and shivering. His mind is confused; spit is dribbling from his curled and clenched mouth. His left eye is shut. They cover him and rush him inside.

Mortality

The unflappable and efficient Jaisinghrao is overwhelmed. His brother looks up at him, wide-eyed and worried. Their father is resting in a room guarded by Surya and Golu personally. Nobody but Kanhoji's maids, the family purohit and his attendant are allowed inside.

'Dada, are you all right? I swear some of your hair has gone grey overnight. See, here,' Sambhaji says, as he touches a lock of grey hair over Sekhoji's temple.

'We have to take him to Kulaba,' Sekhoji says.

'In this weather? It will take weeks by land.'

'We have to. Don't worry, my nakhwa will handle it in the new pal,' Sekhoji says.

'Will he recover?'

'Of course, hopefully. I don't know, I have never seen him sick. Has he fallen sick before?'

'Remember when we went hunting south? My second tiger? He had a stomach ache, then last year, after meeting Shahu Maharaj,' Sambhaji trails off.

'I've never seen him so ill. He has always been on his feet.'

'We can't let anyone see him like this,' Sambhaji whispers.

'No, definitely not. But we must take him to Ai.'

Kanhoji is put in a palanquin and taken on board the pal. They reach the jetty at Alibag, and Kanhoji is taken to Hirakot in

435

the palanquin. The vaids are already waiting for him. They apply their balms of *ashwagandha* and smoke the air with *brahmi*. His junior wives massage his limbs with oil infused with *eranda* and *rasona* as Mathurabai is fervently at prayer at the feet of Khandoba.

It is the day of Ashadha Navratri. Kanhoji is conscious. He can speak, but the words that come out are not the ones he means to speak, and it scares him. His left arm and leg are beyond his will, so he uses his right to chase the vaids away and sends their silver and copper tools clattering to the ground. He tries to get up and falls. His sons put him back on to his bed. Sekho is by his side.

Kanhoji's eyes ask what is happening.

'*Daura**, the vaids say daura, you will be fine—you just need to rest,' Sekhoji says.

'No. Don't. Anybody,' Kanhoji mumbles.

'Don't worry, Baba, nobody has seen you and nobody knows. It's the rains.'

Kanhoji slumps back into his bed and the vaids cautiously reappear to set up their oil drips and apply their compresses.

As the sun sets, a fever begins to grip Kanhoji and his still gelatinous marrow shivers inside his bones. As it rains outside, he perspires indoors. A delirium takes hold of his senses, and his eyes are bloodshot and dilated.

'Find Phangaskar,' he often commands between conversations he is having with long dead relatives and friends.

'There is a village called Phangus on the Bav River, two kos west of Sangameshwar. Do you want somebody from that village?' Sekhoji asks.

'The serpent,' he screams, 'the snake.'

For four days and five nights, he screams and mumbles while coming in and out of consciousness. His face is swelling up. His eyes are swollen shut. He can no longer move and lies motionless on his constantly tended bed. The purohit is by his bed chanting: '*Om*

---

* Stroke.

shri martand bhairavay namah, Om shri martand bhairavay namah, Om shri martand bhairavay namah.'

It is the morning of Masik Durgashtami. It has been raining all night and continues to rain in the morning. It is the day of Lord Shiva. It is the day of the Moon. A trickle of blood seeps out of his right ear and then from the other and then from the nose. His breath does not form, and his chest descends towards the earth for the last time. The rain does not stop. The sun does not come out to shine. Mathurabai collapses in Sekhoji's arms.

'We must have the grandest funeral the Konkan has ever seen,' she says and is supported away by Piloji's wife to begin their lamentations.

The vaids and the purohits begin washing Kanhoji's body and preparing it for its last rites.

Sarkhel Sekhoji Angre summons his brothers and his father's closest aides. They are his now. His heart flutters and bile rises to Jaisinghrao's veined neck.

'This does not get out. The Konkan trembled at his name, and we need it more than ever. Just because Baba is bodily indisposed, does not mean his dream ends. At least till the rains end, let knowledge of his passing stay within the family,' Sekhoji says.

'But how will it look?' asks Dhondoji.

'He is the most renowned man in the Konkan; people will be insulted if they are not told,' adds Manaji.

'What about Baba's dignity?' says Tulaji.

'We will do what you say, Sarkhel Saheb,' Surya quickly adds.

'Raje,' says Piloji looking directly at Sekhoji.

'Yes, Sarkhel Saheb, we will do as you please,' enjoins Sambhaji.

'We will accord Baba all honours of course, but we shall do it privately,' Sekhoji says firmly.

The carpenters are making a high-roofed enclosure for the pyre. The purohit's attendants rush to collect sandalwood. The rain gets heavier, and the sky is dark at noon.

Kanhoji Angria Amar Rahe

When a person dies, there arises this doubt: 'He still exists', say some, 'he does not,' say others.

—Katha Upanishad, I.1.20

The gulls have been scared away and the crows are picking on Pandurao's eyes as his corpse hangs at the gates of Vijaydurg. Hovering overhead, sea hawks and a few brave kites survey the departing armada. A tear comes to the old and distinguished Piloji's eye, standing on the prow of a triple-decked pal with his king. The hawks feel a flutter in the wizened Sardar's chest.

'If Golu were standing behind you, Raje, and Surya had the black of sight in his eyes, this would be the very visage of your father setting out as we did so many times before,' says the immaculately dressed man.

Sambhaji looks at him kindly and folds his hands. Behind him, his dead brother's madman carries the late Golu's axe-pistols and holds his umbrella for him. His younger brother Manaji is by his side.

Sambhaji Raje Angre, or Dajisaheb as the world knows him, is in his father's pagdi. Red and yellow, woven with gold and strung with pearls. That pagri is a crown. On his hip hangs his ancestral sword, the one with a crocodile knuckle guard. He has fashioned his moustache like his father's, and it rises in oiled curls on either side of his large cheeks. Sambhaji Raje is the uncrowned king of the Konkan. Everything from Kulaba to Vengurla is his. The salt in the pans and the salt in the sea are his. We birds belong to him and the fish we catch belong to him. We witness without pleasure, that he feeds the Brahmins twice a year. But when he feeds Yama, we rejoice. All duties due to him are paid to him. His dastak is a well-shaded and cool umbrella under which all trade flourishes. The sea is rich with fish that follow in the wake of his ravenous galbats.

'Sarkhel Saheb, of all your brothers, you resemble Kaka Saheb the most,' says Chimnaji Bhat.

'Dada looked like Ai,' Sambhaji says, glowing with pride.

'He left us too soon, too suddenly,' Chimnaji says.

'Much too soon and with Baba gone just before him,' Sambhaji says pensively.

'Raje is not gone, he was Angria. Now you are Angria, verily you are Kanhoji Angria and let them tremble at the thought,' Piloji says smiling.

'Tremble? These Firangis shit their tight patloons when they hear the name Angria. I have seen it for myself,' Chimnaji says laughing.

'And Saheb, so do the marauders of Yakut Khan, what remains of them,' adds a well-rounded Maloji. His men found Pandurao, the crows led them to him, starving in a ruin.

'Tulaji's fleet from the south has sent its signal, they are at the first post,' relays Sambhaji's chief signalman to him.

'To Chaul,' he commands Maloji.

'Why so many barges?' Chimnaji asks as they are swiftly dragged out past the other vessels.

'All carrying stone shot, Dada is going to level the fort down to its gums,' Manaji says.

'Jai Kanhoji Raje,' cheer the men on the barges.

'And then Vasai,' says Chimnaji, now standing by the gunwale with his compatriot satrap.

'Vasai,' Sambhaji says looking into the sky, his face splashed with the ocean spray.

'Konkan cha Raja,' cheer the Maratha gunners on the galbats docked at the exit of the bay as they spy the Angria. The Koli boarders wave their axes and the Topashis fire off their muskets in salute. The Habshis in their navy ululate their greetings. Every colour, every creed.

'We are Angria,' both the brothers shout to us hawks, their fists clenched. We salute them with our talons.

The bay ripples with a singular chant: Jai Kanhoji Angre. We soar to the clouds above as the Firangi port at Chaul awaits its annihilation.

The Angria is unstoppable. He is the king. Dilli is far, Satara is far.

Jai, Kanhoji Angria

Jai, Konkan cha Raja.

Epilogue

The air is rent with the cawing of crows. Vijaydurg burns. When brother turned against brother, their destiny, that of their family, fled in confused madness.

'I'll take that,' says the Lieutenant Colonel who has just led 500 Marines through the gates of Vijaydurg, grabbing a velvet pouch of exceptionally large gems off the table.

'Lt Colonel Sir, everything will be shared once it is accounted for,' says the young English clerk who has been tasked with labelling and entering the Angrian's property.

'Don't be in such a hurry, mucker, and don't ye bother about the knick-knacks. Wait till our ally's bookkeeper comes up,' the bushy-browed Colonel Clive says to the man not much younger than himself. There is a brutish aroma about the Colonel, and the clerk from Fort George is cowed. He fears this bulbous-nosed brute.

Admiral Watson, who is surveying the room, laughs and the clerk puts down his quill.

Clive walks over to a chest sitting beside a massive, upturned tortoise shell and opens it. He whistles and calls Admiral Watson over.

The Admiral looks inside and signals to one of his petty officers. The Petty Officer orders four Marines to take the chest down to the *HMS Protector*, anchored at a safe distance from Tulaji's burning fleet. Two hundred of Tulaji's galbats and ghurabs are searing the water. The boiled bodies of fish, crab, starfish and squid float on the waters at the mouth of the Vagothan. The burnt corpses of Maratha sailors beside them.

'So, boy, have you found anything else of interest?' Colonel Clive says, walking over to the desk and picking up the sheet of paper the clerk has been writing on.

'Pearls,' the clerk stammers, 'a sack, Lieutenant Colonel, over by those muskets,' the flaxen-haired virgin stammers.

'Too bulky,' says Clive.

'Emeralds?' the clerk asks timidly.

'Green is me favourite shade,' says Clive, winking at the boy and tearing the paper the clerk had been writing on. He throws the shreds on the floor.

The clerk nods to a wooden box on the table.

Clive ambles over and opens it and then puts the box into his coat pocket.

'Don't ye pither, boy, the Murratoes get to keep the fort, we'll just lighten it a bit, and your boss Bourchier will get his,' Clive says chuckling as he continues a light-fingered search of the room. He goes to a wall where a selection of *pistollier* muskets is arrayed in a semicircle. He picks up an exquisite piece with an ivory butt. Picking his nose, he marvels at its workmanship, all the while ascertaining its worth. He palms it into his waistcoat.

Radhoji Jadhav, one of Peshwa Nanasaheb's sardars, is with four musket-wielding silhadars, carrying long swords at their waist, when he enters the vast room. It is a place he had heard of as a child. Ashwatthama's tusk is chained to its ceiling, it has the horn of a unicorn and a stuffed mermaid. His dear uncle had once stood within this room.

Radhoji ignores Admiral Watson, Clive and the Angrezi clerk in the room and heads to the shelves on the wall. Radhoji is going through the various documents on the shelves. Some he throws on the ground, others into a sack held open by a silhadar.

'What about him?' Clive asks the clerk.

The clerk turns to his dubash, who is standing with folded hands behind him.

The young Parsi Dubash is terrified.

'Shriman, the Angrez is asking what you are taking,' the Dubash says in Marathi.

Radhoji does not turn around. He finishes reading the document in hand and then throws it into the sack.

'This fort and everything within it are the property of Shrimant Peshwa Nanasaheb,' Radhoji says as he picks up the next document and without bothering to turn around, peruses it.

'Well, Admiral Watson, it seems we are done here—let's go to greener pastures,' Clive says, and they leave the room.

The fort of Vijaydurg, triple-bastioned, unassailable, is burning. A burning shot hit the main magazine. Colonel Clive and Admiral Watson climb up to the ramparts on the western side of the fort to avoid the smoke that is billowing from the burning township the fort holds. Forests of hardwood timber, teak, rosewood, sal and padauk are blazing so hot, they are cracking the stones of the fort wall. Below them, the ships of Tulaji Angre mirror the flames twice: once in themselves and again on the sea.

The heat is immense from the raging fires all around them. It burns their foreheads, and they worry about the liquid in their eyes coming to a boil.

'Well, Robert, this little expedition will more than make up for what you lost at sea,' Admiral Watson tells his new and fast mate.

'I told you it'd be worth it. 'eard of him from a Member o' Parls, Boone, of his *owd mon*, Connerjee, this famous pirate 'ere, richer than Crisis 'imself.'

'The five six has had a bonny start,' says Admiral Watson, the image of the gold mohurs in the chest seared against the golden fire he is witnessing.

Below, amidst the burning streets of the fort, quarrels and fights have broken out amongst the Angrezi sipahis and the Marathas as each pull on an end of a sword, musket, a bale of silk, a sack of pearls, a chest of silver, a narwhal horn and a tortoise shell. The Munshis and accountants are fighting with their own soldiers: 'This will be shared equally once it is accounted for,' they keep repeating.

The accountants and clerks are flabbergasted at the wealth. A munshi explains to his junior. Tulaji left everything behind when he ran to the Peshwa's tent hoping to negotiate. 'Forgive me, Nanasaheb, I was foolish, I rest at your feet,' he said to Balaji Baji Rao Bhat. Your grandfather and my father were childhood friends, my brothers and your father.

'They knew their place: you do not,' says the Peshwa and has him clasped in crude iron chains. He has been waiting to teach Tulaji a lesson even if the cost is entreating with the Angrez.

Lieutenant Colonel Clive's legs follow his bulbous nose.

'This is the end of the Angrians and their piracy. I'll write Sir Charles tonight itself, the eleventh of February seventeen hundred and five six,' Clive says.

'And you can add a note about me, Rob, if you don't mind. If only I had met you earlier in my career,' says Admiral Watson.

'Course, me dear Admiral, I will. 'Tis a rich, rich land, dear sir, even moderation suffices,' he says to the Admiral.

A red-faced and flustered Marine comes running up to the two men.

'Admiral, there is a treasury down inside and the Murratoes and the boys from Bombay are ransacking it,' the Marine says flushed.

'First we must make sure everything is accounted for, before we share it, not that I shall take a farthing,' says Clive, prodding the Marine to the vault.

'Counted and 'ccounted for,' Clive says, running with childish glee.

A vulture descends to the street and shuffles about, opening and closing its massive wings. The lamenting crows shuffle away in fear.

Acknowledgements

As the author, first of all, I would like to thank Namita Gokhale, without whom this book wouldn't have seen the light of day. For Namitaji's generous encouragement, guidance and support I will always be proudly indebted. My stellar agent, Kaniskha Gupta, whose wisdom is deep and clear, I will always be thankful to. Amish Raj Mulmi, I thank for his time and effort with a long and unwieldy manuscript and his incisive insights and suggestions that threshed the chaff away. In Bhutan, I would like to thank Achu Tshering Tashi, for his generous guidance and indulgence throughout the entire process. I would also like to thank Chirag Thakkar, Saba Nehal and the team at Penguin Random House for making this a reality.

Shri Raghuji Raje Angre and his sister Shrimati Chandrahasha Raje Angre were kind and generous in meeting me at their home in Alibag and letting me interview them on their esteemed ancestor. They patiently went through the manuscript and provided me with jewels of family lore and cultural outlook. I also thank them for providing me with images of seals and coins of Sarkhel Kanhoji Angre.

As a person, I would like to thank the following, for turning me into an author:

My teachers, Ms Sunny, Shanti Vedanayakam, Adam and Brenda Pleasance, Michael Boughn at the University of Toronto and most of all Gautam Sen, who taught me history and the late Phillip Dailey who taught me to read constantly and write simply. I would also like to thank Dr Anjali Chhabria for all her professionalism and help.

Of my family and their friends, I would like to acknowledge the late Sheeroy Sunawala, Rajinder Sawhney and Geoffery Downer for not only imparting their love of reading and history but also opening up their libraries to me and playing the part of guides, through life and this blessed land of ours. My aunt, Zahida Malik and my cousin, Zafar Malik, I must thank for their constant love and exposing me to the rich traditions, temples and culture of southern India. I must thank Kiran Mazumdar Shaw and Harish Salve Esq. as they have always been there for me in so many crucial ways. Amitav Ghosh and William Dalrymple are beacons of craftsmanship and scholarship, and historian Abraham Eraly's work bared the spirit of our history to me.

I cannot thank my wife Dechhen Pelden enough for her trust and faith or my sister Kashvi Rekhy for always egging me on; and my sister-in-law Monisha Macedo and my brother Viraj Chopra for always being a refuge for me.

Lastly, but most importantly, I would like to acknowledge my father the late Shashi Rekhy and my mother Waheeda Rehman for being the best parents one could hope for and for always supporting and encouraging my curiosity and interests, but not before I bow my head to my grandmother the late Ratnavali Ahluwalia who would narrate our never-ending epics to me every evening.

Scan QR code to access the
Penguin Random House India website